YANKEE DOODLE D.O.A.

A closed ebony-and-brass coffin lay in front of the altar. Behind it was a massive, brilliant medley of red, white, and blue flowers arranged in the Yankee logo of top hat and cane. There is none like it. Rupert Huston had owned the Yankees, and with it came the tradition. As the inside of my mouth caked up, I thought instead of Joe Dugan's famous line as he sat in the outdoor heat of Babe Ruth's funeral. "I'd give anything for a beer," Bob Meusel had said to Dugan. "So would the Babe," Joe replied.

In my reverie I didn't notice that Petey had whipped out a pair of opera glasses and was unabashedly scanning the audience.

"Don't you feel it?" Petey said, turning slightly toward me. "Don't you?"

"What's that?"

She leaned into my ear. "Don't you feel the treachery? I mean, Uncle Duffy, don't you just feel the presence of the killer. I think he's *here*. Right here."

I sputtered, trying to do so quietly.

"Snipers don't take mass," I ventured.

Bantam Crime Line Books offer the finest in classic and modern American mysteries. Ask your bookseller for the books you have missed.

Rex Stout
The Black Mountain
Broken Vase
Death of a Dude
Death Times Three
Fer-de-Lance
The Final Deduction
Gambit
Plot It Yourself
The Rubber Band
Some Buried Caesar
Three for the Chair
Too Many Cooks
And Be a Villain
The Father Hunt
Death of a Doxy

Meg O'Brien
The Daphne Decisions
Salmon in the Soup
Coming soon: Hare Today, Gone
        Tomorrow

Virginia Anderson
Blood Lies
King of the Roses

William Murray
When the Fat Man Sings
The King of the Nightcap
The Getaway Blues

Jeffery Deaver
Manhattan Is My Beat
Death of a Blue Movie Star

Robert Goldsborough
Murder in E Minor
Death on Deadline
The Bloodied Ivy
The Last Coincidence
Fade to Black

Denny Martin Flinn
San Francisco Kills
Coming soon: Killer Finish

Sue Grafton
"A" Is for Alibi

"B" Is for Burglar
"C" Is for Corpse
"D" Is for Deadbeat
"E" Is for Evidence
"F" Is for Fugitive

Carolyn Hart
Death on Demand
Design for Murder
Something Wicked
Honeymoon with Murder
A Little Class on Murder
Deadly Valentine

Annette Meyers
The Big Killing
Tender Death
Coming soon: The Deadliest Option

David Handler
The Man Who Died Laughing
The Man Who Lived by Night
The Man Who Would Be
        F. Scott Fitzgerald

M. K. Lorens
Sweet Narcissus
Ropedancer's Fall
Deception Island

Diane K. Shah
As Crime Goes By

Rita Mae Brown
Wish You Were Here

P. M. Carlson
Murder Unrenovated
Murder in the Dog Days

Jane Haddam
Not a Creature Was Stirring
Precious Blood
Coming soon: Act of Darkness
              Quoth the Raven

Crabbe Evers
Murder in Wrigley Field
Murderer's Row
Coming soon: Bleeding Dodger
              Blue

Murderer's Row

Crabbe Evers

BANTAM BOOKS
NEW YORK · TORONTO · LONDON · SYDNEY · AUCKLAND

MURDERER'S ROW

A Bantam Crime Line Book/July 1991

ISBN 0-553-29088-6

Published simultaneously in the United States and Canada

*Bantam Books are published by Bantam Books, a division of
Bantam Doubleday Dell Publishing Group, Inc. Its trademark,
consisting of the words "Bantam Books" and the portrayal of a
rooster, is Registered in U.S. Patent and Trademark Office and in
other countries. Marca Registrada. Bantam Books, 666 Fifth
Avenue, New York, New York 10103.*

PRINTED IN THE UNITED STATES OF AMERICA

RAD   0 9 8 7 6 5 4 3 2 1

For Jerome Holtzman, the Dean

Murderer's Row

Prologue

*". . . now you could take the New York Yankees,
which through the years has had several fairly amazin'
players . . ."*

I offer an apology to ol' Case, or to his ghost, which
hovers somewhere over Gotham, for the following.

*". . . including Babe Ruth and Gehrig and Dickey
and Lazzeri, some of which come along after the '23 Series . . ."*

Whenever anything is written about the New York
Yankees, especially in these lost latter days, when the pinstripes don't seem as magical as they once were, it is fitting
and proper to invoke the wisdom of Mr. Stengel as only he
might commence to deliver it.

*". . . which is where I hit a pair of home runs playing
for Mr. McGraw, even one inside the park, which was
enough to expire a man my age racing around the bases
like that, and I also took one away from Ruth in center
field but he got three anyway and they beat us four games
outta six. They had that Pennock fella too.*

*"That was when that little Miller Huggins was man-
ager as he had put together the first murderers' row of
Ruth, Meusel, Schang, and Pipp, and that same year they
added that young Gehrig fella from Columbia University
which took Pipp's job after his headache the next year.
Speaking of aches, after the Babe had his big stomachache,
Huggins took control of the team until he died of blood
poisoning. Huggins, that is.*

*"Then Jake Ruppert got Joe McCarthy—the manager,
not the senator—to come over from the Cubs and manage
even though Babe wanted the job real bad and never liked*

*Joe after that. But Marse Joe won eight pennants and seven
world championships through '44, which ain't bad.*

"And during McCarthy's time you got DiMaggio
which won it for me in '49 when just about everybody but
the wives was injured and some of them too, and Yogi and
that young man Billy Martin, which was one of my favorites except for that Copacabana thing that commenced in
the washroom.

"And you can't forget Larsen, who pitched game five
in 1956 so splendid it was perfect, to where Pinelli called
the last strike on that Mitchell fella and then retired himself.

"Of course, I'm soft on the New York Yankees, which
you could say was an amazin' ballclub and we had a lot of
'em back then. Why, you could play as low as Class D ball,
which was at Shelbyville, Kentucky, and Class C ball at
Kankakee, Illinois, where I started, but I just go there for a
visit now. I was skipper of the Yankees for several remarkable years, and even a couple stinkers, in which we had
tremendous success thanks to Mr. George Weiss, who always kept track of when I was discharged so he could
reemploy me. Many fans were fairly disgusted when Mr.
Weiss fired Bucky Harris and hired me in 1948 on account
of they thought I was a baseball clown and a managing
failure, at least judging by how some of my previous teams
had ended up. But George was general manager and had a
wonderful wife and provided me with many fine ball
players which could execute and helped win pennants and
world championships. Why, without 'em I couldn't of
done it alone. And my assistant Mr. Berra helped me, as he
was fairly observant and used to learn a lot just by watching, like he should of been when he dropped that foul ball
off Williams when Allie Reynolds was pitching his no-
hitter and then caught another one just like it when Reynolds got Williams to do it again for the last out, and you
got to live a long time to see something like that happen.

"Well, you got all that and more in baseball, like I told
the senators and congressmen in Washington, D.C. when
they called me and Mantle to testify in 1958, which was
the year the club won the World Championship for me
when we was down three games to one. Of course, we had
Turley.

"Now if the senators were calling for testimony today, I guess you would have to point them right up to Yankee Stadium again where some amazin' and disturbing things have happened but not enough of them in the ball games. I never got used to losing, why I hated it, despised it, no matter if you're wearing the Yankee pinstripes or not, which some people said was enough to transform some ordinary players into skilled players, and I saw a lot of that myself.

"Now when I was managing I always paid attention to Gus Mauch, as he was the trainer and kept my broken-down players healthy, and to what Mr. Weiss said, as he was my boss and he was pulling the purse strings for the owners Mr. Webb and Mr. Topping, and they were wealthy men who had their reasons. 'Course I'm not in the position to question the owners except I know when it's time to get out the embalming fluid.

"But I can tell you this: when things happen to the New York Yankees, the whole baseball world, every boys' group and girls' group, every poem and song, takes notice of it. And they all said it just didn't seem like this was the New York Yankees the way Rupert Huston was running the club what with its ups and downs and players grumpin' and groanin' even though they kept the right-field porch close in where now you can poke a ball for a home run with weak wrists, where in my day you had to hit one over a fence about eighteen feet high before you could limber up your home-run trot.

"Well, this here story commences with one of the strangest occurrences in Yankee Stadium, stranger than any I witnessed, and I seen my share, as in 1959 when we didn't win but seventy-nine ball games, 'course the White Sox had the go-go boys, and they won it fair and square with that Al Lopez fella, who I traded twice and still always called him one of my men. No, this mystery was of the kind you see in movie houses and on television shows.

"I could go on and tell you about it and give my opinions about the city of New York, where I lived at Broadway and Forty-seventh Street when I started in the big leagues. The thing is, the fans were shocked, they were amazed, they stopped what they were doing when they heard it, but they were not grieved. The baseball fans I'm *speaking of now. Why, I seen longer faces when DiMaggio burped or when that bad hop hit Kubek in the throat. You see, something strange and different had seized that tremendous baseball town of New York and my Yankees when this was reported in the newspapers.*

"But I can't take the time to talk much more about it on account of Edna is waiting for me in California where we have a nice house and a swimming pool that has held up through earthquakes. Why, most people my age are dead now, and that's what makes life insurance what it is. One of my writers, Mr. Duffy House, who is a fairly amazin' baseball man in his own right, has consented to clarify matters and tell you the ins and outs of this mystery that involves the Yankees and those monuments in center field to Ruth, Gehrig, and Mr. Huggins and the game of baseball, which I was lucky enough to play and to manage on account of I had baseball knuckles and couldn't become a dentist, and you could look it up."

1

The Man at the Top

"So I'm feeling a little smug, Duffy," Chambliss said.

"Don't," I said. "At our age smug is getting through a day without Metamucil."

For me this hadn't been one of those days. The night, however, given what was looking up at me from the dinner plate, was more promising. Lamb chops laced with mint butter, asparagus spears as thin as pencils, and a Caesar salad I came to praise, not bury.

"Let me bask a little," he said. "The game's going good."

"Don't go soft on me, Grand," I said to Granville Canyon Chambliss, the commissioner of baseball, who was sitting at his throne across the table and letting the fumes of some stellar veal chops affect his thinking.

It would be temporary, I knew, because Chambliss was an old soybean trader from the Chicago pits who was made high lord of baseball when the game needed a guy like him. And though it meant that he took up residence in Manhattan and worked in the mahogany and low light of a Park Avenue office instead of the throng in a La Salle Street futures pit, he was still Grand, a torpedo of a guy who dressed badly but had his head screwed on straight. At the moment his tie was loose, his sleeves were rolled up, and he had blue-cheese dressing on his chin.

The dinner was on his expense account because we were on his turf: a well-appointed chunk of West Fifty-ninth Street just around the corner from the Plaza Hotel

and just across the street from horse-drawn carriages and
the heel of Central Park. Why, we had passed that young
actress Miss Angie Dickinson on the sidewalk as we came
in, and she smiled a smile at us that brought the term
femme fatale to my mind.

The joint was called Mickey Mantle's, and while I'm
the last guy to darken a spot with an old ballplayer's name
on it—though I'll go out of my way to clink forks at Rusty
Staub's—Mick's place was okay. My druthers would have
had us in the Carnegie Delicatessen on Seventh Avenue. I
can't begin to say how many hours I spent and how many
pounds I amassed there through the years, and the Stage
Delicatessen before that. The Stage was a required pil-
grimage from the old Sheraton Hotel on Seventh and
Fifty-fourth, where the visiting teams and scribes always
stayed. Besides pudgy writers gorging themselves on the
corned beef, you'd often see Mantle and Bill Skowron in
there. Roger Maris was a regular too, and before them Moe
Berg haunted the place. Skowron and Maris used to dip
their hands into the pickel barrels at the Stage because
they thought the brine toughened up their paws. At least
that was the idea. That was before the joint was sold to
gentiles, who right away put a bar in. Even this gentile
knows you can't sell whiskey in a delicatessen without
eroding the place, so most everybody moved over to the
Carnegie, with those sandwiches that are twice as expensive and too big for one mortal to consume at a single
sitting. Oh my, how we tried though; come to think of it, I
had a taste for one of them right now.

But Chambliss, who is no stranger to the Carnegie, felt
at home here on the wooden chairs and round tables of
Mantle's place. Rouged waitresses in black pants hovered
around him like clubhouse attendants, and the bill of fare
contained provender that Mickey himself would chew on.
The walls were hung with baseball decor, to be sure, but
classy, provocative stuff: paintings and prints in and out of
Yankeedom. They leaked the memories of old sportswriters.

"To hell with ya then," Chambliss went on. He was
eating with his fingers, strip-mining an inch-thick chop.
"I'm not a cheerleader, but attendance is up, revenues are

up, and we got about fourteen teams still in the race—and it's the first week of September."

"The rich get richer," I said.

"You want otherwise? Drugs in the clubhouses? Managers putting down bets? Fans with bags over their heads?"

And he was right. Before Chambliss was invited in, big-league baseball had tried its damnedest to shoot itself in the foot. It was a time, Grand had declared, "when everyone thought they could do anything they wanted." Whenever the league called a press conference, you didn't know whether it was to give out the Cy Young or announce that it was cooperating with a grand jury.

Then Chambliss stepped in, saw the enemy was us, and started spanking. He took up Bart Giamatti's refrain and took it right to the ballplayers themselves. "You guys have a privileged life that most people can't even dream of," he admonished everybody from starting pitchers to batboys, "so live up to it and *obey the damn rules.*" Then he set the rules and smacked anybody who bent them. It was something to see.

I watched intently, even in my semi-emeritus condition within the sporting press. I've personally been around long enough not only to remember when George Herman Ruth was swatting them, but to have had the pleasure of witnessing several of the Bambino's proud prances around the bases. Frank and Estelle House probably would have preferred to see their son pursue a more honorable profession, just as Mr. and Mrs. Stengel of Kansas City once wished that young Charles Dillon had gone into dentistry. It was baseball's good fortune that Casey chose baseball; I don't remember what my excuse was.

At any rate, I was fifteen when I started with the old Chicago *Daily News,* getting an infusion of ink in my veins that never thinned. My beat wasn't the front page (and I knew that Hecht fellow before he went Broadway), except when the boys of summer or autumn won championships and we bannered the results. No, I chronicled the stuff of a pastime, a diversion, the kiss of a ball on red clay, young men cutting and darting on green grass—games.

I was never anything but a sportswriter and never aspired to be anything else. I liked the spectacle and enjoyed reporting it. I've always relished the company of sportsmen, true and otherwise—those who played and those who spectated. As plebeian as it may sound, I echo Will Veeck's sentiment that there is no sight more beautiful, no sound more sweet, than a ballpark full of fans. That won't put Veeck and me up there with Voltaire, but that's okay too.

The bulk of my toil was in the fields of a daily column called "On the House." Thirty years of it, five days a week. That wasn't too original a head, and the column wasn't dictated by the Holy Ghost. What it was, was mud-in-your-eye sports as I saw it, and you could frame it or let the parakeet daub it. But you always got the gist of things athletic: who won and why and how the weather was. And the people must have appreciated that, otherwise the editors would have had me writing obits.

Then it came time to surrender the column to a young Turk, a barb-tongued younker who venerated a well-turned phrase more than the straight dope, a guy who'd rather talk to the player's wife than the player, who didn't like to travel and moaned like hell when the game went longer than two-and-a-half hours. But I won't get started on that. That the *Daily News,* an institution I worshiped, folded shortly after my retirement was, in my most charitable view, only a coincidence.

So I went out to graze, but not completely, since the papers still ask for a piece now and then, usually when some old, once-artful dodger passes. Plus, Mr. Spink's *Sporting News* will still print anything I throw at them; and another publisher, for a sum of money that will not endow my relatives, wants my memoirs. I was working hard on that last item—I mean *memoirs* now, called *One More on the House,* not just a bunch of wormy columns and moldy anecdotes about same—when that Wrigley Field debacle had turned me into a gumshoe.

My meal with Chambliss this night was partially to fete that interlude.

"Hell, I don't think things ever got lower than when the Weaver kid got whacked in Wrigley Field," Chambliss was saying. "Good Lord—the best pitcher in baseball smoked right there in the ivy and the sunshine. Now that depressed me no end."

He tossed the bone onto his plate and used his linen napkin like a paint rag to wipe his digits.

"Saw Red Carney the other day," he continued. "He started in again on the whole thing. What a big hero he was, and your niece—Petey, isn't it?—the old barker is crazy about her. I couldn't shut him up."

I held up my knife and fork lest he go on. We both knew the tale, about Carney, the legendary mike man of the Chicago Cubs, and Petrinella Biggers, my lovely carrot-top niece from Cincinnati, who had spent that summer's weeks before commencing law school as my assistant bloodhound in search of the Wrigley Field killer. The sleuthing was Chambliss's idea: he wanted a baseball man on the inside of the investigation. He wanted a point man to tell him unfiltered versions of what people—cops, players, owners—were saying under their breath in the ballparks and the clubhouses about the murder of one of the game's brightest stars. And I went along with it. And Petey, well, she went along with me. We got lucky, unraveled the unsavory affairs of the Cubs' den, nabbed a fiend before he dispatched us, and restored the element of friendly to the Clark and Addison confines.

But that story is well told elsewhere. Meanwhile, I was in Manhattan as a guest of the commissioner, and his gratitude and baseball's pockets went deep. My real mission in New York, however, was to attend the funeral of a fellow scribe. For some reason—who am I kidding?—because of too much booze and nicotine and room-service food—the roster of my former colleagues was going down like starting pitchers in August. And, as ever, there was no cheering in the press box.

This one was Hugh McGrew, an old Ebbets Field beat man who wrote tighter prose than Red Smith and played the harmonica better than Phil Linz. I always liked Hughie but hadn't seen much of him in later years because he wouldn't ride in airplanes and wouldn't admit to the existence of the Los Angeles Dodgers. The man despised Walter O'Malley.

"Why didn't you bring that doll along with you, Duffy?" Chambliss asked. "I ain't dead yet, ya know."

"Enough's enough, that's why," I replied. "Petey's a

sweet kid with a big brain, and she's on her way to law school where she belongs, dammit."

"I say something made you want to chew on me?"

"Ah criminy, Grand. The kid got infected with that Wrigley Field whodunit. Worse case than Red, who put her on the air and slobbered all over her. She just lit up to the attention like a rookie on opening day.

"Now it's time for her feet to touch down," I added, putting the last of the lamb between my chops.

A long-fingered waitress snatched our empty plates and replaced them with cups of steaming coffee. Chambliss gave her some kind of hand signal, and she returned with a pair of brandy snifters. In them she poured a golden elixir that coated the crystal and sent the smell of fresh peaches aloft.

"I should have such charming problems," Chambliss said.

"Uh-oh," I replied, "here comes the baseball-is-horse-shit-ever-since-those-two-Yankees-swapped-wives routine. So give it to me, and don't ignite that thing."

Chambliss was unwrapping a panatela and lolling the business end of it on the wet of his lips.

"Stopped smoking them years ago," he said. "Doesn't mean I can't suck on them."

"Love 'em and leave 'em," I said, and wished I hadn't.

"All right, you want horseshit? Well, there's horseshit right here and right now in my own backyard. The Yankees and that goddamn Rupert Huston," he said, poking the cigar into the air for emphasis. I could see he wanted to unlimber.

"I'm a Chicago guy, and I always thought I'd enjoy an era when the Yankees were a doormat. After all the beating up they did on the other clubs all those years. I don't have to tell you the record of that franchise is something else.

"Now they're not only down, but Huston is grinding his heel into the club. The whole organization. Doing his best to make the pinstripes and that N-Y logo that flapped on the chests of Ruth and Gehrig and DiMaggio into a laughingstock. A cheap decal."

"Sounds like you got a new perspective, Grand," I said.

"Oh yeah, Duffy. Being commissioner and being east, I see it a little different now. When baseball in New York is down like it is now, it isn't good for baseball in general. I'm convinced of that. And I never thought those words would pass these lips.

"He's *using* the franchise, Duffy. Using it like a toy, an ego toy, instead of caretaking a ballclub with a great legacy. All of his tantrums and hiring and firing are one thing. How he publicly embarrasses his people—some good baseball people—that's his prerogative because he owns the show. I know that too. But dammit, he's—he's—he's corrupting it! He's contaminating it. He's eating away at the guts of baseball ownership worse than all the oil tycoons and real-estate hustlers and cowboys that went before him."

"But Grand," I interrupted, "mismanagement is one of the joys and privileges of ownership."

"Ah horseshit, I don't have to tell *you* what he's doing. I'm just blowing off steam."

With his left hand Grand upended the snifter and drained its sticky contents into his coffee cup. Then he drained the cup. With that he abruptly got up, pushed his chair back, and drew glances from adjoining diners, who already knew who he was and seemed to be enjoying the show.

"Excuse me while I patronize the little-boy's room," he said, and rumbled off, the still-whole, wet cigar sticking out from the knuckles of his right hand.

Chambliss hadn't told me anything new. Like every baseball writer in the land, I'd watched and lamented and written nasty paragraphs about the spectacle of Rupert Huston, the Yankees' egomaniacal, mad czar. Bad press collected like spitballs at Huston's feet, and he stepped through it like a plant owner driving through a picket line. You couldn't phase him, couldn't humiliate or rile him, and you certainly couldn't stop him.

Nobody in New York expected Huston, a beer and real-estate sharpie who had bought the Yankees almost two decades earlier at a bargain-basement price, to be a statesman. He was simply a well-publicized multimillionaire, a wheeler-dealer operating in a town full of them. And Huston came out swinging the moment he got there. As young

Casey Stengel had exclaimed upon being traded to the Giants, "Wake up, muscles, we're in New York now!"

Yet nobody in Gotham expected Huston to do what he did to the Yankees. Nobody expected him to pervert the organization of the baton and top hat, to make it a temporary hitching post for rented players and managers at exorbitant rates, players brought in like mercenaries only to be scorned and excoriated a few months later by Huston himself if they did not perform to his liking. Apple barrels rot from the top down, and it didn't take long for the premises to teem with fruit flies. Despite their fat paychecks, Huston's players soon grew surly and disgruntled. The glow they felt from first becoming a Yankee, a *New York Yankee,* was quickly tarnished by the toxic tactics of the boss, no matter how many times the scoreboard beamed Movietone footage of past legends and the loudspeakers blared Sinatra's "New York, New York." And these players from the provinces, from Oklahoma and Kentucky, wished only to leave. There were no smiling DiMaggios, no shy young Mantles, no grinning Berras. Finally the imports were sold off like unwanted penny stocks.

Huston was the current bane of Commissioner Chambliss's existence. Every time he picked up a tabloid or tuned in the eleven-o'clock news, every time he looked into baseball's mirror, he saw Rupert Huston. Rupert was the ogre of New York, a bigger villain than whatever masochist was posing as mayor, a character so well chronicled the papers did not even use his last name. And yet Chambliss worked for the owners, which included Huston, and while he currently enjoyed support from cooler heads, there was no telling when Huston would marshal the support of incoming owners, the pizza kings, fast-food earls, blue-jean dukes, and real-estate counts who would back him because they had bought into the game the way he had and appreciated his way of doing things.

Chambliss returned with the cigar in his teeth and his hands pink from the blow dryer.

"I put a bug in your head, didn't I? Just bring up that bastard's name, and it gets you going," he said as he sat back down.

"Actually, Grand, my eye caught that pose of Roberto

Clemente over there on the wall. Lost myself wondering how long it's been since I saw Bob run in right field."

"Nice thought," he said, "but you're a liar."

"October 1972. Pirates lost the play-offs to Cincinnati on a wild pitch."

"What I've not done, if you're still paying attention," Grand continued, "is take the jackass head on. Kuhn did that with Finley. Both of them were mud wrestling in a courtroom before it was all over with."

"I've got the complete transcript of that trial," I said. "I ever tell you that?"

"I never asked. Can you imagine me telling Huston he couldn't unload a ball player like Kuhn did with Finley? Look what Rupert did with Bill Wolfe yesterday. Gave him away to Pittsburgh for what—?"

"Three minor-leaguers and change," I answered. "Huston said Wolfe 'wasn't contributing' . . . said he had a bad attitude. I read all about it on the way in. Last year's RBI leader for chopped liver. Couldn't believe my eyes."

"You and the rest of this city," Chambliss said. "They're ready to lynch the bastard. People even call my office, for cryin' out loud. They always call my office."

"What'd John Brush say about the trade?" I asked. "He wasn't even mentioned in my paper."

"Yeah, well, after Huston stalks off the pulpit, his general manager has to stick around and pick up the pieces. I saw a little of the press conference, and Brush looked like he'd been hit by a street cleaner. Which is tough in this town because we don't get much street cleaning."

"Poor bastard," I said. "How'd you like the job of explaining Huston's deals to the world?"

"He tried. Said the Yankees were out of the race and Pittsburgh was willing to part with some good young kids for a power hitter in their stretch drive. The Yankees were building for the future and all that stuff he knew was horseshit. By that time Huston was long gone."

Grand sucked on his dormant tobacco stick.

"And you know, I see the guy all the time. We make the same rubber-chicken affairs, and he treats me like his goddamn roomie. Slaps me on the back and says 'What say we play some pork bellies, Grand?' Jee-zus! I got all I can do to keep from decking the guy!"

I laughed out loud and belched, my belly telling me to stop with the peach brandy already, my waistline pounding at my belt like an angry landlord.

Just then a young fellow brought a phone to the table. It was a portable affair, with a retractable antenna, the Flash Gordon kind of gear that everybody but me takes for granted nowadays. Chambliss threw a suspicious look at the kid, whose hair was parted down the middle and clipped high around the ears, and he snarled at the phone. The commissioner didn't wear a beeper, and he didn't take calls when he was eating dinner. I liked that about him. Somehow, however, he knew he had to take this one.

"Yes, Marjorie," he said, knowing who was on the line.

He listened briefly, then fairly spat the cigar from his mouth.

"Good Lord . . . !" he said, his voice trailing off. His expression dropped somewhere between nonplussed and stupefied; his free hand covered his open ear. He looked at me, then looked away as people do when they're captive to that device.

"Who?" he barked. "Yeah, the Bronx guy. All right, a few minutes. Yeah . . . yeah . . . yeah. Marjorie, c'mon now. . . ."

Then he lowered the phone from his ear, not sure of what to do with it, and turned to me with an expression I had never seen on him before. If I was to guess, I would say he looked like that at the birth of his first child and at the onset of his first kidney stone. His mug was a stew of conflicting emotions, a battleground of exploding capillaries, and he was starting to perspire.

He spoke in a controlled hush, wanting only me to hear what he was saying.

"They just found Rupert Huston," he said. "In Yankee Stadium. The son-of-a-bitch has been shot to death."

2

Death Valley

We hustled out of Mick's as fast as two motivated geriatrics can hustle and didn't wait at the curb more than a few seconds before Chambliss's car rambled up. It was a nondescript Lincoln, as far from a limousine as you can get and still call it chauffeur driven. Chambliss got in front, and I slid in back.

"Yankee Stadium, Norm," Chambliss said.

I craned my head to get a look at Norm, half expecting to see Norm Siebern or some other ex–ball player turned gofer for baseball. Instead I saw a ball of curly hair and a pair of crazy copper earrings attached to a pug-nosed and pretty young lady.

"Duffy House, Norma Perlmutter," Chambliss said, then pulled the car phone from its cradle and started poking its chiclets.

"Love your stuff, Mr. House," Ms. Perlmutter said as she cut the Lincoln east on Fifty-ninth, nearly clipping the hindquarters of a carriage horse at Fifth Avenue.

I smiled. All New Yorkers did their homework. I was sure this one, who couldn't be more than five feet tall and had a ring on every finger of the one hand that gripped the steering wheel, had the complete works of Roger Angell next to her bed.

"How much do you know, Norm?" Chambliss asked, the phone to his ear.

"Only that Marjorie said to get you to Babe Ruth Plaza in a hurry," she said.

"Mr. Commissioner, this is the commissioner," Commissioner Chambliss said. "I'm on my way too. Around Park—"

"And Sixty-fifth," Norma said.

"Sixty-fifth. That means I got you by ten minutes or so. This is no bullshit, right, Larry? In the stadium, for godsakes! Who's your man there? Who? Devery? Do I know him? So I won't worry about it, if you say so. Okay, Larry."

Chambliss put the phone down and turned to me. Our heads lurched and jumped with the barreling locomotion of the Lincoln. Driver Perlmutter was jockeying the heavy automobile down the rutted, potholed avenue like a rumrunner, its shocks and suspension system meeting and exceeding manufacturer's specifications. It was near midnight. Park Avenue was chockablock with cabs and other vehicles pulling onto it from the side streets. Norma goosed the Lincoln between and around them, giving only cursory deference to stoplights.

"That's Larry McGonigle, police commissioner," Chambliss said, turning to me. "You could probably figure it out. He's downtown but on his way. Says Huston was shot in the head—"

"Huston?" Norma Perlmutter exclaimed.

"Watch it, Norm! Dammit!" Chambliss yelled, bracing his hand on the dashboard.

The Lincoln had nearly sideswiped a Yellow cab whose mustachioed driver seemed as hell-bent on breaking in-city speed records as we were.

"Easy, Commish," Norma said, keeping her eyes on the boulevard, then added, "Is he dead?"

"From what I'm told," Chambliss said. "We're sure not going to Yankee Stadium this time of night for a flesh wound."

"Wow!" Norma exhaled. "Answered prayers, huh, Commish?" She broke a smile. I liked this little sprite, even though she drove like Ricky Henderson ran the bases.

"No more of that, Norm. I'm the commissioner of baseball, and one of our own apparently just went limit down. It doesn't matter how I felt about the specific individual."

"I'll never tell," said Norma.

"What else do you know, Grand?" I asked.

"McGonigle said it didn't happen in Huston's office. Somewhere out in the stadium someplace, for crying out loud. Says Brush called him direct."

"John Brush," I said aloud, again bringing up Huston's bright young general manager.

"Is it a murder or—?" I started to ask.

"A suicide? Hell, Duffy, I don't *know.* I assume somebody whacked the bastard. I can't imagine him pulling his own plu—"

We were both jarred nearly out of our seats by another one of Norma's lane shifts. She punched the Lincoln ahead at speeds up to seventy miles per hour. I would say she was making a mockery of speed limits, but I have never been sure of their existence in Manhattan. At this time of night it seems that its one-way avenues are run as straight and fast as possible. Nothing slows the groaning, rattling cabs, ebony limousines, belching buses, and even the sedans of the average driver except an occasional reality of a red light, and then these urban missiles draw to a halt only grudgingly.

Norma Perlmutter, however, the commissioner's driver from hell on a mission to Yankee Stadium, stopped for no light and slowed only when her path was blocked. And she did it all with the aplomb of a mechanic, steering with that single bedecked hand, her eyes focused at least three blocks ahead of our front bumper. I groped for a seat belt, but there was none to be found.

"Get us there in one piece, Norm," Chambliss growled. "The league doesn't need a double funeral."

"Include me out," I added, quoting Yogi.

At 125th we left Manhattan, crossed the Harlem River on the Willis Avenue Bridge, and entered the Bronx and the Major Degan Expressway. That much I knew. The new surroundings, however, blocks and blocks of apartment buildings, housing projects, and intersections that were clogged even at this time of night, grew increasingly foreign to me. During my days on the job, I usually went from the hotel downtown to the ballpark aboard the team bus. And working my fellow riders the way I liked to do, I didn't pay too much attention to the scenery on the way there. Occasionally we cabbed, and sometimes we even took the Lexington Avenue express train, which disgorged us right at the gate. At any rate, like everybody else, I'd heard a lot about the bad, bad Bronx in recent years, and now, despite the darkness and our land speed, I tried to get a fix on the place. I didn't do very well.

Chambliss, with one hand still braced against the dashboard, seemed lost in his own concerns. If he had been informed correctly, the baseball world was about to blow up in his face once again. Indeed, if it was true that some-one had murdered the owner of the New York Yankees, the very bedrock of the game—and its most famous fran-chise—would be tested once again. It was a new crisis that ranked somewhere up there with a players' strike and a World Series earthquake. And Chambliss had to handle it.

In what seemed like no time, driver Perlmutter had us within view of the stadium. Yankee Stadium, that proud white palace, the three-tiered coliseum where the legends live. This, of course, is the new stadium, renovated in 1976 with unobstructed views, escalator towers, plastic seats, and a big-screen entertainment scoreboard. In my mind's eye, however, this will always be the old place, the "house that Ruth built," with posts, a line scoreboard, and the encircling roof hung with that graceful Gothic copper facade. It will always be 281 feet down left, 295 to right, and 490 never-ending feet—Death Valley!—in center where the stone monuments to Ruth, Huggins, and Gehrig stood in play, and center fielders had to run around them to chase down bounding balls as if they were playing stickball in Harlem.

A plume of memory escapes from deep within me, as it does, or should, from every fan who approaches this temple, and I see immortals jumping and dodging and strutting in etched, unforgettable scenes. The Babe, of course, number 3, and Gehrig, number 4, remembering them both when they were thick-muscled and remark-able, and then again when they were ravaged by incurable disease. Lou, just a step too slow because of a scourge we could hardly pronounce and knew almost nothing about, said, "I am the luckiest man on the face of the earth." And Ruth, the wondrous Babe, gutted by cancer to where he leaned on a bat for support on that last July day in 1948, said: "The only real game in the world . . . is baseball."

And Marse Joe McCarthy—after Miller Huggins, who

was before my time—scheming in the dugout, Red Ruffing, Frankie Crosetti, Lefty Gomez, Tommy Henrich. And Joltin' Joe—his velvet swing, the flap of his number 5 jersey against his back, and Al Gionfriddo making that stab of Joe's crushed line drive in the '47 Series, where Joe Page was flawless in relief. Phil Rizzuto, Allie Reynolds, and Jerry Coleman; Mantle, number 7, Berra, number 8 (as was Bill Dickey), Whitey Ford, Elston Howard, Maris, and Billy Martin grabbing that infield pop-up when everybody else froze in game seven of '52, when Bob Kuzava—*Bob Kuzava*—was flawless in relief.

Did I forget Yogi wrapping his legs around Larsen (Larsen said to him, "Gee, you're heavy") after that perfect game? The head swims in recall—at least mine does. I've monitored six decades and viewed hundreds of games within these storied Yankee walls. This rush of sentiment was almost enough to keep me from concentrating on the events at hand, but suddenly we turned onto Ruppert Place and came to a halt in front of the Yankees' main offices on the west side of the stadium. I followed on Chambliss's heels as he scuttled up the steps and into the lobby.

"This way, Mr. Commissioner," said a young uniformed guard. He ushered us through revolving doors into the low light of the main concourse, then turned left and led us through the partially lit corridor toward the left-field seats. The stadium was quiet, huge, and empty, the various concession areas closed tightly, the concourse echoing with our hurried footsteps. The guard's radio scratched with static at his waist. In a few moments, as Chambliss and I began some serious huffing, we came to the end of the concourse and turned into the expanse of stands and the night air of the open Bronx sky.

The guard led us through the fair territory seats of straightaway left field to the concrete steps leading out into the area beyond the fence. To our left was the Yankee bullpen, and beyond that, Monument Park, the garden of nostalgia that holds the plaques and stones of the Yankee greats. As we approached, we could see a knot of figures huddled there. The area was lit with a few auxiliary spotlights, and some of the men held flashlights whose beams cut swaths in the relative darkness.

We stepped quickly past the row of thirteen waist-high plaques beyond the fence in left center, those famous numbers that started with Billy Martin's 1 and ended with Casey's 37, until we got to the patio in center field. At its center, of course, were the granite stones of Ruth, Huggins, and Gehrig, arranged and landscaped with white stones, shrubs, and a flagpole. Behind the stones was the ten-foot-high mint-green wall of bronze plaques commemorating famous Yankee figures from Colonel Jake Ruppert, the baron who acquired Ruth and built the stadium, to Ed Barrow, his thick-browed general manager who molded Ruppert's great Yankee clubs. In between were plaques to everyone from Lefty Gomez and Thurman Munson to a pair of popes, who came to the ballyard ostensibly to give their blessings, but secretly, if you ask me, hoping some of the magic of this place would rub off.

Right now everyone's attention was riveted on the low three-foot retaining wall just opposite the monuments. Slumped against it, in a sitting position but listing to one side, his legs splayed on the red brick walkway, was the body of Yankee owner Rupert Huston.

"Mr. Commissioner," called one of the men standing on the path in front of the body.

It was John Brush, Huston's assistant as well as the Yankee general manager. But the former position, with Huston running the show, held more clout than the latter. I knew Brush and had watched him come up through the management thickets of several organizations until Huston had snagged him a few years back. He was considered throughout the league to be as good a baseball mind as there was in the business. Now, with his shirt-sleeves rolled up and his tie loose, he looked besieged. He came over to meet us.

"John, you know Duffy House here . . . ?" Chambliss said.

"Of course," Brush said, and nodded at me. "Come over here."

He turned and led us over to the others—six men in suits and sport coats and a woman, all of whom looked like police—and the spectacle of the dead Huston.

"Good Lord," Chambliss breathed.

We stared at the crumpled body, the stark victim, the once-indomitable Rupert Huston, billionaire power broker and principal owner of the New York Yankees, now inert, lying like a comatose wino on the sidewalk. His eyes and mouth were closed, his head slack and leaning on his right shoulder. The position allowed full view of a dime-sized black hole in his left temple. Dark blood had coursed from it, staining his carefully razored silver hair and running in a thin line down his tanned jaw to his collar.

That was what was readily apparent. Behind his right shoulder, sprayed against the low wall, was brain and bone —the fierce wreckage of a single slug that took much of the right side of Huston's head when it exited—and more blood. The sight of it sickened me. And the smell—there *was* one—seemed slightly sour, unpleasant. It was the second warm corpse I had seen in a ballpark in too short a span of time, and I didn't like it. I hoped I never would.

Huston lay apparently where he had fallen, and detectives, individuals used to this sort of thing, used ballpoint pens to lightly probe the area of the wound, the bullet's entrance and exit. They did not disturb the body. A photographer was taking dozens of shots from every angle. I noticed Huston's shoes, a pair of soft tasseled black loafers, pointing skyward like disjointed ends of a *W*.

"What happened?" Chambliss asked.

"Sniper. We think from that escalator tower," said the tallest cop, a man with a dark suit coat pulled over a cotton golf shirt. He extended his hand: "Bill Devery, Commissioner. Chief of detectives."

"Damn. I'm sorry," said Brush, turning to both of them.

"You're McGonigle's man," said Chambliss. "This is Duffy House, my associate."

Devery eyed me warily, as if he could smell my media credentials.

"Up there?" Chambliss said, turning to the escalator tower that fed the left-field upper decks.

"From the looks of it. The shell dug itself into the concrete after it passed through the victim. We think he was standing up and thrown back against the wall. It was a hell of a weapon. We don't know the caliber, but it's a good one. Could drop a rhino."

Devery again looked up at the tower. "Angle is about

right. Ain't found nothing up there yet, but we've just started."

"Good God——!" Chambliss bellowed, rubbing his temples and shattering the markedly eerie calm of the scene. The other detectives glanced up at him. "I still don't——I mean, what the *hell* is Rupert Huston doing out in the goddamn center-field patio at midnight? Does anybody know? This is crazy!"

"Well, yes, I can answer that," said John Brush, his hands at his belt. He was a good-looking guy and, at this moment, tightly wound. "Rupert came out here all the time. Usually at night, with the park all closed up. He liked to wander among the monuments. He talked to the stones. He said he believed in ghosts. Honestly. He said he had a direct line to Jake Ruppert and Ed Barrow and McCarthy and Huggins when he came out here. So he did it all the time."

"That's right, Grand," I put in. "It may have been well known only to Yankee watchers. Sort of like Nixon used to roam the White House and talk to paintings of Washington and Jefferson."

"Okay. With Huston I'll buy that," Chambliss said. "But how in hell did someone get in here to get a shot at him?"

"That's what we want to know," said Devery.

Just then a radio, the one held by Brush, came alive.

"Press is here, Mr. Brush," a raspy voice announced.

"Shit. Where's the boss?" said Devery, and went quickly over to where his detectives were roping off the area with yellow "Do-not-cross" plastic tape. They wound it around a knee-high mugho pine, came across the brick path, looped it around the top half of Babe Ruth's stone, and came back to the edge of the low wall to the left of the body. It was a passable semicircle, a barrier against the deluge of the media, a moat between the eyes of the world and the carcass of Rupert Huston. Yet it was not much of anything else, as far as I was concerned. There was no semblance of privacy in this, Huston's most vulnerable state. If the police had a body bag or a sheet, they were in no hurry to produce it. That was obvious to me, and I was just about to point it out to the commissioner when the stampede began.

"Here they come," said a detective.

Suddenly the third-base side of the stadium hemorrhaged reporters, photographers, and camera crews. They scurried down the aisles and between the seats, looking like overdressed fans chasing a foul ball. Now I'm a newshound myself and no stranger to the hungry mob, but this was a frightening scene. What Huston courted in life, the flash of cameras and the hum of Minicams, the thrusting sheaf of microphones and clamoring reporters, was to dog him in death.

I headed for the edges, knowing Chambliss, Brush, and Detective Devery would have their hands full for a good while. None of the herd paid me any attention as I wound my way back over near the Yankee bullpen.

As I turned away from the commotion, the shouts and shoving, I looked once again at the expanse of the stadium. It had always been one of my favorites. Of course, most of my sentiment lies with the old arena, the proud place that was virtually gutted fifteen years ago and replaced—in the name of progress—with what we have today.

The Yankee Stadium I was gawking at was a product of politics and cantilevered architecture and the $100 million mirage of municipal financing. Yankee fans and owners such as Rupert Huston clung dearly to the notion that though the ballpark was changed, the name was the same. I'll give them that, and I'll try to summon the echoes in these grounds. I'll look over the center-field wall at the Grand Concourse Hotel and remember that the famous Yankees lived there and walked to work. I'll look at the field and its dimensions, though softened, and call it the old Yankee edge. I'll hear the feathery, noble tones of Bob Sheppard, that scholar and gentleman, over the public-address system, and believe that nothing has ever changed.

My reverie was interrupted by a quartet of bullnecked men in business suits who were themselves set upon by the media pack as soon as they came on the scene. I guessed that this was Police Commissioner McGonigle and attendants. By this time an ambulance had pulled into the service area behind the bullpen, and uniformed police began the process of removing Huston's body. Mercifully they covered it with a sheet. The camera lights and flashing strobes were blinding, and they seemed almost to render the scene in slow motion. At least that is how it appeared to me, a mute witness to history, I suppose, as I stood alone only yards away from the home plate of the Yankee bull-pen.

In a moment I saw Chambliss break from the crowd. A pair of reporters trailed behind him, lofting clipped questions and pleas. Grand was having none of it as he moved quickly along the outfield fence in my direction. I joined him, and we skipped up the steps toward the stadium's west exits. With one last glance backward, I saw the ambulance bearing the Huston corpse leave through a gate beyond center field. The vehicle's red and blue lights flashed angrily, cutting the New York sky; its siren remained silent.

Chambliss charged ahead, moving in from the stands to the third-base concourse, his head down, his hands thrust into his pants pockets. I could feel heat coming from him. I had all I could do to stay with him as we came to the glass doors leading to the Yankee offices.

"I'm going to need you on this, Duffy," he said.

He *ordered*, I should say.

I took a gulp of the now-dank stadium air and said to myself, *Here we go again*.

3

John T. Brush

The ride back to Manhattan was deliberate and quiet, reminding me of the return trip from a graveyard. Chambliss had a lot to say, but he didn't say any of it. Norma Perlmutter was tired, having expended most of her energy on the sprint over to the stadium. I was also feeling the length of the day, along with its wild finale.

"My phone'll start going at seven A.M.," Grand said finally.

"Like the bell at the old bean pit," I said.

Chambliss smiled—wistfully, I think.

"Let me fight off the hordes, then come by around ten, will you, Duf? We can try to get a handle on this thing."

I wasn't about to object here and now. My New York plans were flexible. I'd have plenty of time to pay Hugh McGrew's kin my respects.

Norma dropped me off at the Summit Hotel on Fifty-first and Lexington, the guest quarters of Chambliss's choice. It was where the umpires stayed, which is a decent recommendation.

"Thank you, my lady," I said to Ms. Perlmutter, and she winked. I like winkers. I was visibly sagging coming out of the elevator, and it was all I could do to push my dogs down the hallway and guide my room key into the lock. It was after two A.M., and I was unconscious before my head hit the pillow.

Dreams carried me for seven hours, the last one—for no logical reason—involving a home-plate tantrum by, of all people, the late Elston Howard, one of my favorite Yankees. I awoke to images of the usually stolid and efficient Ellie in full catcher's garb, with his soft cap turned backwards, the visor up, furiously jawing at Bill Haller—and to a palpable hum in the city around me. It hit me, and I paraphrased, *Wake up, muscles! Rupert Huston has been murdered.* In an A.M. move I almost never make, I went over and switched on the television. Every station was alive with coverage of Huston's death, and I turned up the volume and went off to the bathroom to scrape sleep's barnacles off this old hull.

I had just enough time to grab a bagel and coffee, and I planned to do so until I walked out into the din of Lexington Avenue. I thought I had fallen into a time warp, déjà vu all over again, for on the corner of Fifty-first a skinny vendor with a crooked cap was hawking copies of the *Post,* the *News,* the *Times,* and *Newsday* as if it were V-J Day. With a set of Dutch Rennert–caliber pipes, a paper in each hand, the seventy-two-point "HUSTON SHOT!!!" headlines on the tabloids visible for yards, he howled for customers. I believe he even said, "Read all about it!"

Papers were flying off his stacks, some staying flat out, others creased and tucked beneath armpits. New Yorkers stared at them as they walked, or stopped dead at street corners to linger over the black-and-white photos of the corpse near the monuments and savor the phrases of a half-dozen cityside columnists who, in a deadline dash that must have been a doozy, loosed paragraph after paragraph of lyrical midnight prose on the unbelievable fate of the Yankee boss. Other passersby gawked at blaring TVs in windows of appliance shops. There was one story, and one story only in New York—perhaps in all the country—and it held the populace in its thrall.

I grabbed a couple of tabloids myself, and I felt an odd kinship to the event as I looked at the spreads and scanned the stories. I read as I walked west over to Fifth Avenue, occasionally bumping into people too preoccupied to mind.

If Chambliss had thought he'd have the hordes taken care of by my arrival, he must have badly miscalculated the size of the hordes. Marjorie, his aide, secretary, filing system, and first line of defense, could only manage to lift an eyebrow as she worked the phone. She did squeeze in a nod toward an alcove and a pot of hot coffee—when had anyone found time to make it?—and a supply of almond-filled croissants. Their aromas greeted my nostrils like good news. While I sipped and munched, I could hear Chambliss fielding phone calls from his office. After a few moments Marjorie nodded me inside, and I sat on his office sofa and listened as he tactfully responded to the sallies of reporters who were all too well aware of the commissioner's antipathy for Rupert Huston. Dancing on a grave was not Chambliss's style, however, and he kept his remarks reserved and respectful.

After another four conversations he took the phone away from his ear and cut off Marjorie as she announced the next in line.

"Nope. Put a cork in it for a while, Marj," he said.

He looked at me and all the pastry flakes on my chin.

"Get me a couple of those and a cup of black, will ya, Duf?" he said.

"Slept like a baby last night, how 'bout you?" he began when I returned.

"Babies don't sleep well, Grand," I said.

"To hell with ya. I was dead out until it was time to get in here and face the music. Which hasn't been all that bad. I do an official line of jabber, and then a few soft ad libs."

"I noticed. But be careful, Grand: come off too dry-eyed about Huston, and you'll be considered a suspect."

"Hey! Don't think that hasn't crossed my mind. Hell, I'll be honest with you, Duffy, I can't raise a good goddamn tear for the guy. On the other hand, you can't go shooting people *down*—not players, not coaches, not even sonsabitches who are mucking up franchises.

"My job is to hold things together. I've got to watch every word, every move. I rang all the owners first thing. Had a conference call the size of the United Nations. They're all pretty shook up about this, and I can't blame 'em. Not one of 'em said, 'Hell, Rupert deserved it, so let's just get on with business.' No sir. What they said was, 'It coulda been any one of us.'

"Well, they're wrong there, I believe," Chambliss continued, "but I didn't tell 'em that. A dose of paranoia is good for them. Still, I can't be persuaded that we got open sniper season on baseball owners. Huston courted disaster, especially in this town. Maybe not in the form of an elephant rifle, but he was playing in dangerous territory."

I looked up as Marjorie entered with the pot of coffee. She had remarkable timing.

"Goes back to what you were saying last night," I said.

"It does, and I'm glad you were listening. I'll go that one better. What player was it said, 'You spend your whole life gripping a baseball, and you finally realize that it was the other way around?' Well, the game does that to you. The fires are stoked early, and they burn for years—"

My ears burned. I knew who uttered that quote.

"—and years. You know how we always hated the Yankees? So I got a confession. There was one of 'em I loved. That doggone Lefty Gomez. El Goofy Gomez, with those big ears. I liked how he used to sing and clown and give his relief pitchers—Johnny Murphy, remember him?—all the credit. And DiMaggio, who he said ran down all his mistakes. Hell, remember that time Gomez lit a match at home plate when he had to hit against Bob Feller?"

He was laughing and so was I. The Gay Castillian.

"Umpire said, 'Cut the crap, Lefty. That won't help you see Feller's fastball.' And Goofy said, 'Who cares about seeing his fastball. I just want to be sure Feller sees me!' " Grand cigar-laughed, showering crumbs all over his desk.

"Could you imagine that today?" I asked.

"They'd want me to fine the joker. But that's why he was one of my heroes."

"We had a few back then," I said.

"Yes, Duffy, *heroes.* Goofy could throw pellets and then stand back and enjoy himself. He just loved playing the game. I was but a kid in Chicago and no damn Yankee fan, and that still came through to me. Lefty was something special. And I think that if somebody would have torn Gomez down—I mean, humiliated or degraded him like Huston did his players—it would have affected me. I *know* I would have been torn up.

"I don't think Rupert understood that. I don't think he knew how much he was tampering with when he jacked around the Yankee organization."

With that he pushed aside the last of his coffee.

"So what's the point of all this, Commissioner?" I asked.

"The point is that if we're gonna get the son-of-a-bitch who put Huston's noggin between the cross hairs, we've got to think along the lines of heroes. Hero worship. Huston stepped over the line, and somebody couldn't take it anymore. That's my personal hunch. I been thinking about this all morning, Duffy."

That did it.

"Oh, bullshit. You been on the phone all morning," I groused. "And whattaya mean, 'If *we're* gonna get this son-of-a-bitch'?"

"Excuse me, Mr. Duffy 'Didn't-do-too-bad-in-the-pocketbook-on-the-Weaver-investigation' House. Of course, I want you to come in on this thing. This office depends on it. *I* depend on it."

"I'm a retired sportswriter whose main occupation is attending the wakes of his former colleagues."

"They won't miss you."

I scowled and stewed a little. The almond paste started coming up on me.

"Two things," I finally said. "One, that hero-worship stuff sounds good on the banquet circuit, but it's horseshit as far as Huston is concerned. He had more enemies than the Babe had indiscretions.

"Two, your quote about gripping the baseball comes from Jim Bouton. And should the commissioner of baseball be quoting Bouton?"

"Who do you think I am, Bowie Kuhn?" Chambliss cracked. Then his private phone rang, my time was up, and, like it or not, I had a murder to poke into.

I'll say one thing: Chambliss brought forth from the gut. It struck me on the way back from his office. Here's a guy who has had a good measure of success and acclaim in his time, the kind of thing that translates into all kinds of plaques, awards, dinners, tributes, commendations, and the back-slapping effluvia that people in the fertilizer business tend to heap on each other. Chambliss has also given away a lot of his money. I know that as a fact. So everybody

from the Boy Scouts to his alma maters have named him
Man-of-Some-Year-or-Another. The point of this is that you
would not know any of that from the walls of his office.
Whereas other bigwigs paper their sanctum sanctorums
with medals, personal bunting, and self-portraits, Chambliss's official surroundings are very different. They hold
collages of baseball photos and memorabilia of former
players; souvenir tickets; headlines; baseball cards; baseballs; caps; a signed ten-peso note from Minnie Minoso; an
autograph from Satchel Paige; a framed portrait of Vernon
"Lefty" Gomez, of course; a shot of DiMaggio returning to
the dugout; a scribbled note from Bill Veeck; and a blazing
nighttime photo of Ebbets Field. It is the stuff of baseball,
the game, the kind of thing real devotees collect and savor.
And none of it contains Chambliss's mug. The only evidence that it is the office of the commissioner of baseball is
found in a black-and-white photo of a scowling Kenesaw
Mountain Landis and a framed quote from the late A.
Bartlett Giamatti. The quote reads:

> Whether you like it or not, people will see you as a
> hero. If you really don't want to assume those
> burdens, you should go and do your best imitation
> of Mr. Thoreau. It's said that Americans build up
> their heroes to tear them down. But there's a
> responsibility to maintain that trust. I'm not sure
> heroes don't tear themselves down because
> there's so much pressure on them. You have the
> burden and the glories from having achieved a
> certain level, and you can't shuck off the burdens.

I rather like that, and once I suggested to Grand that it
be printed on the inside visor of every big-league baseball
cap. He smiled. But that is how he feels, and that's where
his heart is. And that's why he spoke as he did about Huston's murder. About heroes. Hero worship. The Yankees.
That grisly sniper's trophy in Monument Park.

I figured that the only guy more harried in New York
today than Grand Chambliss would be John Brush, our
impromptu host of last evening. But I got through to him

at his desk in Yankee Stadium using the clout of the commissioner's office.

"I didn't pay much attention to you last night, Duffy. I'm sorry," Brush said.

"No problem, John. You had worse things to attend to."

"Police were here all night."

"And you?"

"And me. Caught a few hours of sleep this morning. On the couch right here in the office."

"Knowing Huston, it's probably not the first time that's happened."

"You got that right, Duffy."

"Can I get to you today?"

"Today? It's a zoo here, but I'll make time," he said. "It's been a while since I picked your brain."

That was John Brush. He was a big shot, and yet he treated me as if I were Connie Mack. Through the years, as Brush worked for several different teams in different areas —player development and scouting, marketing, administration, assistant general manager—we'd come to know each other, and he used to call me up every so often and barber. He would ask me question after question, good ones pertaining to a player's spine and intelligence, a manager's tact, a scout's instincts, what I'd heard, and how things were playing around the league. I've seen a little of everything through the years, and Brush, I guess, respected my opinions. I can't quarrel with him there. A few years ago I suggested that he consider a particular individual as managerial caliber, and later that person became a Yankee skipper. I'll never divulge just who it was, and Brush won't either. Ultimately Rupert Huston made the hire, of course, and he told the world it was his idea. But it happened just as I have stated.

I had wondered about just how well Brush would fare with Huston. He didn't call me for my opinion on that before he took the job. Of course, I would have told him to take a pass. Huston chewed people up and spit them out, and that would include a thoroughbred like Brush, I feared. I suspect the lure of the Yankees was too strong, and Brush signed on. He knew the tradition, knew he would be sitting in the seat once occupied by Ed Barrow, and later George Weiss. These men were icons to him. His task was to rebuild the Yankees, find prospects and make trades, develop the farm system, nurture new DiMaggios and Mantles, a Tom Tresh, maybe find a stubby Italian catcher in St. Louis. For someone like John Brush, even within ranting distance of Rupert Huston, it was a dream job.

At midafternoon I took a cab up to Yankee Stadium. The ride gave me time to finish the newspapers, the early ones and the new editions that were popping up on the stands by the hour. Apart from the sensation and the details of the crime, coverage had turned to speculation about the possible motives for the murder. They ran the gamut from personal grudge to international terrorist campaign. The casual reader got the distinct impression that every reporter, editor, columnist, and shoe-shine boy in this burg had contemplated such an event before it ever happened. Imagine!

I tore the relevant material from the rags and filed them in my inside suit-coat pocket. It was a muggy, breeze-barren September day in Manhattan. I was wearing lightweight cotton everything and was still feeling uncomfortable. My sport coat wrinkled like a cheap napkin against the seat of the taxi. I perspired and told myself to lose some flab.

Ruppert Place in front of the stadium—named after *Jacob* Ruppert, the owner who had it built—looked like a parking lot for the Minicam Ball. I suspect the crews had been planted there all day, running about the ballyard, the monuments, taping the press conference Brush and his people had held that morning, generally lingering over the scene of the crime. The Yankee lobby was packed. Fortunately Brush had given me an alternate route to his office. To avoid the madding crowd, I slipped out of the lobby into the main concourse. I cleared myself with a guard stationed at the steps leading to the stadium's lower field level. That's the level of the clubhouses as well as the pressroom and dining hall, so this route is well traveled by players, coaches, and the media on game day.

This was not a game day, and security was stringent. I

descended the steps alone and found myself once again in the cavernous bowels of Yankee Stadium. The tunnel on that level follows the contour of the park from left to right field. The cinder-block walls are enameled deep blue. The ceiling is covered with a white fibrous insulation that looks as if it were blown on. Grids of utility lines and pipes run overhead. The air is still and somewhat stuffy, like that of the universal boiler room. There are panels and steel doors, the humming machinery that makes modern structures function, and men in work clothes with tool pouches who understand them. Big-league clubhouses are always tucked somewhere down in the bowels.

I rode an empty elevator up four stops to the executive level and the bank of offices that included Brush's. This was not unfamiliar turf: the 1976 renovation had put the press box and broadcast booths directly in front of these offices. Yankee brass, from the scouting director to the general manager, had only to open the curtains on their office windows to allow members of the press to gawk at their bulletin boards and desks and family photos. Huston's office was on the very end, accessible to his private box behind home plate yet cut off from the press and broadcast rows.

I entered the lobby of the executive offices. Again there was a guard, a friendly young fellow to be sure, but his presence and that of his peers today made me wonder where they all were last night. I stepped past the cases of gleaming World Championship trophies and announced myself to the secretary behind the counter. She acknowledged me, but only slightly. Her phone was buzzing, and she was filling out message memos for Yankee executives as fast as her pencil could move. She would tell her grandchildren about this day—the twenty-four hours after the owner's murder—but right now she was intent only on getting through it.

I found my way to Brush's office, passing others on the way, each one's inhabitant talking on the phone. Except for Brush. I caught him sitting at his desk in the light of a single brass lamp, his head clamped between his hands, his stare searing through the blotter. His phone was quiet. The television screen in the corner—all offices seem to have boob tubes nowadays—was dark. I heard faint strains of a piano concerto. It was slow and mournful, emanating from a deck of stereo components behind Brush. I savored the score—Ravel, I think—and missed Oscar Levant.

Brush sensed my presence and looked up.

"It's not a dirge, if that's what you're thinking," he said.

"Just as well," I said.

"How are you, Duffy?"

He rose and shook my hand, smiled, and came alive. Brush was a solid, good-looking kid of forty-five, fit and trim so that he could pass for ten years younger. He had the thick neck of an athlete, the broad shoulders of Lou Piniella, and a set of healthy teeth highlighted by his tanned skin. He had the hair of a movie star, thick, dark with a sprinkling of gray in it, and a little long, an invitation to someone's thin fingers with long nails. Standing a good six feet two, his height made him look bigger than many of the players he dealt with, men who were, as a rule, smaller out of uniform. I remember a Yankee outfielder, a good one, once telling me that it was hard to negotiate with Brush because he looked more like a ballplayer than the outfielder did. Right now, at three in the afternoon, he was clean-shaven, and even smelled faintly of something robust. He was wearing a long-sleeved pastel blue linen shirt and a wine-colored tie, the slacks to a dark suit, and a pair of black tassled loafers. For a guy who'd slept in his office last night, he looked good.

"Can I pour you something?"

"How 'bout a Ballantine . . ." I said.

"Where's Mel Allen when we need him?" he mused.

We settled for a couple of genuine Pepsis. I took a slug and looked at the walls around me. I was looking at a lot of office walls lately. Brush's were pretty boring. One wall consisted of rosters naming every player on every team in the Yankee organization: squads in Columbus, Albany, Fort Lauderdale, Prince William, Peninsula, Oneonta, and Sarasota. Another held the full rosters of every American League team, and the third offered the National League. The last wall was glass, a view of the field looking down the first-base line and the inside of the Yankee dugout.

"How's the ship of state?" I asked.

"Well, all hell's breaking out on deck, to extend the

metaphor. You saw the lobby. The helm is still under control, however. We'll still show up and play ball games."

"Who's coming at you?"

"Everybody. Cops. Reporters. Agents—whew! Those boys are really nervous now."

"Any G.M.'s?"

"Only for the right reasons. Some of my friends—Roland Hemond, Dombrowski, MacPhail. The other guys are waiting to see what happens. Why? Do you detect the scent of blood in the air?"

"After the Bill Wolfe trade," I said, referring to Huston's blockbuster unloading of his top outfielder two days before. It seemed as if the deal had all but been forgotten now, until I fielded Brush's glare. If wounded looks bled, Brush would be hemorrhaging.

"Duffy, I swear—" He got up and went to the window. The sun was shining rainbows through the mists of a dozen water sprinklers in the outfield.

"The Lundgren trade in July cut the pins out of our rotation. Do you know how I fought that trade? Lundgren had lost three in a row, but he had a sore shoulder. Everybody knew that. But Huston says 'Get rid of the son-of-a-bitch!' Get rid of him! Only the best gun in the majors with Dream Weaver gone, and Rupert says get rid of him. Same thing happened with Wolfe: he goes bad with a hamstring, and he's hitting defensively. He's down on himself, and Rupert says get rid of him. Don't let him heal and find his groove—get rid of him!"

"But you knew that, John," I said. "Huston and his million-dollar tantrums. If he'd been around in the old days, he'd have ridden everybody from Red Ruffing to Allie Reynolds out of town."

Brush exhaled. "Wolfe was a *Yankee*. He loved the sound of it. Wore the pinstripes like armor. A-hundred-and-twelve ribbies for us last year! This year he's hurt and can't push off with his right leg. The trainer swore to it."

"Hell, with Lundgren, do you know, Duffy, his shoulder was so bad, I had a neurologist from Chicago flying in to study his mechanics. Guy named Klawans, you may know him. He studies physical exertion and fatigue—"

"Richard Dotson and J. Rodney Richard."

"That's right. That's the guy. I'm sure he can help us

with Lundgren. I mean, he *could* have helped. Now he helps the Cubs. . . ."

He trailed off, not in anger as much as in injury.

"You know, Duffy, sometimes I wonder whether I should have finished my medical training. I could be rehabilitating these guys now rather than trying to replace them in the roster.

"You mentioned Ruffing, Duffy," he went on. "You remember his second or third season here? He was nine and fourteen for the Yanks. Nine and fourteen. Allie Reynolds had some bum years before he came here. Rupert would have dumped those guys in a minute."

"Huston talk to you about Wolfe?"

Brush snorted.

"After the fact," he said. "Asked me what I thought of the three chances the Pirates offered. I told them they were just that." He looked out his office window over the silent green of the stadium.

"What do you think, Duffy," Brush said suddenly, "was Joe McCarthy the greatest?"

"Of the Yankee managers? You mean compared to Huggins, Stengel—"

"Throw in Houk and Martin."

"Hell, John, I avoid these hot-stove arguments lest I come off like an old fogy. But yeah, I've always been a big fan of McCarthy. 'Course, the Yanks hired him away from the Cubs after he won a flag with them in twenty-nine. I'll never forgive Wrigley for that."

"God, how he dealt with personalities," Brush said. "Ruth, on one hand, who detested him and wanted his job. Gehrig, Lazzeri, and Dickey, who liked his tough hand. Then DiMaggio."

"Even I could manage a DiMaggio," I ventured.

"But what a contrast, Duffy. Here you have Babe— what'd Ping Bodie say, 'I didn't room with the Babe, I roomed with his suitcase.' Then you have DiMaggio—"

"And Eddie Lopat's remark. 'He was the loneliest guy I ever knew. He led the league in room service.' "

"That's it! That's what I mean. And McCarthy had to deal with both of them. Keep them both productive."

"That your vote?" I asked.

"Well," he pondered, "Casey was no slouch at dealing

with personalities. You remember his dictum: 'The art of managing is keeping the five guys who hate you away from the five who are undecided.'"

"A bright man, Casey was. And a brilliant run he had," I said. "You can't argue with five straight World Series wins, ten flags in twelve years. We may never see that again in our lifetimes. I know I sure as hell won't. You know, Bill Veeck once told me that if he had a veteran club, he'd take Stengel over anybody to manage it."

"Platoon, platoon, platoon," Brush said, "and it worked for him."

" 'I got the players who can execute,' he said. And that he did."

Brush smiled. "He had George Weiss too, that cranky old genius," he said, exhaling.

"It's the unending discussion, isn't it? Start talking Yankees, and you can't stop."

He was looking off into thin air, like a kid in a museum. Here he was, a Yankee big shot, a front-office honcho, talking about some people who'd been dead longer than he'd been alive, whose feats he could have only read about, and he was awed by it all. Like a tourist from New Jersey.

"You ever wonder if it's too much, John? All this Yankee tradition? Doesn't it ever feel like a lot of excess baggage? Every night you sit up there and watch the scoreboard rerun that old Movietone footage of Ruth and Gehrig and DiMaggio and Yogi and Mantle and Don Larsen and Thurman Munson. It's like poking a giant yardstick in your face every day, every game. And every time you lose, you seem that much smaller compared to the old days. Hell, John, you got maybe the biggest monkey on your back in the major leagues. You ever feel that way?"

Brush nodded his head slowly. He knew exactly what I was talking about.

"You can look at it that way, of course. Or you can take all those Yankee heroes, all that tradition, heck, just the name itself, *Yankees,* and make it something important. Just like so many people I meet who tell me they grew up hating the Yankees. And that motivated them. They got revved up every time the Yanks came to town. Hey, you know how in World War II the Japanese would shout 'To hell with Babe Ruth!' just to piss off the GIs and make them do something stupid. I figure it made them fight that much harder. You've got to look at it that way. It's what drives you, Duffy. Or it should."

It was an impassioned, impressive little speech, delivered by one who believed it.

"But enough of that," Brush said, shaking himself from his reverie. "The owner of the New York Yankees has been *killed*, and we're sitting here talking baseball.

"Huston was a bastard, Duffy, but he was our bastard, as the saying goes. Say what you will, but he was one decisive individual. He could move. He taught me a lot. A lot about business and a lot about people. More than I ever expected."

"Anything about baseball?"

Brush smiled. Then his face fell once again, and he spoke very quietly. "Rupert didn't know anything about baseball."

That single statement said it all for me. It spoke reams about what the owner of the Yankees had done to this man. It was more than the stupid trades, the outbursts, the feuds with players and managers, the demeaning statements and in-house demotions. It was, I sensed, an undermining of what Brush had worked so hard for, what he carefully constructed for the franchise, his best-laid plans, his strategies and hunches.

"Are the police still here?" I asked, remembering why I was there.

"I'm sure they are. They've been up here since we all were out by the monuments. Wanted specifics. Where was I? When had I last seen Rupert? The phone calls, the guards, the general lay of the land last night. You realize, Duffy, I'm one of the prime suspects. I was *here*."

"Any of Huston's known enemies show up?" I asked.

"His kid Griffith—I think you can include him. And they went at it again. Had to close my door!"

"Again?"

"Long-running family feud," Brush explained. "The kid could piss off his old man with the best of them."

"You know when he left the stadium?" I asked.

"About seven o'clock or a little after."

"He could have come back later, right?"

"Sure, he could have," Brush said. "The security people know him. But the employee service door on a hundred sixty-first had been jimmied or something, did you know that? They think that's how the guy got in. They're trying to figure out who helped him. By the way, are you officially in on this thing?"

"In the eyes of the commissioner, I am. As far as the rest of the world is concerned, I'm undercover."

"If you say so."

"Apart from our friendship that's why I'm here. You were as close to Huston as anyone."

"Well, it's hard to say whether anyone was close to him," he said, looking over at the photo of the two of them embracing after a divisional championship.

He added to my glass, then discarded the empty can.

"If you want motives, just pick up the latest profile. The *Times* did one last spring. Had the wife, dear Lana, and his darling kids. Had a lot on his nonbaseball businesses and his run-ins with the unions. In this town you don't cross the unions. Then there was the art collection and deals with his son. It went on and on. A lot of bad blood and rancor."

"I read it. Berkow, right?"

"Ira and I talked. I like his work. He wrote a book about Maxwell Street in Chicago, you ever see it? Fascinating.

"It seems funny now," Brush went on, "but I actually downplayed the hard feelings between Rupert and the rest of the world. Particularly between him and the players, and managers like Elberfeld. It's part of the process here, I said. Rupert pays you millions, and part of it buys him the right, from time to time, to rip open your soft underbelly."

"Did you say that?" I asked.

"Not in so many words. I didn't have to."

"Was he straight? I mean, apart from the bullshit, did he double-cross people he shouldn't have?"

"Not that I know of. He never did with me. Rupert was a straight-ahead guy. He told me straight up that he was the boss. He said the Yankees were not a democracy. He told his limited partners that that's exactly what they were—limited. If anyone was ever uncomfortable with that, including me, he should get out."

"So where would you look for suspects?" I was thinking out loud.

"I'm not looking for suspects," Brush said.

And indeed he was not. He had an organization to run. I speculated that he would be heavily counted on to keep things going until the fate of the Yankee ownership was determined. Culling through motives and enemies of the late and much-maligned Yankee owner was a job for birds like me. John Brush said he would help me in any way he could.

"Let me tell you something, Duffy. I haven't said this to anyone, and I hope you respect my confidence. The fact is, I always anticipated a day when Rupert would *not* own the Yankees. I think I came here with that notion buried somewhere deep in my hide. I figured, maybe I hoped, that he might tire of his plaything. At the very least maybe his interest would wane and he'd leave it alone, to run without his interference. I don't know.

"And now that it's happened," he continued, "I'm still adrift. I can't focus. I have no idea what will happen next, other than the team will wear black armbands and the purple and black bunting will hang over the door."

I got up and put a paw on his shoulder. It was a fatherly thing to do, and I couldn't resist. I admired John Brush, and I wished his present lot in life were a little more carefree.

"Find somebody to drive in Bill Wolfe's runs," I said. He sagged.

4

Big Bill Devery

As the horsehide bounced, I knew my way around New York. The ballyards and the sportswriters' watering holes, a few delis and too many restaurants (and those, sadly, no longer include Toots Shor's old place, the brick house on West Fifty-first Street, where, as Red Smith always said, "attendance was compulsory"), a hotel or two, and, of course, the commissioner's office. Otherwise I was a tourist. I could no more lift the telephone and arrange to see a varsity detective in the NYPD than I could get an audience with Cardinal O'Connor. On second thought, I've heard that the outspoken churchman is a fan, so maybe he would give me an ear. But Chambliss and his office were going to have to do some heavy blocking for me if I was going to get any help from the gendarmes. I didn't know them, I didn't know the hierarchy, the pecking order, the protocol, or the etiquette. I didn't speak the lingo of New York cops, and I'm sure they didn't much care to learn mine.

Like anybody who has spent a lot of time on airplanes, however, I've read my share of crime novels and police procedurals. Most of them, it seems, are set in New York. There are eight million stories in the Naked City, as it were, and its writers are determined to chronicle each one of them. After reading the good ones, I always felt on a first-name basis with the boys in the precinct houses. But that was in fiction. As far as the real thing was concerned, I was a raw rookie, like the kid Mantle in from Commerce,

Oklahoma, in the spring of '51. Chambliss, however, said not to worry.

Also with the commissioner's blessing, I prevailed upon the Summit's powers that be to transfer me to a suite so I could spread out and get organized. Out of habit, a lifetime of habit you might say, I had brought along my briefcase. In it was my fat dog-eared address book and a half-dozen reporter's notebooks. If I had a nickel for every one of those things I've filled in my time, I'd have a fortune —well, at least a month's salary for one of Huston's utility infielders. I needed the spirals now. Looking into a homicide is a little like putting together a story. You pry and nibble around the edges, talk to people, keep your eyes open and your nose unobstructed, and scribble notes like a Joe Durso.

My scheme was to stick by the book: jaw with police detectives, take note of their scrapings and angles and tests first, and go from there. That meant an appointment with a muckety-muck with a badge. Chambliss took the ball, made a few calls, and phoned to tell me that someone from One Police Plaza would contact me the next morning. In the meantime I had some respects to pay in a little town northeast of Manhattan. At the dinner hour I boarded a commuter train at Grand Central and headed for Rye, New York. It was a little place up along Long Island Sound where Hugh McGrew had breathed his last. I'd shared too many press boxes and broken too much bread with McGrew to let his wake go unattended.

As I rode the train out of Manhattan, its coaches crowded with dour young men and women in gray suits who didn't seem to be enjoying the ride, I thought good thoughts about Hughie. He was a beat guy, one of the many who toiled in the shadows of Grantland Rice and Red Smith and Frank Graham in the salad days of New York sportswriting. Hughie loved those guys, though he didn't have much truck with pundits. He was a hell of a newspaperman, a fact digger, possessor of a clear eye and some of the most efficient and unadorned prose ever printed in the New York *Post*. Daily from his hallowed front-row seat in the Ebbets Field press box, he punched out a wickedly candid assessment of the Bums, and there wasn't a player, a coach, or Walter O'Malley himself, who would dare take issue with him.

At the time there were three clubs in New York, and a dozen or so newspapers, so the fraternity of baseball writers was a considerable one. Each summer the scribes and their better halves got together for an outing, a dinner and dance at a lodge in the Catskills. The fest on a certain August night in 1948, McGrew once told me, was one that none of them ever forgot. They had finished dinner and were dancing in the warm summer air, Hughie said, when someone interrupted the band to announce that Babe Ruth had died. An instant grief fell over the crowd. "Even the wives cried," Hughie said. Then Arthur Mann of the *Herald Tribune* took his mandolin, and as those many grizzled, imperturbable veterans of the sports page stood and held their loved ones, Arthur played "His Memory Will Linger On." Then they all went home.

My visit to Rye was brief. Esther McGrew was happy to see me, and Hughie's casket was closed. I returned to the city and the Summit in time for a nightcap and a waiting message. The latter was from a Captain William Devery, NYPD: I was to meet him at First Avenue and Thirtieth Street the next morning at eight. Devery was, I recalled, the big cop on the scene at the stadium. His glower lingered on, and I made a mental note to be prompt.

But my Boy Scout intentions, I must confess, were sabotaged by a torch singer in Maude's Lounge at the Summit. She was a pretty lady, with teeth as white as the piano keys she tickled and a smile like an arpeggio. Not only that, she smiled at *me*. With no ulterior motives (at my age I kid myself not), and with a warmth that may have come from my second glass of rye, but I wasn't sure, I sidled up to the piano bar and just exuded rhythm without blues. She liked the company and said her name was Julie Field. Then she played and sang "Night and Day" far better than anyone her age, which was little more than thirty-nine, should be allowed. I am a sucker for a set of lyrics, a set of pipes, and some decent phrasing, and Julie had them all. She went from Lorenz Hart to Johnny Mercer to Cole Porter to Ira Gershwin and had me hooked like a sentimental old fool.

Two hours later I said, "You're an artist, ma'am," and stuffed her glass with green. She did a reprise of "Always" and blew me a kiss.

It was clearly into morning when I got back to my room. I was reeking of smoke, rocked from too much rye, and needed slumber. What I got was a ringing phone.

"I don't be-*lieve* it," came the voice. "This is *you*, is it not, Uncle Duffy?"

"And a late-night buss on your cheek, Petrinella," I replied. "I miss you dearly."

My niece wasn't buying it.

"Oh, stop it, Unk. Why haven't you called? You're still in New York —and in a different room, I might add. I think you're into it with Chambliss again."

I didn't like her tone. It clashed with those of Julie Field, which were still coursing through me.

"We had a little event here, Pete," I ventured.

"A little event the whole world knows about. And the commissioner has you on it, right?"

"I didn't say that."

"I did. And I'm on my way."

"Not on your life, my dear," I said.

"We're a team, remember. Tinker to Evers—"

"To law school," I finished. "That's your job. Don't even consider more detective work."

"You're at it, aren't you, Unk? Chambliss has you there on the Huston murder, doesn't he?"

"I'm helping him keep the wolves at bay."

"You're hitting the bricks. And I'm on the first plane out," she said.

"I forbid you, Petrinella. And I mean it."

She exhaled loudly. If impatience were electricity, the connection would have fried me.

"This is not Chicago," I added.

After a series of protestations and whines, each one punctuated with another of my stern refusals to even consider her presence in New York, she rang off. The call was over—Petey had a shrewd sense of how far to push things with me—but I was certain this was not the last of it. Petrinella Biggers, my bright and spunky niece who already had a taste for murder investigations, was not going to sit back and sing little-town blues. It was creeping closer to dawn. She could probably do well in a place that never slept.

As for me, I hit the pillow.

Morning came too soon, but I had no choice. I headed off for my appointment with the police. My local ignorance had led me to believe I was going to a precinct house. Nothing of the sort. For when it hove into view several minutes before eight, the unimpressive building on First Avenue and Thirtieth Street said NEW YORK CITY MEDICAL EXAMINER'S OFFICE over the door. This was the morgue, no doubt the place where Rupert Huston's carcass had been ignominiously filleted and inspected. In death as in birth, the saying goes, we are all naked under the harsh light. I entered the blue-tiled lobby with the spring decidedly missing in my step. When you get to be my age, these places do not inspire vigor in the corpus. I was ambulatory, a working stiff, I reminded myself, which was more than you could say about the majority of the building's inhabitants.

I paused for a moment. People came and went, most of them going up and down the stairs, looking like they knew exactly where they were headed. I did not, which, I had the feeling, may have been Captain Devery's intent. I noticed the verdant house plants near the windows, and then my eye lit on a Latin inscription on a nearby wall. For someone in a morgue, I was being remarkably observant. The text was Greek to me, for other than a few clichés, my Latin vocabulary was moribund.

"Let conversation and laughter cease. This is the place where death delights in helping the living," came a voice over my shoulder. The loose translation was offered by Captain William "Big Bill" Devery.

"Catchy," I said.

"Appropriate," he rejoined.

He turned and headed downstairs, expecting me to follow. Big Bill was not much for introductions, and I was grumbling to myself about that fact when the smell hit me. It was the dank, paralyzing odor of death, and it came on me like a Ryne Duren heater. Devery, the Latin scholar and, I was told later, Columbia-educated head of New

York's vast detective pool, apparently intended that as well.

He led me to a small gray-and-white-tiled office. It was overlit and furnished with only a wooden table and two folding chairs. Devery left the door open. Better to inhale the waft of cadavers and to hear the occasional whine of circular saws as they invaded skulls in the nearby autopsy room, I surmised.

"What is it that you want from the New York Police Department?" he asked, standing and propping himself with a tripod of fingers on the table. His other mitt held a manila folder. Devery was a large man—as nicknames never lie—maybe six four and thick in the chest. He was wearing a light brown summer suit whose coat looked too large even on him, hiding as it did about fifteen extra kilos around his waist. I suspect that, at fifty-five, he was not happy with that. Other than his bulk, his most notable physical feature was a head of thick but remarkably short hair. It was a grizzled mat, very unstylish, and had it been flat on top, he would have been a dead ringer for Roger Maris on Old-Timers Day. He also had Maris's hard, sleepy-eyed stare.

"Is the body here?" I ventured.

"Christ, no."

"Why then are we?"

Devery exhaled and crossed his arms in front of him.

"The police commissioner instructed me to extend every courtesy to the office of the commissioner of baseball," he said. "That, apparently, means you. Which returns me to my first question."

It was as roundabout an answer as a Mel Stottlemyre curveball, but I wasn't going to press things. Devery did not like me—strike that—he wasn't about to appreciate anyone without a badge poking around the biggest case thrown his way since Son of Sam. Homicide gumshoes, like sportswriters, are territorial animals.

"I'm not an investigator, Captain Devery. I cannot and I do not want to do your job. However, the baseball commissioner needs eyes and ears on something like this. If I do some of that, it frees one more of your boys to do the important work."

It was a bone, and Devery took it.

"Good. This ain't Chicago," he said, and I winced.

He tossed the manila folder on the table.

"That's ballistics, forensics, and investigative reports as of this A.M. You can take a look-see. You won't find much more than what you saw the other night at the scene."

I opened the folder and glanced briefly at the top report.

"I heard about your work on that Wrigley Field hit," Devery added grudgingly. "Pretty sharp, but it won't happen here."

"I'm an old sportswriter, Captain, not an operative."

Devery's eyebrows lifted slightly, and I thought I detected an almost imperceptible upturn at the corners of his mouth.

"We think we got point of entry," he went on. "The employee service door on One-hundred sixty-first was pried and taped. No alarm and no sentry. How's that for big-league security?

"The perp must have known this. Once he was in, he went up the escalator tower. Could have sat there all night and nobody knows the difference. He shot from a porch two levels above loge, about one-hundred-fifty feet up. We figure this from the angle of where Huston took the hit, and where the slug hit the wall behind him. The perp didn't leave anything up there, no shells or cigarette butts, but we're pretty sure of it. Had a clear shot, just over the fence between the bullpen and the monuments."

"Isn't there a netting—?" I asked.

"There is. Keeps the fans from getting beaned during batting practice while they're gawking at the plaques in left center. But it stops at the park in center, and if you get high enough up, you don't have to worry about it. Our boys really worked the angles. There's some drawings in there. We think he took one of the only real open shots at the monument area in the park. You can't get one from right field or from the lower left-field stands. It's that escalator tower or nothing. He must have known that too."

That spoke of knowledge of the site, but what about opportunity?

"He also had to know that Huston would walk between his cross hairs," I said.

Devery nodded.

"Shooter was no amateur," he said. "Single shot. Only one—and it put Huston down like an elephant. Blew what brains he had out the back of his head. Weapon was an AR-15 assault rifle. It's a long-bore marksman rifle, comes with a battery-operated sniper scope, high-powered, popular among the Soldier of Fortune set. It's also the only straw we got so far."

"How's that?"

"Two Family hits already this year with the same weapon."

"The Outfit?"

"Surprised us too. They usually go in close. Like to see a guy shit his pants before they pop him. But these two were definitely LCN. That's La Cosa Nostra. Probably one of Farelli's guys, because with him you never know. He'd get a bang out of something like that."

I read *Time* magazine, and I knew of Frank Farelli, the new boss of the Calvino family and New York's current Mafia bad boy. He wasn't Al Capone, or Don Corleone for that matter, but he was a hard guy. And as unpredictable as a Luis Polonia in Milwaukee.

"Huston? Killed by the Mafia? Does this make sense?" I asked.

"I didn't say that. I said the weapon was the same. I said the shooter was a pro. I didn't say it was Mafia."

Devery looked down and fingered the edge of the forensics folder. He was not going to be caught in any speculation with the likes of me.

"Forensics is still incomplete," he continued. "They didn't find much except that Huston probably was epileptic. That would explain some of his bullshit, now, wouldn't it?"

"Your people have done a lot in a hurry," I said.

"The PC has an army on this one. It's the Yankees, you know. The greatest team in the history of baseball until Huston got his hands on them."

"Do I detect a jaundice?" I said.

"I was a fan," Devery said. "What I thought of how he ran the club has nothing to do with it."

"May I have these?"

"No. Take notes. The rest is investigative reports. We're turning the stadium people inside out. We think the perp had help on the inside. From there the whole ball game gets complicated. The man had his enemies."

"What have you ruled out?"

"You should know better than that."

"I know a good cop gets a taste in his mouth."

It was another small bone, but Devery wasn't biting.

"No sir. We're not like sportswriters. We don't go in with an attitude. It's the best way I know of to get burned."

"So how 'bout this," I said. "A mixed-up gun-nut Yankee fan—or Yankee hater, for that matter—acting alone, pried open a service door, made his way to the top of the left-field elevator tower, and sat and waited for the owner of the New York Yankees to take a midnight gambol among the monuments. Then he blew his brains out. Lee Harvey Oswald in the Bronx!"

Devery snorted. "Read the reports, and think what you want. I'll be back shortly. And no, Rupert Huston wasn't shot by a lunatic. It was a professional hit. The victim had many enemies both inside and outside the organization. And you sound like someone a lot more curious than just the 'eyes and ears of the commissioner of baseball.'"

"Habit," I replied.

He left. A minute later the calm was creased by the anguished peal of a skull saw. In my mind I saw a head being topped like a hard-boiled egg. The sound brought back the smell of the place, something that had never really left but had somehow been suppressed in the heat of the discussion. I dug into the reports and tried not to gag.

I learned nothing other than what Devery had told me except for one small bit of information regarding the sniper's perch. Detectives found grains of reddish clay-gravel on the concrete. That soil is found in no other place in the stadium but the monument area, as far as the detectives knew. There wasn't much of it, and it might have been brought up there by a fan. On the other hand, if it came from the shoes of the perpetrator, it meant that he had to have been down by the monuments at some point. Perhaps lining up the angle of his shot? And if so, when? It wasn't much, but I made a note of it.

As far as stadium personnel were concerned, only John Brush, Rupert Huston, and four security guards were present at that time of the night. Brush's statement was lengthy and was made in the presence of four different detectives. He was there, he said, because Huston was there. He made it a habit of leaving only after the boss had left. Huston had been visited by several people—mostly lawyers and business associates—on and off until about eight o'clock that night.

He did have two other notable visitors. One was his acid-tongued daughter, Keeler Huston, the spawn of his first wife. Keeler was accompanied by her boyfriend, a fellow named Herm McFarland, who worked in operations for the Yankees and was at one time viewed as a comer in the organization. The pair had stopped in Huston's office and chatted for a few minutes, at around seven o'clock.

The other visitor was the second Huston offspring, Keeler's brother, Griffith. Griffith's presence surprised me, as it did the detectives, according to the report. It was widely known that Huston and his son had had a falling out a couple of years earlier over Griffith's sexual preference, his life-style, his appearance—he enjoyed being photographed flaunting a Yankee tie tack in his pierced right nostril—the whole wonderful ball of paraffin known as the Generation Gap. Griffith Huston's current interest, however, lay in the world of fine arts, and Brush affirmed the widely known fact that the kid had shaped up his act enough to draw some of his father's investment bucks into art.

Griffith had left, according to Brush, between ten and eleven. Huston stayed on until midnight, something not uncommon for him. He often wandered alone in the empty ballpark, sometimes asking Brush to join him, sometimes going off without telling anyone. Brush became suspicious only after the Yankee owner was gone longer than usual and could not be found by security.

There were two sets of guards on duty, and neither saw or heard anything. Two were stationed in the Yankee lobby. The other two were supposed to make roving checks of the premises. That night, however, the latter duo did not do much roving. In fact, all four of them were in the lobby when the shooting took place. Their specific responsibility, they seemed to believe, lay in the front-office and lobby areas. Exterior doors were locked and electronically controlled, with the exception of the overhead steel and delivery doors beyond the outfield area. The security station had a half-dozen video monitors, but none of them was placed out in the ballpark or the monument area. Finally, nobody had seen Huston go out to the monuments, though each guard, plus a couple of maintenance men, testified that they had seen him do so many times in the past. One guard noticed the elevator descending from the executive offices past the lobby to the field level. The time corresponded, as well as he could recall, with the approximate time Huston supposedly left his office. Sometime later, no more than forty minutes, John Brush had called security to inquire of Huston's whereabouts. Then he came down to the lobby and with one of the security guards went out into the stadium to look for Huston. They found the body, and Brush personally notified the police.

Other reports included interviews in the neighborhood. Detectives fanned out all along 157th Street and talked to a bevy of characters in Crazy Stan's Sport Shops, the Ball Park Bowling Lanes, and the other joints hunkered in the shadows of the stadium and the elevated tracks. It was tedious stuff—and not a bit of it helpful. If any neighborhood mope had seen a professional killer carrying a high-powered assault rifle with a silencer and a battery-powered scope, he wasn't saying so to any of Big Bill Devery's cops.

I was still reading when a figure caught my attention just outside the open door. It was one of the laboratory personnel—at least he had on a white coat—a little guy, maybe fifty years old, with thick glasses and bushy gray-black hair that stuck up around his ears like a court jester. He was looking in at me through the open door. I ignored him at first, but each time I paused and lifted my eyes from the reports, I saw this guy gawking at me. Once he even waved. Business must have been slack—if you could say that down there—or the guy just wasn't used to seeing bodies that breathed. I kept reading.

In a moment a voice came from the doorway.

"I knew it. I *knew* it," the voice said. "It's you, Duffy House, Chicago *Daily News*. Chicago's best. Boy isn't this something!"

My laboratory voyeur came in with his hand out-stretched.

"Dave Fultz here," he said. "Born and raised in Bridgeport. Played ball with Richie Daley when he was snot nose. He was pretty good, you know. I was one of your biggest fans, Mr. House."

That explained it, and I shook his zealous hand.

"My fans are far-flung," I said, not wanting to get into it with this guy.

"If I had my way, I'd be back in the old neighborhood. I'd be cuttin' up in Cook County with Stein. Hey, is old Stein still there? But my wife, she comes from Jersey, I met her in college, so I been out here ever since. You know where I was when Fire Commissioner Quinn blew off the sirens when the Sox clinched—"

"If you say McCuddy's, I'll call you a liar."

"Yeah! Yeah! I was! Me and Bill O'Connell and Chuck Belanger."

He laughed, and his glasses slid down his nose, and I noticed he had some nasty-looking stains on his coat.

"Hey, nice to meet ya—"

"Fultz. F-U-L-T-Z. Toxicology. Here's my card. I'm on the Huston case. Hey, could you imagine someone taking a potshot at ol' Bill Veeck? Huh . . . huh? That's the differ-ence here, if you want my two centavos."

"Actually, Eddie Gaedel was pretty sore at Veeck for taking him out of that game once he walked."

"Hey, yeah. I forgot about that. You got the Huston file there? Top drawer. Hush-hush. You got some real clout to even get a peep at it."

I shrugged.

"So you need something, you call me. Eleventh Ward, Mr. House. Dad was Streets and San. I won't forget how you've tried to get Nellie Fox into the Hall of Fame. Do I gotta say more?"

With that he looked behind him and backed out of the office with a wave. Then he popped back in again.

"Geez! Duffy House right here in my lab. Boy, do you take me back, huh?"

He was gone again, into the dull business and the keen smells of the morgue. I fingered his card and tucked it into my notebook.

Some time later, long enough for me to thoroughly peruse the police reports, Devery returned. He collected the file like a stern proctor and showed me the door. I was more than ready to leave. In the lobby he handed me his business card. I was beginning to feel like a mobile Rolodex.

"You're to contact me if you need to know something," he said. "Me and nobody else. Don't suck up to the others."

"I and the commissioner thank you," I said, meaning nothing of the sort.

Devery chuckled.

"I read the sports pages, like I told you, Mr. House," he said. "Grew up with Red Smith and Dick Young. If you were back in the sports section, I'm sure I would be a fan of yours. In homicide I'm not."

Then he and I left the place where death delights in helping the living.

5

Petey

Upon stepping out onto First Avenue, I gulped the air like a drowning man. It was not fresh—as New York City air has not been fresh since the days of Home Run Baker—but to my besieged nostrils and buffeted lungs, the breeze off the boulevard was baby's breath. A morgue will do that to you.

I decided to walk back to the hotel. I went north up First Avenue, catching a glimpse or two of the East River to my right, coming upon the NYU Medical Center. It was midmorning in Manhattan: shopkeepers had their doors ajar, fresh flowers and hot pretzels were for sale on the corners, and this side of the island seemed content.

At Forty-second Street, where Franklin Delano Roosevelt Drive turns into the city, the avenue became United Nations Plaza. I'd always admired the architecture, its whiteness and fountains, even though the idea behind the place has never fully hatched. I swung west down Forty-fourth Street and eyed the fluted spire of the Chrysler Building. That was my idea of a skyscraper, a needle poking the clouds, Manhattan's tallest building when Ruth was cleaning up behind Koenig, Lazzeri, and Jumpin' Joe Dugan.

In no time I was in the hustle of Lexington Avenue as it moved uptown to my hotel on Fifty-first. I stopped at the desk, where the clerks were beginning to know me on sight, to check my messages. I had three. All were from "P.

Biggers." All said to call immediately. I stuffed the memos into my shirt pocket like ticket stubs.

Petrinella—an old family name that was shortened to Petey before the ink on the birth certificate was dry— Biggers is my kid sister Betty's daughter. She's a twenty-three-year-old redhead, a freckle-faced knockout who got her looks and her quick mind from her mother's side of the family. Betty had prevailed upon me back in the spring to look after Petey when she came to Chicago to go to law school. I did just that, giving her shelter until she could find her own place, and enjoyed the heck out of the kid. Her spunk and gift of gab made up for the void my place had known ever since the passing of Wilma, the late Mrs. House.

Petey blew into town with a ragtag wardrobe, except for the running shoes, which were many, a library of tapes for that little machine clipped to her waist, more knowledge of the game of baseball than many sportswriters I know, and just about the best, most optimistic, blithe spirit you could imagine. She was ready for the big City of Broad Shoulders and loved every inch of it. Just walking down Michigan Avenue at night made her swell, and she gushed like Marilyn next to DiMaggio.

Even though she plundered my refrigerator, inflated my telephone bill, and left everything she touched on the floor, I liked having her around. Her arrival coincided with the Dream Weaver murder in Wrigley Field, and she dove into that intrigue with me like a latter-day Nora Charles. Her zeal came in handy, given my knack for being in the wrong place with the wrong people at the wrong time. It also convinced her that I needed looking after, and she would have been all too willing to lodge with me indefinitely. But it wasn't healthy. She was becoming a little too enamored of the shady world of sportswriting. And as much as I am flattered by imitation, it was not, as I say, healthy.

Finally I moved her out of my overpriced lakeside digs into an overpriced apartment of her own. She needed her own routine, and she had to get on with the business of an education in law. As much as I liked having a rookie in camp, I had promised her mother that I would keep Petey's nose pointed in the direction of torts and precedents. There would always be time to hang around the ballyard and talk garbage with an old eyeshade.

She appreciated my concern for fundamentals about as much as Bill Skowron getting the bunt sign from Frankie Crosetti. That she'd had a whiff of a murder probe, one that had taken her from a stadium's tunnels to its skyboxes, didn't help matters. When I took off for New York to feed off the commissioner's expense account and bury an old peer, she had wanted to go along. Not on your life, kid, I had said.

That was my first mistake. Being in Manhattan when Rupert Huston was expunged was my second. I knew very well the messages would pile up at the desk like overdue bills. The chase was afoot, Watson, and Petey Biggers, irrepressible niece with her appetite for mayhem whetted, wanted in. Not this time, kid. I would be adamant, counting on distance and my stern, less-than-avuncular warnings as an ally. I had a feeling I had said "kid" once too often.

In the hotel room I collated my notes taken from Devery's reports and collected my thoughts. My skull also slumped into my palms. It was early afternoon after a night of too little sleep and a morning in the morgue. The walk back from the morgue had cleared my head and tapped me out. I was contemplating suspects and motives, hired gunmen and deranged Yankee fanatics, if the latter isn't redundant, when the knock on the door startled me. I had dropped off.

"Room service," came the muted voice.

"Not for me. Check your order."

"For you, sir. Compliments of the management," came the reply.

Good Lord, I fumed. I can only stand so much largesse. The Summit had already slathered me with enough pillow chocolates and white wine. I went to the door anyway, perhaps out of sympathy for the bellboy who had schlepped the "compliments" all the way up here.

I opened the door, and she burst into a cackle.

"You fell for it, Unk!" Petey yelped.

Bedecked with a canvas bag, sunglasses, that shock of

red hair, and a grin as cocky as Jim Bouton's, my niece leapt over the threshold and gave me a bear hug. She smelled wonderful.

"What the—!" I growled.

"I'm here, Uncle Duffy. New York, New York!" she said.

With a sideways fling she sent her bags flying into the closet and headed into the suite.

"Get a gander at this, will ya!" she barked, spreading her arms and pirouetting as if she had just homered in the bottom of the ninth.

Her dramatic entry and pirouette caused her to lose her balance, and suddenly she tripped over a prone copy of the Manhattan phone directory and fell headlong onto the floor. The carpet notwithstanding, it was a hell of a stumble.

She rolled and held her knee and writhed.

"My knee! My knee!" she protested, a bit too loudly.

"Mickey Mantle, 1951," I said.

"Was that a phone book or a sprinkler head?" she replied.

"Smart kid," I said.

She sat up, suddenly free of pain, and looked up at me like Opening Day.

"How good would Mickey have been if he'd had good knees?" she asked.

"He made a lot of people forget DiMaggio with his bad ones," I replied.

"Mmm," she agreed, looking off and seeing, I'm sure, one of the Mick's splendid shots into the upper-deck facade of right field.

"So," she resumed, "tell me you're glad to see me."

"I won't. I know what you're up to. Where'd you get the funds to fly out here?"

"The glory of plastic, Unk. What's that you always say about my generation and credit?"

"Don't humor me."

"Why not! C'mon, Uncle Duffy. You knew the commissioner would sign you up again after Huston caught it. I could feel the vibes all the way back on Lake Shore Drive. And I said to myself, 'Self, how ya gonna keep the girl on the farm when there's murder in the Big Apple?'"

I shook my head and smiled. I smiled a lot around this niece. She was a tonic, I always said, for whatever ailed me.

"You are chipper," I said.

"That's for sure."

"How'd you find my room? No, let me guess. The commissioner probably all but drove you over here."

"They were very helpful, especially when I told them I had to deliver some of your special heart medicine."

"What the—"

She cackled again.

"Mr. Chambliss also said he'd put me on retainer until we cracked this thing. Retroactive to the moment I stepped from my apartment."

"Baloney. I know the man, and he wouldn't give that deal to Travis McGee."

"Okay, you're right," she said, "but it's a great idea, don't you think?"

"No," I said. "No. No. No. We're not in for a Wrigley Field reprise. I'm not gonna let you—"

"We've had this conversation before, Uncle Duffy, so just chill out. We're a double-play combo. Rizzuto to Gordon. Kubek to Richardson. Dent to Randolph . . ."

"Tinker to Evers—and leave nothing to Chance," I said, anticipating her topper.

She glowed. And bobbed her head up and down.

"Besides," she said, "we have a funeral to go to tomorrow morning."

The cathedral of St. Patrick's, that grand monument to belief, was only a few blocks away at Fiftieth and Fifth Avenue. The weather had turned muggy, the air still. It was as if someone had put a fetid dome over the city, and as I've said in many a column, I don't like domes. A crowd had begun to collect within a block of the church. It was the usual gaggle of gawkers, fans, and those city denizens who seem to have a scent for celebrity. The mood, I immediately sensed, was anything but somber. They were there to see Yankees past and present, the famous and the more famous: Mantle, Reggie, Whitey Ford, Bobby Murcer, maybe even DiMaggio himself. They were also there, I fear, to dance on Huston's grave.

Petey and I pushed our way through the throng. She was armed with two passes from the commissioner's office, so our access was assured. Suddenly I was stopped dead by the strong outstretched arm of a police officer. A certain dignitary had appeared, and the officer was assuring him a wide berth. The crowd craned to see, and a collective murmur swept about us. Walking in with his inimitable hunched shoulders, his arms motionless at his sides, was one of the biggest Yankee fans of all time, Richard Nixon. He smiled his peculiar smile and went inside.

After much jostling we followed. My eyes tried to adjust to the low light of the cathedral. It was nearly full. A large portion of pews had been cordoned off for Huston's family; the Yankee family, including John Brush, manager Jack O'Connor, some coaches and players; former Yankee greats and baseball dignitaries—Chambliss was there with Vincent, Ueberroth, and Kuhn—New York's political luminaries; business tycoons; and a good number of famous faces from show biz. These were people in Huston's track, I mused, most of them indebted to him for something, and he to them. It's really a very small club, and the players know each other well.

All sat somberly, facing forward, as news cameras situated in a sort of bullpen off to the side panned them. A closed ebony-and-brass coffin lay in front of the altar. Behind it was a massive, brilliant medley of red, white, and blue flowers arranged in the Yankee logo of top hat and cane. There is none like it. The same arrangement, sadly enough, had flanked Billy Martin's pine box. I imagine a similar bouquet was placed behind the Babe's bier when he lay in state in the lobby of Yankee Stadium in the summer of 1948. I shuddered at the comparison, but it was inevitable. Rupert Huston had owned the Yankees, and with it came the tradition. As the inside of my mouth caked up, I thought instead of Joe Dugan's famous line as he sat in the outdoor heat of Ruth's funeral. "I'd give anything for a beer," Bob Meusel had said to Dugan. "So would the Babe," Joe replied.

In my reverie I didn't notice that Petey had whipped out a pair of small opera glasses and was unabashedly scanning the audience.

"There's Sinatra," she whispered. "And Bill Bradley. And Trump! There's Trump!"

"What the hell are you doing?" I stage-whispered at her. "This isn't the ballpark!"

"I want to see who's here. There's Ford and Mantle and Yogi. God, all in a row . . ."

"Petey, in the name of privacy, put that thing away," I hissed.

She lowered the glasses but kept her eyes fixed on the celebrity pews. "God, is that Gloria Steinem? Gloria, a Yankee fan? Couldn't be," she said mostly to herself.

The organ began to play something suitably somber and baroque. At Bill Veeck's memorial a trumpeter played Copland's "Fanfare for the Common Man." For Huston, fat chance.

"Don't you feel it?" Petey said, turning slightly toward me. "Don't you?"

"What's that?"

She leaned into my ear. "Don't you feel the treachery? I mean, Uncle Duffy, don't you just feel the presence of the killer? I think he's *here*. Right here."

I sputtered, trying to do so quietly.

"Snipers don't take mass," I ventured.

"No, not the triggerman," she said. "I mean the person who plotted the deed. The force. I think he's sitting so close, he could jump into the coffin and straighten Huston's tie."

I closed my eyes. It was the only response. Petey returned to her people watching. I did what an old uncle in church has to do with his fidgety and squirming niece—give her a peppermint, look down his nose, and try to keep her in line with a frown. I wasn't terribly comfortable doing that, or sitting here for that matter. I have always worshiped in the temple of baseball, to borrow a phrase, and gone to breakfast instead of church. I didn't know how much time Petey had spent in houses of worship in her life. Precious little, I judged. But not too harshly, given my personal bent.

Just then a priest emerged from an alcove, followed by three people in black. The first was Lana Huston, Rupert's third and current wife, an ambitious woman as well known to the public and press as Huston himself. Every mourner stopped in midfidget and followed her entrance, all of them, including me, wondering whether Lana was worth more with Rupert dead or alive. Lana was followed by Griffith and Keeler Huston. Each appeared suitably solemn, a condition that wears well on the surface and under black veils. I don't mean to be catty, but the Huston family spats were legend.

"Keeler and Griffith, right?" said Petey.

I nodded.

"Who are they sitting with?" she said, but didn't expect an answer.

As the first eulogy began—one, I must say, that nicely tap-danced its way around Huston's true self—Petey reverted to her antsy self. She pulled a pad and pencil out of her purse and began writing. I listened to the priest, more out of curiosity than sentiment. Paid to circumlocute, clergymen were Stengels in cassocks. I wondered if a Yankee player would get up and say anything. I doubted it. I knew both Huston and Thurman Munson, and Huston was no Munson. In death as in life, considerate words for Rupert Huston would come from those on the payroll. With the rest of the audience, I sat and endured.

Petey kept writing, not a narrative or a poem or a personal reverie in this house of mourning, but a list with headings and numbers. I leaned in for a look and saw the words *sniper, Mafia, spouse, passion,* and *greed.* Petey was deducing, working the crossword puzzle of Rupert Huston's murder, the chips in her brain tripping and blipping. Touch her, and the electricity would arc.

Finally the churchman put a nut on his euphemisms, and the crowd rustled as another speaker approached the pulpit.

"Who's *that*?" Petey gushed, suddenly forgetting her jottings.

I lifted my head and recognized the tanned, handsome mug of John Brush. He unfolded a piece of paper, ran a hand through his salt-and-pepper locks, and prepared, with all seriousness, to speak. He reminded me of Robert Redford addressing a Greenpeace convention. The crowd quieted.

"That's Brush," I whispered. "Huston's G.M."

"That's John Brush?" Petey gushed. Her interest was

undisguised. Her eyebrows raised, and her green eyes glowed. She raised those damned binoculars and trained them on Brush as he collected himself. Her ogling was shameless.

"In the 1970s," Brush began, "something was happening in this city that New Yorkers were not used to. The proud Yankee tradition seemed a memory. After a last-place finish in 1966, the team struggled just to win as many games as it lost. The World Series, that annual event usually staged in the roasted-chestnut air of Yankee Stadium, took place in distant cities with players not wearing pinstripes, players not named DiMaggio, Mantle, and Berra. . . ."

"Listen to him," Petey breathed.

". . . the rest of the baseball world may have gloried in the Yankees' demise, but to those of us raised on the Yankee tradition, it was a tragedy. And it looked like one that wasn't going to end soon. At that sorry point a man came on the scene who was determined to bring back the Yankees. He was a man who, like so many of us, was moved to tears by Lou Gehrig's farewell speech, by the Babe, by the black-and-white films of the great DiMaggio, of Yogi hugging Don Larsen on that remarkable day in 1956. That man was Rupert Huston. . . ."

At that Brush paused. The tabernacle was so quiet you could hear the flicker of candles. Petey was among the transfixed, having lowered the glasses to hang on Brush's every word. I had to admit that I was just as rapt. I didn't know the kid had it in him. It's one thing to be a good baseball man; it's quite another to wax poetic about it. And he was doing it in homage to Rupert Huston, a skunk.

I waited for the hammer to fall. Brush was too much of a realist to let Huston pass unscathed.

". . . You may have quarreled with his style, with his decisions, with his temper and his tantrums. Rupert Huston was not a serene man. But you cannot quarrel with his intent or with his results. He made the team a winner. He brought pride back to the Yankees, and nobody can take that away from him.

"Rupert Huston did not go gentle into that good night, and I don't think anybody expected him to do so. He should be remembered, however, for reviving the Yankees in a difficult time. I'm proud to have worked with him in that. He made the Yankees a power once again, a presence, a team worthy of its legacy. Rupert Huston loved the Yankees."

With that Brush stepped down. It was a brief, eloquent speech, and for the first time I detected some genuinely moist eyes in the crowd.

"That was wonderful," whispered Petey.

The final act was almost as good. Frank Sinatra got up and sang "Abide with Me." No doubt someone had decided that a rendition of "New York, New York" might not float. He sang it a cappella, and it was nice, though perhaps at points his pitch was a little less than perfect. Then again, who am I to talk about somebody else losing pitch?

The service concluded, and Petey and I were among the first to walk out of church. The dazzling light of outdoors rudely jarred me back to reality after our little encounter with mysticism.

"Look at the crowd," said Petey, her eyes adjusting to the light more quickly than mine.

Indeed, an army of media and camera artillery flanked a crowd that spilled into the street. Gleaming black, white, and burgundy limousines were strewn about the curbside like derailed boxcars. It was one of those circus times.

"Let's get out of here," I said, clutching Petey's elbow.

"Go ahead, Unk. I'm sticking around to see what I can see," she said.

"C'mon. People don't look like much when they're in mourning."

She looked sideways at me.

"How many of them do you think are mourning?" she said.

It was a good question. I was jostled by the crowd. It surged to get a look at Lana Huston, the grieving widow, and her two somber stepchildren as they left the cathedral. Petey stood on tiptoes to get a look at the Hustons.

"Which is which, Unk?" she said, without taking her eyes off them.

"Keeler, the weer one, is the daughter," I said.

"So she is," Petey said, scarcely concealing her fascination.

I decided right there that it would have been useless

to try to persuade my niece to come along with me back to the hotel.

"You know where my room is," I said. "We have work to do."

She smiled and winked.

"I'm way ahead of you, Unk," she said, and lost herself in the throng.

6

Lana

There was no sense in fighting it. Petey was in Manhattan to stay, and I would just have to steel my jaw and hang in there. I felt like Ron Cey righting himself after registering that Gossage pellet in the noggin in the series of seventy-eight. Well, maybe I wasn't that beaned, but at my age you try to simplify things, and Petey was scrambling the roster like George Weiss in a pennant race.

The Summit made things easier by settling Petey into the adjoining room. Now she had her privacy and her own key and was but a knobless door away. The tab was baseball's, of course, as was the whole mess that kept me here in the first place. I also called my building manager back in Chicago and had her send me a little more of my wardrobe. I'm no dandy, but my traveling clothes were getting a little familiar. I would have to make do in New York for the duration, something not all that damnable given my many years of living out of a suitcase. What I missed most was my library, that wall of resources and frigates that allow me to travel lands and arenas faraway, not to mention the statistics that enable me to settle batting-average arguments with Petey.

In the meantime I plowed through the prose of the local papers. Few cities in the universe can churn the inky waters of newsprint like New York. The murder of one of their most flamboyant, wealthy, and public personalities was a city editor's dream. And the boys on the sports desk weren't exactly dormant either. Reporters from a half-dozen dailies covered every inch of the story and created a few inches that weren't there. Police-beat regulars called in their markers. Columnists returned every phone call. Sports reporters unraveled Huston and his Yankees like a cheap sweater. Mafia reporters sought out their informants. Feature and society reporters scraped the gilt-edged veneers of the Huston families, of Lady Lana, of Keeler and Griffith, of friends and relatives, neighbors and paramours real or assumed, and the warts festered.

As I read, I took a few notes, and compared them with the ones I'd gleaned from the police reports. The papers graphically recreated the crime—the time sequence, the angle of the shot, the specifications of the rifle, and its availability worldwide. Unfortunately, it was as available as a cough drop to just about any lunatic competent enough to fill out a mail-order form. They speculated on every possible method of entry and exit available to the perpetrator. They accounted for the movements of every person known to be inside Yankee Stadium that night and then researched each personal history as if its subject were a Supreme Court nominee. (A part-time electrician with a habit of renting she-male porno videos fared miserably in that probe.) They provided maps, graphs, overlays, and illustrated scenarios in edition after edition. It was, for the most part, pretty solid background material, and it saved me a lot of legwork as well as another meeting with Big Bill Devery in the near future.

The papers also elicited a half-dozen muttered confessions, some from professional crooks or unnamed button men deep inside organized crime families, others from pathetic creatures with glassy eyes who knew Bellevue as a second home. A crazy in the Bronx proclaimed that he not only had done the deed but would snipe at the owners of the other New York teams if they didn't shape up their franchises. Such outbursts created headlines tall and howling. Each new run of the papers, the *Times* as well as the tabloids, hit the streets like a grass fire—"I SOLD SNIPER RIFLE! Buyer Had 'Killer Stare,' Says Gun Dealer"—no matter how solid the newest lead or how credible the latest admission.

And yet, even the most cursory reading revealed palpable frustration. It was evident even to this out-of-town, part-time gumshoe that the police, the on-camera muck-ety-mucks in dark suits and worried brows, and the face-less but relentless brick detectives who knew the underside of every rock in their home boroughs, were not even close to disturbing the sleep of the stadium sniper.

Awash in all this roaring journalism, I was rattled by the ring of the telephone.

The voice was masculine, the delivery curt.

"Mr. Duffy House, please," it said.

"In the flesh," I replied.

"Please hold the line for Mrs. Rupert Huston."

With that command I stayed on the line like Graig Nettles in the late innings. I wondered what kind of good fortune, or what kind of clout, had brought the eye of the storm to this navigator. I had little time to wonder.

"Mr. House," she said with a clarity reminiscent of a midwestern schoolmarm but the inflection of a New Jersey manicurist, "I was told you desire an audience with me. I thought I'd save you the inconvenience of rooting about."

"This old rooter appreciates that," I said.

"Tomorrow morning at ten-fifteen," she said. "If the light is not too bright for you."

"I function well in daylight now that I've given up all my bad habits."

"That's a shame," she said, her voice lightening a bit.

"It's nice of you to see me . . . given the circum-stances," I added.

"It *is* nice," she said.

"I'm curious, how did you know my intentions before I even knew them?"

"Your employer," she said. "Grand Chambliss is a dear friend. After all, he made Huston's life miserable, and I like that in a man."

I laughed, perhaps a bit too quickly.

"Tomorrow then. Shall I have a driver pick you up?" she asked.

"Nah. Hey, you've done enough already."

"We shall see. Good-bye."

I was left listening to dead air. I smiled to myself, and I had jotted "Lana: 10:15 A.M." on the hotel pad before it hit me: I didn't know where she lived. Some operative I am. A phone call to the commissioner's office remedied that.

Grand wasn't in and therefore unable to explain how he
persuaded Mrs. Huston to ring me up. But Marjorie, his
secretary and all-knowing resource, supplied me with the
address of the Huston digs, as well as Lana's private line. I
told Marjorie she was invaluable. "I know," she replied. If I
had had any doubts about the pith of New York women,
these last two ladies had pinned back my ears.

Petey returned from stargazing about two hours later
than I expected—she was always later than I expected.
Her sunglasses were perched on top of her head, and the
heavy Manhattan air had not dulled her. Nothing that I
knew of could dull her.

"Now that was a send-off," she said. "Trump, Bill Bradley, Sinatra—"

"And John Brush," I said, reading her mind.

"Hmm," she said.

She didn't elaborate. Nor did she share what tack she
had pursued after the proceedings. Having been through
these waters before, however, I had a feel for the way
Petey liked to do things. She had a secretive, scheming
nature about her. The wheels were always spinning, and
she didn't like to jabber about things until they took shape.
That might make her a good, if unorthodox, spouse some-
day; but the habit was aggravating in the business of detec-
tion, where leads, clues, intuitions, and hunches have to be
aired if for no other reason than that they can trigger a
connection in a partner's mind. And I was that partner.

"You learn anything about the Huston kids?" I asked,
deciding to cut through the silence.

Petey glanced up from her reading of a tabloid.

"Oh, uh, yeah. Griffith. He's into art. I got an address
of a gallery," she said.

"Thank you," I said. "In the meantime I have an appointment with Lana Huston tomorrow morning. Care to
join me?"

"What? I mean, Uncle Duffy, you already got to her?"

I nodded. She looked impressed, and while I knew I
owed the appointment to the good offices of the commish,
I could keep a secret too.

That night Petey and I found a Thai restaurant on the

Lower East Side and over pud prik and pork satay we discussed matters fiscal and professional. Apart from room service, which, I insisted, she plunder responsibly, I asked her how she was going to get by on this expensive island. Pocket money, I had found out, is not Petey's strong suit. She looked at me, batted her lashes recklessly, and exuded blithe unconcern. "A girl's gonna get by," she said expectantly. The babies of the late sixties, even more than the baby boomers, have a way of believing that money will always be there.

I sighed, hemmed, threw in a haw, and offered her a ration of my daily cash stipend from the commissioner's office. She smiled. She knew she was valuable, and she knew I knew it.

Once the haggling was over, she settled down for some business talk.

"How much will Lana tell us?" she asked.

"I suspect not much more than we already know from the papers. Take a read of the *Times* piece on the family. I'm more interested in where Mrs. Huston points us. Or where she *thinks* she is pointing us."

"Motive?"

"From what I see, not financial. This is a wealthy lady with Rupert Huston alive or dead. She might fear probate, but I doubt it. The truly rich have lawyers who draw up things for these occasions. I'd bet Lana made sure she was taken care of in any event.

"On the other hand, hatred, disaffection, venality— those are always possibilities. Throw in power plays, control, and plenty of greed, of course. There's been a lot of positioning going on between the missus and Rupert's kids, especially the daughter."

"Sweet Keeler," said Petey, staring off, sharpening her hooks.

"So we'll see," I said. "If this is a family affair, then some very nasty and expensive moves have been made behind the scenes. You don't have somebody scoped with a high-powered rifle on whim."

"I love it," Petey said, leaning closer to me. "We're gonna get the *smell* of this thing, I know it. If Lana is what I think she is, she'll send out vibes and daggers and all that good stuff. It'll drip off the crystal. And we'll lap it up, Unk."

"Please, Pete, try to work up some enthusiasm for this visit," I cautioned.

The next morning we stepped onto Lexington Avenue in front of a cab. You have to be aggressive in this city, which the redhead at my side seemed to pick up before I gave her any lessons.

"Ten Gracie Square," I declared.

The cabbie was a white-haired, pencil-thin fellow with lines on his neck that matched the grids of Manhattan's streets. He was on the doorstep of social security if he was a day, wearing a golf hat and sporting a remarkable white mustache and a closely trimmed goatee that took me back to the Village Gate in the early Dave Brubeck days. Petey looked at him, smiled, turned to me, and said, "Papa Smurf." I had no idea what she was talking about.

"Gracie Square," the cabbie said in a voice that registered gravel on the tone bar.

His hack license, number 20541, revealed him to be one Arnold Langer. It had a nice American ring to it.

"No offense, but most people going to that address don't get there by jitney," Arnold said, as he waded into traffic with his left arm hanging out the window.

"We're slumming," I said.

"Ha! Ha! Ha!" Arnold laughed hoarsely, his head dipping toward the wheel. He straightened. "That's a very special block. Very special. It reeks of aristocracy and power. Old, old money."

He spoke slowly, a true orator of the boulevards.

"The widow lives there, you know," he went on. "The grieving widow. Ha! I would call her the first lady of the Yankees, but I have too much respect for the greatest baseball team in the history of the game."

Petey perked up, smiling at me. We had stumbled onto a baseball fan, and we knew he was about to hold court.

"My father first took me to Yankee Stadium in 1936. We bought general-admission seats. One dollar and ten cents. We walked up the ramp because my father liked to sit in the third tier. The third tier! Section five, behind home plate. We could see the foul lines.

"You see, the first four rows of the third tier were reserved. They cost one dollar and sixty-five cents. But right behind them were ten rows of general admission. General admission, if you can believe it! You got a lot of foul balls, and you were right on top of the field.

"And there I was, walking through the ramp and seeing the field for the first time. I remember thinking, *I can't believe it. It's a fantasy.* I had my glove with me. It was DiMaggio's rookie year. Gehrig on first base. Dickey catching. Crosetti at short. I saw Joe DiMaggio in center field, and I knew I was seeing something more graceful than I had ever seen in my life. A fellow named Gomez was pitching. They were playing Cleveland. . . ."

At that he trailed off. We were already in the Eighties and heading toward the river. Arnold Langer was quiet for a time, lost in an era past. I knew the feeling.

Then suddenly he turned and said, "You know what Gomez said about Cliff Melton, you 'member that big pitcher who won twenty in thirty-seven? Lefty said he had such big ears he 'looked like a cab with both doors open'! Ha! Ha! Ha! Now I can picture that!"

It was a good line and a good prologue to our upcoming tryst with the new proprietor of the Yankees of today.

Arnold turned onto East Eighty-fourth Street, a short dead-end block that was the two-hundred-year-old Gracie Square enclave. A few blocks north was Gracie Mansion, the mayor's place. Ten Gracie Square was one of three low-rise buildings, a regal, exquisite structure with three towers. It was a cooperative owned by some of New York's oldest, proudest money, and it was, as Arnold Langer had said, American aristocracy. The apartments were spacious by anyone's standard, with dozens of rooms, several baths, fireplaces, two-story living rooms, and grand views of the East River. Attendants and security were subtle, but everywhere.

"Thank you, Mr. Langer," I said as we pulled up.

"I enjoyed talking with you," he said, turning and making no move to accept my tender. "If you want my opinion, I'll tell you. No man knows the situation like I do. I don't wish violence on anyone, but Rupert Huston was a disgrace to the Yankees. He was a tragedy. He—he—he was *tampering* with the legacy! My Yankees! And he had no right! If they catch the guy who shot him, no jury will convict him. We're all Yankee fans!"

With that he took the fare, and I waved away the change.

"Thank you," Arnold said. He held up his hand, not wanting us to flee just yet.

"One more thing. She didn't do it. The Mrs. Huston here," he went on. "She didn't kill him. She didn't have the heart for it. A Yankee fan murdered the bum. And she was no Yankee fan."

We left Arnold, his pronouncement, and the raised temperature inside his cab. We had tapped a vein.

"A Yankee fan," Petey said, and said it all.

We were ushered into the Huston home by a maid and immediately found ourselves delivered from the sticky East River air to the rich fumes of polished mahogany and soft leather. Our shoes padded on pre-Ayatollah Persian rugs. Fresh flowers bloomed amid floral prints. Chandeliers tinkled. Original art works, paintings, and sculpture appreciated quietly. Chimes like soft thunder marked the quarter hour. I expected Alistair Cooke to appear at any moment.

Such muted opulence, I should add, was not something Lana Huston was born to. She had acquired it. She had scraped her way into these surroundings and into New York's high society, and once arrived, had set out to rule them. Had I not been apprised of her background by no less an authority than Grand Chambliss himself, I might have scoffed at it. Nevertheless, Lana Davidovich was the daughter of a *mohel* in Brooklyn. That fact led to untold numbers of jokes, most of which should have remained untold, in parlors, pressrooms, and clubhouses everywhere.

With a mind as sharp as a two-edged knife, she used her spunk, grit, and overachiever mentality, an average education, and a remarkable nose for where the action was to get what she wanted. That path had taken several turns. At various stages of her business career, she had sold stocks, real estate, and beauty-school franchises; she had been a travel agent and a lonely-hearts-club entrepreneur; she had operated a string of pet crematoriums. Lana skated in and out of business ventures like other women changed hairdos. Her last enterprise was a psychological consulting group that evaluated the worth of corporate employees. That was how she got the eye, and ultimately the hand, of Rupert Huston. He loved to evaluate employees; then he would fire them anyway. It was his third marriage, Lana's first.

The nuptial elevated Lana to the helm of several of the Huston businesses, excluding the Yankees. That was Rupert's toy. She handled hers—a few cosmetic lines, a commuter airline, an Arizona hotel and resort development—and did so with flare and brass. Her chiseled and oft-renovated face was everywhere, particularly in advertisements for Huston's holdings. Likewise, she insinuated herself into New York society, into its ballet companies and museums, its boards and commissions. She was Lady Lana, a woman with a profound if gratuitous taste for the trappings of royalty, American style. Like Rupert, she reveled in the media eye, courting its stars, snapping at its vipers. The two of them had been a well-suited, predictably tempestuous team.

"Hello, Mr. House," came a voice from a side parlor.

We were shown inside and came into Lana's view as she peered over reading glasses from a Louis XIV table littered with papers. The room was lined with bookshelves and low-lit with green-shaded lamps, a library turned home office, as far as I could see. The widow Huston seemed hard at work. There was no evidence of mourning, no pile of damp tissues.

She got up to greet us. She was dressed in slacks and an elegant off-white silk blouse that clung just enough to give evidence of her considerable curves. She was a young lady, no more than forty-five, with rich black hair and black eyes. She was striking but not a beauty, yet all the enhancements, the skin tighteners and softeners, the coiffure, the subtle tucks and cosmetic surgeries, had transformed a bright but not ravishing Brooklyn girl into a stated elegance. A hint of a costly *parfum* wafted my way. I shook a hand laden with carats.

The same hand was not offered to Petey, I noticed. And I checked my sleeve for cinders.

"And is this your Girl Friday?" she said.

Petey smiled and held her tongue. She didn't grind her teeth, scowl, or narrow her eyes. She was growing up magnificently.

"Miss Biggers, my assistant," I said.

"Assistant. Cute," Lana dismissed.

Petey responded by sitting down on a white velvet chair before Mrs. Huston had sat, which I'm sure wasn't often done in this room.

"Granville tells me you were a famous sportswriter. I used to read Red Smith in college," she said. "And now you work for the commissioner's office?"

"That's right," I said. "Keeping tabs on things, things like the death of your husband. Which I am very sorry about."

"Thank you," she said. "I imagine those other idiots who call themselves owners are a little nervous right now."

"Murder is bad for baseball," I said.

Her upper lip arched slightly. "You'd get an argument on that.

"If you were writing this up," she continued, "I wouldn't speak to you. I'm not granting interviews. According to the papers and television, I'm a suspect in my own husband's murder. That's how ridiculous things are. But this is New York, home of the Mayflower Madam and preppy murder."

"You stand to benefit financially from his death," Petey made bold to interject.

Lana turned and stapled a glower on her.

"I think that's the conventional assumption in the media, Mrs. Huston," I offered, ever the diplomat.

"Rupe and I worked as a team. I built up what he gave me. Doubled and tripled revenues. I hardly needed him to *die* to 'benefit financially,' as your cute little assistant puts it. That is too petty for words."

"A stout defense," I said.

Lana lowered her head and looked directly at me. She removed her glasses.

"Okay, let's get it up front. Rupe and I had our public quarrels. He was a hard person to get along with. So am I.

People took bets on who would dump whom first. And they all crapped out."

"Did you love him?" I asked, surprising myself. It was a Barbara Walters lob that I didn't know I had in me. Petey threw a sideways glance at my plaintive chops.

"Stop it, Mr. House," Lana said. "We're both too shrewd for that."

The room was deathly quiet. You could hear sarcasm drip.

"Others surely stood to benefit from your husband's death," I said, moving right along.

"*That* is for sure. Start your list right there, detective. I told the deputy commissioner that. He is the only police officer I've spoken with. And I filled his notebook.

"Rupe had enemies like jockeys have hemorrhoids," she went on. "Now there's something the press hasn't written. All of his so-called associates in business, baseball, the track, unions, real estate, you name it—they're all suspects. Rupe played games with mobsters, gamblers, hustlers, con men, lawyers, politicians, agents—everybody. None of them were worth a pitcher of warm spit."

I scratched my head and tried to figure out where that "warm spit" line came from. I liked it, but Lana had stolen it from someone.

Lana paused, quickly snatched a tissue, and sneezed loudly into it. Her nasal passages were in fine working order.

She went on. "Rupe liked dickering with 'em, the rougher the better. In his mind he could handle all of them before he went to lunch. And you know what? He was right. Somewhere along the line, mark my words, Mr. House, he had their nuts on a platter. Parboiled. That's the way he did business."

Petey chuckled. Between hemorrhoids and scrota, Lana had not left much below the belt undamaged.

But I almost missed it, because I was still racking my damn skull trying to locate that "pitcher of warm spit" quote.

"In ten years of marriage," she continued, "I saw him take more midnight meetings and suspicious phone calls than a Park Avenue hooker. You know how he dealt with people, all the shouting and the threats.

"But I'll tell you this, he wasn't afraid of anybody. He had no fear. That's why they had to kill him with a rifle at long range. He'd have laughed in their faces if they came straight at him.

"I'll tell you a story."

She stopped and turned to Petey. Here was a woman who could talk, and she was making certain the room's junior, and prettier, female presence paid attention. She got up from her chair and walked into the low shadows of the room. We followed her like an audience follows a diva.

"One night Rupe and I were dining and dancing at the Waldorf with friends, and we left very late. And Rupe said, 'Let's take a walk in the Park.' I said, 'Rupert, dear, you can't just do that. No one walks in Central Park after dark.' And he said, 'Ah, bullshit. People who show fear invite the punks. The park is an institution, and it's ours.' So we took a walk in the park. Arm in arm. Power is an aphrodisiac, you know, and it cuts both ways. The night was very nice. And sure enough, out popped a dirty, greasy kid with a knife. I was scared to death. 'Give it up, man,' the kid said, or something stupid like that. He was waving that knife like they do on TV. I knew exactly how that Goetz character felt. Exactly. So what did Rupe do? He started laughing. Laughing! He had his hand in his pocket, and he stuck it out a little and said, 'I got more power than you got, kid. I'm not giving you a thing unless you wanna work for it.' The boy got real nervous, and I was shaking hard, and my head was pounding. 'I'm with the Yankees. You want to work for the Yankees?' Rupe said. 'Yeah, man, like you some kinda Huston guy or somethin'?' said the kid, and Rupe laughed and said, 'Yeah, some kind of Huston guy.' I guess the kid believed him, or he was nervous, but he just said, 'I'll get you later, man,' and ran off. He just ran away. 'See? That kid was more scared than us,' Rupe said. Except that Rupert wasn't scared. The man, I repeat, was without fear."

Lana paused and slowly rubbed the palms of her hands. I detected a definite trace of emotion.

"That's quite a story," I said.

"Whew," said Petey. "I never read that in the papers."

"The *papers*," she snapped. "The papers are trash. Hotshot reporters, and not a damn one of them even asks what Rupert was doing out there in the first place. It's September! His allergies make him miserable outside this time of year. He takes four kinds of antihistamines and stays inside. The only place he can breathe is in air-conditioning. And he's supposed to be out walking by the monuments? Give me strength!"

"I didn't read that," I said.

"No, not when they've got *me* to write about," Lana whined.

"And his children?" Petey asked.

Lana stiffened.

"The less said about them, the better. They're worthless. Scum. Griffith's a degenerate, Keeler's psychotic. I won't let them in this house. I haven't for months.

"They're going to go after what they don't deserve out of this," she continued. "And I'll fight them. Oh, they don't know, those little worms. Think they're going to carve up the Huston empire, and they'll get a fight on their hands like they never thought possible. Black and blue. To the death."

A blister broke out on my forehead. Petey sat erect in her chair.

Then Lana smiled, the same toothsome smile that graced full-page rotogravure ads for her resort properties and spas in monthly magazines.

I had it. It was Garner. Nance Garner, one of FDR's vice presidents. The warm-spit remark came when someone asked him what he thought of his job, if I'm not mistaken. I was so proud of myself that I almost missed Lana's parting salvo to her stepkids.

"I'll skin them alive. Don't think I didn't learn something from their father."

7

Den of Yanks

I'm not one for phony mystique and cheap perfume, but I admit that no clubhouse beguiles me like the Yankee clubhouse does. Walk in the place, and there's legend in every corner. Put all the stones and plaques you want in center field, and that's fine, but the stirrings are felt inside the clubhouse, the place where Ruffing, Reynolds, and Raschi iced down their golden wings, where Rizzuto read his mail, where DiMaggio drank coffee in half cups, where Mantle's aching knees were wrapped in ice packs until they looked like frozen turkeys, where Munson looked into the mirror and scowled, and where Reggie strutted nude.

For fifty-eight years, starting in '26, the clubhouse was Pete Sheehy's domain, and in his grumpy, lovable way that grizzled old Irishman cared for and fed his Yankee boys like a father. He loved them and adored them, almost as much as his ice cream, which he ate in big bricks. After he passed away a few years ago, they named the room after him—put his name in bronze on the door, and I hope it stays there forever.

The clubhouse is all modern and acoustical now, with carpeting, wide white cubicles, and those boom-box stereos I'll never get used to. Million-dollar utility infielders with pearl earrings, gold necklaces, and hair full of Brilliantine preen in front of the mirrors. In my mind, however, it is still that place where Casey assembled "my writers" and held court, and "Marse" Joe McCarthy before him. It is the place where mere mortals, or so we were told, donned those pinstripes, laid that NY on their chests, and were transformed into Yankees. More champagne flowed there than in Guy Lombardo's dreams. Year after year, it seemed, flashbulbs popped in the grinning mugs of disheveled October heroes. The den of Yanks—could there have been a pride more famous?

So I decided to go back there right now. I'd had enough of police officers, cathedrals, and moneyed widows. The crime was against baseball, in one of its storied arenas, and I wanted to rub against the bricks. I've always felt a ballpark was like an opera house, full of niches and caverns, and, of course, alive with phantoms. No matter what kind of fee I cadge off the commissioner, I'm still a writer at heart, and to get a story, you have to dig around, seek out slivers of light beneath doorways.

I left Petey to her own devices, which she was to direct at the Huston menagerie. Our audience with Lana had piqued Petey's whiskers, and she was eager to sniff through the family's soiled laundry.

The Yanks, now with black-banded sleeves, were opening a series in the stadium that night against Boston. It was late morning, and while it would be hours before the players showed up, I knew the coaches would be around. Manager Jack O'Connor himself was accused of never leaving the place, a situation that, if true, would have been convenient a few nights back. I'd known Jack for twenty years, but—and I don't say this unkindly—I didn't have much of an opinion about him. He'd been a Yankee player for a couple years, and he'd been the proverbial sparkplug of an infielder. That kind too often becomes manager, and, apart from the conventional wisdom of the scrappy-little-guy-overcomes-the-odds, I'm not sure why.

It wasn't O'Connor's past or his scrap that bothered me; it was his off-the-rack approach to managing. Don't get me wrong, he didn't embarrass himself. He had his pitchers bunt when he was in the National League. He sent up righties against lefties and vice versa. He seldom let his starter go past the seventh inning. His teams won as many as they lost. He kept the boys hustling and never said a discouraging word. He became a lifetime member of the old-boys network of white, crew-cut managers whose treads never seemed to wear thin. Put a walnut-sized plug in their cheeks, and they all look the same. But Jack was a company man, and safe for Rupert Huston. He answered Huston's dugout phone calls in midgame, and no self-respecting son-of-a-bitch would ever do that.

I caught him in his underwear mixing up one of those diet milk-shake concoctions.

"Lemme get ya a beer, Jack," I said.

"Oh boy, I got the beer. Right here!" he yelled, patting his inner tube.

"Duffy House, where's the fire?" he said, and offered a handshake.

I took it. The clubhouse echoed with Jack's chatter. I expected him to whistle through his teeth and chirp, "Hum babe. Come awn, hum babe."

"Don't drink that slop," I said.

"Hey, I gotta deal with the manufacturer, Duffy. Lose thirty dingers on the bathroom scale, and they put me in a commercial. Where's the fire, huh?"

"Fire's in your shorts," I said, "if I know how that stuff works."

"Haven't changed, you peckerwood."

"How are things, Jack?"

"They're all right. Considering. Heyya, Duffy, 'tween you and me, things have been tough. But we're pulling together. Putting this thing behind us. Getting some consistency. This is a good ballclub, Duffy. 'Course, we ain't like the good Cub teams of the eighties, but who is?"

"C'mon, Jack. I'm not writin' anything. Cut the horseshit."

He pulled back a step.

"What's that supposed to mean?"

"Nothin'. I apologize."

"You're a knocker, Duffy. That's not what we need right now. Nobody knows what's gonna happen around here. So don't go knockin'."

"All right, drink up, Jack. And tell me how things were running in the clubhouse before it happened."

"Not writing anything, huh? Well, they were like they shoulda been. A ballclub's a ballclub. Don't mean shit what they say in the locker room. I don't listen to 'em."

He was interrupted by the ring of a phone in his office.

"You gonna be around, Duffy? I'll tell ya some things,"

he said. He winked and went off, his slippers slapping against his chubby heels.

It was as comfortable an exit as any.

"Don't be so hard on the guy," said a voice in the corner.

I put up a wet finger to test the wind direction. The words came from a human medicine ball propped up by a pair of pink, hairless legs and perched on a stool. It went by the name of Ed Sweeney, an old catcher who made Clint Courtney look petite. Now he was a first-base coach, one of the best, and probably the wiliest sign stealer in the big leagues. Sweeney had been stuffed in his cubicle the whole time. Missing him was like missing a full moon.

He was reading what I took to be a magazine but turned out to be a catalog full of power tools and gadgets.

"You work those things, Ed?" I asked.

"What's it to ya, ya Chicago gangster?" he said. "How's Al Capone?"

"I've missed ya, Ed. That needle of yours."

I shook his hand, and he stayed sitting on his stool. He was dressed in his underwear and a pair of thin, casing-tight sanitary hose that made his legs look like uncooked Italian sausages.

"Built me a compost holder over the winter," he said.

"For the clubhouse?" I said.

"Get outta here," he snorted.

"I thought things would be a little looser on the premises without the old man around, Ed."

"You did, eh? Well, you said you ain't writin' nothin' down, so you didn't hear it from me."

"Huh?" I said, looking around for Yogi.

"This place is still too full of contracts," said Sweeney. "Guys bought for too much money after havin' a year like they won't have again until the pope shits in the woods. I got a name for it. It's called bein' Oscar Gambled. And these Gambles get here, and none of 'em are Yankees. They're goldbrickers."

Sweeney turned a page of his catalog. He was going. If I'd have been on the beat, I'd have had half a column out of him already.

"Whattaya call 'em? Soldiers of fortune?" he asked.

"Prussians."

"What?"

"Mercenaries."

"That's it. And they come here and don't like New York this and New York that, instead of thinkin' *Yankees*. Something special. Fuckin' layover, that's what it comes down to. Told ya, Duffy, I don't gilt the fuckin' lily. You can call this team the New York Prussians. I like that. All because of you-know-who and his fuckin' money.

"So now heaven answers our prayers. No shit. Gimme a nickel for all the times I heard in this place 'I'd like to fuckin' kill the fuckin' guy.' Bingo! It happens, but instead of singin', they're all up in the air. Now they don't know what's comin' next, the fuckin' preema donnas, and that scares the hell outta them. They're hangin'. Like when you take a physic and you're waiting for it to kick in, you know?"

I knew, so help me.

"Now these mercenaries are nervous about their contracts. With no Huston around who's gonna come up with the same numbers? They got the wives and girlfriends in jewels and furs, and them bills got to be paid.

"But I said too much already, what the fuck do you care, anyway?"

I laughed out loud.

"Compost bins," I finally said.

"We're all in the fertilizer business, Duffy," Sweeney said.

I laughed again.

"You leave the door open, and the cat drags in anything that walks."

The remark did not come from Sweeney but from the pipes of somebody behind me. The place was crawling with echoes—and with Irishmen. This one, however, I knew right off.

Handsome Harry Howell came in with a box of baseballs for the autograph table. Howell was Pete Sheehy's successor, the man who had been Pete's right-hand man for as long as anyone could remember. Howell was a mick from Flatbush, a guy born under a toadstool with a bit of a brogue and a line of blarney that made Dylan Thomas sound tongue-tied. But it was his looks that lent him his moniker, for Harry was a smooth, handsome guy with clear eyes and a smirk, an Irish smirk. His black hair had turned silver now, but he looked as good as ever.

"Talk to Sweeney here, and you get washed by the bubblin' fount of ignorance," said Harry, giving me a bear hug.

I'd forgotten how long I'd been away from these guys.

"Welcome to the Yankees. The team God smiles on," Harry said, sweeping his hand around the empty locker room. "No matter what Sweeney here says."

"Ed was just talking about answered prayers," I said.

Harry raised an eyebrow. Then he motioned me closer, a true conspirator. He whispered.

"Day after, as sure as I'm standing here, there were boys looked in the mirror and grinned from ear to ear. It was like the weight of England being taken off the place, Duffy."

"I hear now they're not so sure," I said.

"There's reason for that too. See, these boys got heaps of money, but they're not money players. Not by a stretch. Not like Catfish and Reggie, Nettles, or Thurman—"

"Fuck, Harry, you're talkin' another league now," Sweeney interrupted.

"—see, those boys could get the big paycheck and play. Put the green on the table, and Fish'd pick it up. Nothin' bothered 'em, fact is, they played better when they had red asses. But not these birds. They don't got the *whiskey* in 'em. Like Sparky, he was a good one for that. So Mr. Huston now, he was wearin' 'em down. Man could do that to you."

"What Harry's trying to tell you, Duf, is that these candy asses don't know money," said Sweeney. "They want guarantees, that's all. No risk, just a guarantee. And Huston didn't give 'em a guarantee. After the big contract up front, he said, 'Now go out and fuckin' earn it.' He gave 'em shit, and the player you got today can't take shit. When the shit comes down, they shit."

"The man's a poet," said Harry Howell.

I felt as if I were caught in a traffic jam, with drivers honking front and rear.

"Now I'll tell you straight," Harry went on. "Mr. Huston, he brought talent in here. Money does that. Real talent. But he abused 'em. That was the sorry thing. He tore at their livers."

"Ah, to hell with their livers," said Sweeney as he rose from his stool, stretched, passed a *blat* of near lethal flatulence, and went off toward the hard-boiled-egg pile.

"You ever think someone *here* would kill the man?" I said, gesturing around the empty clubhouse.

Harry shook his head and ran a hand through his silver hair.

"Never to my dying day, Duffy, and I'll tell you why. You need fire in your soul to kill, and these boys don't got it. When Mr. Huston ripped them, they threw a bat or punched a locker, but that was the long and short of it. They went whimpering to their agents is what they did." Harry paused, and then continued. "Oh, the DeFord thing was hot. There was a lot more to *that* than the people know."

He turned his head and coughed. I made a mental note of Alfonzo DeFord, the moody free agent who had come to the Yankees when Artie Elberfeld was the field manager.

"Only man in this place who possessed the demons has been gone a while now. You know who I mean," Howell continued, reading my mind.

He took a few steps closer, cocking his head, catching me out of the top corners of his eyes. A trace of perspiration lay just above the neck of his T-shirt.

"Artie. Little Artie. Now that lad had the fire. You'd take up for him. I saw the blood in his eye, Duffy, and don't think Mr. Huston didn't see it there too. Reason he fired Artie three times—you know all about that. Now the boys in this room are callow from the first. Always have been. Young Joe. Young Mick. They come here not knowin' much about life. But they learned from Artie, 'cause he spoke the truth. He was sacked for tellin' the truth. 'Owners don't like that,' he always said. But the boys, they did. They went to war for that man, for Artie, God love him. Fought for him. Mr. Huston—they went to the bank for him. He had the boys' pocketbooks. Artie, he had their souls."

He drew a breath, then apparently decided he'd said enough. His tenor tones rang in my ears, and I felt as though I'd been to an IRA rally. My throat was dry, and my bones stirred. Howell was an Irishman, and he was possessed of an Irishman's gifts.

"You want fire in the belly, Duffy, look up Artie," Harry said. "Don't look around here. This is a laundromat."

With that Handsome Harry Howell raised his palms in supplication. Then he broke a smile like a rainbow.

"But why are we bellyachin'? This is the Yankees. The New York *Yankees,* as sure as my mother rests in the ould sod. And we all know God smiles on the Yankees."

Actually Howell was only half-right about the fire to be found in Yankee Stadium nowadays, for some live embers still smoldered in the person of Alfonzo DeFord. One of Huston's famous multimillion-dollar free-agent purchases a few years before, DeFord, a great ball player with an even greater opinion of himself, was a Huston attempt at bringing back the likes of Reggie Jackson and Dave Winfield to Yankee Stadium. Like those two, DeFord brought with him a potent bat—for three years running he'd stroked thirty homers and stolen thirty bases—and produced a lot of runs for Huston's Yankees.

Unfortunately, DeFord was a proud, defensive black, reminiscent of Dick Allen, and his arrogance often overshadowed his statistics. I liked him because he always had an opinion, and as Sparky Lyle said of Reggie, even if he didn't have anything to say, he was always quotable. Columnists bow and scrape in front of guys like that. It was Reggie who once proclaimed that he could spout off as long he could "hit the ball over the wall," and he could always do that.

DeFord and Huston—along with former manager Artie Elberfeld —kept up a long-running feud, a soap opera of insults, taunts, and charges that salted the headlines but wearied the fans. When Huston got rid of Bill Wolfe, his close friend, DeFord, as expected, was furious. "Get me off the DL"—he was currently out of action due to lower back spasms—"and this sharecropper is gone too," he groused.

I had not read what he'd said about Huston's death, and I was curious. Ed Sweeney told me that DeFord was working himself back into form by taking batting practice in the cage just beneath the stands down the first-base side. For reasons known only to him, DeFord preferred the ministrations of a mechanical pitcher to a live one. That is what sent me in the direction of right field after I exited the clubhouse.

And DeFord was there, alone, wearing a pair of baggy navy Yankee sweats, which were soaked with sweat. His nearly shaved skull was a sheet of perspiration. He was a massive and powerful man, a left-handed swinger who coiled like a Winfield and hitched like a Jackson and pasted the ball like a DeFord. Pitched balls thwocked off his bat and hissed into the netting. He looked fit.

I was standing inside the door no more than ten seconds when he stopped and looked over at me. His eyes were dull and heavy, black and intolerant. He was in no mood, no mood at all, at least it seemed that way until he opened his mouth.

"Still think I should bunt more?" he said with a voice that gave nothing away to Paul Robeson.

I smiled. I had once written that a man with his speed and power could get thirty extra hits a year by laying down a few bunts on low fastballs with the third baseman playing deep.

"Get you out of slumps quicker. That was Rod Carew's favorite trick," I said, which had also been part of the column.

He smiled.

"I ain't Carew," he said.

The pitching machine was out of baseballs, and its arm whistled through the air delivering nothing. DeFord stepped on a foot pedal, and it stopped.

"What's happenin', House? I been lookin' for your book," he said.

Then he grabbed a wire basket and began filling it with baseballs off the floor. It was something to see: a multi-millionaire shagging his own swings.

"Don't look too hard, Al," I replied. "The book's still in the typewriter until people stop getting killed in ballparks."

"No comment," DeFord said, emptying his basket of balls into the machine's basket.

"How's the back?"

"Achin'. But it's time to play. Time to toil for all the Babe Ruth writers, you dig?"

"Not sure."

"You don't work here, House. You don't put up with the Ruth shit every day. Ruth this, Ruth that, long as I been here. From guys who forget all about Henry and Willie."

He lifted his shirt from his belly and wiped his face. It didn't help much.

"That's hot-stove talk, Al," I said. "And you'll lose everytime."

"You too?"

"Mays stole more bases, and Aaron hit more homers. Give you that. But Ruth had a three forty-two *lifetime* batting average over twenty-one years. You ever hit that high for a whole season, and for power too? But here's another thing, Al: ol' George Herman was the best left-handed pitcher in baseball before he came to the Yanks. Beat Walter Johnson more than Johnson beat him. Had the most scoreless innings in World Series games until Whitey Ford broke his record. Should I go on?"

"Ah, shit . . ." DeFord said. "I'm talkin' to the wrong man."

"No, you're not, 'cuz I loved Aaron and Mays. They could do things nobody could do," I said, scrambling to keep his attention. "Which reminds me, how'd the Wolfe thing go down with you?"

"The hell! Didn't go down at all. The Wolfer got mugged."

"You communicate with Huston about it?"

"Yeah. I got me a rifle and shot him through the head. . . ."

"Don't say that so quick," I said.

"I'm the Joker, House. Jack Nicholson got nothin' on me. Truth is, I wanted to do it. Somebody beat me to it, didn't they?"

"Police talk to you?"

"Hell, what for? I get paid if the bastard's dead or alive," DeFord said. "Hey, every guy on this Yankee team wanted to put a slug in Huston's ass one time or other. Traded Lundgren, shit. Now Billy. If I'd seen him on the street after I heard about Wolfer goin', I'd of taken him out right there. Done it with my hands. And no jury here in New York would convict me. Have to try the case in Zimbabwe to get me guilty. Howdaya like that shit?"

He wasn't smiling. He picked up his bat and stretched, arching his back, grunting, trying to chase the demons that lived in his spine. Then he turned the pitching machine back on and looked back at me with a smirk.

"How 'bout this, House: my trouble is that I couldn't stand the man. He was a racist plantation boss who thought he owned my ass. But check it out: I ain't enough of a Yankee lover to dust him."

With that he got into a hitter's stance in front of the plate, and he actually started laying down some bunts.

8

Artie

From the Yankee pressroom, I called the hotel and left a message for Petey, suggesting she wrap up her digging by late afternoon and join me for dinner at Yankee Stadium. John Brush had told me to make myself at home while I was in town, and that meant partaking of the good food in the stadium's press and hospitality-room restaurant. If I had a nickel for all the meals I've eaten in stadium clubs, I'd be Howard Johnson. Most of them, the meals and the facilities, I should add, are first-rate.

You might not know it from their prose, but sportswriters are well fed and watered by the host clubs. They line up at the home team's hot buffet tables, laden with everything from fried chicken to prime rib, and usually go back for seconds. The rolls are warm, the desserts gooey. Free feed of the peanut and hot-dog variety continues in the press boxes, with only a gratuity to the servers expected. It is a fact of the sporting press not readily known to the public, and one that has always made me chafe. Of course, such talk among my fellow ink-stained wretches is heresy. But my colleagues in City Hall, the courts, or on the police beat are not routinely dined by those they write about. Sportswriters always are. We're all in the fertilizer business, as Ed Sweeney said.

In the meantime I had most of the afternoon to use, and I took a stab at making contact with Artie Elberfeld. Harry Howell's words burned in my head, and I wanted to get close to the flame Harry spoke of. I knew Artie had a home in Duchess County, the same one he bought when he began his first of three tours as Yankee manager some fifteen years ago, even though he'd skippered other clubs in between. Ailing, undermotivated ballclubs we always have with us, as well as the occasional owner so close to his rope's end that he considers ringing up Elberfeld. Rope's end or wit's end, it took either one to fetch Artie. He was currently unemployed, but he always answered his phone.

Of course, I knew Elberfeld, the Tabasco Kid, as they used to call him; no baseball writer in the last quarter century could have avoided knowing him. But he was not a friend of mine. No baseball writer in the last quarter century was Artie's friend. Yet I had his home phone number. Artie was like that: he might tell you to go to hell and how to get there, but he'd make sure you could reach him so he could do it personally.

I dialed and he answered. It was as simple as that. I heard the chatter of a television in the background, and I sensed from a couple of indistinct consonants that Artie had melted some ice already this day. But he said he'd bend my ear. "Meet me halfway, House," he said. "I know a place with a good satellite dish and a better barmaid." He gave me directions to a bedroom town in Westchester County called Briarcliff Manor, which he said was an hour away by train.

His directions sounded simple. I toyed with the idea of cabbing to Grand Central and riding the railroad; but after a few indecisive minutes, I called Marjorie at the commissioner's office instead. She told me to sit tight and wait. "It's about time we heard from you," she said. "We were getting worried." She added that it would be only a few minutes before Norma Perlmutter, the office chauffeur and our navigator of a few nights back, would be honking out front on Ruppert Drive. I thanked her, apologizing for not having checked in sooner. "Noted," said Marjorie.

I found a pair of newspapers to devour on the ride and settled in to read them in the stadium lobby. Instead, I ended up reflecting on Artie Elberfeld. I knew a lot about him, having devoted several column inches through the years to his highs and lows, his triumphs and tragedies. Here was one of those tough kids who grew up in an ethnic ghetto—a real ghetto—more than half a century ago in

Newark, New Jersey, where your passport was your fists, and you had to show it at every block.

His father died when Artie was a toddler, which meant his mother had to take menial jobs in other people's houses. Artie scraped and scrapped for everything. He had a big mouth, a short fuse, and a quick right fist. During World War II he played sandlot ball around Newark, outfield and catcher, and slapped hard line drives between the infielders. He dug in at the plate and was afraid of no one, least of all the opposing pitcher. Throw at the Tabasco Kid, and he'd charge the mound and go for your throat.

After the War he was signed by the Yankees and cut a swath through minor-league towns from Oneonta to Columbus. He was loud and fiery, a short kid fighting with teammates who thought him too runty and with opponents who threw at him or slid into the plate too high. He got a lot of base hits and threw a lot of runners out at second with his strong arm. His teams always did well, and on one of those minor-league teams Artie hit .368. His managers alternately loved him and hated him, and never for a minute forgot that he was around.

When Elberfeld came up to the Yankees, Casey Stengel had been the skipper for a couple of years. He had had such success with another diminutive scrapper, Billy Martin, that he took Artie under his wing even when some of the veterans were hazing him. In those days before multi-year contracts and guaranteed job security, veterans made no bones about intimidating newcomers to try keeping them off the roster. When they ragged on him about being too small to make it in the big leagues, and claimed his hitting accomplishments were bush-league feats, Casey said something like, "A lot of you guys didn't hit like him in high school! Welcome to the Yankees, son." That was the beginning of a long and warm relationship between Artie and the old man. Then Casey told him to hang around with Billy Martin and learn the game from him. And Artie did learn about major-league ball from Martin—and a lot more.

Billy and Artie, though they both had a fiery temperament, became fast friends, always defending each other against attacks from opponents. And Casey was the great mentor and father figure they both had in common. You can make something out of Casey being without a son and both Billy and Artie being fatherless. I don't know about that, but I do know chemistry when I see it, and those three men had it.

Like Martin, Elberfeld brought along his share of trouble, and George Weiss, unlike Casey, didn't think much of his scrappy personality. He was still the abrasive kid from the tough neighborhood who fought too much. When he felt aggrieved, he came out swinging. He carried a long-standing hatred for Red Wilson of the Tigers and duked it out with that tough nut more than once before he was traded to the Tigers.

On top of all that, Artie also had a reputation for late nights, liquor, and women—baseball's lethal off-the-diamond triple play. The Yankee management fretted about his influence on players such as Whitey Ford, Mantle, and Yogi Berra. Never mind that those guys were capable of being frisky on their own. The front office groused nonetheless.

Stengel, on the other hand, liked him and won with him. Especially in the World Series. Artie Elberfeld, in the field and at bat, was a player, a battler, the kind of money player Ed Sweeney and Harry Howell had said the Yankees didn't have anymore.

Just then a car honked, and I was shaken from my homework by Norma Perlmutter. It was good to see the impish, curly-haired pilot. I swung my bulk into the front seat and spotted her leather driving half-gloves, the leather ending at the knuckles and her naked fingertips and their magenta-polished nails curled around the wheel.

"Hiya, Mr. House. Where we goin'?" she chirped, wheeling out into traffic as if she already knew. On her forehead, I swear, she was wearing a green eyeshade. She looked like a brunette Harpo Marx if Harpo had been a bookie.

"Whattaya have in mind?" I said.

"Blow in my ear, and I'll take you anywhere," she said.

I laughed. The trip would be a pleasure. I told her that we had to go to a town called Briarcliff Manor, and added some of Elberfeld's directions. She nodded confidently and pulled onto the Major Degan Expressway.

"Ever been there?" I asked.

"No. I don't feel safe in the suburbs," Norma said.

She got the expected glance out of me.

"That's a joke," she assured me.

"Where *do* you live?"

"Kew Gardens. Queens," she said, with an accent stolen from Fiorello La Guardia.

"Who lives there . . . this Briar place?" she asked.

"I don't know. It's Artie's idea. Artie Elberfeld."

"Great!" she said. "He's the best."

She made a fist as she said it but kept her eyes on traffic, fishtailing in and out of lanes. I snapped my seat belt on. She approved. "You never know," she said.

"I heard Huston was gonna rehire Artie," she went on. "Artie always said he was ready. Said he would manage them without pay just to give 'em back their pride."

"I don't doubt that," I said.

"Why'd Huston fire him in the first place?"

"And the second place . . ."

"Whatta jerk," she muttered.

"Well, Norma, neither man was easy to get along with."

She sniffed and worked the pedals. I watched the road signs and saw that we had progressed to the Thomas E. Dewey New York State Thruway. I silently raised an homage or two to the old crime fighter. I thought of Virginia Hill.

"You ever see Artie play?" I asked.

"Mr. House," she said, looking my way. "I wasn't even born yet!"

"I guess that rules out the Copacabana episode," I added.

"Where are you comin' from?" she said.

I chuckled. Where was Petey when I needed her?

"I thought people from Kew Gardens knew all that Yankee history," I said. "Nineteen fifty-seven. Big fight at the Copacabana nightclub with a bunch of players. And not too long after that, Artie Elberfeld wasn't a Yankee anymore."

"Yeah, I heard of it. What happened?" Norma said.

I did not mind refreshing her infertile memory. I waded into a replay of that May night when Yogi, Whitey Ford, Mickey Mantle, Hank Bauer, Johnny Kucks, Billy

Martin, and Artie all went out with their wives or girl-friends to celebrate Yogi's and Billy's birthdays. They ended up at the Copa on East Sixtieth for the Sammy Davis, Jr., show.

"There are plenty of versions of what happened, but most people say that a drunk made a racist crack about Sammy Davis, and it made Hank Bauer pretty hot," I said. "Bauer's roommate at the time was Ellie Howard, who was the Yankees' first black player in 1955. . . ."

"I know that," Norma snipped.

"Anyway, words were exchanged, and even Sammy Davis himself told the hecklers to shut up or get out. Bauer, you may not have known, was one of the strongest men in the game of baseball—Casey Stengel once said he was so strong, he could 'pinch off your eyebrows'—"

"I love it!"

"—well, Bauer got up and went after one of the heck-lers. Then Johnny Kucks, who was a middling thrower who had a good year in fifty-six, and Yogi got up and grabbed Bauer. But things by that time were up for grabs, with bouncers and everybody mixing it up, including Artie and Billy. When the chairs and tables stopped flying, one of the bums was on the floor with a concussion and a broken jaw. The next day the papers were red hot with stories about the fight. All the Yankees were called on the carpet by Dan Topping and George Weiss. To a man the players pled innocent. Yogi said something like 'We were amazed when we heard anybody was hit, because none of our guys hit him.' He said he was holding onto Bauer, so he 'couldn't of hit nobody.' Then Yogi came up with one of his famous lines: 'Nobody did nothin' to nobody.' "

Norma, who was enjoying the story immensely, burst into laughter at that.

"Of course, George Weiss didn't see it that way," I went on. "And even though he didn't do anything right at the time, he started getting rid of some of those guys who weren't big stars as the season went on. He traded Billy Martin to Kansas City, and Artie went to the Tigers. I don't think Johnny Kucks lasted the year either. Even Casey, who was always saving somebody's neck—"

"Like . . . like—don't help me—" Norma interjected "—like when Don Larsen got in trouble in spring training. Got drunk and ran his car off the road."

"Precisely. But he couldn't save Martin and Elberfeld this time. Being traded really hurt Billy and Artie. Weiss, the horse trader, picked up Ryne Duren, the blind Dutchmen—you remember him, don't you?"

"Get out of here."

"And Harry Simpson, who was best known as 'Suitcase.' "

Norma Perlmutter nodded her head vigorously at my rendition of this page of Yankee history.

"And all this time I thought the Copacabana was just a bad Barry Manilow song," she said.

I marveled at such a frame of reference on life.

By this time we had progressed to the Saw Mill River Parkway and then over to the Taconic Parkway. The scenery had greened considerably. This was pretty territory in any man's eye. Norma drove as if she were a regular commuter. At Chappaqua Road we left the parkway and traveled on old Route 100. The trip took us a little less than the hour Artie had estimated it would. I had a feeling Norma often beat estimated arrival times.

We slowed and nosed our way until we found the place, called Torchia's Ristorante, and the smell of sweet Italian sausage filled the air. It was nothing special to look at, a kind of low brick-and-stucco building that looked as if it had had spontaneous additions slapped on through the years, and I immediately liked it. Wagon wheels covered a pair of front windows. Norma pulled into the parking lot and killed the engine. I thought she would come inside, but she stayed put.

"Not on your business," she said, and pulled out a copy of something called *Delta of Venus*.

"Wouldn't you like to meet Artie?"

"I'd *love* to meet him," she said. "Give me a wave when you're done."

The place was dark but not foreboding. A bar dominated its center area, and dining rooms branched off to the right and the rear. My brogans clumped on the flagstone floor as I took in the decor of knotty-pine Americana with a touch of largesse from liquor distributors. The tables were covered with oilcloth. It was midafternoon, so the clam-

and-linguine lunch trade had thinned, and the place was nearly empty. A few plaid-shirted guys with harmless vocabularies were funning with a zaftig waitress who wore an oversized shirt with two considerable pockets in front. Her laugh suggested that she enjoyed being funned with.

The jocular young lady did come right over to me, however, and directed me to the figure in the corner. It was Artie Elberfeld all right, the guy who used to attract crowds wherever he went. A short wild-eyed guy who brought crowds to their feet when he ran onto the infield of Yankee Stadium, who had managed the Bombers to titles, who sprayed tears, love, and acrimony like his line drives, who was loved and hated, shunned and adored, and now, finally, in this small bar in a little New York village, alone.

He was about sixty-five now, a little grizzled on the sides and lined in the cheeks, but he still had that glint, that schoolyard flash. It was the greatest "intensity" a good many sportswriters had ever seen. For years I'd had the feeling that Artie Elberfeld was on the psychological edge, his mind spiking with surges and short circuits, his emotional equilibrium tenuous at best. Part of what made him a great manager, that quirky, unpredictable energy, also tortured him, kept him with one foot on the dugout step, and stapled a squinting, strained look on his face. That same visage was now staring up at a daytime TV drama of love and treachery. He gripped a glass of caramel-colored liquid in each hand. He'd removed the maraschinos. He had a long start on me.

"Whattaya think of this place?" Artie said to me. "Some people around here wanna knock it down. Well, not me. I wanna buy it. And it ain't for sale."

The words ran together, the delivery only slightly reminiscent of Artie's famous pistol-shot diction. The pistol had just been oiled a little too much. I ordered a bottle of Genessee beer.

"Hey, Tracie," Artie called out. "This guy named House. From the sports pages, you ever read him? What's your first name, Duffy, and don't give me any of that Irish shit."

Tracie leaned down to where her eyelashes nearly

dusted clean my forehead. A hank of auburn hair fell over an opalescent peeper.

"I've read every word you've ever written," Tracie said, nearly knocking me off my stool with a wink.

"This is the one I was tellin' you about, Duffy," Artie said, leered, and fielded a clicking sound from somewhere deep in Tracie's throat.

I apologized for having arrived in midentendre.

Tracie exhaled magnificently and left us in a fog of cologne somewhere between Old Spice and Afternoon Delight.

"It's all smoke," Artie said. "She's locked, stocked, and barreled with two kids and an ex-convict in a house trailer. Trust me on that."

"It's a good smoke," I said.

Artie took a big gulp of one of his drinks, then turned to me.

"If you read the fish wrappers lately, you're sittin' next to a murderer. I had Rupert Huston whacked. Howdaya like that? I had a fight with the bastard a few nights before, and the next thing you know, I hired a guy with an elephant gun, and he shot the son-of-a-bitch from the cheap seats. At midnight. Can you top that?"

"I'm no Mickey Spillane, Artie."

"Who'd he play for?"

I grimaced.

"We used to pass *I, the Jury* under the table at school, so up yours, House."

I smiled and pulled on my beer.

"I made commercials with Huston," Artie went on. "Why would I wanna have him hit? He was my meal ticket."

"Was he going to put you back in the dugout?"

" 'Course he was. Question is, was I gonna go?"

"Answer?"

"In a minute! Never cleaned out my locker. How do you like that? Seriously, the Yanks aren't what they're s'posed ta be, and I wanted to do something about it. Give 'em their pride back."

"Is that what you were talking about a few nights back?"

He snorted.

"Funny thing, Duffy. I went up to the son-of-a-bitch's office, and I tore him a new asshole. I always did when I'd had a few belts. The team's playing horseshit, and I knew he was gonna do something stupid. That Wolfe trade—I could see it coming. I told him to let the hell go. Let the *hell* go. Stick with his real estate, his Indy cars, or any damn thing, but let go of the Yankees.

"See, I can tell him that. I put up with what most people hated about the guy. His big mouth, all his interference. He and I are a lot alike in that way, so it never bothered me. I didn't give a shit about him buying every contract in sight. I didn't even give a shit when he'd fire a guy in the middle of an inning. I done that myself.

"I didn't care that he didn't know the game. You remember that story Sparky Lyle used to tell about Rupert thinking we'd tied a game up because the guy from third crossed the plate before the third out was made at first? That didn't bother me; I'd just rag his ass and send a ten-year-old kid up to explain it for him.

"All his fights with the commissioner and his crazy stuff with the umpires—you remember when he publicly called that one ump an Arab terrorist, and Grand Chambliss fined his ass thirty K? I hate the goddamn umps most of the time myself.

"Didn't bother me how two-faced the son-of-a-bitch was 'cuz I never listened to him anyway. I'm a little moody myself. I'd needle him about his financial scandals. He used to get a good laugh out of it, then tell me where to go. Good goddamn laugh. Rupert was like water over a rock to me. Hell, when he fired me, I usually said, What the hell took you so long!

"That's no shit, Duffy. This is me talking, not the booze. My head gets real clear when the subject of the Yankees comes up. See, I worked to get back there. After I quit playin', I started out as a scout, for cryin' out loud, lowest damn rung on the ladder just to get in the front door. Managed the Mud Hens, then coached for that silly shit Mayo Smith, 'member how he tried his best to keep those good Tiger teams in the sixties from winning? Then I got the Angels, Texas, and Milwaukee—you know I did my time and turned some pissant clubs around. It's on paper, I'm not tellin' you anything new.

" 'Cuz all the time I'm shootin' for one job and one job only. Only place I wanted to be in baseball. I learned that from Mr. Stengel, the greatest manager who ever lived. You want a hero from me, Duffy, and that's who you get. You can take Joe and Yogi and Billy Martin, those guys, 'cuz they were heroes in my book, and I won't argue with you. But I'll take 'em behind Casey. That old man. Forgot more about baseball than most guys who call themselves managers today ever knew. And *he* knew he had the best job in baseball when he had number thirty-seven on pinstripes.

"So finally that goofy-ass Huston called me and made it sound like it was his big idea. Made me manager of the New York Yankees. Casey's job. The only job I ever wanted, even though it's the easiest one in the world to lose.

"But that's all part of it. Listen up, House. As soon as they hire a manager, they stick a fuse up your ass and light it. You can hear it hissin' and burnin' down every time you turn around. Only man didn't have one was Connie Mack, and he owned his damn team. Sat in the dugout and didn't even have a uniform on. Wore a suit, for chrissakes. God knows, they stuck a fuse in my ass, and I heard it. Had cordite on my cheeks.

"That was the thing with Rupert and me. I could live with that. Didn't bother me."

His voice cracked slightly, and he emptied his second glass. It hit the bar a little too solidly. Artie was flushed and sweating heavily. I could actually feel the heat of the man.

"So you got the best job in baseball, and you can live with the worst son-of-a-bitch in the game, and you got a fuse burning in your ass. So what in hell *did* bother you, Artie?"

"Glad you asked. Glad you came up here. It's nice, this place, ain't it? Tracie over there. The locals don't bother you. Play a few hands.

"What tore at my guts," he resumed, "was when Rupert wouldn't give it up. He was on this King Rupert thing. Trying to convince the world that he was bigger than the Yankees. Him! Huston! Bigger than the New York Yankees, which is bigger than all of us. So that night I told Rupert that I'd sooner put a stake through his heart than sit back and see him tear all that down. Make the Yankees a joke.

He had to let go. He had to step aside. Put Brush in there or get Gabe Paul or Al Rosen back or some damn thing, but he had to get the hell out of the way!

"I did threaten the son-of-a-bitch! I told him I'd sooner see him dead than see the franchise pissed on! I didn't say it behind closed doors, and some Huston kiss-asses like that McFarland jerk—now there's another story—heard it and they think I meant it! Well, they're right. I'd a loved to a killed the prick. But like Sinatra, I just said that about my friends in the Mob as a joke. That was no threat. There's lots of people out there hate the ground I walk on, and they'll spread some stories and tie me to it, which is kind of a joke because I ain't been doing much but watching baseball games on my dish and turning down offers to manage in Seattle and Atlanta and every junior-college team on the Eastern Seaboard. That and too many elbow curls with the sauce."

He swayed, grabbed the stool for support, and missed. I reached over to him, but he regained his balance. He was an old catcher, still able to make the peg and avoid the hitter's high swing at a pitchout.

"Whattaya doin'? Writing? You say you were in the commissioner's office? What in hell'd I hear from you for?"

"I'm—"

"Who cares what you're doin'. I always liked your stuff, Duffy. Never read it, but I liked it. I always told Red Smith he was fulla shit, and I never read his stuff either."

"You read every word," I said.

"Nah, that's Tracie over there. But forget about her until later, 'cuz if you're serious about this shit, you got to turn over the DeFord business. Big bad Alfonzo. Rupert shucked him. And Al don't take that shit. He makes me look like a stiff. Gets that look in his eye. Man."

Tracie had brought over a cup of coffee, and Artie slurped at it noisily. I didn't cut in. The mention of Alfonzo DeFord interested me.

"DeFord," Artie went on. "Him and me never did get along. There's another guy thinks he's bigger than the Yankees. I told him once that he and Huston were made for each other, and the bastard came at me. Shit. But Fonzo's got the balls—and the contacts—to do it. You know, waste a guy. Think about that, Duffy. And while you're doing it, I gotta bleed the weasel."

He scuffled off toward the men's room.

I looked at my watch and decided I had to get back. I went out and fetched Norma. She propped her eyeshade on top of her curls and eagerly accompanied me back inside.

I introduced her to Artie.

"You are one of my all-time heroes," she said.

Artie hauled off and hugged her, just clutched her to him as if she were a lost daughter. When he pulled back, I noticed that his eyes were moist. I marveled. The guy had made a career of wearing his emotions on his sleeve. He wanted to be back in baseball more than ever, and the mere supplication of a fan made him ache.

Norma bubbled as we retraced our route into the city. Instead of an autograph, Artie had written her a rambling paragraph. She was starstruck, and she jabbered. I was left with my usual musings. Artie had touched a chord. The game is made up of heroes. Artie himself venerated Casey, his mentor and surrogate father. He played in the shadows of Ruth, Gehrig, and DiMaggio, heroes all. He despaired for anyone who didn't feel the way he did. He despised those who thought themselves somehow bigger, more important, more imposing than the tradition, the game. He spat in the eye of Rupert Huston.

And I wondered, as I thought back on that fiery little shell of a man on the edge, sitting in a dark corner of a small-town gin mill, how desperate was he?

9

Petey and Brush

An empty open-air stadium in late afternoon is a sight
as tranquil and gorgeous as a meadow. The late sun catches
the angles and outlines the facades. It lengthens shadows
over the rich grass and the red clay. The empty seats tick
and creak as they cool. Sounds of supply trucks and park
workers occasionally crease the silence, echo through the
vast arena, then die away. A few players wearing warm-up
uniforms lope and work out here and there. A stillness
pervades, a readiness, the anticipation of crowds and noise
and the crack of the bat. All only a few hours from now.

It was at that golden moment that Petey met me at
the press gate where her credentials were waiting. She
was smartly dressed in a pair of pleated slacks with a cop-
per-colored belt around the waist, an olive green short-
sleeved sweater, her burnt red hair swept back into a
bushy cluster, and a light scent of musk. As usual she
turned heads like rear-end collisions do on freeways, and I
paused to buss a peaches-and-cream cheek. For the benefit
of the security guards, it was more than avuncular. Petey
gave me a look.

She then looked past me to the expanse beyond my
shoulder. I'd forgotten: she had never been to Yankee Stadium, and I knew the words of the cab driver upon first
seeing Yankee Stadium—"this is a *fantasy*"— were burning in her ears. Ballparks have a power over the young and
impressionable of America—those, that is, who were
raised right. Petey was one of them.

We walked through the concourse and the field-level entrance, which opened to an expanse of reserved grandstand seats just above and behind third base. Petey stopped and took in the panorama.

"Yankee Stadium," she intoned.

She let her eyes roam over the ocean of deep blue seats and the fabled playing field, the expanse of the outfield, the steeply tiered seats overhead, and the Victorian facade, a replica of the one that once skirted the entire roof, far above the center-field wall.

Colonel Ruppert used to call the stadium a "mistake, not mine, but the Giants'." The Yankees, of course, were originally the New York Highlanders, part of the fledgling American League at the turn of the century. They played at Hilltop Park, at 165th and Broadway, the highest point in Manhattan, hence the ballclub's name. The park was one of those wooden, covered grandstands common to the era. It held about fifteen thousand fans, though thousands more—in the days before liability suits—would stand along the foul lines.

The Yankees also played in the shadow of the mighty New York Giants and John McGraw, who ruled baseball from the nearby Polo Grounds at 155th and Eighth Avenue. McGraw, of course, never thought much of the American League, much less the Highlanders. Nevertheless, in 1913 the Giants allowed the Highlanders, who became known as the Yankees after headline writers grumbled over the length of the name, to play in the Polo Grounds, and they did so for ten years. Why, Babe Ruth hit his first home run as a Yankee there in 1920. It sailed over the right-field wall, which was a meager 254 feet away from home plate, and went clear out of the stadium and into the midst of a sandlot game.

When the Yankees decided to build their own stadium in the Bronx, it was with McGraw's blessing. "Once they go up there," McGraw said, "they will be forgotten." In 1921 Jake Ruppert paid six hundred thousand dollars to the William Waldorf Astor estate for 11.6 acres of farmland just across the Harlem River from the Polo Grounds. Two years and $2.3 million later, after a frantic 284 construction days, Yankee Stadium opened for the 1923 season. There was mud and construction debris everywhere, but the stately arena was ready. Governor Al Smith threw out the first ball, baseball commissioner Kenesaw Mountain Landis observed sternly, and John Philip Sousa led a marching band through the opening festivities.

"This is like going to church," Petey said. "Babe Ruth, Lou Gehrig, Joe DiMaggio . . ."

"A holy trinity if you're a Yankee fan," I said.

"I always hated the Yankees," she replied. "But that's irrelevant now, isn't it?"

"No, that's part of it."

She smiled.

"We have time for a tour?" she asked.

We had time—and clearance, thanks to John Brush— and I led her down the aisle and out toward the left-field stands. It was the same route I had taken a few nights earlier. Petey took in the sights like a person who had seen a few ballyards, some from the inside out, in her time. Like everybody else, she wanted to see Monument Park, so we stepped out of the stands behind the left-field fence and went down onto the field level.

"Is this park different for you? I mean, from the old stadium?" she said.

"Yup. And for good reason," I said.

The original stadium was "the house that Ruth built," as the great Fred Lieb wrote in the *New York Evening Telegram,* and a lot of fans wanted it named after the Babe even then. As it was, the dimensions of the field catered to his strength with its intimate right-field porch. With Ruth not only anchoring the Yankee lineup but with his power hitting changing the very face of baseball, the Yankees and their new stadium hit the ground sprinting and never looked back. Over sixty thousand fans packed the place on Opening Day, and Ruth delighted them all by parking a slow curve from Boston's Howard Ehmke in the bleachers.

It all came back to me as I toured with Petey. I told her of the Polo Grounds, now razed, and McGraw's mighty Giants, indeed—gone west. Why, even Little Napoleon's style of play, the so-called "inside" baseball of scraping and sacrificing for a single run, was swept away by Ruth's clouts, and the game itself was saved from boredom. That too was all part of the old Yankee Stadium.

"But I'm not jealous about the old place," I said. "They

moved a few things around—the bullpens, and the monuments, shoot, they used to be right out in play in center field. They changed the dimensions: the right-field porch was all of two-hundred-ninety-six feet away. That's longer now. And that little, low railing—it couldn't have been more than three-and-a-half feet high the way the right-fielders used to push off it.

"But to tell you the truth, Pete, it's the players I see, not the park. The Yankees had real *teams*, with guys like Andy Carey and Gil McDougald, who you don't hear about much today, but they just fit in and produced. Roy White— now there was a fixture in the boxscore. The magic of the pinstripes. It was right here. Other teams around the league would have killed for it.

"There was Yogi and Larsen, Maris and that great season of his, Hank Bauer, Mantle—oh, how he crushed the ball—those guys. That bad-hop grounder hitting Kubek in the throat in the sixty series —'course, that happened in Forbes Field. Casey, always with his hands in his back pockets. The mind has a way of petrifying those scenes."

"I wish I were you, Unk," Petey said.

"Hah! These old bones? My blood pressure? Forget it."

"No, your memories. Everything you've *seen.*"

"It's funny, Pete, but I look around, and I think of things I didn't see. I never saw Josh Gibson play here. They say he nearly put a few out of the park. I didn't see Gehrig's farewell. DiMaggio practiced perfection here every day, but I only caught a fraction of his play."

I could feel myself being sucked into Yankee Stadium's vast hole of nostalgia. I fought its pull. We had other things to think about, and I nudged Petey on toward Monument Park.

We got to the tray-table monuments designating numbers the Yankees have retired, then to the garden itself with the three stone markers for Ruth, Gehrig, and Huggins, and the lime-green rear wall of bronze plaques. Petey lingered long, reading every word.

"Did you know Ed Barrow?" she asked, eyeing the plaque commemorating the brilliant general manager of the Jacob Ruppert era.

"He was an old man when I met him. He scared the hell out of me."

"He did?"

"A great baseball mind. I'm easily intimidated."

"He sure had bushy eyebrows," Petey mused.

"So do I."

She winked.

Then she turned and walked back to face the stone markers. She stepped back and turned to look at the low wall behind her. She ran her fingers along the stain where cleaning solvents had removed the blood. Then she turned and stared up at the escalator tower above left field. Baseball was no longer on her mind.

"The cops probably measured every angle," she finally said.

"So did the sniper. It was a hell of a shot."

"Did you go up there?"

"Yeah. Felt like Oswald in the window of the Texas Book Depository," I said. I really hadn't, but the thought occurred to me just now.

"A lone sniper?" Petey said.

"One bullet. You're standing right about where Rupert was. He never knew what hit him."

Petey absently brushed a wisp of hair away from her left temple. It was also on about the very spot.

"Pity," she said.

We retraced our steps and continued the tour by heading into the restricted tunnel area of the stadium's lower depths. We followed the semicircular main corridor as it led from left field around to home plate and back out again to right field. This was not Petey's first foray underneath a major-league stadium; we had done extensive work in the bowels of Wrigley Field a few months earlier on the Dream Weaver case. Yet each stadium is different, and Yankee Stadium, renovated and 1976 modern, has a few quirks of its own. The tunnels are well lit and glossily painted, however, giving the renovated stadium's underbelly little of the damp, eerie quality the old joint had. The tunnel ceiling is a mass of insulated cables and pipes, the dry air alive with the humming sound of machinery. Nooks and crannies seem to have been designed out of existence. The phantoms coming and going were electricians and maintenance men, a member of the grounds crew, a few vendors.

Although Petey craned to look into doorways and alcoves, she saw little. The look on her face was familiar to me: she was alert and interested, yet somewhat disappointed. The antiseptic guts of Yankee Stadium didn't seem like a suitable lair for a killer. We passed the Stadium Club, vendors' offices, security offices, storage rooms, and a machine shop. We passed the entrances to the clubhouses, the umpires' room, the players' Nautilus room. She perked up a bit when we looked into the players' batting cage beneath the stands on the far right-field side. It was empty now, but equipment, mats, and netting were strewn everywhere.

We walked leisurely, with Petey's low heels clicking on the tile floor, unhurried and unchecked by security. That was something to be noted. A person properly outfitted, or with authentic-looking credentials dangling from the lapel, seemed to attract little attention. I wondered if the same could be said about the night of the murder. Doubling back, we once again approached the Yankee clubhouse, where activity was picking up. Batting practice had begun, and players, reporters, and club personnel shuttled in and out of the locker room. They shot glances like one-hoppers at Petey, and she fielded them and tossed them off like Willie Randolph.

The boys stationed outside the clubhouse wanted to barber, but I brushed them off. Instead, I guided my niece through the pressroom filled with tables and telephones and into the adjoining dining room, where we filled our plates with prime rib and baked potato.

After we sat and arranged ourselves, buttered our rolls, and ladled dollops of sour cream on the Idahos, Petey raised the question.

"You sense anything at all out there, Unk?"

"Hmm," I mumbled. "Big ballpark. Business as usual behind the scenes. No mourning, that's for sure. So no, I don't feel a thing."

"No looks, no suspicious eyes, no . . . no edginess. It's as if he were killed somewhere else," she said. "On his yacht or in Florida or in his bedroom. Not in the house that Ruth built."

"If there's any treachery out there—"

"Treachery? No way," she cut in. "More like relief."

We dug into the food, and the *jus* ran red on the plate. Petey asked about my rendezvous with Artie Elberfeld, and I related the details, briefly editorializing on Artie's fitness as a suspect. Dessert was a devil's food sheet cake, and Petey had two helpings. On her second helping we were surprised by the cool presence of John Brush, who had suddenly walked in from the pressroom entrance. As usual he was dressed for the boardroom, with wing tips and a pair of navy slacks. His yellow silk tie was tightly knotted, the sleeves of his blue Oxford-cloth shirt rolled to the elbows.

"Duffy, you're holding out on me," he said with a smile so self-assured it could have sold Thurman Munson a set of encyclopedias. He was concentrating, I observed, on Petey.

"John, this is my niece and assistant, Petrinella Biggers, if that's what you're talking about," I said.

Petey went glassy-eyed.

"Hi," she said, and when he held out a tanned hand, she poked it with her fork full of cake. I'd seldom seen her so rattled.

"John Brush," he said. "It's nice to see Duffy here with a female in the press mess hall. He's gone on record as not wanting them anywhere near the clubhouse."

The SOB. I'd written a couple snide columns about women in the locker room, particularly about a gal from Toronto who rubbed me the wrong way, and apparently Brush had come across them. I've mellowed considerably since then—about women in the locker room, that is—for whatever damn good it did me right then.

Petey scowled at me.

"Duffy," she said, as if she were scolding a bad dog. Not even "Uncle" Duffy, and I couldn't remember when she'd addressed me like that.

"Wait a minute," I began, but the two of them were off and sniggering at each other.

"Petey is what everybody calls me . . . and I'm not a sportswriter," she said, suddenly regaining her cool and offering Brush a very warm handclasp. Brush took it like a snake on a rodent.

Some small talk ensued, but it was plain that Brush had to get going, which he did shortly. He invited us to stop by his office during the game. Several eyes throughout the room followed him as he went out. He was the top hat of the Yankees now, and everyone knew it.

"He's something," Petey said, eating her cake and having it too.

A while later we followed the flow of sportswriters up the elevators to the press box. High above and just to the right of home plate, the press box follows the contour of the ballpark and is situated in front of the Yankee executive offices. Starting from the first-base end and separated by glass partitions are the organist, the stadium scoreboard keeper, the public-address announcer, a long three-rowed press section, broadcast booths, more press rows, and finally, the executive boxes—the Huston gallery. The setup allows just about everyone to see what everyone else is doing, from John Rooney, Bobby Murcer, Phil Rizzuto and assorted echoes at the mikes to the beat writers of the *Times, Daily News, Post,* and the other dailies. In an aisle seat in the back row of the main press section sits Red Foley, the official scorer and a Yankee Stadium fixture for years.

Petey and I took an unreserved pair of seats down from Red in the back row, and I pointed out some of the personnel: the younger beat guys who tap out their stories on their computer keyboards as the game progresses, the columnists and color guys who gum cigars and wait for the Muse or a gust of insight worth twelve column inches, and the radio guys who keep track of the score and get their grist from the locker room afterwards. I dropped a few items of press-box protocol, including the ban on cheering or any other partisan outbursts. Petey winced.

"What old fart came up with that?" she said.

"All press-box rules spring from and are enforced by the Baseball Writers of America, an august organization of old farts of which I am a lifetime member."

"Excuse me," she said with characteristic irreverence, "but the no-cheering thing is still a stupid rule."

As sharp as Petey was, she knew not of what she spoke, so I ignored the remark.

During our chitchat I got my share of nods and howdy-dos from boys whom I'd worked with through the years. But Petey got as much if not more attention. Sports stiffs are salivators of the worst sort, and Petey had their glands churning. We stood for a tape of Robert Merrill singing "God Bless America"—just one of many Merrill tapes that come on any time the crowd has to be led in song—which was the day's substitute for the national anthem. Now I revere Irving Berlin as much as the next fellow, but I prefer Francis Scott Key's authentic patriotic article and sung in person by an American with his hand over his heart. If it was good enough for Fort Sumter, it's good enough for Yankee Stadium, dammit.

I communicated same under my breath and out the side of my mouth.

"Aren't *we* in a good mood," Petey said as we retook our seats.

About two pitches into the game, fellow old-time scribe Dick Bennett came by to schmooze. Bennett was a longtime member of the New York sportswriters' fraternity, and in no time he was off and running about some of our mutual memorabilia. Out of the corner of my eye I noticed that Petey had gone off on her own. I saw her moseying along the aisle behind the press box, pausing to watch the activity in the broadcast booths, peeking into the executive offices behind her. I had a solid idea of whom she was looking for.

A couple of scoreless innings later, she came back with a hot dog and a hot pretzel—criminy! where did she put it? —and provided me with a break from Dick Bennett's bout of nostalgia.

"Remarkable," she uttered with her mouth full. "The refreshment-stand guy—he says 'hot dorgs and sorsages,' I love it—he runs out of mustard and actually goes down to the commissary and commandeers some Poupon for me."

"Remarkable," I said.

"Yeah, but catch this, Unk. The P.A. announcer over there, he's reading Shakespeare between batters. I swear! *Twelfth Night.* Can you believe it?"

Bennett and I laughed.

"That's Bob Sheppard," Bennett said. "He's a professor of English at St. John's."

I started to fill Petey in. "A legend. Been behind the mike for a long time—"

"Forty years. Started in fifty-one," Bennett said.

Sheppard's deliberate, precise, and foggy tones punctuated our conversation. His style was inimitable. Yankee fans can hear him in their sleep.

"He doesn't miss a thing," said Petey.

"He's had a while to get his timing down," I said.

Just then John Brush appeared in the aisle behind us. He leaned on the railing just above our heads. For a guy as busy as he should have been, he was giving us plenty of idle moments. Between wide-angle perusals of the playing field, he cast none too furtive looks at Petey. Uncles, or anybody with two eyes, can spot these things.

"Not too much excitement for you yet, Duffy?" Brush asked.

"Oh, my niece here just discovered Bob Sheppard and his Shakespeare," I said.

"Twelfth Night," Petey said.

Brush laughed.

"Brilliant man," he said.

The organist chose the moment just before the new inning began to break "Take the *A* Train" out of his repertoire and dust it off.

"And the organist plays Ellington," Petey said, definitely feeling her oats.

Brush leaned in. "Unfortunately, stadium organists and everybody else plays that tune. I remember how Lawrence Welk's guys used to play it, and Welk announced it as 'Take a Train.' "

I lifted my brow. Lawrence Welk?

"What a great tune!" Petey said, unfazed by Brush's geriatric reference.

"A lover of Shakespeare, Ellington, and baseball," Brush said, raising his eyebrows in my direction. "This lady has class, Duffy."

Petey glowed. I lifted my feet.

"I've really come to appreciate the great jazz tradition in the last few years," she said.

What last few years? I thought. *A few years ago you were fighting acne and listening to Michael Jackson.*

"Is that right?" said Brush. "Well, you've come to the right city for it. What's your favorite jazz format?"

By this time Brush was not even faking a look in my direction. I felt like a towel boy at a nudist colony.

"That's a tough one, given this smorgasbord," Petey said. "I'd love to hear a big band, a regular seventeen-piece, since this would be the place for it. Then again, I'm always a sucker for the individual artistry of solo piano."

I listened in awe. Petey was good with the patter.

"You can hear both on the same night in this town," Brush said, not so much making conversation, I realized, as plans. "A young cat named Tom Still is playing at Bemelmans' Bar in the Carlyle Hotel. He's as good as they come."

Petey had anticipation written all over her mustard-blotched chin. Suddenly the crack of a line drive ignited the crowd, and the place shook with cheering as a Yankee speedster legged out a triple. Even Brush interrupted himself.

"Nagy. Kid's coming on," he mused.

Then he returned to his quarry. "Look, what with everything going on here, it's been a while since I loosened my tie. I could really use a jazz fix, and Tom Still's blend of influences from Art Tatum and Bud Powell through Oscar Peterson, with even a little Randy Weston thrown in, could be just the ticket."

Petey arched her back. I wasn't sure she knew what Brush was talking about. On the other hand, I'd cut my teeth on Bix Beiderbecke, Jelly Roll Morton, Charlie Christian, and Fletcher Henderson's band, so Brush was talking my language. But it was a twenty-three-year-old redhead he had just met who was his jazz aficionada of choice.

"What say you join me after the game?" he said, letting his eyes move over toward me.

"Great!" Petey said. "Isn't it, Unk?"

"We can hit a few clubs," Brush continued, not waiting for my two cents. "What'd Ellington used to say?—'the great savory pot-au-feu called New York.'"

"For cryin' out loud, John, this is a ball game," I said.

He waved me off and bid us drop by his office after the game.

His invitation infused Petey, and she fairly bounced

up and down in her seat for the rest of the game. To my right Dick Bennett kept up the Yankee trivia, noting that the last game in the old stadium was an 8–5 loss to the Tigers. Fritz Peterson took the defeat, and Duke Sims hit the final home run. I took Dick's word for it and hummed "*A* Train" under my breath. I couldn't get the tune out of my mind. The ball game had the pace of a Broadway bus at rush hour—plodding but with many interruptions. It was what sportswriters charitably term a pitcher's duel when they don't want to call weak hitting weak hitting. The Yankees won 2–1, and when the game was over, Old Blue Eyes pounded out "New York Squared" on tape, a post-game tradition that was starting to get on my nerves.

Less than a half hour later, Brush appeared—showered and freshly shaven. He was an immensely handsome man, now wearing casual slacks and an open V-neck sweater, and he swept us along into his chauffeured car. The ride was pleasant enough, with Brush, sitting in the front seat, quietly assessing his team.

"It's not a deep, confident squad, Duffy," he said, and went from position to position to make his case. It was G.M. shoptalk. I listened more than I spoke. Petey never took her eyes off Brush.

"The Wolfe trade killed us. It was not just a bad trade, it was ill timed. So ill timed," he said, trailing off.

In the meantime our car, with its silent driver, sped south into nighttime Manhattan. Brush turned momentarily and looked out into the darkness of Central Park.

Petey leaned forward. "Your eulogy at the funeral was really beautiful, John," she said. "I was touched."

He looked at her and smiled slightly.

"Thank you," he said softly, his expression now distant, funereal. "It was important to me."

I nodded agreement. The air was heavy.

"Enough of baseball," Brush said, and not a minute too soon. "We could stop at the Algonquin. The Oak Room."

" 'In the lobby people come and go, speaking of Lerner and Loew,' or something like that," I said. "They banged out *My Fair Lady* here, legend holds."

Brush smiled and said, "A nice torch singer works it now."

"And Dorothy Parker weeps," Petey said.

We were outdoing ourselves in the name-dropping category.

"Or the Carlyle. How 'bout that? It's the domain of Bobby Short, you know. His Shortness began playing there in sixty-eight. And there's Bemelmans', which I mentioned, across the hall."

"You're the host, John," I said.

In no time we pulled up at Madison and seventy-sixth and the Carlyle Hotel. The café was a small, well-upholstered room decorated with murals by some guy named Marcel, who was partial to nudes in front of easels, leaping poodles, and other standard stuff. After poking our heads in, Brush ushered us on by, however, and across to Bemelmans' Bar. The place was named, Brush said, after Ludwig Bemelmans himself, who painted the walls with bulldogs and rabbits, and school children in the park. We walked in and were buffeted by a big piano chord, a bass-note stinger, and animated applause from a medium-sized crowd. If anybody recognized John Brush, nobody made a fuss about him. He'd chosen well.

"We're lucky," Brush said, "sometimes this place is shoulder to shoulder."

A good corner table was ours, and seconds later three very cold glasses of an English ale were put in front of us. I didn't remember ordering, but Petey smiled, and I figured some quick communication had gone on without me. More of the silent variety continued as Petey sat in the middle of us, with an edge distinctly to John. The two of them started talking between themselves, as if they'd done this before. I wouldn't say sparks were flying, more like coals glowing. They were a smart, comely couple. Of course, Brush was much too old for my niece as far as I or any right-thinking person was concerned. I had the definite impression that Petey didn't share that opinion. She was coming down the line like Mattingly covering a sacrifice bunt. The performer was Tom Still, the guy Brush had ballyhooed, a strong-jawed fellow who played the keyboard the economical way the Celtics used to play defense. He was now improvising on a Gershwin number.

Brush lifted his nose out of Petey's ear long enough to bob his head with the beat.

"Gershwin loved to come down to the clubs and work

out with the jazz guys," he said. "Even when he was the biggest thing around. They say he could take any tune and do variations on it. A genius. A Mozart."

Brush knew his stuff, Petey was floating, and the kid at the keyboard held the room. I drank my beer and noticed Petey hook a pinky on Brush's wrist. It was a nice move. I tried to concentrate on the playing, the keyboard variety that is, which was first-rate.

Suddenly he ended the piece, and the palms clapped loudly.

Brush spoke over the applause: "You hear the way he moved from the rubato of his introduction into the walking bass with the left hand when he got into the tune? And that up-tempo riff with his right hand where you could just about hear the brushes come in. Even though they weren't there."

I swallowed. I would have said, "The kid sure has a left hand on him," and left it at that. But Brush was working overtime, the redheaded idolater at his side lapping it up. Was this the way it used to be? I had to relieve myself, and I headed for the latrine.

On the way past the bar, I thought I heard a familiar caterwaul coming from a familiar white-haired head. I looked in, and sure enough, there was Studs Terkel at the bar. He was nursing a beer, destroying a cigar, and lecturing the bartender on the minimum-wage law. I'd known this raconteur, actor, and, finally, big-name author for years. It seems like as far back as the Babe's called-shot homer, which was in the Series of '32, but maybe I'm stretching things.

"Leave the man alone," I called in. "He works on tips, not barflies."

"Heyyyyy, whattaya say, House!" Studs said when he eyed me. "I heard you were in town. Chambliss! Workin' the Huston thing, eh? What a story! What a story! Finally a robber baron gets what's comin' to him! Shoulda happened to Comiskey. The Old Roman. Why, Shoeless Joe'd be in the Hall of Fame now!"

Studs went from there to every topic on the front page and plenty on the inside sections.

"I'm here interviewing Ossie Davis and Henry LeTang, the dancer, choreographer, oh, great talent!

Taught the Hines boys every step they know. So I stop in here 'cuz they said that kid named Still was playin' in the club. Chicago boy. D'you know that? Real good. I wanted to hear him 'fore I go to bed. You stayin' here? Not me. I'm flopped at the Algonquin, for cripes' sake. Used to stay across the street at the Royalton. 'Member that place? Where Algren used to stay. Perfectly fine old fleabag hotel like my mother used to run until the developers got their hands on it and turned it into a three-hundred-dollar-a-night joint for swells.

"Hey, how 'bout that Huston thing? Holy smokes. Dead in center field! You got a line on it, Duffy?"

Studs's red-checked shirt was unbuttoned at the top, and his knit tie was loose and revealed the top of a red T-shirt. Heavy odds had it that he was wearing red socks and Hush Puppies. I didn't even have to look. Man was a millionaire, and he still dressed like Bill Veeck, who was also pretty well fixed and dressed like he forgot his pants.

"It was an inside job, that's all I know," I said.

Studs, who is older than I am and has twice the energy, jerked his cigar out of his mouth.

"Hey! How do you know?" he barked.

"Guy was perched up in the escalator tower," I said. "That's inside as far as I'm concerned."

"I got you, Duffy. For a minute I thought you were on to something."

"Nobody is, as far as I know."

My bladder screamed for immediate attention.

"Hey, get back to Chicago, Duffy. Come on the show if I still got it when I get back. To Christ! You heard what they're doing to the station? We'll do a whole hour on this thing."

It was a promise, and I hurriedly left Studs to educating the bartender on the history of organized labor in the U.S.

When I returned to the room and paused at the door, Petey and Brush were locked in gab, their heads inches apart, Petey's coppery hair, now lying over one shoulder, contrasting with Brush's darker locks. I made a mental note to do a little background check on his nocturnal reputation. The piano player was taking a break. Petey, for her part, was plunging into the breach. Nearing the table, I realized that the subject was front-office baseball. Brush was dispensing insight like a latter-day George Weiss. Petey hung on his words, but she held her own in the conversation, and he was plainly taken with her. They were quite a match.

Brush warmly acknowledged my reappearance; Petey treated me like a waiter. I was not sure I knew my niece when she was stalking, and less certain I liked her in that posture. That, or I was just exhausted, a bit sodden from the beer, and I needed to dent a pillow.

"I'm a tired Indian. The last sets are all yours," I said to them both.

"Oh, don't go, Unk," Petey said with all the sincerity of a sidewalk watch salesman.

"Duffy, if you're tired, you should run along," Brush said, a bit too quickly. "Your niece is in good hands."

"That's what I'm afraid of," I said.

Petey did an eye roll.

"I'll be home early, Uncle Duffy. I have a geography class first thing tomorrow."

"Make sure you tell John your plans for law school. Remember, Pete?"

She didn't even bother to look up at me.

"Enjoy yourselves," I said.

Then I yawned and wondered, *Had I given them an idea?*

10

Farelli

The hour at which Petey's key nudged the tumblers of her room's lock was lost to my deep sleep. I wouldn't ask her for an accounting. Suffice it to say that I was up and at things just after eight the next morning, figuring I'd have a few hours before she'd be conscious enough to touch base.

I put an obligatory call in to Inspector Devery and was told he'd get back to me. I didn't want to get on the wrong side of Big Bill. Then I made a call to Chicago.

Although I'd interviewed a number of people who would have gladly taken out a hit contract on Huston and had the means to do so, the sniper part of the murder was still the key ingredient. I needed an objective, no-bullshit opinion on what kinds of professionals—or amateurs—favored that murder weapon. And I knew I could tap Del Howard, the FBI agent I'd rubbed elbows with in the early innings of the Wrigley Field affair. My time zone had an hour on Chicago, and I knew it was good to get to agents early, before they hit the bricks. Howard answered my call on the first ring.

"Good luck, my friend, you're in New York now," he responded when he heard my long-distance query about the weapon and its adherents.

I'd certainly heard that before, but not in tones as disparaging as Howard's. He said he'd done some time on the East Coast and didn't think much of the place, and I told him I didn't need a tour guide.

"They do things different there, Mr. House," he said.

"Like murdering owners with high-powered rifles?"

"For starters. Hey, it got the job done, didn't it? A few more neutralizings like that, and club owners all over would shape up their organizations, don't you think?"

"Can we be sure?" I asked.

"Who's running the Yanks now, the wife?"

"Forget it. I think she's waiting for the dust to clear and for her accountants to see how much is coming her way."

"I like that general manager—what's-his-name?"

"Brush. John Brush. And I like him too, but I didn't call to talk baseball, Del. No offense."

"Touchy, touchy."

"Can you help me out on the Mob side? Tell me if there's something to the sniper part of it. That sit well with you?"

"My East Coast guys tell me the Calvino family did two like that recently. Same kind of barrel. It ain't close up and personal, like they like it. Twenty-two in the back of the head is their favorite. Scrambles things. But then again, it's New York, and they got a different sense of humor out there. That Farelli, now he's a piece of work."

"So I notice. Plays the press around here like a harmonica," I said, visualizing the steely eyes of New York's biggest and brashest godfather.

"A regular Phil Linz. How's that, Mr. House?"

"Remarkable, Del."

"Anyway, the problem is they can't put him away. They keep investigating, but they can't ever make a case. Bad cases, bad wires—whatever."

"Can I talk to him?" I asked. "Or is that a pipe dream?"

"No, from what I hear," Howard said. "He ain't like the goombahs here. They stay low, don't talk to nobody. Farelli, hell, he'll buy ya lunch."

"Is that right? Can you help me out?"

"I'll make some calls. As long as you promise you'll keep me on the hook. Let me know what happens."

"No promises," I said.

"There's always promises, Mr. House. What's your number there?"

As I rang off, I heard a tap on my door. I opened it to

Petey, who came in with a fresh pot of coffee, a tray full of breakfast, and a countenance of sunnyside up. It was amazing, a little maddening. The resilience of youth is wasted on the young, or something like that.

"Morning, Unk!" she said, and hefted the tray over to the table. She was barefoot and wearing a soft maroon jogging suit. I half expected her to say that she'd paced out a few miles already this morning. She didn't.

Instead she sat across from me, dug into a Danish, and gushed, "What a night! What a city! What a man!"

I poured some coffee and buttered an overpriced croissant.

"Try to cheer up, kid," I said.

"He is so smart. So cool. So self-assured . . ."

She trailed off into the marmalade.

"My, my. Hook, line, and sinker," I mumbled into the croissant.

She silently took offense.

"Say whatever you want. I just had a good time. I had an exciting, terrific, *electric* time," she said.

"Stay at the Carlyle, uh, at Bemelmans', I mean?"

"Slipped there, didn't you? But yeah, for a while. Then we went to this club called Sweet Basil on Seventh Avenue in the Village, which was the opposite of Bemelmans'. Crowded, smoky, and loud—with Gil Evans's big band. Black-and-white pictures of Coltrane and Mingus all over the walls—John calls them 'jazz demigods.' It was great. They had to kick us out."

"Get any sleep?"

"Enough."

"So what happens now? Do you sit around and wait for him to call?"

"Get a grip, Unk. That's so ancient. I did what any twenty-three-year-old single woman in Manhattan would do on a great date with a gorgeous, sexy, delicious guy—I asked him out."

"What?"

"Yes, I did," she replied. "I'm not going to sit back and let him think about things. No. Men don't do well when they get time to think. And he said he was booked tonight, but tomorrow night is a wrap, and we're going to take up where we left off."

She gobbled a piece of cantaloupe far too big for a single mouth.

"You're quite an operator," I said.

She chewed and shook her head.

"No," she said quietly, "I just really like him."

"I like John too, but are you forgetting that he's still a suspect in this thing?"

"Don't get itchy, Uncle Duffy. You're the one who introduced us, and you're in my will for that. Besides, John threw out some great leads on the case, because who better knows the poop on Huston and that family of his? I've got loads to follow up on."

"That was my next question," I said.

"Okay. Listen up. John said the daughter, Keeler, keeps house with a guy named McFarland, who works in operations or something, some middle job, with the Yankees. Huston gave him his job, John said, but he could never stand the guy, so he sort of froze him. McFarland, on the other hand, figures his hot hand with Keeler makes him upwardly mobile in the company, so he's always pushing and treating people like shit. Push finally came to shove with Rupert, John said, and there were some nasty scenes between Keeler and Daddy. John doesn't think Keeler is so bad; in fact, he said he kind of likes her. But he said McFarland is a real scuzzball and kind of bogus, and John doesn't trust him any farther than he can throw him.

"That's number one, which I like," Petey continued, "but I *love* number two. It's the skinny on darling son Griffith, emphasis on *darling*. Seems he runs with the fine-arts crowd, emphasis on *fine*. Ol' Rupert had a series of shit fits through the years as Griffith's brush stroke became more and more fine—"

"Such a metaphor, Petey."

"Translate that fey—because Rupert Huston's kid runs with the silk-scarf crowd in the gallery scene. Thing is, John said—now get this, Unk—even though Griffith is this huge embarrassment to his old man because of the way he swings, it seems he got Rupert in on the money side of the art scene. And investing in art is big nowadays—big, big bucks, John said. So on one hand Rupert's sweeping the kid under the rug, or putting him in the closet, if you will, and on the other hand he's got his fingers in gallery games with Griffith and his gay friends. Don't you love it?"

The breeze from all that cooled her coffee, and she went for warm.

"That's an earful," I said. "Seems your man Brush was very talkative."

"We talked and talked, Uncle Duffy. So maybe I was working on him. I mean, I'm crazy about the guy, but you don't think I'd forget what we're doing here in this town?"

I smiled.

"Liar," I said.

Petey giggled and flicked the ends of her fingers through her hair. She was a parakeet in the morning sun.

"John's such a sharp guy," she said. "He knows so much outside of baseball. He reads people. And I definitely think he likes the fact that I'm interested."

"So do I."

"You do?"

The phone rang.

"Is that your plan for today—Griffith and Keeler?" I asked as I got up.

"Uh-huh."

The phone was Del Howard. He had the name of a New York FBI agent to touch base with on setting up the Farelli talk. Howard was a good man who, I wanted to believe, was doing this for the good of baseball. Fat chance. He said I owed him one. I suggested a pair of souvenir Yankee wristbands.

"Think large, Mr. House," he corrected.

Howard's New York contact was available right off. He made a point of the fact that I was to present myself to the Farelli people as a baseball writer. Farelli would like that, he emphasized. Then he gave me the phone number of a café in Little Italy. I should ask for a Mr. Bozzo, which was pronounced *bot-zo* and not *bozo*, a point exceedingly important to remember, and then tell him exactly who I was. The rest was up to Frank Farelli.

It all seemed a little too easy, and it was. I waited until late morning, after Petey had set out on her own, to dial Mr. Bozzo. It was hard to know what was on the other end of the line. It grunted, possessed a slight wheeze with each breath, asked me who I was three separate times, though it never identified itself, and, when I said I wanted to talk to Mr. Farelli, did not seem to comprehend the request. It did not, however, hang up on me.

After a long, stammering delay, the voice gave me an address on Canal Street and told me to be there in two hours. That was the easy part. The queasy installment came when I decided to take the Lexington Avenue subway downtown. Now streetcars and subways go way back with me. I rode them as a kid when they were a nickel, and I didn't think anything of it. I grab one now and then in Chicago and basically think mass transportation is the lifeline of a city. But my descent into the Manhattan tube did not bring about a wave of nostalgia or a renewed confidence in the system. I don't mind the crowds, the teeth-grinding noise, the indecipherable announcements, or trains marked "North something" that are headed south. What was hard to take was the stifling, cottonmouth air, the tomb odors, the sleeping bodies, the wide-awake panhandlers, and the stares from a few psychopaths whose spooky brain waves registered me either as a former British prime minister or a quick mark. When my train came, it looked like a Halloween float. Say what you will about the energy and sweep of graffiti art, I say the New York trains look like hell.

Nevertheless, my squealing, psychedelic bullet got me to the Canal Street station, and I exited within a dumpling's throw of Chinatown. The sidewalks were crammed with goods and vendors; lower Manhattan was a hive of ethnic enterprise. I poked my head into fish markets and fruit stands. I was jostled and bumped dozens of times and felt no worse for wear. It was an overcast day, but there was no feel of rain in the air.

My address was a luncheonette just off Broadway. The appointed time came and went as I walked back and forth and forth and back in the general vicinity. I bought a paper and looked for stories I hadn't already read. I fended off panhandlers. I bought an apple and ate it. I paced, and I stood in one place and quite obviously looked like a man being stood up. I waited a full hour, and nobody nudged my elbow or made any contact that I could detect, though I was sure there was somebody out there looking me over. It was maddening. I don't care how important or paranoid the Mob wiseguys are, I was there when they told me to be there, dammit. I'm too old for their hazings. I finally left and walked over to Mulberry Street, a scowl like a scar affixed to my mug. At an outdoor café I bought a home-made cannoli, and it tasted lousy.

My spirits had not lifted any by the time I got back to the Summit, where a phone message was waiting, as I had figured, and I ripped into the number. A voice not much different from the disembodied charmer I'd talked at that morning told me to meet Mr. Farelli that night at another address. Before I could chew him a new ass, the line went dead.

In the time that intervened, I stewed about gangsters and the Mob and the Mafia mystique or whatever they're calling it nowadays. I don't have much truck with it. Harry Steinfeldt, the old gangland reporter back in Chicago, used to rib me about that. Harry insisted that the hood beat was no different from the sports pages: "My stats are as good as yours. You keep track of hits and runs, Duffy. In my game a guy is hit and gets the runs." Then Harry would have himself a chuckle.

But Steinfeldt had a point: people read about mob-sters and ballplayers, hit men and hurlers, bookies and rookies, rubouts and grand slams with equal glee. They keep track of the players, memorize the nicknames, and tally the boxscores. And they do it for the same reason: the two worlds are pretty far removed from their own, and the action is diverting. Whether the play takes place in Yankee Stadium or on Mulberry Street, your average straphanger has as much in common with an overweight Mob juice-loan operator as he does with an overpaid Yan-kee right-fielder, so what's the difference?

My problem is that I honor the traditions and intrica-cies of baseball, but I scoff at the same in gangsterdom. It's a failing, I guess, a weakness not unlike my inability to appreciate pan pipes, modern dance, and sushi. Specifi-cally, what I don't buy in the gangster game is its hokey set of social rules, most of which were set up somewhere in Sicily a hundred years ago, and all of them based on an overpublicized ethnic bond. *Omertà*, schmerta. Their army functions like every other army does, with the rituals and pecking order well understood by all the soldiers. Ev-

ery soldier sucks up to the guy above him and treats the
guy below him like hell, which is the way all closed, tightly
disciplined armies work—whether it's the Mob or the FBI.
What I will grant them is their heightened level of paranoia. You don't have to take a gander at too many photographs of guys like Joe Columbo getting whacked in the
middle of a crowded park to get a little edgy.

Well, I had no choice in the matter. I needed to talk to
a don of the Mafia rather than the Mattingly persuasion,
and I had to get to him his way or not at all. As for Farelli,
head of the Calvino family and often referred to as the
most powerful gangster in America—an appellation easy
to bestow and, I should add, as impossible to verify as
"most valuable player"—he was what the tabloids called a
"modern" godfather. I'm not sure what that really means
other than that Farelli was more likely to enjoy baseball
than boccie ball. He also did not smoke, watched his cholesterol intake, and did not have a nickname.

As for his personal style, Farelli was young as dons go
—no more than fifty-five—loud, and as brazen as they
make them. He went where he wanted to and when,
never hid his face from a camera, and said what was on his
mind. He was the Donald Trump of the New York underworld, if you will, and with an ego to match. Unlike his
secretive, Old World predecessors, the snarling, no-com-
ment Mustache Petes, Farelli made no secret of his charm.
He relished the camera and the visible microphone, and
he was very good with them.

Still, the stories went, Farelli didn't get to the head of a
family through P.R. He had been a brutal Calvino soldier, a
vicious contract killer who had come up through the ranks
by taking out whoever stood in his way and brooking no
insult or injury. One of the stories with some currency in
the local press had it that a fairly harmless union operative
had unknowingly tipped off an undercover cop to some
drug dealing by Farelli's brother-in-law. The brother-in-
law had been rousted but naturally never went to trial on
any charges. Some weeks later the unwitting informer disappeared and was never heard from again. Everybody
seemed to assume that it was a Farelli act of retribution.
But nothing ever came of it.

This was my host that night.

The place was called Casa Bella, on Mulberry and Prince streets in Little Italy, and my cabbie had no difficulty finding it. The feast of San Gennaro, a yearly Little Italy blowout of colored lights and cannolis, was coming up in a few weeks, so the cabbies would be taking a lot of tourists down here. Mulberry Street is made for out-of-towners: just narrow and gritty enough, clogged with restaurants and bakeries, to give it an Old World feel. Every so often an Italian-speaking couple double-parks and argues loudly over a bag of laundry or shouts up at a head sticking out of a third-story window.

The hack paid no mind to the two overweight gentlemen standing in front of the restaurant. To him they looked like a couple of jowly guys who never wore neckties and who were softer in the middle than Marv Throneberry. To me they were a pair of torpedoes, amusing caricatures had it not been for the fact that they both probably packed firearms, and one of them had probably been my phonemate that morning and was responsible for my wasted trip to Canal Street. Both eyed me like a walking rash and followed me inside the Bella. Things were busy, and the smell of Parmesan cheese was in the air. Waiters with order pads tucked in the smalls of their backs hoisted steaming platters of garlic-laced mollusks and glasses of dark wine. Before I could even get a squeak out about who I was there to see, I was led to a table in the far rear of the restaurant.

Sitting with his wide back to the wall, his square head bedecked with a great swept-back pompadour of curly charcoal-gray hair, looking as if he'd just jumped off the pages of *Time,* was Frank Farelli. He was a handsome guy, a Johnny Blanchard with maybe twenty extra pounds, wearing a worsted suit coat and a light-colored turtleneck. The only thing missing was the neck.

"Mr. Duffy House of Chicago," he said in a basso profundo. He remained seated and extended a paw. I thought of Moose Skowron, shook his hand, which was soft —the man was definitely not a roustabout—but viselike, and I switched thoughts to Jumbo Brown.

I sat down with my back to the restaurant and nodded at a fellow sitting at Farelli's right elbow. On his nose was an oversized pair of horn-rimmed glasses. He bobbed his head almost imperceptibly and was not introduced.

"I like the way you write baseball, Mr. House," Farelli said. "Always did. I read you in the *Sporting News* for years. My father brought it home. So how do you like that?"

He grinned and offered a fine set of teeth. His presence fairly towered over me, and I wondered if his chair might not be an inch or two higher than mine. No, it was his head, I decided. It was bull-like, his forehead so vast that he had what can only be described as a tall face. In the center was a substantial nose, which looked to have been cracked a few times and set fairly close but not exactly back on its original moorings. Farelli was resplendent, to be sure, his clothing expensive, his hair razor cut and perfect. A pair of half-inch lateral scars to the left of his chin and above his right eye seemed placed in the terrain of his tanned olive skin by a character artist. His nails were manicured and caught the light.

"I like that," I said, responding to his reference to the *Sporting News*. "I've put down a few paragraphs in there through the years."

Farelli thumped the table with an open palm, and I winced.

"A few? Hey, Joe, this is a book, a *library* right here. Take Red Smith and Dick Young and Til Ferdenzi and roll 'em up in a ball, and you got Duffy House here. You'd a writ in New York, Mr. House, and you couldn't pay for a meal in this town, you know that?"

I waved him off.

"So what'd I tell you about this guy, Joe? Huh?"

Joe, the silent and—I quickly deduced—deadly shadow, gave a less-than-awed nod.

"You know, I'm proud to get to meet you," Farelli went on. "All these years I'm reading you. Not just on the Yankees. All the teams. I kept track since I was a kid. So, how do you like my place?"

He spread both arms out wide, like a preacher giving —or asking for—a blessing. "You want calamari? You gotta have the calamari in my place. I insist. You're a calamari man, and this is the best you'll find on this street. In all of New York. Hell, best in the New World, how do you like that? My chef's from Sicily. Brought him in myself. Makes calamari like it should be."

If my tongue was tied, who'd have known? A plate of lightly breaded, deep-fried calamari, which I mightily savor, was slid in front of me like an offering.

"My people tell me you're snoopin' around on the Yankee thing," Farelli continued. "Huston, the cocksucker. My people say you're thick with the commissioner. Helped out when that kid pitcher got offed in the Chicago ballpark. I heard all about that. Kid could throw."

"Your people leave me breathing fumes on Canal Street today?" I asked casually, looking up and squeezing a wedge of lemon over a morsel.

Farelli's seatmate rubbed his chin.

"Hey, Joe. Listen to this guy. Hey, what's your thirst? Aldo!" he called. "A Brunello. It'll get the fumes out."

Farelli smiled, enjoying himself. He was a pro at holding court.

"Whatta we—sixteen games out? Make it twenty-six, and it don't matter. Team's got no nuts, not like the Yankees you and I used to know, Duffy. How 'bout this: a story you did on Johnny Murphy, the old reliever. I remember reading it on the living-room floor. I liked Murphy. We got nobody with his stuff in the pen. And then Huston gives up Wolfe, who could hit. Could break a game open when you needed it, and now whatta we got? Where are we? DeFord, the shine, he don't know if he's gonna show up and put in a full day or not. And this is the Yankees I'm talkin' about, Mr. House."

I wasn't sure where to come in on that, or if Farelli wanted me to. I well remembered Johnny Murphy, but not the piece I'd done. I was still wondering if Farelli really knew I was a sucker for fried calamari or if he assumed I should be. Wondering about these things, I drained some of the wine without paying attention; but I knew right off that it wasn't Riunite. I smelled the grapes, not the yeast, and enjoyed the sensation so much that my eyes must have widened a little. Farelli let a smile creep across his mouth, though he said nothing.

I cracked open a crust of bread and took in the surroundings. The place was well appointed. The tablecloths were very thick, very white linen. The walls held some interesting American art, not those inane Italian scenes by Utrillo you see in every *ristorante* this side of Mama Leone's. Imported Italian leather caressed this old behind, and I sat across from a man wearing immaculate clothes and manicured nails. Mozart's *Don Giovanni* played over the din. I had to remind myself that the gracious host of this prosperous table had probably used his own hands to squeeze the life out of some poor union guy whose only mistake was to be in the wrong place at the wrong time.

"So, Mr. House, talk me some baseball. When I talk baseball—I talk about guys like Nick Etten and Spud Chandler and Billy Johnson and Snuffy Stirnweiss—people look at me like I took a powder. Know what I mean?"

"Etten? Stirnweiss? I knew those guys—but you?" I marveled.

"I was a kid," he said. "Sittin' behind the dugout with my father. So yeah, I knew those guys like my sisters."

"Tell me this," he went on, never looking past my eyes, though the restaurant around us was alive with diners, "what's your fix on the Mets?"

"The Mets?" I stalled, trying to figure.

"The Mets."

"Okay. The Mets. Best pitching staff in baseball, and they'll still lose."

"Knew it," said Farelli. "You ask an expert, and you get it back straight. No bullshittin' the bullshitter."

"Then again, pitching is power," I said. "Don't hold it against them."

"Casey always said pitching was seventy-five percent of the game, and the other half is hitting," he said, and started a chuckle.

"That was Yogi," I corrected. "Casey said, 'Good pitching will always beat good hitting, and vice versa.'"

That cracked Farelli up. A few beat-up Yogi-Casey bromides go a long way. Even Joe, the elbow ogre, broke a grin. With that Farelli looked over my shoulder for the first time and nodded away the two slugs who'd ushered me inside. I'd almost forgotten that they were standing there, quiet guardians that they were.

Then Farelli zeroed in on my eyebrows again.

"I ask Mr. House an offhand question about the Mets, and he gives me an offhand answer. He knows I don't give a shit about a bunch of Queens fags. My loyalties are with the New York Yankees. I ask what's going to happen to the New York Yankees. That's the real question, Mr. House. But I don't ask out of not knowing. Huston's out, it's a wonder nobody didn't whack the bastard before. He's out, and what's happening is something I don't take lightly.

"My father took me to the games, Mr. House," he went on. "His father, an immigrant from Naples, took him. We went to the house of Crosetti, Lazzeri, DiMaggio, Rizzuto, Berra, and Billy Martin—he was *paesan*, you know."

"Don't forget Ping Bodie," I said. "His real name was Francesco Stephano Pezzolo."

Farelli nodded and smiled. "My father talked to DiMaggio like I'm talking to you. Never talked baseball because what could you tell the great DiMaggio about baseball? He talked to Joe about what people had inside them, how you could read them. When Joe hit in fifty-six straight, he was doing what my father said to do. The thing with Joe is that you couldn't read him. Not a chance. He's up to the plate, and you don't know, lookin' at his face, if the count is oh-two or three-and-oh. They talked about that.

"And then once my father said, 'Hey, Joe, take a pitch now and then. Learn how to refuse 'em. It ain't gonna kill ya.' How do you like that! To DiMaggio! I saw Joe the other day, and he remembers it like yesterday."

The calamari was gone, and the plates were swept away. Empty new ones appeared, shiny, hot, freshly plucked from the dishwasher. Then, from both sides, the table was loaded with food. Three platters of veal, a plate of pasta, a platter of shrimp, spinach, eggplant, and red peppers. They settled in front of us like barges.

"We eat," Farelli declared.

Between slicing and chewing, alternating great swabs of his napkin across his chin, his arms reaching family style for platters, Farelli concluded on the Yankees.

"The family is shit. It was Huston and Huston alone, and he was scum. A stupid man. He was stupid in business, but stupid men still make fortunes. And he had a fortune. He was stupid in baseball with the Yankees because he didn't know nothing about the tradition. His problem was . . . he allowed his mind to be overcome by bullshit."

Farelli had spoken profoundly, and he stared off as he washed down some veal with fine red wine.

"He wasn't from New York," he went on. "He never was from New York. As far as the Yankees are concerned, Huston was a fake, a *fugazy*. He never knew about my father and his father before him, and he didn't care.

"Nobody could talk to the man. I know, Mr. House. I tried to talk to the man. Now the team *has* to go to someone. Huston's family is nothing. Worse than nothing. The son you wouldn't want. Tell your commissioner that, Mr. House. Tell him for me."

I listened patiently. I had no choice, even though my patience was growing in the opposite direction of my waistline.

"Tell me something," I finally said, eager to air out my tongue. "Who kills a man with a rifle at midnight in Yankee Stadium?"

He shook his head and waved the back of his hand in the air, like a man shooing a fly.

"It wasn't business. Not our business. Huston had real estate, and we got interests in real estate. He was a stupid man, and he made enemies where he shouldn't a made enemies, like in Miami. Man can find consequences that way. But there's no connection, Mr. House. I'm saying it didn't happen. Forget about the weapon. That's newspaper talk."

I raised my hands off the table.

"I don't know. Some people from one of the other families were dropped with one just like it."

He took a great drink of wine and daubed the corners of his mouth. He looked irritated.

"I'm not going to tell you what you read or what you don't read. You talk to people. You had a sit-down with Artie up north, and it's right that you did. You're a smart man of baseball. So is Artie."

Artie? I thought. *How did Farelli find out about me and Artie? Who talked to whom?*

"You and that lady friend of yours are casting around," Farelli went on. "She's a looker, and I'm told she's blood relation to you."

My face must have paled. It was a one-two punch.

Farelli smiled. "A man in my position has a superb

intelligence network, Mr. House," Farelli said. He smiled again, almost sweetly. "And it helps to have superb intelligence.

"So I tell you this. People say things. The police say things. When they can't explain something another way, they point to us. They say Frank Farelli this and Frank Farelli that, as if that explains it all. It's convenient for them. It also don't mean a damn thing, and it don't lead to a damn thing, and they know it, and we know it, but still people say we use sniper rifles. Sniper rifles—like this is Vietnam or something. I don't bother with it, Mr. House, and you shouldn't either.

"This is what I'm saying to you: the Yankees are part of me, and I couldn't stand to see what the cocksucker was doing with the team. I took my boy to see them, and I had to explain it to him the way it was—because it ain't there no more. When I went to the games at his age, the players were seven feet tall! They were my heroes—DiMaggio— he was a *god* to me! To my kid? The New York Yankees to him are just a name on a baseball card."

His free hand was clenched. A thin bead of perspiration formed just beneath his sideburns.

"Look at Yogi. Left the team and said he'd never come back until there was a different owner. Not for old-timers' day or nothin'. Yogi . . . not wanting to come back to Yankee Stadium. Is that a fuckin' shame or what?"

He pulled a piece of bread apart, then left it lying there. He continued in subdued tones.

"If Huston had to be taken out, he would have been taken out. Disappeared. You can quote me on that, Mr. House. But it didn't happen. So don't bark up that fuckin' tree. You'll find what I tell you every time."

I swallowed a last exquisite morsel of veal wrapped in bacon.

"Do I have a choice in the matter?" I asked.

"You're a great writer. You're a smart man. You have a choice."

"So I leave here," I said, "with a full stomach and a trail as empty as my wineglass."

It was a statement, but he took it as a query.

"No. I asked you here because I sincerely appreciate

what you do for the game. And I got some information for you."

"Good," I said.

"This is what nobody knows, what I'm givin' you. There was somebody inside the stadium when it happened. Somebody nobody knows about. He seen a few things. You might want to talk to him."

I looked at Farelli incredulously.

"Name is Ganzello. He's a breaker, an inside guy does safes and boxes. Good driller. Works 'em like a dentist. We know this guy Ganzello. He ain't connected, but we can work with him. That's what my people tell me.

"Now here's the turn. This Ganzello's got a weakness, a very bad weakness. He's a Mets guy. Mets, Mets, everything's Mets. And he takes it with him on the street. Seems he thinks breaking Yankee Stadium is some kind of special thing for him to do. He tells everybody he's gonna drill whatever box the Yankees got there, and it don't matter what he gets, cuz he's gonna leave something behind from the Mets. Like a little kid, or something."

He looked at me significantly, but I didn't know what he was talking about.

"So that's what he done. He's there that night, and he seen some things. I'll make it so that he'll want to tell you what he seen. A favor to me. A favor to me and from me to you."

"Inside the stadium? The guy was inside that night? You sure about this?" I asked. The very idea of it had my wheels whirring.

"You don't have to ask, Mr. House," Farelli said.

I pushed my plate away. The food had been wonderful, but it was now secondary.

"This is the first warm one I've had on this," I said.

"You can find this Ganzello kook in Queens. My boys'll help. Take you to see him if you want. That way you don't worry about things."

"An address and a little contact beforehand is enough, if that's all right. You've done too much already, Mr. Farelli," I responded. I couldn't picture riding around the city in the company of the two heavies who had ushered me into the Casa Bella.

"Frank. Make it Frank. Consider it done."

I tarried some through coffee and a bevy of truly glorious pastries and cannolis that sent my cholesterol level reeling. Farelli didn't touch the sweets or the coffee, and he turned somewhat subdued. The pug at his side, who had eaten voraciously, sat like a stone. Farelli asked what World Series games I'd seen through the years and nodded almost wistfully when I said that, but for the last five years or so, I had just about seen them all.

"My favorite was forty-seven," he said.

"Al Gionfriddo."

"How'd you know?"

"Yankees still won in seven."

"Yeah," Farelli said, his eyes distant and in his mind seeing DiMaggio kick second base in disgust after the five-foot-six-inch part-time outfielder for Brooklyn ran down his line shot into left center, a hit that would have knotted up the ball game.

"I felt great for that little dago. Gionfriddo. Even on Brooklyn. Didn't play but thirty-some games for the Dodgers and didn't nobody even know his name until that one catch. But nobody'll never forget him now. Least of all Joe."

I nodded. His every word was on the mark.

"What a game, this baseball," Farelli, the godfather, said.

11

Keeler

Tuesday came up dark and wet, one of those A.M.'s where you want to order up room service, turn the appointment book face down, and have yourself transported to the Florida Keys via a Travis McGee caper. Or Carl Hiaasen. The rain daubed diagonal streaks against the windows; the water dripped and puddled on the sills; the outside air was a soup so damp that it curled hair and chilled joints. If you let it, weather like this could set a mood, like a virus, in you. If you let it.

Any local innings were a dead issue by ten o'clock. All the possibilities out there—ten men on the playing field, another forty waiting to be heard from, four irascible umpires, any number of pitches and swings, three outs, eight-and-one-half innings or more—were awash. Which is refreshing once in a while. Baseball is a lot of things, but not, unless you perform in one of those abominable indoor stages, guaranteed.

I considered all that in the shower, the bathroom variety. I also considered a much-needed comparison of notes with Red Carney, my flushed friend and audio-video raconteur with the Cubs in Chicago. The topic would not be baseball, at least not in the truest sense. Red got around, hoisted many a stein, and had chased plenty of skirts in his day. As for the final category, I was curious to know what he knew about John Brush. I don't care what anybody says or how old and independent Petey is, it was a glimpse of her ankle he was coveting, and uncles have certain inalienable rights in these matters.

It took a little phone tag before Red lit up my line.

"Holy cow, Duffy! Chicago's a *boneyard* without you! Half the gin mills are closin' down! Nobody reads the newspapers anymore! The butcher shops—" Red started in.

"Put a cork in it, Red, for cripes' sakes. I'm ensconced on this island, and I don't want to hear about how good you got it back there."

"How's Petey?"

"She's too damn good, if you want to know."

"Get off your horse, Duffy. There's a peach of a kid, that's what."

"And that's why I'm calling, Red. Whattaya hear about the mating habits of John Brush?"

"Brush? John Brush. Guy stepped out of a shirt ad without the eye patch? That Brush? Oh boy, Duffy, now you got me. I'm a National Leaguer—you can't expect me to know about the junior circuit."

"Give it to me, Red."

"Brush and Petey—omigod. I'm readin' you, Duffy. Loud and clear. Cue the organ, cut to a thirty-second spot—"

"Cut the horseshit, Red," I interrupted emphatically. "What do you know about this guy's sniffin'?"

"Ladies love him. I'll tell you that, and he loves the ladies. Who wouldn't? Good-lookin' guy. Single. General manager of the Yankees. Plenty of dough. Kid's got it *made.* Like the hosiery salesman, you know what I mean?"

"The hosiery salesman? Okay, Red, let me hear it."

"Yeah, the guy liked to pull down two or three sales a week—haw, haw, haw!"

I let Red ripple with that one for a while. Finally he came back.

"I'll betcha Petey warmed up to Brush like clam sauce on linguine."

"Something like that."

"Well, she's a grown-up girl, don't worry about it. Give Brush credit for good taste. Pete's a smart kid too, Duffy, don't sell her short, which is what you tend to do with people once in a while."

"Yeah, well, he ever been married?"

"Not that I know of."

"Anything foul? Any Bouton or Wade Boggs shenani-gans, or Steve Garvey, for that matter?"

"You mean, would Brush screw a bush if he thought there was a snake in it?"

"Red, for cryin' out loud, this is my niece we're talkin' about!"

"Boy oh boy, Duffy, your ass is raw, ain't it? You takin' a fire extinguisher to the john with ya? It's that Huston thing eatin' you up, I'll bet. Hell, everybody here's happy as shit that the sumbitch caught it. 'Cept maybe the White Sox."

"I'm all right, forget about it. Half the time I worry about what Petey's up to, and the other half I try to convince myself I got to smoke out the guy who did baseball a favor."

"Chambliss payin' you good?"

"Almost as much as a weak-stick utility infielder from Venezuela."

"So don't stew about it," Red said. "You got a tab runnin' in Gotham, and that can't be too bad. They pick up the garbage in that city yet?"

"They stack it on the sidewalks like sandbags. Before dawn the garbage trucks come and wake me up, and when I walk outside later, the trash is there like it was never even picked up. You figure it out."

"So get the job done and get back here where we got alleys and you don't see the shit. Plant your old broad ass in the friendly confines for a one-twenty start. Wind's always blowin' out, you know."

"All right, Red . . . ," I closed.

"Hey, Duffy, we miss you around here," Red said, God love him.

Not long after I laid the receiver in its cradle, a knock rattled the door. It was the door to the adjoining suite, not the hallway, and I opened it to a smiling Petey. Speak of the devil, or the devil's playground.

"Update time," she sang, and marched into my room.

I never refused an offer by Petey to fill me in. It was her nickel, and she started off.

"Mr. Chambliss is a real keeper, Unk. He got me right to Keeler Huston, and she's not talking to *anybody*. I mean, right in the front door."

She went over to the sofa and took a notebook no bigger than a compact out of her jeans' rear pocket.

"I wrote it all down as soon as I left," she said, flipping the pages.

The commissioner, she said, had made a personal call to Huston's daughter on Petey's behalf. It was entrée few others possessed.

Keeler Huston lived in an airy, light, nine-room, rent-controlled apartment on Central Park West in the eighties, Petey said. I've never comprehended the intricacies of New York City's rent control, something that doesn't exist in other cities: the manner in which these properties are passed along, or how people with the resources of a Keeler Huston got to live in them. I also had no time for such knuckleheaded concerns, for Petey was racing on.

She digressed about how she had ridden the subway uptown and added a brief soliloquy about how she loved mass transit.

Each day, waving aside my cautions about the subway as old-fogyisms, after she'd consumed a complimentary hotel continental breakfast or two eggs over easy at Two Jays deli around the block, she had been off on the subway.

"Must be the scent of urine," I said.

"Here we go again," she said. "Somebody pee on your leg on the platform, Unk?"

"How would I know?" I said.

She sniffed and read nicely worded details from her notes about a Hispanic girl with a leather-fringed purse reading Tursula Perrin's *Old Devotions;* a trio of black teenaged boys with boom boxes and wearing open-tongued, floppy, high-priced tennis shoes and designer sweatshirts, who laughed and joked, but when they opened their mouths, an African language tumbled out; a beggar walking from car to car with his pants half-off; a swarthy, aging, droopy-eyed gigolo or would-be gigolo in a suit and shirt unbuttoned to his navel and displaying a torso of gold chains and an inch-thick chest carpet. Her words were flowery to the point of romanticism, for she had yet to grow weary, jaded, or, perhaps, realistic about the scrabble of mankind in the Black Hole of Manhattan.

"What do you say to the pervert grinding his pelvis into your hip?" I asked.

"He gets an elbow in the ribs or a knee in the nuts," Petey said. "I'm not stupid."

Nevertheless, Petey, newcomer to the Big Apple, this harrowing city, clung to the notion of the world of the subway as being fascinating, rich, and remarkable. She had not been radically rubbed, grabbed, fondled, goosed, or, God forbid, mugged, and I hoped she never would be. The subway was your frigate, she said, as long as you were smart and quick and tactful enough to avoid its trouble.

"*Frigate* is the wrong word to use when discussing the subway," I said.

"You're nasty," Petey responded.

She began her narrative. "Just after ten or so I was up in the West Eighties. Neat part of town. Not far from where John Lennon lived . . ." I could clearly picture her eagerly sniffing through the Upper West Side like a beagle on a hare's trail.

It was not difficult to find Keeler Huston's place. In the rain, moisture glistened on the apartment buildings' dark stones like sweat on Elston Howard during the backside of a Sunday afternoon doubleheader. Petey's umbrellaless walk brought out the ringlets in her curly hair. In the day's gloom only her green eyes shone.

A doorman called up to clear her way, and she entered the building's inside hallway, where she proceeded to Keeler's ninth-floor apartment. There she was telescoped through the door's eye, then admitted by Miss Huston herself. The heiress scanned Petey with a tentative, feral look, one she had no doubt honed on her stepmother before she had turned on Lana altogether.

The apartment was old and grand, with high, coved ceilings and long hallways, fireplaces, loads of wicker and teak furniture, and a mishmash of expensive appointments and decorations, all of which were arranged in what Petey called "a planned, sloppy elegance." Keeler, who had a couple years and a couple trust funds on Petey, walked ahead of her across a series of Oriental rugs.

Keeler's apparel matched her digs: the tails of a baggy,

unpressed long-sleeved shirt that looked as if she had grabbed it off Herm McFarland's laundry pile hung over an exquisite pair of gray suede slacks. Her tanned feet were bare, the toenails painted black. She held a lit cigarette, oddly, between the tips of her middle and ring fingers; in fact, she was not to be without a cigarette between those fingertips. She wore no makeup, and some would have helped, Petey noted. I passed that off as an editorial comment. Keeler's hair was tousled, bordering on unruly, giving her, in all, a kind of stick-it-in-your-eye, this-side-of-Bohemia look that probably had driven her stepmother to distraction. What it did for Rupert was anybody's guess.

Without being either rude or particularly hospitable, she showed Petey into a well-lit solarium with no plants. They sat across from each other on the coral-colored cushions of two matching wicker divans. A short-haired, tailless cat appeared from behind an oversized raku pot, eyed Petey, arched its back as if Petey were an Airedale, and sauntered off. On the walls were stark, shadowy, black-and-white photos of a nude female with remarkable crevasses. Petey tried for a tactful compliment but could not for the life of her summon one, so she said nothing. She thought she smelled roasted almonds. Or arsenic.

"So why are you here—exactly?" Keeler led. She had her father's voice: nasal and Jersey bred.

"Because the commissioner of baseball convinced you to see me," Petey said. "I'm sorry about your father."

"Sorry enough to consider me a suspect?"

"No. I have a really difficult time with the idea of daughters murdering their fathers."

"Even if they're rotten bastards?"

"The daughters or fathers?"

"Take your pick," Keeler replied. "Anyway, I didn't kill my father, I didn't hate him enough for that. If you get the jerk who killed him, that's fine. It'll make probate a lot easier."

"You're jumping ahead of me."

"Look, Paula—"

"Petey, as in Petrinella."

"That's too bad."

"Excuse me?"

"I didn't mean that. I'm a real bitch lately, and you

would be too. My father, who I was actually getting along with at the time, not only got himself killed but left us in a pissing contest with his third wife, a person who does not deserve breath. Getting what you need, so far?"

"I'm not sure I know what I need. That's why I'm here, to answer your first question."

"Lot of people think the commissioner's office had my father terminated. It would make sense."

"Do you know Mr. Chambliss?"

"No."

"I didn't think so."

"He works for the owners, that's all I have to know. Great group. Father used to call them morons with ballparks."

"So did Charlie Finley. Anyway, how much did you hate your father?"

"My, my, we do change the subject, don't we? And I think Petey is a nice name. Keeler's no bargain, you know."

"Truce," Petey said. "I'm not here to piss you off."

"Whatever. Let's just say Father was never much of a father. I called him that just to remind him—and me. He was too taken with himself and his power. He loved the very ground he walked on. He'd put his arm up to his nose and *smell* himself. Get a rush."

"But you stuck around," Petey suggested.

"The children of the rich always do. The velvet trench —ever heard that phrase? My brother and I can cash a check as well as anybody. Father sent me to Smith, a couple years in Paris, then Copenhagen, and then I got my tush right back home. That way Father had to take care of me. You can't let the world see Rupert Huston's kids lacking, know what I mean?"

"Stop me if I'm wrong, and I'm no shrink, but you don't say all this with much, uh . . . well, I mean, *disgust.*"

"Who's disgusted? My life's a beach. Daughter of a famous, wealthy man. Life-style of the rich and famous. Ski in Gstaad and scuba in Belize. Nosh at Le Cirque. So I'm gonna complain about that? No way.

"Sure, he may dump on the guy I live with," she went on, "and he messed up my brother so bad that he doesn't know to wear a pair of pants or a skirt, but I got it good. Real good. I eat one-half of a cantaloupe and throw the other half away. Barbra Streisand said that. And when we win in court against the bitch—and we're gonna win—I'll have it better. Hoot. Frankly, I'm pretty straight on things, and I always have been."

"So maybe I should be talking to your brother."

"Maybe you should be."

She stretched her arms and tucked a leg underneath her.

"Look," she went on. "I was really shook up when Father was killed. Who wouldn't be? I'm not *that* much of a cold fish. And I felt bad for my mother, my real mother. She met Father before he became a world-class creep, and she took this hard. Nobody knows much about my mother, and they never will, but that's the truth."

"She give you your stuff?"

"My stuff?"

"Moxie."

"What's that?"

"Uh, chutzpah."

"Sure."

"And Griffith had to get his from the old man."

Keeler smiled slightly—an honest, pained, slight smile.

"Tell me about him."

"I haven't got the time. He's a mess."

"You two have any relationship at all?"

"Oh, sure, he calls up at three in the morning sometimes crying his eyes out. That's cool, huh? I don't let him in the house unless he's alone—he hangs out with fungus—and clean. I mean nose clean."

"What does your husband—"

"Husband? Please! Herm is my live-in, but he's not Mr. Keeler Huston, though he sure would eat that up. Lordee. Where was I? People start talking about Herm and me being mister and missus, and I lose it in a hurry. . . ."

"Herm and Griffith."

"Oh, yeah. Well, they're not drinking buddies. Herm sort of watches himself around Griffith. You don't want to get on the shit list of the boss's kid even though the kid is on the boss's shit list. Did that make any sense?"

Petey sighed.

"Does anybody get a free pass from you, Keeler?" she asked.

"Oh, I'm not *that* bad. I don't hate my little brother, I'm just sick of him. He wears you down. Take any pop psychology you want—shoot, get it from the checkout line at a grocery store—and it fits Grif. The poor little rich boy who had everything but his old man's love and respect, blah, blah, blah. Loves his mother and she loves him, but she gets the heave-ho from the old man. He turns gay. You know, all the easy stuff.

"When Grif was about twelve, Father used to make him wear a Yankee uniform at the stadium and play catch with the players. It was pretty pathetic. Tony Perkins has a better arm. His shrinks had a field day with that.

"Then he quits Williams College and starts packing his nose and wearing ascots and harem pants and swishing around SoHo calling himself an aesthete."

"And your father had a fit?" Petey cut in.

"Shit fit. Capital *S*, capital *F*. But that was kind of neat, see, because it was about the only thing that gave Grif some power over Father. Grif says he likes boys, and he'll do what he wants to do, and Father says then he'll pull the plug on the allowance and throw him out on the street, and Grif says you can't because I'll scream bloody murder to the *Post*. So Father backed off on that one mucho rapido. Grif told me it felt good."

"How long ago was this?"

"Long enough for the two of them to make kind of a deal—that's what Father did best, you know. Grif stays out of the papers and far away from Yankee Stadium, and he gets to keep his inheritance and all his Gold Cards."

By this time Petey's throat was dry, and she could have used a cup of coffee. Keeler wasn't offering one. The tailless cat stood in the doorway and scowled.

"And the deal held?"

"Always touch and go. Griffith's a cokehead, and you know how it is with them. Father always threatened to send him off somewhere to detox, even threatened to cut Grif off unless he did it. Threat, threat, threat. Father said he'd stage the whole thing, just come right out in public, go on 'Sixty Minutes' or something, and say what a problem his poor son had and as a father he had no choice. That never happened, though. Grif cleaned up his act. Then he played another hand."

Petey leaned forward, wishing she had the courage to take notes. Keeler pulled her shirt away from her chest and fluttered the material. She smiled again, that treacly, spoiled smile that heiresses assume seconds after birth.

"Why, I'm just telling you everything, aren't I?" she said.

She made the face of that sneering Manx cat. If Petey had had a length of piano wire, she would have looped it around Keeler's gullet and petrified that expression for history.

"Anyway, my slick little brother Griffith got Father involved in the art scene, that's the most recent. You know, masterpieces. Buy high and sell higher. Sotheby's and all that. Oh, Father started going for them like free agents. Grif was introducing him to all these gallery honeys with their hot items—probably hotter than Grif knew—and Father was buying the stuff like junk bonds. So the two of them were suddenly big buddies. How do you like that?"

"I'm not sure," Petey said. "I don't know much about that scene."

"Neither did Father, but did that stop him? Baseball, art, real-estate deals, oil paintings—what the hell's the difference? You want to sniff around for Commissioner Chambliss—and that's a laugh—about who had an interest in killing Father, you should go down to SoHo and talk to a queen named Monte Beville."

"Who's that?"

"A dealer—art, that is—a pervert and, I'm sorry to say, my brother's current, uh, lover. He's really a piece of side-trash with a double chin and eye shadow and a wardrobe full of designer bowling shirts. Were you at Father's funeral? He was there with his collection of walking doilies. They looked great standing outside St. Patrick's next to Mickey Mantle and Joe DiMaggio."

"What would be the motive?" Petey asked. "Especially if Griffith brought your father in as a client."

"Get a snootful of Monte and figure it out for yourself," Keeler said. "But try to catch him and Grif when they're straight, whenever that is."

"Is that what you told the police?"

"The cops, hah, they were all over my brother and me like lice, so I didn't have to tell them anything. I'm just being nice to you."

"I'm flattered."

"You should be. And I've got a lunch date."

With that she unscissored her legs and pushed herself off the couch and walked from the room. The interview was apparently concluded. Petey, with no other choice, followed. The tailless cat followed Petey until Petey suddenly whirled midway through the living room and quietly hissed at the animal. Once again it arched and stalked off.

"You think your brother had something to do with your father's murder?" Petey asked as she once again trailed behind.

"No," Keeler said, not turning her head. "I think my brother just hangs out with sleazoids. Personally, I think Lana had my father killed. How about that?"

By that time she was at the front door. She turned and leaned against a carved hall tree, and jagged shadows from a crystal overhead light marked her face. She was not an unattractive woman, but by no means a beauty, her looks certainly not enhanced by the fact that she emitted as much warmth as a turnstile. She bore only a faint physical resemblance to her father, except, Petey now well knew, in the category of charm.

Keeler crossed her arms in front of her.

"There was no prenup with them. Father married her and made her the sole beneficiary of everything. Said it was a vote of confidence. The boob. He laid that on me and Grif first thing. Just to piss us off, I think. Lana used to remind me of it every time we met. You could see it in her little eyes.

"But Father was getting sick of the bitch, and he told me he was going to change things. Change the will and buy her out. Another one of his talents, you know. And I think Lana found out and killed him before he could pull it off. So there."

Petey squared herself a few feet from Keeler.

"A little too blunt for me," Petey said.

"Lana rhymes with blunt. With a capital *C,*" Keeler said.

Reluctantly, and shaking her head as an uncle might with a sassy but clever niece, Petey smiled.

Keeler Huston, the rhymer, didn't bite.

"I've done what the commissioner asked me to do," she said as she cracked the door. "I hope you take my advice."

As Petey was about to offer a parting phrase, a cat meowed somewhere in the apartment. It was one of those guttural feline howls that usually emanate from dark alleyways and connote fangs and claws and barbed appendages.

". . . so I left without saying anything," Petey concluded. "Not a thing."

12

Ganzello

Petey's encounter with caustic Keeler Huston and her tip about the lipid Monte Beville made for good listening, and I listened well. Petey related details beautifully, with fine elocution, dash, and ample tartness. There was a good bit of the reporter in her, an eye for the curled lip to go along with a well-oiled bullshit meter. But I didn't tell her as much. The slightest praise might push her into my former trade, and her fingernails were too clean for that.

But she was aflame.

"I think we got motive, Unk," she exclaimed. "Real motive. You got some real dirtballs in pretty clothes mixed up with a lot of money and a kid who got his old man into this thing. One word for it: *wow!*"

I listened patiently—and encouragingly. I wasn't about to head her off any warm trail unless I had something warmer, which I thought I did. In fact, I had choice meat on the skillet: Farelli's tip sizzled. Without playing can-you-top-this, I filled Petey in, and her eyes widened like Chris Chambliss's when his bottom-of-the-ninth, right-field tater won the Yankees the flag in '76. Even with her own probe in hand, I could tell she wanted in on this one.

"A *safecracker*," she swooned, as if it were something exotic.

"A common thief with steel toothpicks and a cordless drill," I suggested.

Nevertheless, she relished the idea of meeting John Henry Ganzello. I didn't say no, but I did say that these birds had a thing about talking solo. The whole time I was thinking that I didn't want Petey anywhere near this low-life.

"It'll take some setting up. Farelli's calling the shots on this one."

"Hey, Unk, we gotta get beepers," she said. "Then we could shoot around on our own and stay in touch. You get the Farelli call and you beep me, and I'm in your lap in no time."

"A beeper? Thing doctors wear that looks like a garage-door opener? Goes off like a stuck guinea pig during the adagio movement of Ravel's Piano Concerto in G Major?"

"Aren't we highbrow today? Anyway, you can get vibrating beepers that go off in your pants."

"I don't like foreign objects in my trousers," I said. "And don't answer that one."

Petey's grin bordered on a leer.

"I'll make a call to the commish," she said. "He'll go for it, you watch."

"Maybe he will, but I won't. I like the privacy of being away from a phone. And I don't want an antenna sticking out of my head like a cat's whisker and—"

"And you've gone all these years without one, blah, blah, blah. And do you still phone in your stories or, better yet, send them in with carrier pigeons?"

"We actually did that! Back when I was in Chicago, we had pigeons at Wrigley Field that used to fly photo canisters back to the office—"

"Geez, Unk, give it a rest! We're in the decade before the twenty-first century. We should be in constant touch with each other. Period."

She knew nothing about the glory of carrier pigeons.

"I'll look into it. In the meantime I'm off to SoHo. Scare up Griffith and his crowd."

"What's your passport?"

"Right now, my smile," she said. "And with this crowd that may not be enough."

"Be smart. Be safe. We'll hook back up tonight," I said.

"I've got a date," she said, and beamed, then bussed

my cheek and took off, leaving me nothing but her tail wind.

She was gone but a few minutes when the phone rang.

"You got something for me, House?" came the voice.

I searched my memory, then placed it.

"How do you mean, Chief Devery?"

"Frank Farelli doesn't see people unless they got something to give him."

"Your office has good eyes, Inspector."

He didn't respond.

"Or ears," I added.

"We're close on this thing, House. If you got a piece we need, you give it. That's the way we work here. I got detectives in every borough wringing this thing dry. We know where you been. We don't keep nothin' to ourselves."

"Farelli's a baseball fan," I said. "He cut his teeth on DiMaggio and the gang in Yankee Stadium. We talked shop."

"His or yours?"

I paused.

"A little of both."

"So?"

"So he told me his people had nothing to do with it."

"Bullshit," Devery said, a little too loudly.

"All right, let me try this on you: the rifle. Farelli said you guys were making a big thing about the sniper rifle. And he said forget the rifle."

I could hear a faint snort.

"Gimme a break, House. Farelli'll put his schlong back in his pants when we produce the weapon and tie it to one of his *goombata*."

"Look, Chief, if you're close, score. Touch home and end the ball game. Don't wait for me. I'd just as soon get back to Chicago and day baseball."

"Book your flight," Devery said, and hung up.

A pleasant man, I reflected, and thought of Ralph Houk, whom Devery resembled physically. But Houk, the old marine, was a pensive guy. I retrieved a dial tone and tried to make contact with an equally cheery bunch on the other side of the badge. Farelli had said he'd have the Ganzello meet set up by sometime today. A voice finally gave me an address in Queens. "Clam Bar," the hood said. "Main and Roo-sevelt." That was it. No specific time or any other tribal instructions.

I didn't pause to consider my tack on this Ganzello encounter. I'm no rookie, and my knees are shot, so I wasn't afraid of the danger involved in all of this. At my age it's dangerous to go to bed at night without walking the dog and patting the will. Jeez, a lady with drop-dead good looks could probably do just that for me. So the specter of hitting against Ganzello wasn't going to scare me off. Hell, I don't even carry protection, except for my Blue Cross and organ-donor cards. A firearm under my sport coat would probably look more like a colostomy bag. And besides, I figured that if Farelli had set me up with this guy, his boys would be somewhere close to make sure it went off okay. Big bruddah, or something like that.

Hailing—or just slightly venerating—a cab, I wished for a reprise with Arnold, the Yankee fan. Instead my hack was a stolid, overfed Mesopotamian young man whose backrest was a blanket of nut-sized beads. He waded into Lexington Avenue traffic with his left arm hanging out the window and pushing away other vehicles as he wedged the groaning Checker cab from lane to lane. I said, "Shea Stadium." He said nothing. On the front seat was a small transistor radio that was vainly striving to pick up a frequency offering what is referred to as "rap music" but was getting static instead. But I'm the wrong one to try to tell the difference.

The day was cool and overcast, still damp from the rains, and rather than watch the grayness of Manhattan roll by, I caught up on the papers, which I happened to have with me. Huston's murder was off the front page, but teams of reporters were still draining it. You could, however, just about read the frustration in their prose. They were not getting much. I looked for Devery's name and a few quotes but didn't find them. I read but did not finish the obligatory story of a contract killer in Florida who was supposedly spotted in Manhattan at the time of the shoot. I looked up to see prematurely graying walls covered with graffiti as we crossed over into Queens.

Soon the cab was drawing in on Willets Point and Shea Stadium. My mum driver stopped beneath the elevated station on Roosevelt, across from the stadium, and wordlessly took my cash. His two-way radio squawked gibberish. I got out and stretched my legs and decided to take a slight detour.

A wide boardwalk leads from the train stop and away from Shea toward the grounds of the United States Tennis Association. That's the American equivalent of Wimbledon and enough of a spectacle during the U.S. Open to nudge even my normally moribund interest in the ace-deuce-love game. Jim Murray once said, "You know tennis in this country is in scandalous condition when a couple of guys named Boris and Ivan are playing for our national Open title." A chestnut if I've ever heard one. I never made any pretense of being nuts about every sport, and I made a personal promise not to write about any one of them whose rules were foreign to me. To this day, I will admit, I am not sure what constitutes an icing penalty.

The boardwalk was deserted except when a Number 7 train would disgorge a few passengers, so my shoes tapped a lonely rhythm on the boards as I walked over the vast train and bus yards and maintenance houses below. My attention was taken by the shiny silver spirals of concertina wire looped atop the train-yard fences to thwart trespassers. The anticipated interlopers are usually "taggers," those spray-painting lizards who turn entire fleets into something resembling a caravan from an LSD hell. The protective wire looked merciless—a mass of razor-sharp, jagged Honda logos—as angry and forbidding as the barbed strands on concentration camps. I couldn't take my eyes off it and was depressed about it until I was over the boardwalk and onto the green and sycamore-lined park land of the USTA grounds. Its massive concrete main stadium and surrounding courts make up a remarkable complex, a mecca for the fuzzy chartreuse ball and its tanned, racqueted floggers. I won't pull any tenuous social dictum out of the presence of tennis courts and concertina wire within a soft lob of each other, but I thought about it.

I watched a few matches in progress on the outdoor courts for a while, then retraced my steps over the boardwalk and back to Roosevelt Avenue. I walked up to 126th, gawking at Willets Point Industrial Park and the Feinstein Iron Works, an auto part and hubcap jamboree just across from the vast stadium parking lot. Every crankshaft and mag wheel known to man seemed to be in these acres, and plenty of grease jockeys were picking through them. I kept going. The area below the roadway was swampy and desolate, a sort of urban wetlands in a greenish hue that finally gave way to the bustle of Flushing.

After a public-housing project or two, the blocks before Main became a miniature Chinatown, a hive of fish markets and green groceries teeming with Asian proprietors and customers. At Main, however, the old Flushing neighborhood of Woolworth's, Alexander's, and a branch of the Chase Manhattan Bank reasserted itself. The intersection was crowded and noisy: traffic was backed up, cabby and civilian horns prodded drivers, and bumpers nudged over the walk line as if to nose walkers out of the way. Pedestrians five deep crossed the streets. It was weekday business as usual in an old borough hub, and no business was more usual, I quickly noted, than that of the Clam Bar on the northwest corner. My designated joint.

From its corner entrance on Main, the place ran like a boxcar along Roosevelt: a long bar, the window on Main full of franks on a grill, a ham slicer, and piles of corned and roast beef. It had a rear door, or escape, on Roosevelt near the pay phone but before the toilet. Besides sitting at a bar stool, a customer could stand up along the Roosevelt wall to drink beer and eat clam chowder and littleneck or cherrystone clams. A TV played constantly in a distant corner above the bar; the phone against the wall was seldom without a patron hunched over its box.

I took in all of that in a single sweep. I'd been in hundreds of dives like this on thousands of street corners. They were the currency of a decent intersection. I found a stool at the half-occupied bar and ordered a beer, lifted my elbows as the Formica was wiped off by a chum in a T-shirt, and sniffed the onions and grease from the grill. Nobody paid any attention to me. I have nothing against these places, but you couldn't say they have much going for them either. Guys like John Henry Ganzello, on the other hand, use them as executive suites.

I swung around on my stool and took a look around.

Besides the bartender in the white T-shirt and white apron, a grill man in a matching white T-shirt and apron tended the glistening stacks of artery cloggers in front of him. The two of them kept a running patter with a handful of regulars, a truly motley crew of idlers, some of them seated, some of them standing at the open doorways or cruising over to the phone or pausing to take in a few mindless minutes of sports television. Every so often a dish man, maybe the cook, in a white shirt and white apron, waddled in from a back room. People came and left, some grabbing food before the bus came, a beer or a soda. The clams didn't seem to be moving.

My attention was soon taken by the bar politician, a kind of garrulous, self-appointed greeter and social commentator who was working the bar like a precinct rally. No more than thirty-five, with a head of dirty red hair that grew down his neck and onto his back, he sucked on a cheroot with a brown, unappetizing set of protruding teeth and a grin that left saliva pods on the corners of his mouth. The cigar left flecks of tobacco on his lower lip.

"Oh, momma," he crowed, rubbing a belly the size of a feed bag, at a young woman in black tights as she disappeared into the subway. "She comin' back? She smell it on me?" he added, then cackled like a landlord and hitched up a pair of baggy, beltless jeans just before they exposed the gulch of his rear. The pants-hitch revealed a pair of scuffed cowboy boots.

"There she is again—"

He also needed a shave; in fact, his mug was a moist mat of two-day growth. Now, I will give a ball player the right to go unshaven into that good night game, given the fact that a razor and a palm full of after-shave tends to abrade the skin and make it pretty sore in the heat and perspiration of a ball game. I never begrudged Thurman Munson or Catfish Hunter their scruffy looks. But this guy, this assault on every tenet of appropriate personal hygiene, was a slob, the type who makes you immediately check on the status of your last gamma globulin inoculation. Still, while he was as wholesome as the pond scum I had crossed over at Willets Pond, and his verbal sallies at passing young ladies made those of hod carriers look chivalrous, this guy was in a swaggering good mood, jolly, full of chatter, a clam-bar bon vivant.

When the phone rang, he pounced on it.

"What's the line on Doc?" he shouted to the bar.

"Five and a half, six and a half," came the reply from the counterman.

"Take it," he muffled into the receiver. "It's found money."

I took a stab with the bartender in the white T-shirt.

"That Ganzello?"

"Could be," came the answer.

I kept my eyes on him as he sauntered about. It took another beer on my part, two more pathetic peals at innocent females entering the subway, three phone calls on games in Houston, Philadelphia, and Baltimore, and a corned-beef sandwich on his behalf before he fixed on me.

"What's up, Commissioner?" he said on his next pass.

He had known who I was all the time. I pondered the power of Frank Farelli. He nodded over to the deserted counter along the far wall, and I took my beer with me.

"So who wants to know?" he said, leaning on the counter and facing the wall.

"You've been told, I presume," I said, my back to the wall.

He scowled, gurgled somewhere in the caverns of his throat, then put his cheroot in his teeth and looked sideways at me. He had watery eyes, and one focused a little off center.

"I got some real heat on this," Ganzello said.

I wasn't going to console him.

"Real fuckin' heat. Major league. Shudda kept my mouth shut. But what good is it if nobody knows? You got your fuckin' trees fallin' in the forest all day, and who's hearin' 'em, right? So that's my bind, and now it's a federal case, am I right?"

"Make some sense," I said.

"Fuckin' A. I ain't tellin' you nuthin'. I was warm that night, that's what, Jack. I ain't sayin' how I got that way, but it was flawless. I'm inside Yankee-fuckin'-Stadium, can you handle that slice? Me. I'm Mets allaway. John Henry Ganzello. Fuckin' pregnant in the joint that Ruth built! See, I ain't sayin' I'm an inside man total, but let's just say I *been* inside before. I can pick. Give me time, and I'll punch anything made. I got Carborundum bits'll chew through fuckin' krypton."

By that time he had blown a cloud of oral swamp gas my way that was so noxious the beer couldn't cut it.

"Look, Ganzello. Frank Farelli said you had something important to tell me. He said you *would* tell me something important. He did not say you would filibuster like Casey Stengel on ether."

Ganzello pulled his cigar out of his mouth and held it like a half-dessicated stick of licorice. I looked directly into his veiny eyes. Suddenly he grinned.

"The big man knows me. Little ol' fuckin' John Henry in Flushing, and the big *goombah* knows me. Such a deal."

He walked over to the rear entrance and spat—I would say he hawked a clam, but it seems inappropriate given the menu—onto the sidewalk. Nobody seemed to mind.

"That's cuz I cracked his fuckin' team, you got that? The wops down there love the Yanks—second only to linguine and pussy. So I know there's a safe in the place, don't ask me how, and get this, I don't even *care* what's in it. Listen to me, Jack, you're not listening, I care more about a dime bet on the Mariners than I care about what's inside the box. As far as John Henry is concerned, me a person who was born into this world hating the Yankees like I hate porgies, it's an honor just to break that stadium and leave a picture of Darryl Strawberry inside. Listen up, all you Mets fans, break the Yankees' fuckin' bank!"

I was amused, but I tried not to show it. I walked over to the bar to escape the fumes momentarily and get another draught.

"That's mine, Bobby," Ganzello said.

"No, it's not," I said, and put a sawbuck on the bar.

"Man can't buy ya a beer, you gotta problem," he said.

"Thanks anyway. But don't let me interrupt," I said.

"So I got in. I was in the stadium, in the basement. I had it knocked—"

"You cracked the safe?"

"Don't get ahead of yerself. I didn't say that. I said I was warm when I seen what I seen. Gimme a break. You don't believe me, you check out some of them doors down there and see if they been picked. I left a few marks. Was gonna fuckin' write my name down there, or maybe HoJo's number, he's my man."

"What time were you inside?"

" 'Round eleven."

"Around isn't good enough."

"Fuck you."

"Where were you?"

"In the guts. From around first base, you know, by the locker room. Was gonna cop some bats or something—get me a Mattingly full a pine tar and shit. But fuck it. That ain't far from the middle where they got a counting room don't nobody know about. Cashiers take it from the ticket windows down on the inside. Like Vegas. Room's got a blank door and a seven-foot Mosler like banks use for little shit behind the tellers. Goes from there for the switch out to center field on a cart when Purolator's inside. That good enough for ya, smart ass?"

"And you got in the counting room?"

"Hell, I got in the *box*."

I took a drink. The beer was going warm.

"You go find a big man with the Yankees, my friend, and you can ask if somebody didn't open the box and find a little Metsie helmet like you buy for a kid. Compliments of me. I left it there."

I smiled.

"A safecracker with a sense of humor," I said.

"You got it. Shove it up the Yanks' ass! And the biggest asshole, Huston."

"So where were you when the shit hit the fan?" I asked.

"Long gone at that point in time. That ain't the issue."

"What is?"

"I seen somethin' interesting, Jack. Somethin' ain't nobody wrote about, okay? You know where them main elevators come down the middle? Right there. I hear a cart or a forklift or somethin', and I about shit. I grab my equipment and head out. I got my blowout plan in case some-thin' happens, and I look out, I see this cart by the elevators. Like a golf cart they use to move shit around in the park or bring a reliever like they used to. Had a bag on the back. Looked like a great big batbag. Yankee blue with the logo, you know. Kinda layin' sideways off the back. And the guy took off with it."

"Where?"

"Down the tunnel. One goin' out to left field."

"Who was driving the cart? What'd he look like?"

"Some fuckin' guy—who am I, Joe Friday? Saw his back. Blue shirt, maybe like a stadium guy wears. Fuckin' Yankee hat on, like they all wear."

"See anything else? Hair or something?"

"I was watchin' *my* ass. Not his. As soon as the cart took off, so did I."

"Just like that?"

"I don't need a blueprint, Jack. Took me months to lay out my invasion here. I got people I know where they're supposed to be every minute I'm inside, and when some fucker shows up surpriselike, my ass is gone. That's the first rule of inside."

The phone rang, and Ganzello was on it. My mind was running Watergate-style with the possibilities: the scene as Ganzello had described it, the existence of a cart with an oversized batbag on the rear end only minutes before Rupert Huston was murdered. This was all virgin stuff, and some of it did not mesh with the time frames already established. And nobody—not anyone inside the Yankee front office or one of Devery's detectives—had mentioned anything about the counting room or, more significantly, a monumental breach of its security. If what Ganzello said was true, the events going on inside the ballpark on that incredible night made the mind reel: not only had a sniper invaded the stadium and potted its owner, but only a few hundred feet away, the club cash box had been cracked by a Mets fanatic. It was an incredible scenario. A few people at the core of the Yankees' organization had some explaining to do.

Ganzello returned. He'd unsheathed a new mocha-colored eighty-cent pacifier.

"Looks like I got a few things to check out," I said.

"You could say that. And tell Farelli."

"Tell me this—you get much?"

Ganzello snorted.

"I don't say that to nobody. Nobody gotta know that. Let's just be suffice that I left 'em with somethin'. Most guys in my line of work like to leave a callin' card. Now me —I give 'em the Metsie helmet like I said, and one other thing I won't say but trust me it was *be*-yutiful, you hear what I'm sayin'? I'm a sportsman. Life's a game of chance with me, and if I go to my grave, I know at least what I done that night in fuckin' Yankee Stadium. Can't nobody take that away from me."

"One more thing. You hear the shot?"

"What shot?"

"The sniper, for cryin' out loud."

"Gotcha. No. I was gone, man."

"Is that right?"

"You got it, Jack. I'm not stayin' around for fireworks. I'm on the Major Degan and outta there when that shit come down."

"How do you think he got in?"

"The shooter? Shit. Dozen ways. Big barn like that. You got ingresses and exgresses all over the place. Sittin' right there by the tracks and stuff—that ain't no Fort Knox, Jack. And a lot of people don't know Huston cut down the security runs, cut 'em way down, after he bought the club. Cheap ass. He bought his lunch that way, mark my word. There ain't but a few sleepy asses watchin' the TV screens on a park that big, and they're mostly eyeballin' around the front-office part on the Plaza. They'd tune in 'Sanford and Son' if they could. Assholes. I ain't divulgin' any more about that, but you can read between the lines. Lotta guys ain't even as good as me could penetrate."

I realized that I might have to lift my legs for fear of getting both shoes full of what Ganzello was slinging, but it was his turf, and it was his nickel.

"Looks like one of 'em did," I said.

"That's where you come in, in the first place."

"Huh?"

"Farelli, your fuckin' rabbi. You figure out the why of that yet? C'mon now, Jack, you got a few miles on your loafers, so it ever hit you why the old man is gonna have a sit-down with you and give me over? That's what happened, and I'm tickled as shit you asked, because here goes the theory according to John Henry Ganzello. Goes like this: ain't nobody but the families take out someone like they did Huston. Fuckin' sniper! Farelli likes that shit.

Scope 'em, man. He done it two times, and the street knows damn well there ain't but one shooter can do it. Ain't no Zip either, 'cuz they use them Sicilians on up-close juice. Those bastards'll look right at you and pour battery acid down your throat or put a pick in your eyeball, and the whole time you're sayin', 'Who the hell is this guy?' But with somebody like Rupert fuckin' Huston, shit, you gonna take him out, it's gotta be first-division problems. Some big fuckin' sore won't go away. Huston pulled the old man's chain one time too many and *zzzzzt!* he's out. No more extra innings, Jack."

He stopped, walked to the door, and expectorated another misdemeanor onto the sidewalk.

"And he gives you *me*?" he continued. "Me? Shit! He can pump smoke up your ass better 'n that, you know what I'm sayin'?"

He was getting edgy. There comes a time when even John Henry Ganzello tires of the sound of his own voice.

"Sniper. You've got to admit, that's a hell of a hit," I said, looking for slack.

"Nothing but the best for the Yankees," he said, and broke a shallow smile.

"Between that and you in the countinghouse, I'd say the Bombers had a rough night."

He liked that and grinned like an underworld chipmunk.

"I'm a *rogue*, ain't I?" he said, and started to laugh. He leaned over and coughed, still laughing, the cough a raspy, frightening, guttural bellow, and laughed even harder. His equilibrium seemed in danger as he roared and tried to clear his cluttered esophagus. I looked away in case all hell, or his trousers, were to break loose.

He raised up, clenched his fist, and shouted for the world to hear: "I'm a wild-ass Mets maniac Yankee-killin' rogue!"

13

Deposit

After an overly lengthy stop at what can only be called the Clam Bar latrine, a gamey subterranean cell where, it struck me as I stared at mildewed lines of grout and the urinals packed with ice cubes, John Henry Ganzello had no doubt consummated some of his business dealings, I hit the sidewalk. I needed a clean telephone, and I found one in Woolworth's next to the tropical fish. They had a good buy on kissing gouramis. I dialed Devery. I needed some background from him without giving away the case.

"Detective Chief Devery. House, whattaya got?"

The sound of his voice caught me off guard. You don't expect to get through to the big possums in a bureaucracy even if they are at the bureau.

"Got a name I want to run by you."

"That's more like it. Shoot."

"Ganzello."

"Two *l*'s? Got it. I'll run it through. Where you gonna be?"

"In transit."

"Gloria," Devery said.

A rare mood, I thought.

"Whatever. I can come around within the hour."

"Downtown. Centre Street."

I hung up and was about to cruise my favorite five-and-dime when a buck-toothed ogre blocked my path near the Rubbermaid display.

"You got what you wanted, now get the fuck outta my neighborhood," Ganzello said.

No more wild-ass Mets maniac, no more offers to cover my tab. Ganzello glared at me like an umpire who had just seen his call contradicted by the stadium replay.

"Just browsing," I said, and headed down the aisle.

He followed right behind me, his dank breath on my neck. Once through the revolving door, I paused to get my bearings, and he was on me. Suddenly my ribs exploded, and my breath was sucked from me. I doubled over, seeing black and hearing sirens. Ganzello had shot an elbow into my torso, flush on the rib cage, and it like to collapsed my lung.

"What the—!" I gasped, holding my left side.

"Don't come suckin' around no more, I don't give a fuck who sent ya," he growled.

I gulped for a decent lungful of air and lurched toward the subway station. My heart thumped. I tasted blood in my throat. Ganzello let me be. Just before I reached the corner, I spotted an empty cab.

Upon massaging my ribs I decided I had had the wind knocked out of me and was more startled than hurt. The cab took off toward Manhattan, its faceless driver unconcerned about my labored breathing. Ganzello's elbow woke me up, however, and I spent the trip back to Manhattan putting things together. His sudden fury told me something; that it had manifested itself outside the friendly confines of the Clam Bar told me more. I took out a reporter's notebook and scribbled, trying to remember most of what the punk hustler had said and more of what he had implied.

The stadium sniper was nothing extraordinary in Ganzello's skewed perspective, and it had Farelli written all over it. He said the street knew who the shooter was— or at least, I figured, who was talented enough to carry out Family hits using a high-powered rifle. As sleazy as Ganzello was, there was something to the fact that he pointed back at the Farelli organization in this whole thing. Hitting Rupert Huston was no spontaneous act by a little man: it had contract killer pasted all over it. It was carried off without a hitch, and that smacked of some help from inside the stadium. The killer got in and got out of a high-profile, closely guarded arena. Or *was* it closely guarded, and just how good had the Mob been at getting someone inside?

This was well-worked territory, I figured. The police had been all over the ballpark's security guys from the beginning. The New York press and their irrepressible Mob reporters were exhaustively picking through Huston's organized-crime closet, detailing his dealings in hotels and his relationships with various Mob-dominated labor unions associated with the construction business. Names like Hoffa and Giacalone—and Farelli—had come up over and over again.

Just as I had never joined the gang of reporters who tackled the goat or the hero after a ball game, I didn't relish joining them this time. I also didn't cotton to John Henry Ganzello's split personality. And I wondered what to make of the fact that he said he never heard the shot.

My cabbie knew what Centre Street and One Police Plaza were all about, and he got me there for under thirty bucks. Even though I was on the commissioner's pad, the fares were murder. I paid and tucked the receipt into my wallet. Entering the cavernous corridors of the NYPD HQ, I wandered a while before I found Devery's sanctum.

He was waiting for me behind a desk as wide as a home club's buffet table. The walls of the office climbed to ceilings at least fourteen feet high. Plaques, awards, commendations, medals, ribbons, and photos of Devery with everybody from Cardinal O'Connor to Mario Cuomo made the place look like the anteroom of a Tammany Hall politician.

"You look like you've pitched middle relief," he said. "Relax and have a chair."

I did, feeling the soreness in my ribs as I settled in. I spotted a photo of Devery with a Yankee in uniform and saw it was the late Ellie Howard. It was an odd, telling memento. The first great black Yankee.

"What'd you think of Jimmy Cannon?" he suddenly asked.

The question took me off guard. It shouldn't have.

"A fellow professional. I never knocked any one of 'em."

"Okay, that out of the way, what'd you think of him?"

I chuckled.

"He could write better than Hemingway. And Hemingway knew it."

Devery liked that one.

"I read him every day when I was a kid. Memorized his good lines. Thought he was a lion."

"So did Jimmy."

He nodded.

"I miss him," he went on. "But you know who I miss more? Frank Graham. Of the old *Journal-American*."

"Frank Graham," I said wistfully, remembering many a press box I shared with the man. Graham was to Cannon in the flamboyance category what Dan Topping was to George Steinbrenner.

"Now there was a craftsman," I offered.

"Red Smith had a great quote from Graham about Cannon," said Devery. "Graham said Jimmy was like a left-handed pitcher with great speed and no control."

I smiled and pictured Graham saying it.

"I didn't know you had such a place in your heart for old sportswriters," I said.

"I try not to let on. Especially in their presence. But I gotta hand it to you on this one," he said.

He raised a file in front of him.

"For a guy who's only the eyes and ears of the commissioner's office, you got into some deep territory. This Ganzello pooch. Where'd you come on him?"

"An anonymous friend of the commissioner's," I replied. "Told me to check him out. That's why I'm here."

"My people know him. He's a book up in Flushing. Got paper on him in three states. Pays his street taxes and keeps out of harm's way. Not a made guy."

"I think I understand that: a bookie with a record who is not a full-fledged member of the Mob?"

"That's it. But that ain't what you want, is it?"

"I'm not sure," I said.

Devery was toying. He looked at the Ganzello file as if he were a teacher and I was the struggling pupil.

"One thing you might like in here is that this guy has a few pinches for safecracking. Seems he likes to go inside once in a while."

I tried not to let on. But Ganzello did have some credentials; I hadn't been put on.

"Can't be very good if he was caught," I said.

"On the contrary," said Devery. "He's real good. So good that my people think his action is a cover. As a book he's a loser. He'd give you odds on when the ball's gonna come down in Times Square on New Year's Eve."

I pondered that.

"Fingers like his could get into a locked ballpark pretty easy," Devery added. " 'Cept this guy is no shooter. Only has one good eye."

"Only takes one," I said.

It was Devery's turn to smile. He swiveled his chair, put his hand behind his massive head, and looked off in the direction of shots of Paul O'Dwyer and Abe Beame. He was a wily old-school cop who'd made it as high as you can go as a New York detective. I could see why.

"Any signs? Your guys find anything that fits Ganzello's technique?" I asked.

"Nothing. The employee door was tampered with—you knew that—but it wasn't picked. We think we know how it got left open, but it doesn't help us much. The security guys played real dumb, and now they got lawyers sittin' on them."

"One more thing," he added, turning back to me. "Don't try to find this guy. He's not a made Family guy, so he don't abide by their rules. These fringe players—the ice thieves, safecrackers, home invaders—they live in a no-man's-land. Half of 'em are feeding a habit or paying off heavy juice. They're dangerous assholes. Duffy, you even get close to Ganzello, and there's no telling what he'd do. It's not like tracking down ol' Ralph Terry and talking about how he pitched McCovey in the sixty-two Series. This Ganzello's in a different league."

I nodded solemnly, so advised. Devery wasn't finished.

"For your information, and for your information only, Duffy, Ganzello is the first new name that's stuck to the wall in this thing," he said. "And I won't forget where it came from. I appreciate your coming to me."

"I wouldn't have if you'd been at the morgue again," I said.

He laughed.

"Still, Chief, where does it get either of us?"

"It gets us real close. We think we know who the shooter is, and we think we can put him in the area. We think we got a trail on the rifle. Now if Ganzello checks out, we think we know how our boy got in."

"You think it's the late innings?" I asked.

"And we got Yo-Yo Arroyo with his best stuff on the hill," he said.

He got up from his high-backed seat.

"Let me give you my direct line," he said.

I pocketed his card and considered my heightened status.

"Tell me," I said as he came around toward me, "is this Albert Seedman's old desk?"

He lifted his eyebrows and nodded in acknowledgment of one of his famous predecessors.

"Seedman. How do you know of Seedman?"

"I read his book," I said.

He whistled slightly and put a healthy mitt on my shoulder.

"You got a hell of a reading list," he said.

It had been a hell of a day for this old geezer, and I decided to unwind at the ballpark. The Yanks were finishing up their home stand after the rainout, and I was hungry for some good pressroom chow. I'd lived much of my life out of a suitcase, so being holed up in the Summit was not cruel and unusual for me. A good sports columnist is used to running from the Masters in Augusta to the marathon in Boston to a ball game in Baltimore and a fight in Atlantic City. He lives in a place where somebody takes in the mail, the newspapers, the handbills, and the meter readers. If he is single, he owns no pets; his plants are cacti. Phone machines have remedied the message problem, but before they were around, I simply left my black rotary on the front-room table to ring until it hurt. To hell with 'em, I figured; if they didn't know I was out of town by my byline, they didn't deserve my ear. If he is courageous, perhaps foolhardy, a columnist—and a beat writer for that matter —takes a spouse, an independent, self-sufficient, infinitely tolerant, bordering on saintly human being who looks upon his prolonged absences as mental-health days.

I needed an answer to a vital question: had Yankee Stadium been penetrated by one John Henry Ganzello? By late afternoon Petey was still not around, so I left her a note revealing my Yankee Stadium destination. Traffic was obscene, not to mention the tirades of the cabbies, and I arrived at 161st Street in the Bronx well into the dinner hour. Before heading into the dining room, I nosed around the lower corridor on the first-base side.

There were plenty of reporters and assorted individuals with current-date credentials milling around, so nobody paid much attention to me. I was looking for the unmarked door that led to the inner hallway and the counting room Ganzello had mentioned. Suddenly it seemed that there were too many doors, too many choices. To the untrained eye—or at least to one who historically knew how to find only the clubhouse, the pressroom, and the dining hall—the underground level of the stadium was a maze.

At last I decided on a certain portal. It was unmarked and innocuous, and after a quick glance over my shoulder, I leaned down to examine its jamb. I am no evidence technician, but the steel striker plate had what seemed like several pry marks on it. They were horizontal grooves, apparently fresh, the kind of marks I know I'd leave if I had to bust into my place with a screwdriver. Ganzello had insisted that he'd left them there intentionally. I wondered. I wondered if I was being suckered. I felt a little silly, and very hungry; after another fleeting glance I left for the dining room.

Already into a pork chop and baked-apple compote was my niece. She was sitting alone.

"Unk!" Petey said, waving the chop at me.

"Nice of you to make contact," I said. "Your beeper must be on the blink."

"Oh, John called and suggested I come down early," she said. "You weren't anywhere to be found, so I hopped up here."

I muttered unintelligibly and went over to the bar for a glass of Ballantine on draught. When I returned, Petey leaned in on my chin.

"What happened? Did you make contact with the guy? What was he like?" she asked all in a rush.

I looked around me.

"Are we alone?" I asked.

She made a face.

"What was he like?" I repeated. "I wouldn't let him in my house."

"You wouldn't have to," she said.

"Don't interrupt. Let's just say I had to wash my hands after ten minutes with him. But—and this is a big but—if what this mug said is on the square, we've finally got something to go on." I went on to relate Ganzello's foray into the stadium's inner chambers.

Petey listened raptly, yet never missing a bite.

"Who knows about it here? John?" she asked.

"I intend to ask him. But that's just for openers. You have any idea who's head of operations here? The person who watches the receipts . . . ?"

"Come on."

"Herm McFarland. Ring a bell?"

Petey's magnificent eyes gleamed.

"*Keeler*," she breathed.

Just after the third inning of a good ball game with plenty of base hits and some great baserunning, I went to find Brush. Petey, knowing this might be sensitive for her friend, offered to stay in the press box.

Brush motioned me into his office. He kept the game monitor on but turned down the sound. Without watching we both knew the tide of the game by the pitch of the crowd.

"You aware of any other breach of security that night?" I asked.

"I'm not with you, Duffy," Brush said. He was in uniform: the impeccable ice-blue dress shirt, a yellow tie, the tailored navy blue suit pants, black wing tips. His concession to casual was rolling up his sleeves to midforearm.

"A burglary. Specifically, in the stadium's counting room and safe."

"You serious?" he said, sitting straight up.

"Sure am."

"You're saying somebody broke into the ballpark and robbed us? Down in operations?"

"Exactly."

"When?"

"About the time of the murder."

"My God. That's impossible. What else do you know?"

"Very little. That's why I came to you."

He picked up his phone and punched an extension.

"Herm there? This is John Brush. Tell him to stay put. I'm coming down."

He got up.

"Come along. I want to get straight on this myself."

An elevator ride and a few nods at security personnel, and we were in the stadium operations office, Hermus McFarland presiding. I scanned the surroundings, trying not to gawk. Against the wall, with its door wide open, was a standing safe.

"Got a minute, Herm? This is Duffy House," Brush said.

If McFarland wondered who I was or what I was doing there, he didn't say anything. Brush's presence seemed to take care of that. McFarland was in his thirties, a thin guy with a receding hairline. In his shirtsleeves, his tie loose, and in the bustle of the operations office around him, he looked like an accountant. To speculate about what Keeler Huston saw in him was to wade, I'm afraid, in murky waters.

"Hit the door," Brush said.

We stood in a characterless clutter of file cabinets, in-out bins, computers, and stacks of printouts. Unlike the memorabilia-strewn dens of the brass upstairs, it could have been any office anywhere. Even the crowd noise did not penetrate the walls.

"Was there a break-in here the night Rupert was killed?" Brush asked when the door was closed and it was just the three of us.

Fastball down the middle.

"Well, whattaya mean, John?" McFarland said.

"Just what I said. Somebody burglarize this office that night?"

"Okay. Burglary? No, I wouldn't say that. We had a, uh . . . we had an irregularity, if you wanna call it anything."

"Cut the shit, Herm. What happened?"

"I'm not being funny with you, John. It's just that—

okay John, I'm gonna give it to you straight now. I mean, I got people on account of my situation here would like to see me embarrassed. So things happen, and I don't go running upstairs."

"What happened?"

"We had a shortfall, okay? A couple thousand . . . which is no big thing, and it still could come out in the tapes, but for now I can't find it."

He itched his elbows as he spoke. He was as uncomfortable as a kid who'd just been caught shoplifting.

"With no burglary? No break-in? Where'd the money go?" Brush said, his voice pitch rising. I watched him. He was tattooing McFarland pretty good.

"I don't know, okay? You could call it a burglary depending on your definition of the term—"

"The safe. Anything happen to the safe?" I asked.

McFarland looked sharply at me. He exhaled and ran a moist hand over his face.

"Okay. You want straight, John, I'll give you straight," he said. "The safe was opened. It was drilled."

"Drilled?!" Brush exclaimed. "You mean, as in cracked? The safe was cracked?"

"I guess so."

"And you don't call that a burglary? You got people working here who can do that kind of thing?"

"Look, I don't know—" McFarland said.

The guy was now a mess.

"Anything else peculiar? This person leave a mark or something?" I inquired.

At that McFarland sat down and tried to regain some color.

"Here's the whole thing. I came here with Keeler that night because of her father. But I didn't come down here into the office. The next morning I got a call from Nicole real early. I was still whipped from being up half the night.

"I got here as soon as I could, maybe ten, and you know what a mess it was with the cops and the media. What I saw out there was the open safe. A lot of papers and things were moved around, but it wasn't really ransacked. The cash we keep—hell, it's change, about enough to carry a Nedick's overnight. Maybe a couple thousand bucks, give or take. But it ain't anything a big-timer would go after. We do the bulk of our ticket business by credit card, and we get armored-car service for the cash. The vendors handle their own. Nobody got in over there from what they tell me. What else can I say?"

Brush slapped the wall with an open palm.

McFarland swallowed, then said, "Look, there was money gone. But this is why I thought something might be fishy, or maybe there was someone in the office pulling a prank. Because, well, inside the safe was this little blue batting helmet. A thing you'd buy for a baby. A Mets helmet. And on the table—"

With that McFarland sighed, looked away, looked back at us, then looked down at his own desk.

"—on the table was a pile of shit, okay? I'm not making this up. Nicole almost threw up. And a little pennant was stuck in it, a Mets pennant.

"And that's the straight dope."

I was stunned. I turned away to keep from breaking a grin the size of John Henry Ganzello. The son-of-a-bitch *had* taken a dump on the Yankees.

Brush was incredulous.

"Somebody took a shit on the table out there? And put a Mets pennant in it? And it happened that very night? Someone was in this room? In the stadium?"

McFarland nodded.

"And you didn't report this to the police?" Brush said.

"Would you?" McFarland said.

He didn't get an answer. We went out to the counting room, where McFarland showed us the safe. He'd had a locksmith come in and service the safe's locking mechanism. The small drill hole had been puttied over and painted and was nearly unnoticeable. The doorjamb revealed pry marks similar to the ones I'd spotted earlier.

McFarland pointed at a low table in the middle of the room.

"The deposit was—"

"Never mind," Brush snapped, "I got an imagination."

He led us back into McFarland's office and closed the door.

"Who knows about this?" he asked.

"Me. Nicole. Now you two," he said.

"Nobody in vending?"

"No."

"Keep it that way," Brush ordered. "Keep me apprised of anything you hear. Anything that happens. This goes no farther than this office.

"Goddamn embarrassing, Herm. And I don't think you or the Yankee organization needs any more embarrassment right now," he added as he motioned me to the door. "I'll make some inquiries with people who can help us on this. In the meantime you keep your mouth shut."

McFarland, whose cohabitation with the daughter of the slain owner of the Yankees had no doubt featured worse ultimatums over brunch, meekly nodded his head.

Brush strode quickly out of the office. I had all I could do to keep up with him as we retraced our steps back to the upper deck and his suite.

"Unbelievable," he growled quietly. Then he added, "I really appreciate your bringing this to me, Duffy. This place is having a nervous breakdown."

"How you gonna handle it?" I asked, not certain if I had a right to.

"As I said, I'll make a few calls. I trust you'll keep confidence, as a friend and a professional. McFarland is another matter. Between you and me, he's got an agenda of his own."

"Can you keep this thing in the building?" I asked.

"I've got to," he said. "The papers would have kittens. Can you imagine the *Post*?" he said.

"The shit would hit the proverbial fan," I said, and then laughed. "Sorry, John, I couldn't resist."

He didn't smile, didn't share my cheap amusement. To say the least, he appeared preoccupied.

As anxious as I was to get back to the ballgame—I find myself enjoying them more now that I don't have to look for a column in them—I found my thoughts nowhere close to the action. Bob Sheppard's tones announced every batter, and the scoreboard regaled the crowd with that vintage Movietone action of past Yankee glories, but I was replaying the phlegmy phonetics of John Henry Ganzello. He *had* been inside. He *had* punched the safe and shat on the Yankees. And if he was telling the truth about that, could he not be believed about seeing someone in a blue shirt driving a motorized cart with an equipment bag on the back? Who was that? Did the security detail know anything about it? Had they even been asked?

Petey was all over me for details when I returned, but the press box was not the place to fill her in.

"Things are breaking, Pete," I did say, cracking open a peanut. "Ganzello got in. McFarland's ass is on the griddle. Brush is fit to be tied."

She squeezed my wrist and flashed a clenched-teeth grin.

"I love it," she said.

A 6–5 Yankee win saved by a backhanded stab of a bases-loaded drive just over third base brought the crowd to its feet and the smug sounds of Sinatra to the P.A. Any notion of comparing notes with Petey during a ride home were dashed by her now standard, maddening little remark, "I'm going with John."

But she did say that she had a plan and needed to talk about it with me in the morning. I cabbed home alone and nearly fell asleep before we got to Central Park. My message light was ablinking when I got to the room, but I ignored it and slept an unapologetic sleep.

I was certain that I had not warmed the pillow for any longer than twelve minutes when the phone went berserk. I had strictly forbidden this to happen, and the front desk knew it. A fossil such as I does not have a lot of sleep left in this noisy world, and at my age I have decided to enjoy it.

"What!" I barked, searching for my glasses.

"House? Devery. Your man Ganzello was popped."

My head cleared.

"How? Where?"

"Got him outside a joint he darkens up in Queens. Two hours ago."

"Sniper?"

"No. They whacked him at close range when he walked out of the place. Two slugs in the back of the neck."

"Good God. What's your make on it?"

"Oh, they got him all right," Devery said. "His people. Question of why."

I exhaled audibly.

"I wake you up?"

"No, I just came in from jogging," I wheezed. "Keep me in on this, will you, Chief?"

"One more thing you might find cute," Devery added.

"What's that?"

"They put a brand-new Yankee cap on his head. Stuffed a pair of tickets in his hand. Sunday game against the Tigers."

14

ℳonte Beville

Sniffing the gamey odor of sibling treachery and soiled family laundry, Petey's plan had been to move quickly from Keeler Huston to brother Griffith. Not only were her ears primed with bile straight from the mouths of Lana and Keeler, but her vision had been blurred by the daily stream of painted prose dished forth by the New York tabloids concerning the family Huston. She read every word, and now, a deadline having passed since the night of the murder, she lapped up several gossipy, anecdotal articles from New York's feisty set of weekly magazines. They left no gallstone unturned. Her room was papered with them, many with pages ripped out and passages underlined. Petey, with her personal contact and special perspective on the players, was like a female I. F. Stone, mining nuggets from buried paragraphs and throwaway lines, eager to stitch them into a coherent tableau that would account for the bullet that coursed through Rupert Huston's brain.

Griffith Huston and his arty friends were her next targets, and in order to get a look at their turf, she pulled what I fondly call "a Petey." That is, she rushed in full of zip and zeal but not a heck of a lot of design. The afternoon before, while I had been buttonholing Ganzello, she had hopped a downtown train out of Grand Central and several minutes later sought the light above ground at Spring Street in SoHo.

She had decided to blend in with the background and

thus had dressed as a jogger. But Petey in jogging togs is to camouflage what neon is to moonlight. She wore—and magnificently so, I say with a keen reporter's eye—a pink tank top, skintight silver spandex leotards, and silver gray Avia running shoes. Her russet hair was set off by a pink headband. Perfect disguise, she thought. Perfect, of course, for the stockbroker jogging course in Central Park on Sunday morning. On a weekday afternoon in the heart of Manhattan's gallery district, however, where your average denizen, male or female, dresses in the baggy black cottons of Chinese peasants, Petey stood out like Dave Winfield at a convention of albino midgets.

But she was there, and she had to make the best of it. She jog-walked west on Spring Street, turned north on Broadway up to Prince, then went west again. She knew that the Beville Gallery was around here somewhere — rather than having looked it up, she was ad-libbing—and she would just have to wander until she found it. At West Broadway she went south again, back toward Spring Street, passing the John Dellaria Gallery, and Scott Hanson's on the left side of the street, where John Visser and Paul V'Soske were exhibiting their recent work. In front, sitting on a flatbed truck trailer that looked like it belonged in Iowa, was a huge block of wood. A sculpture in progress, perhaps, or just a big hunk of tree that might have been better off turned into a couple dozen Louisville Sluggers.

She stopped and eyeballed the SoHo Fruit and Vegetable market, the Susan Schreiber Gallery, the Center for Tapestry Arts. But no Beville. Just then, looking east up Spring Street, she caught a glimpse of banners hanging over the sidewalk a little past the Spring Street Market. There it was, with gold and fuchsia streamers announcing its glory, the Monte Beville Gallery.

Petey broke into a less-than-dedicated trot, running in place at the corner, then pausing when she finally reached the premises and taking in as much as she could. Turning left at the corner, she jogged by the long side of the gallery on Mercer Street and peered in. The place had glistening wood floors punctuated by Persian rugs and twisting waist-high sculptures in brass, wood, and mixed materials. The walls were collages of oversized prints—Dalis, O'Keefes,

Ertés. Even in her initial short glimpse of the place, Petey sensed that it could suck in the holders of new fortunes like a magnet does steel shavings.

Petey did a loop in her jog at the corner of Prince and Mercer and headed back on the other side of the street for one more good look. She saw no one; indeed, the gallery seemed uninhabited. She noted a couple of conspicuous double-parked cars out front: one was a deep green low-slung Jaguar, the other a camel-colored Mercedes convertible. They were rich, luscious automobiles, and as Petey cast her gaze lovingly upon them, she suddenly noticed two figures who had appeared in the front window of the Beville Gallery. They were staring directly at her. To anyone's gaze it was a tasty stew: mint, overpriced flivvers reflecting red hair and bouncing, carved muscles beneath silver spandex. Petey, sensing her cover had been blown halfway to Coney Island, kept jogging up Spring Street until she had stepped off the three blocks to the subway station. She quickly disappeared below street level, where she soon wished she had brought along a baggy sweatshirt. Instead she endured the ride, which included three overt and somewhat salacious proposals of marriage, until she was safely back to the Summit.

Petey related all of this back to me the next morning and could not hide her sheepishness over her choice of garb. She was setting me up, however, eating a little humble pie in order to throw a bigger order at me.

"Unk, I'm going back as a buyer," she said. "An interior designer or consultant or some bozza-rozza like that. Here's the skit. I make an appointment personally with Monte Beville. Tell him that as a designer I have a fat budget and a fatter client who needs a quick art fix. One of these I-don't-know-art-but-I-know-what-I-like guys that is putty in my hands. I put on the look, you know, stylish professional woman with little artsy-fartsy touches. Get a car and driver. Walk into his front door with cash hanging out of my purse and wait for his tongue to wag."

"Such a ruse," I said.

"I mean it. I'll paint myself the color of money, and that's what these gallery owners are really all about. Long green."

"Can you talk their language?"

"Uh, I think so. I pulled an art minor in college, and my girlfriend Bridget worked in a gallery in Cincinnati. The jargon's no sweat, and I'll kite some lines from a few reviews. It's easy to find out who's hot right now," she said, totally convinced. "Plus, I'm a good listener. Don't forget that."

"Sounds harmless. But will it get you the skinny on Griffith Huston?"

"We'll see. Right now my problem is spiffing up. I need some serious clothes, Unk."

"Huh?"

"Really. Donna Karan, Giorgio Armani, Calvin Klein, Gillian, Oscar de la Renta—"

"You talking apparel? Or jockeys?"

"Wardrobe, Unk. Good stuff. I need a credit line of a thousand to start."

"Dollars? Ouch."

"Hey. I can't walk in there with something from Filene's basement. I've got to look like what I represent. I guarantee you Monte Beville will notice."

"He won't see a poor kid from Cincinnati whose mother choked every nickel to pay the bills? He won't see a girl who worked her way through college? How're you gonna manage that?"

"Same way Meryl Streep played both *Sophie's Choice* and *Out of Africa*—acting. You've never seen me act, Unk."

"Oh, I don't know about that," I said, and smiled. Petey was flying with this thing, and confidence fairly oozed from her pores.

"A thousand bucks on your back. A limousine—"

"Think the commissioner would free up his car and driver?"

"—and a mouth full of pop-art baloney. And a phony client."

Petey grinned and nodded her head up and down. She looked like a Punch-and-Judy swinger about to get a chance to pinch-hit with men on base.

I thought of just the guy, and added, "As Frenchy Bordagaray said to a confounded Casey Stengel when he was caught stealing home with two outs in the ninth, 'You ain't seen nuthin' yet!' "

"Exactly," said Petey.

I harrumphed a Casey harrumph and left it up to her to negotiate with Grand Chambliss. He was taken with the sprite and would probably respond docilely, as do most men when they are in whispering distance of beautiful young women. I had every reason to believe that Monte Beville was not above board in his business dealings—the old guilty-until-proven-otherwise syndrome that investigators are good at. But I did not consider him dangerous. So I said nothing. If nothing else Petey's foray might smoke out Griffith and thus fill in the final piece of the Huston family puzzle. But if Keeler had tipped off her brother, Petey would have to navigate through that thicket on her own. I saw little harm in it and thought the exercise a good piece better than Petey dating randy players, or managers, especially since we were dealing with a world of a completely different persuasion. I also did not fill her in on the demise of the scatological safecracker.

Petey moved with the speed of a subpoena in getting to Chambliss and prying an added chit for her wardrobe out of him. Chambliss thought her SoHo charade was a fine idea. He didn't even have a problem with Petey using his name as a referral, if she thought it was necessary. Chambliss was baseball, and baseball was Rupert Huston, and, from what we knew, Rupert Huston had been one of Monte Beville's favorite cash cows.

The use of the commissioner's auto was another matter. Grand greeted the request with a friendly wave of his hand. But his driver, the spiky Norma Perlmutter, glowered. Norm probably would have driven *me* around Manhattan for days without a sigh; but Petey was her age, no sharper than she by her lights, and getting much too much attention. Norma's miff went for naught, however, and Petey quickly got into the limo and gave her directions.

After a few hours in Bloomingdale's, Petey was bedecked, accessoried, and ready to go. She came by the Summit to give me a look that afternoon, when I was trying to figure out what to do with a dead Ganzello and a very live Herm McFarland. Her look was from some guy named Isaac Mizrahi, and it was full of color and flaps and looked fine to me as long as I didn't have to see the price tag. A purse the size of an equipment bag hung over her shoulder. She had put some English on her locks, stuck two earrings in one ear and none in the other. I may have been dreaming, or just overly suspicious, but one of her earrings, coated though it was with some kind of acrylic paint, looked remarkably like a rolled-up prophylactic! A rubber! What we used to call "safes" and kept buried in our wallets.

"Uh, Petrinella," I ventured. "That on your lobe. It *isn't* what I think it is, is it?"

"Condom jewelry!" she exclaimed. "Yes, Unk. It is so nineties, and you are so sharp."

"Forgive me," I sighed.

This was Big Apple Petey, not the old Dr. Denton's muppet or the frisky sneakers-and-blue-jeans rocket I used to know.

"My car here yet?" she sniffed, and then burst into laughter.

She had called ahead and chatted up Monte Beville directly. He bit. Grand Chambliss's imprimatur was the impeccable ticket. She made an appointment with Beville for late afternoon, and in short order the icy Norma Perlmutter, who made the drive without offering a word, pulled the commissioner's car in front of the Beville Gallery at Spring and Mercer streets. Petey told her to sit out front until she returned. Norma's expression put frost on the windshield.

"Mzz Biggerzz. Welcome," oozed Monte when Petey introduced herself. No man had ever polished her moniker with greater sibilance. His eyes skated over her like water bugs, and apparently they liked the terrain. He offered a hand so warm it felt as if it had been baked.

Beville was tall, tanned to the gills, yet with looks that strained to overcome bad bones. He wore makeup, Petey noticed, a little base to cover what his tan could not. He had a hammy double chin that he probably detested. His teeth were capped but large. His ink black hair was moussed, shiny, and swept back to a little rat's ponytail. Whatever torso he had was lost in a layered, roomy ensemble of black pleated slacks and a double-breasted gray silk jacket. A string tie with a bison's head split a black buttonless shirt.

In all, as Petey discerned in an instantaneous scan as exacting as Beville's had been of her, Monte was a production, a gust of pattern, shadows, and a pair of gunmetal gray Italian leather shoes that barely peeked out from beneath his cuffs. Small feet, Petey noted. Her mother had once warned her about tall men with small feet. Her mother had once warned her about women without lips. The two admonitions rolled in her head. *Mene, mene, tekel, upharsin.*

"Like what you see?" Beville said, interrupting her lapse.

"It's very impressive, Mr. Beville," Petey gushed, quickly looking around the gallery.

"Monte, I insist. The commissioner of baseball—a nifty client," he said.

"An old friend of my uncle. He's a doll. And he's serious."

Petey's eye caught a Dubuffet, a Hockney, a Roger Brown.

Beville went on. "A wood or bronze sculpture? I get good trade from sportsmen on those. Sort of like selling the old Remington cavalry charges. Dreadful stuff, but I wish I had a hundred of them."

He was in full stride now, tossing off the good, the bad, and the ugly according to his jaundiced eye.

"Original oils? Something contemporary?"

"What about a rare Chagall—cheap?" Petey asked, suddenly making eye contact.

"My, my. I can get Marc for you, but it won't be cheap. I can get anything you're after, Ms. Biggers—I mean, I represent a network of dealers and artists," he said, and then he varnished a smile across his chops meant to win the confidence of the most suspicious heart.

Petey rubbed her hands together in front of her chin as she strolled, her eyes roving, her steps measured and silent on the costly floor coverings, her thoughts hurtling. The art around her was glossy and colorful, meticulously matted and framed, most of it upbeat and fairly representational. A few surreal Dalis and abstract efforts by artists Petey didn't recognize interrupted the menu.

"I'm sure Mr. Chambliss is knowledgeable about the art world," Beville ventured.

"Don't be so sure," Petey countered. "Put it this way: he's a smart guy who knows what he likes."

"A good start. And what kind of motifs and colors would we be working with in the Chambliss home?"

Petey considered fast.

"Mr. Chambliss isn't the kind of person who wants his art to match the paint on his walls. . . ."

"Of course not!" Beville responded quickly.

Calm down, Petey told herself. Beville smiled again, assuming an oiled, assured countenance—facial cruise control. He was an operator and very effective: one part culture maven, one part boiler-room salesman.

"I wonder if Mr. Chambliss would bite on a Dali print . . ." Petey ventured.

"*Excellent.* And daring. These photolithograph prints were signed by the artist before he died in 1987."

"How many in the edition?"

"Five hundred—as expressly called for by Dali himself. Each one signed in pencil."

"How much for each print?"

"Four thousand."

"Very impressive—" Petey said, then paused, and reached for some mustard: "—that is, if they're authentic."

It was a quick pitch, and it caught Beville with his weight on his left foot. He righted himself and narrowed his eyes into mail slots.

"Please, Ms. Biggers. Of course they're authentic. But that's not the real question, is it? All art is an illusion. People pay us to give them an illusion, don't you agree? You and I are simply the link between those who don't know what they're doing—the artists—and those who don't know what they want—the buyers."

"Hmm," said Petey, not sure whether she agreed with him or wanted to join his confederacy.

"You see, artists are interested in their 'principles,' which is elitist excrement to me. To them, dealers and designers have no principles but money. Now some people would call the relationship between dealer and artist and collector a parasitic relationship; I prefer to call it 'symbiotic.' We take care of them, and they keep us in a strong cash-flow position.

"And most artists are grateful to us for taking over the business part of their lives," he continued. "They need people like us just to be their go-between with the people who buy their work. I can't tell you how many artists have told me that they can't stand the kind of people who buy their work. Artists and rich people simply don't mix very well at all.

"As far as I'm concerned, with one group that has so much money they don't know what to do with it, and the other group clearly not knowing how to handle it—I think we should be the ones profiting from this situation. This is business, Ms. Biggers.

"Plus, there's no accounting for taste," Beville hammered. "Who was it that said, 'Some people have taste, and some people think otherwise'?"

"I don't think anybody said that," Petey replied.

He scowled.

"But they should have," Petey said, and then smiled, easing up a bit.

Beville smiled, reflexively and mirthlessly, back at her. He dearly appreciated a tart tongue; indeed, he made his living in bitchery. Ms. Biggers was a contender, and he welcomed her quick rejoinders.

"A businesswoman, I do declare," he said. "I am a businessman. If it sells, it's art, thank you. Do you know of Frank Lloyd? Certainly one of the most famous gallery owners in Europe and America. Frank said, 'I don't give a damn what anybody says, there is only one measure of success in running a gallery: making money. Any dealer who says it's not is a hypocrite or will soon be closing his doors.' That's right. He'd *been* there."

Now Beville was going.

"So we hook up with rich people, and we give them whatever they need to make them feel whatever it is they need to feel—cultured, artsy, intelligent, whatever.

"So it is with you and your Mr. Chambliss. You don't have anything to do with whether the baseball commissar has a wonderful life or not. You just work with him, caress his ego, direct him the way you want him to go. He feels good, you feel good, we wrap the canvas."

"I don't like to think of it as crass manipulation," Petey said.

"Call it what you will," Monte interrupted. "But it's what we do, Ms. Biggers. And as long as people believe they are satisfied, we're doing our job. Remember, we have to be students of human nature and push the right buttons."

"Mr. Chambliss said you worked with Rupert Huston," Petey said abruptly.

"So I did, between you and me. I told the press we had a client-buyer relationship, and that was that. Piss on those barbarians. Hard copy, my ass."

Monte was swiftly moving from the showroom into the boiler room.

"Rupert was a collector I helped with some important pieces," he continued. "And he got my nose into his dealings, thank you. What blew me away—and I'm not easily blown—was watching him wheel and deal in *his* business. The way he peddled horseflesh on that team! The way he set 'em up and knocked 'em down! My God, he made Lee Iacocca look like Erté!"

"Do you know Griffith?" Petey asked, reaching, looking at a Warhol as she spoke.

"Griffith?" Beville said, his tone of voice reaching for a neighbor note.

"Huston. I know he's into the art scene," Petey said. "Mr. Chambliss said he was quite involved and even got his father interested. Since Rupert was your client, I made the connection."

Beville pursed his lips and exhaled through his nose.

"For you to know," he answered, "Griffith is a part of my business now. A valuable part."

"Rupert's collection is fabulous, I've heard," Petey went on. "Mr. Chambliss is envious, I think."

"It is, and they always are," Beville responded.

"Nice business if you can get it," Petey said.

"And I got it, thank you," Beville said. "So how about you? Will we take a chance on anything for your Mr. Chambliss? I'd love to get you on my books. I think we'd do well together, Ms. Biggers. This is New York, you know, and there are fish to fry."

"The Dali prints. These two. Let me take them along to see how they'll work in the Chambliss living room."

"Stunning! They exude style," Monte exuded. "I know you'll be able to sell him on them."

Sell, Petey said to herself. Monte Beville was quietly ecstatic, consumed. Petey could almost feel the paper burn from his register tape. He was more than she had imagined, a highbrow entrepreneur without rein. He had motive dripping from him like cerulean blue from a freshly opened tube. And Griffith Huston was in his stable, an apprentice, an abettor.

Then Petey turned and mustered an intense look deep into Monte Beville's eyeballs. She spoke like a surgeon to her scrub nurse.

"What I really want, Monte, is a Chagall. A good one. I want it hanging right in Commissioner Chambliss's office for every baseball owner and every agent and superstar to see. It should knock their lights out.

"Can you get one? Can you? It's important to me," she said, mustering a whole cliché's worth of cheerleader-decorator.

He returned her stare, cocked his head like a Doberman, and nodded like a jewel thief. Not a word passed his lips, just a brief, nearly imperceptible, but definite nod. Petey had a feeling the masterpiece was being procured as they breathed.

She left him with the necessary credit data and a handshake. He reciprocated with a hand embrace, his left paw cupped over the back of her hand up to her wrist: a candle snuffer, a catcher's mitt, a Venus's-flytrap. Petey couldn't decide which.

Through the whole gallery episode Norma Perlmutter had sat in the commissioner's Lincoln listening to a tape of Rickie Lee Jones and scowling. She paid no attention to passersby, and they didn't blink at her or the car. Chauffeur-driven automobiles, stretch limousines or showroom models, stood in front of galleries every day of the year. Their owners might be famous, but the occupants, the designers and consultants that Petey mimicked, were known only to gallery owners. But known they were. Saliva coursed inside the cheeks of the Monte Bevilles all over SoHo the moment one of these culture scouts cracked open the rear door.

When Petey got into the limo, Norma started the car without a word, and eased it into gear heading west on Spring Street. Petey's thoughts were hurtling. Monte Beville's operation was a sea of sleaze, she was sure of it. He had pounced on her overture for a Chagall like a chicken hawk on a poularde. Griffith was his altar boy. She had to make some connections, find the warts that were definitely there. The two plainly wrapped Dalis lay next to her on the seat.

"Don't look now, but we've been followed from the gallery by a green Jag," Norma said.

Petey whipped her head around to look out the back window.

"Oh, *real* good, lady. I say don't look, and you take a home video," Norma said, her eyes fixed on the rearview mirror.

Petey guiltily spun back around.

"Too late. Shit. Shit. He knows we registered him," Norma said.

She turned right on West Broadway and proceeded up the wide, busy thoroughfare. Another car pulled between them and the Jaguar.

"There he goes," Norma said.

Petey turned again and got a glimpse of the Jaguar's rear end as it cut down a side street.

"You see the driver?" she asked.

"I didn't grope him, but I saw a little. Bad hair. Like Phil Collins. Big nose. Like Johnny Depp."

"He make our car?" Petey said.

"Unless he's brain damaged. This boat stands out like the Staten Island Ferry. You want back to the office?"

"I want," Petey said.

"Your gallery owner's been all over us like a virus," Marjorie said the moment Petey stepped into the commissioner's office. "He wanted to know about you and Mr. Chambliss and just what you all had in mind."

Petey grimaced.

"Don't worry," Marjorie said. "I've concocted better stories for stranger birds than him. It was kind of fun."

She spoke over a straw-thin telephone mike. Her computer hummed, and papers, documents, and memos littered her desk. She was in total control.

"Thank you," Petey said, instantly liking the commissioner's assistant.

"I wish I could have gone along," Marjorie said.

"A sentiment not shared by your driver," Petey said.

Marjorie smiled.

"That's Norm's way of marking," she said. "Don't be offended. She's good. She'll help you when you need it. She really will."

"Speaking of help, I need some."

"Somebody to bounce Monte Beville off of?"

"Yes!"

Marjorie winked.

"You smell a slimy gallery owner, a Fire Island phony who took a rich, stupid baseball owner for a pile of money—"

"Yes!"

"—and this same owner's rich but screwed-up son—"

"Who is now Monte Beville's business partner . . ."

"—Really!—"

"Yes!"

"—and they're all in bed together."

"In flagrante delicto!"

"In what?" Marjorie asked.

"Legal term," Petey replied. "Having to do with being in the act."

"The act!" Marjorie said.

The two of them broke up.

Once Marjorie regained her efficient office form, she handed Petey a memo.

"This is just the man for you," she said. "He knows the scene. He knows Monte Beville. And get this: he knows Rupert Huston's collection."

"You're remarkable, Marjorie."

"All knowledge passes through the office of baseball," she said. "And I am it."

"You're a gold mine, and I'm lucky to know you," Petey said.

"I'm cement, Petey," Marjorie said. "Glue. I keep things together. We New York girls do it best. And you're one of us now."

"Honored," Petey said, and meant it.

15

Wid Conroy

The Ganzello murder had made no splash in the press. It was the player-to-be-named-later finally named. TV missed it, as far as I saw. The *Times* ignored it. The *News* had no room for it. The *Post* and *Newsday* found mouse holes eighteen pages inside late editions. Ganzello was described as a bookie and small-time thief. A Queens detective speculated that he fell behind in his street taxes, or did not cut the Mob in on his swag, or made a pass at a hood's moll. Pick one or all of the above—but don't get carried away with the last. No tears were shed. No connections were made. Devery, to his credit, had raised no flags, not even to his pet press conduits—and I knew he had them—so the secret was ours.

For my part, I knew. Farelli's boys had gone out of their way to make it as clear as a boxscore. Ganzello had desecrated the Yankees, Farelli's personal holy of holies, an entity in the godfather's life almost as dear as his father's memory. Ganzello, in his street-smart stupidity, had sullied something that Farelli preferred pure, and then shot his mouth off about it. You can hit a homer in someone else's ballpark, but you should not come out of the dugout and tip your cap to the crowd. Farelli had killed people for less than this. The question remained: Had he killed somebody else for more?

I had been ready to toss this around with Petey the night before, but she had not returned to her room. I presumed she was now sharing toothpaste with John

Brush, a man I now needed to talk to. The identity of John Henry Ganzello, exactly where he had been the night of Huston's murder, what he had seen in those few minutes, and finally, his recent demise, would intrigue the Yankee G.M., I was sure. What Brush had found out about Herm McFarland now keenly interested me. We were close to the shooter, I was certain of it. How close we'd finally get was another question.

I heard Petey cross her threshold, and seconds later my phone rang. Yes, I was up, and we needed to compare notes.

"Nice night?" I said.

"The best," she cooed.

There was no other word for it: my niece was smitten. The sandman had delivered. I only hoped that in the interim, when she was not walking on air and blowing kisses, she could concentrate on business.

"Let me fill you in," I said.

I began to run through the encounter with Herm Mc-Farland when she interrupted.

"John told me. I couldn't believe it! A dump right on the table!" she interjected.

"Brush didn't think much of it."

"I know, but *I* did."

"What else did Brush say?"

"That he's going after McFarland. He thinks there's something there—you know, Keeler, Lana, the whole family thing. They've been real cool to him since the murder. As for Hermie, John inherited him, and he doesn't trust him much."

"He won't trust him at all when he hears that the defecating burglar was murdered last night."

"What? Dead? They killed the safecracker?"

"Up in Queens. Put a slug in the back of his head at close range. Didn't screw around. Then they put a Yankee cap on his head and a pair of tickets in his mitts. Just for cutes."

"Get out! That's like the old Al Capone gang murders."

"You got it. In case we didn't get the message."

Petey marveled and ran her hand through her tousled, hastily pinned hair. She was a morning person, as bright in the A.M. as butter and warm Danish, but she had not spent a lot of this morning in front of a mirror.

"That's really bad news, isn't it, Unk? I mean, this guy could have cracked it wide open for us."

"I don't know about that. I think he said all he was going to say. Maybe all he knew. And he only did that because Farelli was leaning on him. Devery thinks he'll have the rifle soon—he didn't tell me how—and that he can tie Ganzello to the gun."

"What do you think?"

"Me? Old 'On the House'? Sportswriter turned part-time op. Holed up in a strange city with a niece what's left me for another man—"

"Oh, stop it."

"—and I'm going around in circles with a case where there's a lot of nibbles but no bites. Like Whitey Ford when he was really fine, which was most of the time."

"What are you talking about?"

"Well, Devery thinks it's the Mob cum Ganzello, Brush—who apparently doesn't know about John Henry's death—thinks McFarland's involved, and you're running with Griffith and Beville. In any event, we may find out who did it—a pro, I think, underwritten by the Mob—it all points that way. And we may come up with a dozen motives, because Huston made enemies of a lot of nasty people. Guys whose eyelids don't open all the way. Probably screwed one of 'em once too often.

"But—and here's a *but* that's kept me guessing longer than I've spent trying to figure out how anybody ever struck out Joe Sewell—we won't get anywhere close to who hired the trigger finger. Not anywhere close, Pete. And time will pass, and things will cool, and the case will fade like Tom Tresh's batting average. Grand Chambliss'll get tired of it, we'll check out of here, and the case will sit through the ages like that pile on Herm McFarland's counting table. Petrified. Unsolved."

Petey's eyes lowered.

"You're down," she said.

I made a face.

"Well, *I'm* not," she exclaimed. "John thinks I'm onto something. I told him what I have learned about Keeler and Lana, and now Griffith and the art scene, and he told

me about a lot of new dirt that was being shoveled between Rupert and the family. Real trouble, John said. He
thinks it was getting too strong even for Rupert, and that's
saying something. In those last days there were a lot of
meetings with a guy named Portes, a lawyer Rupert used
mostly for trusts and things. John thinks Rupert made
some big changes in the way the family purse strings were
drawn and who was going to get what."

"Could be. But did that turn them into killers? Would
any one of them have the guts to gore the golden ox?"

"That's what I'm going to find out. John also told me
all about Griffith and his old man. Griffith had started
showing up at the stadium like he owned the place. That's
how John finally met him. The same Griffith with an earful
of silver earrings and a half moon cut into the hair on the
side of his head. The dreamy boy who was banned from his
old man's ballpark when he started hanging out with the
swish crowd in SoHo, remember?"

"So I do."

"Except he became Griffith, the art curator. The masterpiece kid. From Monte Beville's inventory to his old
man's walls."

I rubbed my rough old cheeks. I needed another cup
of coffee. Petey was young and not easily deterred.

"Your pooper said he saw somebody on a cart, right?"

"My pooper?"

"You know who I mean."

"Jeez! . . ."

"And now we learn that the late owner's prodigal son
has started showing up in his private box talking abstracts
instead of Astroturf."

"You like this Griffith angle, don't you?"

"Like it a lot," Petey said, "and that's where I'm going.
I have a date today with a guy who knows the whole scene.
Time to smoke out li'l Grif boy."

Then she came over and put her arm on my shoulder.

"Buck up, Unk. What we've got is a trail still warm, not
a petrified turd."

A comforting thought.

Without a car, a wardrobe, or a ruse, Petey hoofed uptown to Columbia University. She had an appointment with Professor William Conroy, art historian and expert. Marjorie from Chambliss's office had done the advance work and had given Conroy her highest recommendation. With Petey that was golden. Finding her way past the public exhibits at Columbia and into the art history department offices, Petey walked down a corridor of beige, unadorned doors. For a coop of art lovers, the decor was downright depressing, she thought. She found Conroy's, and it was also bare save for a small card with his name and his office hours: "3–4, Wednesday" printed on it. Nothing else. She knocked and received no answer. She had an appointment for 2:30, and she was exactly on time. She knocked again. Still nothing.

Petey waited at the end of the hallway, occasionally venturing down connected hallways in search of Gary Larson pinups. She was beginning to fear she had been stood up when a figure finally hove into view down the corridor. He was a rotund man of middle age, shuffling along pigeon-toed with his head down. His pants swished together at the thighs. He was carrying an aluminum attaché case and wearing a cylindrical kind of hat that looked to Petey as if it had been lifted off the pate of a Roman Catholic prelate from another century. The man stopped at Conroy's door and worked the lock. It was three o'clock, a full half hour after their scheduled meeting. Professor Conroy was not counting.

Petey went over immediately and tapped on the partially open door.

"Good news or money?" came the reply.

"Good news," she said. "I'm Petey Biggers."

She poked her head inside, and Conroy, standing amidst an office stuffed floor to ceiling with papers, small art objects, photographs, books, and assorted artifacts, did not look up. He stood at his desk going through mail. The cap was off, revealing a magnificently shiny bald dome; what hair he did have was a dark fringe that ringed his squat head and exploded into a full, curly salt-and-pepper beard. He looked to Petey like one of Santa's veteran elves, complete with a radish-red nose. A pair of round blue-rimmed glasses were perched on it. A tabloid headline taped to a bookcase Petey could see directly behind him read, "It's True: Bald Men *Are* More Intelligent."

"So you are," he said, peering at her over the tops of his glasses, and offered a few fingers to shake.

"Have a seat while I look at my mail. This is junk, mainly. Oh yes, good, a reply from the Walker. Hmm. Hmm. What would I do with a Subaru? Ah, my airline tickets to Stanford. A lecture next month on ancient Near East relics, you know."

Petey, not having anything else to do, nodded.

Suddenly Conroy sat down, his girth pushing a hiss of air out of his chair's cushion.

"So," he began, "Marjorie called from the office of the commissioner of baseball and was very persistent. I happen to be an admirer of Grand Chambliss. After some of the pompous blowhards in that office, Chambliss is the real McCoy. I told her that."

He had teeth like a chipmunk, and when he spoke, they pecked at his lower lip.

"You got to me first, young lady," he continued. "Maybe last too. Police, lawyers, journalists—none of them found Wid Conroy, the person who investigated Rupert Huston's collection."

His chest visibly swelled.

"So you know of the Beville Gallery?" Petey asked.

"I am aware of Mr. Huston's connection to Beville. That should be your first question. Let's not dissemble. We're better off if we both know whom we're dealing with."

Petey fidgeted. She had forgotten that small offices all over the city held professors like this.

"Your next question concerns the Monte Beville Gallery. Well, it's a nice shiny gallery—filled with nothing but fakes. And he's a fraud. He doesn't have an authentic piece of art in the whole place. I exaggerate, but it's close."

Petey was amazed.

"Is that true?" she asked.

"Miss Biggers, I've been in this business for more than thirty years. My eye is my livelihood. I am hired by the Getty, MOMA, the Whitney, and hosts of private collectors to authenticate their collections. Sometimes I know immediately, sometimes it takes me somewhat longer. In the case of Mr. Beville, any legitimate New York art person knows what that gallery is peddling. . . ."

"Hold on a minute, Dr. Conroy. You mean people know Monte Beville is selling fake art, and they don't turn him in? I mean, he's one of the most popular in SoHo. His gallery—it's not a second-floor closet. How could he be in business—how could he get away with it?"

Conroy chortled. If he'd had a pipe, it would have emitted two well-spaced, smug plumes of smoke.

"Caveat emptor, my dear young lady," he said. "Let me explain. It's a very tricky business. I, an art expert, cannot go to the police or the federal attorney's office and say this guy is dealing in fake art. I'd be in court for the rest of my life.

"Do you know you can ask anybody in the legal community or any prosecutor, just what is a fake? What is an original? What about reproductions? They don't know. There is very little legal theory or machinery to deal with it.

"God knows, *I* don't need the aggravation. If people don't know enough about art to realize they're being taken, or to hire somebody like me to authenticate the stuff *before* they buy it, then they deserve what they get."

It was an uninterrupted speech, and Petey was quite certain Conroy delivered it often.

"How much of this is going on?" she said.

"It's very big business right now—very big. A couple of favorable conditions exist. You have the market, first of all. In the old days only a certain aristocracy were art collectors. There were fewer of them, and there was less art around. They knew what they wanted, they knew where it was, and they pretty much knew how to get it.

"Today you have a whole new class of people with large disposable incomes—you know the creatures I mean —who want to invest in art as a commodity but know absolutely nothing about it. They are at the mercy of dealers and gallery owners. When you have fools with money, you will always have someone who will gladly help them part with it. And when art becomes a commodity, and when it hits the marketplace, it is no longer an ethereal, noble thing. It's just as dirty as everything else is."

Petey took it all in, nonplussed, not expecting such an

unequivocal tidal wave of scorn for the business of Monte Beville.

"Look, Professor Conroy. Indulge my ignorance. Tell me how they do it."

"High technology, Miss Biggers. In the old days, fakes were harder to make; and it took real artistic talent to make them. Plus, they were easier to detect. Today, printing processes have evolved remarkably."

"Prints?"

"Yes. Prints have long been a mainstay medium of the art world—intaglio etchings, seriographs, lithographs, even prints reproduced on a printing press. Now the traditional way of establishing value in these prints was for the artist to destroy the block or stone or whatever he printed off after he had made a certain number of prints, right?

"Nowadays we're faced with reproduction by the process of photolithography. Sophisticated cameras are used to take a picture of the painting, then the film is broken down into color plates, and it is mass-produced by print on high-powered computers. Some artists have authorized the use of photolithography for their paintings.

"I'll give you an example. Not many years ago Salvador Dali supposedly signed a contract authorizing this process for some of his paintings. He signed five hundred blank sheets of paper on which the photolithographs were to be printed. The going price was to be two to four thousand dollars. But these prints were virtually indistinguishable from the five thousand or fifty thousand that were printed illegitimately. If you bought one of those, you bought a three- or four-thousand-dollar poster."

Petey felt a jutting pang in her lower back. Dali. One of her personal favorites. She saw those two prints—a cool eight-thousand simoleons worth—sitting beside her in the backseat of the commissioner's car. They were only on approval, thanks be to God.

"Is there any way of verifying those prints?"

"It usually comes down to the paper used. You discover the year the paper was manufactured and compare it to the alleged year the print was made. But it's tricky. The whole thing is tricky. What is an original? What is a reproduction? People walking into an art gallery aren't bringing along an art expert. And a Monte Beville has no trouble in talking them into it. An 'investment' in art, right? Monte even has the documents to prove that a given piece was bought and sold for so much, establishing its value. Except that even the documents are phony. A ring of crooked dealers passes them around like lottery tickets."

There was not a brush stroke of doubt in his voice. "In fact," he said, "photolithography has become a favorite of the Mafia—only they use it for pornography and money laundering. As you can see, it's like printing money."

"And this is Beville's stock in trade?"

"Well put. His stock. His trade. He is an operator—very smooth, very bright, and totally amoral. One of the recent scams of these shysters, by the way, is *inventing* an artist."

"Come now . . ."

"Yes. Now remember, we are generally speaking about a ring of crooks working closely together. They invent an artist and call him, let's say, Marcel Duchamp the Younger. Then they actually create a Duchamp look-alike, with a few noticeable deviations.

"They then send gratis prints to the Louvre, or to the Mellon Foundation, maybe the Nancy Reagan collection—I had to throw that in—and they get a response back stating something to the effect that the museum has cataloged the work in their collection. That acknowledgment is gold, because they can show it to the buyer and claim the artist's work is quite legitimate because it is in the Louvre. Of course, it is in a warehouse in the south of France with a million other like pieces. But so what? Legitimacy has been established. Let the bidding begin.

"Oh, it goes on and on. They invent Israeli painters fresh off a kibbutz or Latin American freedom-fighter painters, Armenian protester painters, South African antiapartheid painters, you name it. Of course, the work is done by some guy in the Village, but there's the genius: these aren't truly fakes because the originals don't exist. The *artist* doesn't exist."

Petey shook her head. Wid Conroy once again chortled. His levity was undeniable, his humor that of a limb collector at a leprosy sanatorium.

"Don't people who buy these pieces know anything?" Petey said.

"Frankly, no. They think the art market is respectable and a man like Monte Beville trustworthy. 'Art, not money, is his only love,' they gush. And they are so wrong. Beville has worked all the scams I've described and more.

"Which brings me to your next question, which you've been slow to ask . . ." Conroy said.

"I'm overwhelmed," Petey said.

"Ah, I have that effect on women. Ha, ha. But you must want to know about my appraisal of the Rupert Huston collection."

Petey smiled. "You amaze me, Professor Conroy. You're fearless. What you're saying is dynamite, but . . ."

"Let them come at me, the fakers. I've got the big artillery, and they know it. So, anyway, I was contacted by the daughter—"

"Keeler."

"—yes, Keeler. Somehow she became suspicious of the art her father was buying. Her brother, you may or may not know, has a relationship with this Beville character, and I know there is no love lost between the siblings. That may have been the spark that sent her to me. An appraisal date was set up, with Huston himself in attendance. I usually insist on that, for reasons I'll get to.

"On the appointed day I appeared at his home on Gracie Square. The place is sumptuous, and the walls are full of paintings—"

"I've been there."

"Fine. But before I looked at even one of them, I told him my fee. Thirty-five hundred dollars. You see, Miss Biggers, I've learned how to deal with these people. You'd be amazed at how many want to refuse payment when they find out that their art is phony. So I don't twitch until my price is agreed to.

"Huston agreed, and he showed me through some of the dozen-odd rooms, all of them hung with slick-looking forgeries. We went down into a billiard room—you know, I don't think I've ever met anyone who actually played that game—and it had artwork leaning up against the walls. And there was a room adjoining it which was full of even more work. Recent acquisitions. He had me look all around.

"Finally he ushered me to a fine Eames chair, offered

me a brandy, which I accepted, and said, 'Well, Mr. Conroy, what do you think?'

"With drink in hand I said, 'The fee is up front, Mr. Huston.' He looked disappointed in me, like an admonishing schoolmarm with a recalcitrant boy. 'You know what they are, don't you?' he said, with a supremely confident glow.

"I kept my best poker face on and said, 'From years of experience, Mr. Huston, I don't comment until I have the fee in my hot little hand.'

" 'I don't want to pay that kind of money just to find out I've got a bunch of fakes,' said he.

" 'I know you don't—just like a lot of people don't,' " said I. 'But that's simply the operational given in my world, Mr. Huston.' And I raised my drink, set it down, put my hat on my head, and went for the door. 'No, wait a minute,' he said.

"I paused. I tell you, young lady, to have the most powerful man in New York resigning himself to the fact that he needed me, well, that was quite a moment."

Petey leaned forward. "Was there a standoff?" she asked.

"Not much of one, really. I have dealt with the wealthy, and most of them feel they have attained power over almost anybody because they have money. But Huston truly needed me right then, not the other way around, and he was no match for me."

Petey marveled. Conroy beamed. He was clearly having a wonderful time.

"I've said it many times: I simply don't inhabit a world in which people like Rupert Huston have any relevance. Wealthy people are my métier, young lady. Some are gracious, and some are cretins. And Huston, it seemed to me, was one of the more ignorant cretins."

"So he paid you?"

"Had some difficulty coming up with a check—they all do, you know. But finally he wrote it, signed it, and personally placed it in my mitt. I made sure it was authentic—heh, heh—and then I said to him, 'Your gut feeling is correct: you've got a houseful of fakes.'

"The look that came over Rupert Huston's face was one I'll never forget. It fell like a crumbling dam. The color drained like a bad landscape. His visage made Van Gogh's look downright merry.

"I don't think that man got taken very often or very easily, and like the man of great machismo that he was, or thought he was, he did not take very kindly to it," Conroy concluded.

"Incredible! Then what happened? You told him he had all fakes and left?"

"No, my dear, I'm not *that* crass. First of all, I played him a bit, for dramatic effect, you know. There were a few authentic pieces there; and I did investigate a number of pieces quite thoroughly, showing him how either the paper or the material or the style made it a phony piece of art. I also rendered advice on taxes—how he could declare the equivalent of a business loss, and so forth. This is all part of my fee, especially when the news is bad.

"I don't know how much of it made an impression. Huston was an angry man by then."

"Was Mrs. Huston—Lana—there?"

"I didn't meet her."

"Did Huston say anything? Make any threats? Give you any idea of what he might do?"

"Oh, he did at first what so many try to do—he tried to argue with me, to refute my findings. He ran over to several pieces and extolled their beauty. 'This can't be a fake!' he said about one piece, I can't remember which. 'It's too beautiful!' And I told him they often are.

"I had to educate the man, as is often the case. I told him, for example, of grave robbers—"

"Grave robbers?"

"Indeed. In the case of archaeological digs that are sponsored by a government or university, the recovered artworks go to an official museum. But many private, clandestine diggers—grave robbers, pure and simple—work hand in glove with art crooks. When they find something, the objects go on the art market, but they are copied before they go on the market. That means when a 'discovery' is announced to the world, there may be as many as ten copies out there.

"Why, the Royal Brussels Museum was burned by one of these. They wanted a certain Egyptian fish vase of the eighteenth dynasty to fill a hole in their collection, and they wanted it very badly. The art crooks knew this, of course. They read the same art magazines and journals that curators do. Three came on the market, two of them real, one a fake. But the fake was a little bigger and more beautiful than the real ones. So the curator at the Brussels set the value of the real vases at one million dollars each and the fake at two million—and the museum bought the fake! Don't forget, a fake is always *beguiling,* so beguiling. And Mr. Huston was beguiled."

"Holy Indiana Jones," Petey whistled.

Conroy sniffed.

Petey quickly added, "What can Huston, I mean the estate, get back in resale value?"

"Nothing. *Nada.* You see, the ultimate definition of a fake or a forgery is that it has no resale value. These galleries don't offer money-back guarantees. Oh, they might take a piece back in trade—for another phony piece maybe? So you're stuck with a bunch of pretty posters that you can't get rid of anywhere."

Petey ran her hands over her face and shook her head as if she'd just slid hard into second base to break up a double play. Her head was filled with possibilities, with Huston's rancor and resentment, with fraud to the tune of millions of dollars, with motive.

"Do you think Monte Beville, or Griffith Huston—if he knew, that is—thought Rupert would never find out about the fakes?" she finally asked.

Conroy ran the tips of his fingers over the mat of his beard.

"Maybe . . . maybe not. Beville's pretty slippery. He's rather committed to what he does and the life-style it affords him. The difference between thieves and you and me is that they can sleep at night. Remorse is as foreign to them as smallpox.

"We're in the realm of speculation now, but I think perhaps if Huston called him on the fakes, Beville might have pushed his hand and invited him to get in on the scam. He may have offered to take back the art if Rupert would set him up in another gallery, in Miami or Scotts-dale, or somewhere where the pickings are virgin.

"I don't know. What I do know is that the Monte Beville Gallery is where Mr. Rupert Huston said he acquired most of his collection, and what he had was a text-book collection of phony art. What he did about it we may never know."

He chortled anew, as he had done in summary of so many like episodes, not with malice but with resignation.

"I'll know. I'll find out," Petey announced.

She sensed that Professor Conroy's lecture was at a close. It was not.

"It was tragic what happened to the man. I hope it wasn't related to this," Conroy reflected. "But this is an increasingly violent world, and my business is not untouched by it.

"I must say, however, that as much as I rue the fate of Mr. Huston, I feel more for some of Monte Beville's other victims."

"How's that? I thought you said earlier that his clients deserved—" Petey said.

"Not all of them. Monte Beville has looted some fortunes that belonged to kindly elderly ladies. They were fools, to be sure, but they did not deserve what happened to them. I'm suggesting something quite treacherous, Miss Biggers."

"What? You've lost me."

"It's very simple. Beville, I have every reason to believe, perpetrated his deceptions on wealthy but lonely old ladies, some of whom came to me, but too late, and a couple of whom died of very unnatural causes. Very unnatural causes."

"How do you mean?" Petey asked.

"I think they were poisoned. Plain and simple. One dear soul in particular. I'm convinced of it, as convinced as I am of the forgeries and fakes I discovered in their collections. I brought the cases to the attention of the police, but they seem to have ignored me. If you ever have the time or inclination to look into this, please come back."

It was a footnote, and Petey took heed of it.

"It's all quite amazing, and kind of depressing," Petey mused as she stood to leave.

"If you mean my dear ladies, yes, yes, it is," Conroy said, rising, the cherubic glint momentarily absent.

"Thank you, Professor," Petey said. "I'm lucky I found you. You're . . . you're the genuine article."

"That I am," he agreed, then bowed from his ample waist, chuckled, and offered Petey a doughy, unadorned, but sincere handshake.

Forgers, fakes, grave robbers, Petey thought as she descended the long, shallow stone steps of Columbia. She was dizzy with facts and insights, anxious to spew them to me, to run out and all but put manacles on Monte Beville and his man Griffith. In her mind right then, she admitted to me later, the case was solved. The evidence hung on the Huston mansion walls, the perpetrators were fingered, the motive was clear. It was too good to be true. All Petey lacked were the mechanics: a mail-order receipt for the rifle perhaps, the shooter, the sequence of the execution, a confession.

All of that she would squeeze—and she was certain of this—out of Griffith. She immediately hit a telephone on the sidewalk and tried to reach me. She missed because I had left the Summit for an appointment of my own. The sun had come out, the weather was as nice as it gets in Manhattan, the late-afternoon air along Broadway relatively fresh, so Petey decided to walk. She was a hoofer, a healthy kid with good habits—apart from the nighttime hours she kept—and she walked with her arms swinging and her head high. She walked south toward 110th Street, past kids, hustlers, panhandlers, old ladies, and mothers with strollers.

But, she later recollected, she was as preoccupied as a professor, and she noticed little around her. Her thoughts jumped back and forth among the images and realities just heaped upon her by Conroy. *Beguiling,* she said to herself, the word he had so artfully chosen. She applied it not to the phony art but to the two principals: Monte Beville and Professor William "Wid" Conroy. There was Beville with his lavish trappings, a tony gallery full of varnish, chrome, Lucite, and walls hung with beguiling art. There was Conroy with his musty, cluttered burrow of an office, his funny hat, his frumpy clothes and cultivated little beard, his beguiling temperament. They were two eccentric men molded by the world of art. One, however, was a poseur, a conniving felon; the other a deadly earnest academic but an art lover. Petey's mind fixated on the images of both men, their mugs side by side in her head. And she saw them for what they were: Beville a fake, Conroy the real item.

She wondered how far to take this, whether or not it was a phenomenon peculiar to New York, this heightened place that never slept, this arena where people created surreal personalities and outrageous shticks and then strained to keep up with them. Monte Beville was a lurid example, but Petey considered whether or not it translated to Rupert Huston, to the Yankees, to the fact of a sniper in the upper deck. By this time she had made her way to Central Park West and the green of the park. She kept walking, telling herself she would catch a bus or a cab but enjoying the stroll. And she never noticed that she was being followed, and had been since she'd left Columbia.

At the juncture of the sidewalk and an asphalt path leading into the park, he suddenly came up behind her. Petey had no purse, but rather a nylon pouch that went around her waist like a belt. It held her wallet, her notebook, makeup, and a few other small items, and she instinctively clutched it when she felt a presence behind her. Then someone grabbed her arm. A young male, a kid maybe—but who was a kid anymore?—yet anything more she could not tell unless she were to turn and face him.

"Keep walkin' in the park, and you won't get hurt," he rasped.

To her credit Petey kept calm, kept moving. She was the type to turn and rap him one. She had the temper of a Billy Martin and the toughness of a Hank Bauer. She might throw an elbow or dropkick him in the essentials. Or she might just bolt and see if the punk had any speed and stamina. She considered all of the above, got mad at the prospect of being mugged, took a deep breath, and stayed on the path. She looked around for another person, a cop, a jogger, anyone who might help, and she thought, *Is this what it's like?*

As she walked, her throat constricted, her breathing became short, her knees shook. And then she realized the person behind her seemed to be suffering from the same labored condition. That frightened her, for she knew from her short romance with big cities that the biggest danger was a nervous, edgy punk, a hopped-up little junkie with a weapon. Anything might set him off, cause him to panic, to cut her or shoot her. So she tried to stay cool. Under her loose-fitting blouse, perspiration rolled down her rib cage.

"Over by the tree," the kid said.

It was a large, aging walnut, its trunk abused through the years by knives and bottle openers, squirrels and urine. Still, it gave shade, and the bushes behind it formed an alcove of sorts. It was a perfect and horrible spot. Petey paused as she neared it, wondering how far she would let herself be pushed.

"My sister hire you?" he suddenly said, letting go of her arm.

Petey turned and finally got a look at her assailant. He was a kid in his early twenties with a pasty face, dirty blond hair as short as an army cut, and an ear full of spikes, all of which gave him the appearance of a skinhead, one of those European thugs seen at neo-Nazi rallies who maim each other at soccer games or rallies or over a needle on some Amsterdam street. You see a kid like that, and you get smug for being childless.

Yet this guy, Petey saw immediately, though unkempt and red-eyed, was outfitted. His clothes had labels, unpressed to be sure, but togs from guys named Calvin and Giorgio. He shuffled in a pair of Spike Lee Nikes that retailed for more than this reporter made in a month as a cub. Studded black leather bands girded each wrist. The kid, despite his tough-guy swagger, seemed to need all the support he could get in the wrist department. He was, of course, Griffith Huston.

He squared up in front of her, a foot or so away, pawing the dirt like a horse, spitting like a horse's ass.

"I ain't gonna rob ya or worse, man," he began. "But yer fuckin' with me, okay, bitch?"

"Griffith," Petey said.

"I don't introduce myself. Fuck it. You got business with me, then do business. But don't fuck around."

"Cut the tough-guy Brooklyn shit," Petey said, though I'm not sure she'd ever been to Brooklyn.

He cocked his head, angry, off kilter. He spat again for effect and tried to sneer at her. It wasn't the kind of thing he was good at. Petey had sliced through it.

"Hey, bitch—!"

"Don't 'bitch' me," Petey said. "You got something to say, say it. I'm not working for your sister, if that's what you think."

"You been at the gallery—"

"I've been all over. I'm a private investigator trying to find out who killed your father. If that bothers you, then you got a problem."

"Fuck you. I didn't kill him."

"Who did?"

"Ask my sister. She and my ol' man went at it, man, she tell you about that? No way. She's pushin' him about Herm the worm. Dad was pissed. Herm's ass was supposed to be canned, ya know. History. Keeler was having a shit fit about it. Yeah, she tell you that?"

"No, she didn't."

"No way. She fuckin' put you on *my* case, instead. And on the gallery and the blow, man, and all the ways I'm supposed to be gettin' over on my ol' man. She laid all that shit on you good, right?"

"Keeler can talk."

"Mouth on the bitch."

"That your favorite word?"

"Hey—"

He spat again or at least made the gesture, but nothing came out. His mouth was as dry as Petey's.

"I ain't gonna rap with ya. You fuckin' stay outta my face, man, or things could happen. I don't know who you are or who yer workin' for, and I don't give a fuck. I didn't zip my dad, okay? No fuckin' way. But I know some people, right? And they can get rid of you like an itch, man."

"Is that a threat? I mean, come on, Griffith, are you throwin' it down?"

"Fuck off."

"No. Face up to it. I'm on your case—why not? You come up full of holes. Your father couldn't stand your friends. He threatened to cut you off if you didn't get straight. He knew you're a junkie—"

"Shit!" he wailed, and spun around like a rookie taking a called third strike.

Then he turned and, his eyes aflame, advanced at Petey. She held her ground even as she felt his quickened breath. He stuck a finger between her eyes. She steeled herself and was suddenly very afraid of this kid.

"My sister, dammit—! Dammit—!"

"Hold it!" Petey exclaimed, and slapped his finger out of her face.

With that he faltered, still huffing, and stepped back.

"Enough of this crap. Let me clue you in, Griffith," Petey said. "I work for the baseball commissioner. His office wants an answer to this thing. I don't know who killed your father. I talked to your sister and your stepmother—"

"You bullshitted your way into the gallery!"

"I had to. It was the only way. The point is, nobody's clean on this thing until we find out who murdered your father. And the sooner you get off your horse, the better."

"Fuck off."

"Oh, give me a break, kid. For your information Keeler didn't finger you. She doesn't like the way you live, but she doesn't have it in for you. And she's not the one saying you killed your father. You hear me?"

"Look, I'm outta here. I told you what can happen if you keep messing me over. You can shove my sister up your ass. She's been fucked up about my ol' man for years, I don't care what she says. She hates the world, man. Me. The ol' lady—"

"Lana?"

"Her too. But I meant my real mother. Keeler don't talk to her. No way. She tell you that? Bet she didn't. Hates her worse than Lana. And she'd run Lana down on the street like a squirrel if she had the chance. Then back up and do it again."

Petey put her hands on her hips and sighed.

"Nice people," she said.

"Who asked you?"

She glared at him.

"Lana said she's coming after both you and your sister in court," she suggested.

He sneered.

"She's nothing. My ol' man settled up with her. He told me before he was killed. There ain't gonna be no court fight, no way. He bought and paid for her ass long ago."

"How about yours?"

He looked past her at the approach of a pair of joggers and again appeared as if he were about to flee. However, he still had a point to make.

"My ol' man was gettin' into my thing. We did business. We had an account, man. That's all I'm gonna say cuz that's all you gotta know. Like you don't take out someone you're doin' business with."

"Unless the deal goes sour," Petey said.

"Fuck off, you hear? If you still wanna breathe, bitch."

Then he ran. He turned and ran back onto the path, up an embankment, and disappeared.

Petey, drained and out of breath, stood and let the breeze buffet her. Then she shook herself and began walking toward the path leading out of the park. Once she reached the street, she would hail a cab. She strode with her head down and had no idea of what was coming on her. Suddenly she was slammed in the back, blindsided like an innocent umpire in the middle of a bench-clearing brawl. She screamed as the force knocked the wind out of her and sent her sprawling headlong onto the dirty macadam of the path. Her hands and arms scraped harshly against the pavement. Her right knee came down on a spleen-sized rock, and it sliced into the skin.

It was over in seconds, her attacker sprinting off as quickly as he had swooped down. She sat up, her legs and arms a jumble of dirt and dust, torn pants and bloody scrapes. Her mouth was full of grit, and her eyes watered. Her knee burned, and her wrists were numb. She was still short of breath. Her left shoe had come off and lay upright on the other side of the path.

"But you're alive, *faygeleh*," said a white-haired man with glazed eyes as he bent over her and studied strands of her lovely hair.

16

Dave Fultz

When Petey got back to the Summit, she looked awful. Her hands and arms were scraped and raw. She had a strawberry on her right elbow as big as the ones Willie Randolph used to get with headfirst slides. Her lower lip was puffy, her slacks were torn, and she had a major-league hip pointer that stung like hell and made her eyes water.

And yet she had a smile on her face. It was tortured, like that of a pitcher who's just grabbed a line shot with his bare hand, but a smile nevertheless.

"I got him, Unk," she said, leaning gingerly against my dining-room table. "I got the little bastard."

"You got creamed, that's what you got. What happened, Pete?"

"It's a long story, and I'll tell you the whole thing over a warm washcloth and some first-aid cream," she said.

A few minutes later she returned in her terry-cloth robe, barefoot, her hands full of ointments. She was limping. She set up her personal MASH unit in my kitchenette and began cleaning her wounds, but not before she had dropped her robe off her shoulders.

"Petey!" I objected. She still had her underwear on, but such immodesty unnerves me.

"Unk, get a grip. You've seen better in locker rooms," she scoffed.

"Not the kind *I* trespass," I said, averting my eyes. A product of an age where a glimpse of too much stocking was scandalous, I cannot easily lose my prudery. My great-uncle used to tell a story about the time he was helping a young lady out of a carriage and she slipped. Her dress flew up, he said, and he got an extended look at the bare flesh above her ankle. "I did the right thing, however," Uncle Dink said. "I married her."

Petey, on the other hand, was sitting on the countertop, one knee raised to her chin, daubing the bruised and abraded skin of her arms and legs like a Rubens model. And she was oblivious to her exhibition, well into a recap of her conversation with Wid Conroy.

"Millions, Uncle Duffy! Beville and Griffith took Huston for millions. A houseful of fakes—that's what Professor Conroy said he found. Can you imagine how *pissed off* Rupert was? His own kid!"

And as if to punctuate her suspicions, Griffith, speak of the devil, had pulled off his awkward confrontation in Central Park, she added.

"He's unstable, Unk. He's a messed-up kid. And messed-up kids with money have a way of knocking off their parents. The best-seller lists are full of them."

"You think he decked you?"

"Of course! I mean, maybe not him personally. Maybe one of his buddies just waiting for him to give the signal. Who knows? But the beauty of it, Unk, is that it doesn't matter! I got him dead in the water, and he knows it. He threatened me. Now he's running scared, and he's going to make a mistake. They always do."

As much as I wanted to slow her headlong jump to a conclusion, I couldn't fault her reasoning. Griffith and Monte Beville fairly dripped motive.

"Now where do we go?" I asked, deliberately choosing the collective pronoun.

"Weapon, Unk," Petey said. "We've got to put the smoking gun in their hands. We know Beville's a killer—he's poisoned some of the old ladies he's done business with."

"Whoa! Throw that curve again."

"Listen to this: Conroy said he's sure some of Beville's wealthy clients have had their prune juice spiked. He's serious. He said he's got evidence they were poisoned. And for the same reason: Monte sold them a bunch of fakes, and they got wise to it."

I shook my head and chewed on that assortment of facts.

"A vast leap of reasoning, don't you think, Petey? From arsenic and old lace to an AR-fifteen above third base?" I said, and immediately winced.

"Great, Unk. Nobody's better," Petey gushed.

I waved a hand and said, "Question still on the floor."

"Got ya. We got plenty of work to do before ordering play-off tickets."

She finished balming her wounds. She was pink and smelling of unguents as she rewrapped her robe and shook out her great head of hair.

"You'll take it easy tonight, I suggest," I said.

"Best way I know how: John's picking me up at nine, and we're off to the Vanguard," she announced.

Then she pecked my cold, frowning cheek as only she can, reminding me that her welfare was out of my hands.

The Yankees were out of town and far away—playing games against expansion teams in California and Washington. They were mostly night contests, which meant the first pitch was thrown near my bedtime. That was fine; I had plenty of reading backed up on me. Some crafted prose from Ross Thomas beckoned. Beneath it lay a galley copy of a book about relief pitchers that included some guys named Lyle, Page, Murphy, Duren, and Gossage. It had been sent to me by an editor at some Manhattan publishing house in the hope that out of the kindness of my heart and the sound judgment of my years, I'd say something nice about it, which he could slobber on the dust jacket. Then people all over America will pick up the book, notice my blurb, and say, "Gee, if Duffy House liked it, I've got to have it." It's fairly amazin', as Casey used to say.

Finally, I meant to get to a tome sent over by Grand Chambliss's office. It was a dog-eared thing written by a friend of Bowie Kuhn and published back when you could buy a book for under ten bucks. Entitled *Post-Mortem,* it was written by a sawbones named David Spain who used to be a medical examiner around these parts and gained some notoriety as a coroner-for-hire in some big murder investigations around the nation. For obvious reasons the subject matter was right in my strike zone. Grand had sent it over innocently; at least there was no handwritten note saying I was doing a horseshit job and maybe this would help.

So I turned on station WNYC-FM, coated the inside of a tumbler with some brandy, and let my eyeballs race. Deep into Dr. Spain's account of the Alice Crimmins case, I heard Petey's door open and close. *Her* evening was yet young.

The Spain book absorbed me, and I read case after case with more than passing interest. The dead speak, the canny coroner wrote, if only you know how to listen. I had half a mind to grab the phone and see if the fellow was still around and might want to moonlight with me.

My morning came early, only a few hours, I later learned, after Petey's night ended. Brush had taken her to the Village Vanguard, that jazz shrine on Seventh Avenue in the Village and a place Brush knew almost as well as Yankee Stadium. As a college kid in the sixties, he told Petey, he had visited the place often and said he never wanted to leave. That was music to Petey's ears, and she hung on his elbow and his words as he gave her a guided historical tour of the place.

Brush said he'd known the late Max Gordon, the guy who opened the club in 1934, when the Yankees had Ruffing and Gomez but couldn't get the flag from the Tigers of Greenberg and Gehringer. Ol' Max, with his stogie and his ear for a riff, soon put one murderers' row after another on stage, and the Vanguard became the Yankee Stadium of jazz. Brush had heard them all, idolized every one, pointed out their photos on the walls as if they were family snapshots.

"A bar where jazz is being played," he said, "is still the most integrated place in America—because there's mutual respect between the races—and Max's place was just that."

Gordon, Brush said, called them "cats"—"hep" cats, "cool" cats, and just about any other cat that came to mind —and he let the talent run wild. Charlie Parker, Sarah Vaughan, John Coltrane, an ardent baseball lover, a young Miles Davis, Dizzy Gillespie, and the ill-tempered Charlie

Mingus, who once tore the Vanguard's door off. Their photos, those sweaty, laughing, jumpy photos were priceless and everywhere, frozen moments of jazz history. There was Art Tatum, the blind genius of the keyboard who used to roll a set of ball bearings in his hands when he wasn't playing. And Coleman Hawkins playing "Body and Soul" on his tenor sax. A more famous piece of jazz may not exist, Brush said, unless it was Thelonius Monk's " 'Round Midnight."

Brush went on and on, stealing lines from Gordon himself. When Leadbelly played the Vanguard, he said, people used to call and ask, "Is Mr. Belly in the club tonight?"

He told stories of other acts, of Lenny Bruce and Woodie Guthrie; Peter, Paul, and Mary; the Monday-night big bands of Thad Jones and Mel Lewis; the blues and scat singers; the bebop brass and reeds; Harry Belafonte; Miriam Makeba; even Billie Holiday, who was before John's time, but he didn't let on. Petey said that people around them strained to hear his narrative, his seemingly inexhaustible cache of trivia and background on Max Gordon and the Vanguard and just about every name who ever swung in the joint.

Freddie Hubbard's new young quintet was playing a savory stew of blues, standards, and originals, with even a waltz thrown in. Petey noticed that his brilliant young white pianist was wearing a mustache to disguise the fact that he wasn't out of college yet. She was sure he was younger than she was! Petey was swept away. She loved the music, ached to learn more about jazz, and venerated the Vanguard. It melded with her love of tradition, something she immediately realized to be as important to jazz as it was to baseball. And Brush was tapping that sensibility like a leech on a thigh. It was early morning before they left the club, proceeding as usual to Brush's place. As she replayed the tryst for me a few hours later, I could fairly feel the glow.

"He's just the smartest man I've ever known, Unk," she said about Brush, which is what she often said about Brush, and which, I guess, was a better reason to go gaga over a person than most kids come up with nowadays.

"He knows so much about everything. Baseball, music. He travels all over. He's a skier—"

"I should have known," I interjected.

"No, seriously," she said. "He skis competitively. Next winter he wants to take me to Vermont with him."

I shook my head. Petey was aglow. As I listened to her, I wondered if I'd have a seatmate on the return flight to Chicago, whenever that might be.

Petey, however, said she had not tripped the light fandango to the extent that she forgot to fill Brush in on the clip of her investigation. In the muted denouement of the evening, she said, she launched into her findings, her meeting with Professor Conroy, his scathing indictments of Monte Beville, and his finding of fakes on Huston's walls. Into all that she tucked Griffith Huston, citing his renewed accreditation with Dad, his sleazy relationship with Beville both in and out of the gallery. To Petey it was an anatomy of a murder, brimming with money, greed, bad blood, and treachery. And she had the marks to prove it. Her bruises and her aching hip were a clear sign to her that she had gotten too close, and Griffith had panicked.

John, she said, found it all fascinating and plausible. It explained Griffith's reappearance at the stadium, he said. The kid seemed to resent him, Brush mentioned, perhaps seeing him as a competitor, a person on whom Rupert Huston had bestowed trust and responsibility, two things Griffith never earned. Brush also said he was certain Griffith's new status with his father had injected yet another level of intrigue into the Huston family rivalries, especially with Keeler. And to Brush, Keeler, not the shrill Lana, was the dangerous one, the machinator.

"That's why he was so edgy about that thing with Herm McFarland," Petey said. "Did he tell you that? Of the whole Huston family, John likes Keeler best, but he doesn't trust her. He's convinced Keeler's in the middle of it somehow."

"Then he told me to be careful, Unk. John said there's nothing those people wouldn't do if they were backed into a corner. 'Never forget, they've got their father's genes,' he said. He personally gets jeeters from Griffith, and I know what he means. The kid's got junkie eyes. He does.

That burnt-out look. Gives me the creeps. And Keeler isn't exactly Shirley Temple.

With that she grimaced as she moved in an attempt to flex her right side. It was midmorning when she related all this, and Petey was showing some wear.

"You still hurting?" I asked.

"My hip is bummed," she said. "Cramps my style."

"I don't want to hear about it."

She winked.

"John thinks I've struck gold, Unk," she said.

"I think he thinks *he* has too," I added.

She winked again.

"Where are you headed?" I asked.

"To bed. Recharge the batteries and slam this thing in the P.M."

"Your routine stinks."

"Well, a girl has to do what a girl has to do," she said, going out the door.

I had no idea what that meant, and I didn't wait for an explanation.

While I was in the midst of making a few calls and setting up some appointments, my phone rang. The call came from downtown—the morgue, to be exact. It was Dave Fultz, the little Scooter Rizzuto of a technician I'd met when I'd gone with Chief Devery to the slab room.

"Come see me down here, Duffy, and I'll give you something'll make it worth your while," Fultz said.

"Bait the hook, Fultz."

"Tox runs. Huston. Good stuff," he said with the buzz-saw laugh of a guy who's been shaking beakers too long.

"That didn't make any sense, Dave."

"Toxicology, Duffy. What was running through Rupert's insides when he was poached. Might change your ball game, champ." He chuckled again.

"Spray some Airwick and meet me at the door," I said, and hung up.

I was back down on East Thirtieth Street and inside those morbid walls within the half hour.

Fultz was waiting for me at the bottom of the stairs, once again within earshot of the saws and the smells of that human meat locker. He was smiling and nodding his head up and down like Mortimer Snerd.

"Sox did it again, Duf! Blew a three-run lead in the ninth. That new park! It's a disease! A carcinogen—the revenge of Cominsky!"

"Dave, Dave. How long you been in New York? You've got to forget about the pale hose."

"Didn't hear that, Duffy. I didn't hear it," he said, and led me, his lab coat flapping, to his cubicle.

He closed the door, then went over to a stack of *Sporting News* and pulled a folder from under the stack.

"Can't take the chance of having these swiped, so I put 'em under my Bibles," he said.

He held the file in front of him and paused as if he were Bob Sheppard about to announce the next batter.

"Your man," he began, "the late owner of the New York Yankees, Rupert Rollins Huston, had a river of chlorpheniramine running through his tubes. That's a whammy of an antihistamine. And it was mixed with a monoamine oxidase inhibitor. Bad news.

"Now don't roll your eyes. I'll make it simple. The guy had allergies. He was on prescription-level antihistamines. But the level I found in him was way too high. And mixed with an inhibitor—which you use for hypertension, among other things—and the system short-circuits. In this case it was enough to mickey the guy, Duffy."

"Hold it. Time out. Run that by me again."

"It's just that. He had levels of a toxic drug in his system enough to level him. Add the oxidase inhibitor, and the guy could OD. Plain as the nose on your face. Coulda done it himself. Somebody coulda done it for him. Who knows?"

"When'd you find this out?"

"Yesterday."

"Why the delay?"

"Hey! It wasn't easy, and these things take time. Plus, there wasn't no rush on it. Cause of death was a gunshot wound. Half his cranium looked like a bad cantaloupe, so toxicology is an afterthought. Unless you're the guy s'posed to do it."

"You stumbled on this?"

"Stumble, no. I don't stumble. We do tissue-and-organ

toxicology runs as a matter of course. But unless we're looking for a cause of death, we get to them when we can. This is a busy place. I like baseball history as much as the next man, so I jumped at Huston's run."

"Devery didn't press you?"

"As I said, he had a corpse with the head blown off. He didn't much care what was in the guy's liver."

"So what does this mean, Dave. What do I do with it?"

"Hey, I'm no Columbo. But I'm glad you asked. See, if Huston had a bad running nose, he coulda swallowed one too many capsules. Possible. Then again, if somebody knew he took those things, they coulda helped him along."

"How does the stuff work?"

"Strong. But side effects—drowsiness, the usual mopery is real bad. There's much better stuff around. Anyway, too much woulda knocked him down. Mix in the inhibitor, and he coulda been out for the count."

"Hang on, Dave. I'm running for days on the premise that Huston was killed by a sniper. You're saying he might have been poisoned."

"Yup."

"When?"

"Don't exactly know, but he had it in his organs, so give him at least a half hour, maybe more."

"Holy mackerel," I said, trying to put things together. "What killed him then?" I added.

"Don't know. This stuff coulda. The bullet sure as shootin' coulda. I mean, all in all, ol' Rupert didn't have much of a chance."

"The drug was enough to kill him—"

"Hey, I don't know for sure . . . but those levels coulda put him down like an elephant."

I tried to regroup. I flipped through the lab reports, trying to make sense of the jargon but not really concentrating on anything else but Fultz's shocker.

"This is a real slip pitch," I said.

"Want my two cents?"

"I'll take your whole wallet."

"Heh, heh. Well, Duffy, you were at the scene. You seen the body. You tell me: Was there a lot of blood?"

"Uh, yeah. I guess. It was a mess. There was, whattaya call it—gray matter?—kind of all over the place."

"But blood? Red stuff. I mean, was there a good bucket of it?"

"Well . . . ah shit, Dave, I didn't really take a decent look. I'm a sportswriter. I don't cover the cop shop. I've seen plenty of charley horses and a few bloody noses. Herb Score gushed pretty bad when McDougald tagged him in the face. But to tell you the honest-to-God truth, I don't know squat about bloodshed."

"Gushed," he said. "That's the word, Duffy. It makes all the difference in the world on this thing. If Huston was dead before he got shot, his heart wouldn't pump blood. It woulda spilled, but it wouldn't have any pressure. If there wasn't much blood, then somebody got to him, poisoned the son-of-a-bitch before he was shot."

"Just to make sure, you mean?"

"Maybe. Or maybe to throw everybody off. I mean, who's lookin' for poison when you got a hole through your head? That's how the good illusionists work, you know. Keep you lookin' at one thing, and do the big stuff somewhere else."

I put the file on the desk and went for my hanky. It felt like the old days when I was back in the front row of the press box, on deadline in the last inning with my lead all composed and the story line just about to bed, only to have a couple of walks, a booted squibber, and a wild pitch threaten to blow the whole thing.

"But if he was dead, how'd he get out there?" I asked, thinking out loud.

"That's your ball game, Duffy. I'm a lab rat. If I were you, I'd do a whole new postmortem on the thing. Need help?"

I snapped to quickly enough to politely decline.

"One more thing, what happens with this stuff now?" I asked.

"Right to the boss. Devery gets everything. What he does with it is his business. Why, you need some time?"

"More like a miracle."

"Well," Fultz said, "you're dealin' with the Yankees, you know."

They were words from a lifelong White Sox fan, rueful, to be sure, but I knew exactly what he meant. It was time to get back to the ballpark.

17

Monument Park

I never thought I would compete with my niece for a source. Then again, I never thought DiMaggio's heel would come around in '49. I never thought Roger Maris would be traded for Charlie Smith, and I never thought Bucky Dent was a power hitter. But Petey's investigative antennae were on my mind when I called John Brush, who was in town trying to make trades rather than on the West Coast with the team. He couldn't find time for me during the day but suggested I come around to the stadium for a bite when the sun began to set.

And my niece?

"Why," he laughed, "she asked for the night off."

A return of good sense, I hoped, or the lure of a trail too warm to ignore. It was neither, I later learned. Petey was so spent from her outrageous hours and so sore from her bump-and-run in the park that she lost the rest of the day and night to sleep. It served her right.

In the meantime I touched a few bases. I bantered long distance with Red Carney, who said he was coming in to New York to broadcast a Mets-Cubs series and would buy me dinner tomorrow night. I caught Grand Chambliss between league brushfires and brought him up to date. He couldn't stifle a guffaw when I told him Huston had a houseful of fake paintings. It was not very charitable or commissionerlike of him, God knows, but he roared anyway. After hanging up with Grand, I asked myself out loud if I should make contact with Chief Devery and decided against it. He wasn't exactly burning up my phone lines.

Then I did something that old print guys like me are wont to do: I wrote it all down. I went over what I knew about whom, who was where at what time, and what made sense. Before I drained a beat at the *Daily News*, I was a makeup guy. Yes, I was. Back then we made up the pages with slugs of lead hot from the linotype machines. I spent a lot of time with the printers putting pages together on the third floor, and I was good at it too. To this day I can read a newspaper upside down, which is how the pages composed in lead looked to you. When I put things together, lay them out, crop the photos, get rid of the widows, the tombstones, and the wrong fonts, I get a feel for the whole picture. Some things you never lose.

So that's how it was in my suite that afternoon, with Manhattan grating and grinding below, my niece sawing logs in dreamland next door. I sat down and took a bunch of hot clues and cold-blooded suspects and tried to compose a page of murder.

It was closing in on six P.M. when I leaned onto Lexington Avenue and hailed a cab for the Bronx. I had an appetite and a thirst, and I was genuinely eager to compare notes with John Brush. The traffic was heavy and the air smarting as my hack quit the bumper tag of the Major Degan Expressway and dropped me at the Yankees' front office. Kids were playing basketball and wallball in the parks across the street, their shouts mingling with their stereos. A lot of other legs were churning in games in the green fields across 161st Street. Flags flapped on poles. It was all urban bucolic and kind of nice, unless you are of a mind that nothing can be nice in the Bronx.

It wasn't a game day, so I missed the smell of roasted chestnuts and hot pretzels. After a security check an elevator took me to the executive level and Brush's office. Although a bunch of other men and women in shirtsleeves were still around, Brush appeared to be in his office alone, sitting behind his desk, absorbed in what was on top of it. The corner TV was turned on to a national-network talking head.

Brush was his usual tanned, masculine portrait of health. Everything on him looked fit. The office was cluttered but under control, just as I had remembered it from my earlier visit, except for a framed advertisement that hung on one wall. It hearkened back to the days when Ike was in office, and it showed a young, grinning player touting Chesterfield cigarettes. From where I was sitting, it looked like Yogi. Smoking and ballplayers was no big thing back then, and Yogi always was a great salesman. I remembered when he bought a big life-insurance policy and a teammate asked him why. "Well," Yogi said, "I'll get it when I die."

"Take your deals off the table," I said, tapping the open door as I entered. "You got a spy in the house."

Brush stood up to greet me.

"I'd call you first before I did anything, Duffy. You know that," he said, and motioned me to the sofa.

"Whattaya after?" I asked.

"I'm going crazy looking for a starting pitcher—if for no other reason, just to show 'em we're not folding in the wake of Rupert's death. But all the noncontenders are dealing their available arms to the clubs in the races—and for ridiculous rates. I may have to stand pat until the winter meetings."

I could feel the frustration. A G.M. is an unseen genius when the club is going good and every roster change he made over the winter comes up golden. When things are floundering, when his blue-chippers are dubious and his doubtfuls are dreadful, he is a buffoon. Brush, like his team, was somewhere tilting toward the middle.

"How's the shamus business?" he asked.

I made a face.

"Don't play the dummy with me, John. You got a pipeline into a certain redhead gives you more dope on this thing than me."

He grinned.

"She is *something*, isn't she, Duffy? Probably the sharpest young woman I've ever met."

Oh no, I thought, *Brush too*. A grown man stung worse than the child. The other deck of the Manhattan Love Boat pitching and reeling in the waves. Would anything he said make sense at all? I indulged him.

"She has fine, fine genes, if I do say so myself. And

watch your step with her, John, because in her uncle's eyes she can do no wrong."

"I stand well advised," he said.

"You don't stand at all," I rejoined. "You got worse knees than Mantle. How bad is this thing really getting between you two?"

He rubbed his hands through his hair, terrain I knew my niece had traversed, and smiled. A bit sheepishly, I thought.

"Bad," he said.

"Good," I said, and threw an avuncular smile at him. "The family could do worse than to have you in the clubhouse."

"Hmm," Brush considered.

The stadium outside his office window, with the exception of a few pops and groans that always emanate from an empty arena cooling off at the end of a day, was quiet.

"Eat in or you want to run out?" he asked.

"In is fine with me. Whattaya got?"

"Matzo-ball soup, kreplach, potato pancakes, corned-beef hash, brisket—all from the last kosher restaurant in the Bronx."

"Rye bread and beer and I'm yours, John."

For the next half hour we talked baseball, specifically Yankee baseball, which wasn't a happy prospect. The team had not been in the hunt for a long time. Seventeen games out of first and dropping like a stone, which was depressing even at the end of the season. Brush ran his lineup by me, mixing statistics with margin notes. He paused to hear my retorts, to note as much about what I was not saying as what I was. The guy had a way of listening when he conversed, like a good interviewer, and there aren't many of those around anymore. Too many baseball big shots do nothing but expound, in love with the sound of their just-mouthed wisdoms, and you can't get a word in edgewise. I once sat at the foot of Dallas Green, who held a brief and dismal tenure with the Yankees, as he regaled me with the contention that he personally removed the loser's look from the ushers at Wrigley Field when he took over the Cubs organization. From the *ushers,* for crying out loud.

But there was none of that now. Brush, instead, was picking my brain, not underestimating it, so much so that I wished I had better things to offer him. Too much of my wisdom with regard to his current club was sports-page stuff, and by the time it gets there, it's often too late. Did I know of another Mattingly in the hustings? A Guidry? Was there a veteran somewhere, a Wilcy Moore or a Ewell "The Whip" Blackwell, who might come alive in Yankee pinstripes?

On the other hand, Brush may well have been humoring me. He knew major-league horseflesh as well as anybody. He also knew what kind of stuff the names on his wall —those minor-league wannabees—had inside them and whether or not there were any championship seasons gestating in the Yankee bushes.

"Rupert proved after he bought a pennant that you can't buy a pennant," Brush said. "You can buy talent, but you can't buy desire or pride or chemistry or luck. We haven't had much of those around here lately."

"How much can you do personally? What's the state of the front office?" I asked.

"If anything I've got a freer hand. Until the club is sold or whatever, I'm general manager, descendent of Barrow and Weiss—"

"And Lou Piniella and Syd Thrift."

"Knock that off, Duffy. But anyway, I'm gonna bust my butt until somebody tells me to take a hike. This is the Yankees, after all, the greatest franchise in baseball."

"Wake up the echoes, John."

"That's it, Duffy," he said. "That's precisely it."

At that moment a guard brought up our dinner, a stack of containers and wrappers and kosher goodies that would have made Ron Blomberg weep. Two pickles the size of fungo bats wafted the smell of garlic and brine beneath our nostrils. Brush liberated a few cold beers from his private cooler, and we moved the feast out to the front row of the press box, where it spread out in front of us like a table at a bar mitzvah. With the open air and green grass of the stadium before us, we ate like backup catchers.

"You knew they found the guy who burgled your counting room, didn't you, John?"

"They did?"

"Yup—Petey didn't tell you?"

"No, I guess she was too caught up with an art dealer. Hey, that's a big break in this thing, isn't it?"

"It was."

"What do you mean?"

"Guy was a professional thief. Safecracker, home invader. The kind of mechanic who could get into the place almost without leaving a scratch. And he was a degenerate Mets fan, which explains the mementos."

"You're kidding me—"

"No, sir. A real sweetheart from Queens. The thing with him is that he worked for the Mob once in a while. Kind of a journeyman. He shared his take with the Outfit guys, and they let him operate."

"He broke in here for them?"

"I don't know, neither do the cops. He could have broken in for a lot of reasons. The way it was explained to me is that on a big killing like this, these guys like to have an inside man. He cases the place, maybe he cracks the door on One hundred sixty-first Street, maybe he provides a diversion if something goes wrong."

"That would fit," Brush said. "I mean, he broke in, but he didn't take much of anything."

"And he left a lot more."

"Don't mention it."

"On the other hand, maybe he wasn't working for the Mob," I continued. "I'm no expert on the sharkskin-suit league, but this kind of a job isn't their style. He could have been working for somebody else. Say Herm McFarland?"

"Wait on that, Duffy," Brush said, wiping sour cream from his chin.

He continued. "Forget Herm. Making him a killer is like turning Benny Bengough into a slugger. I worked over his file after that pile-of-crap episode. Made some calls. Found out some things. There's motive there, sure. Rupert hired him and led him to believe he was a star. The daughter was behind that. Keeler. She's the climber. She stuck it to Rupert about her 'Hermie' all the time. And then Rupert would blow him off. Herm wasn't going anywhere in the organization, and he knew it.

"But, Duffy, Herm hasn't got it. He's a utility infielder with a weak stick. Indecisive as hell. A wimp. He couldn't pull a trigger at a penny arcade."

"Could he hire someone to do it?"

"Possibly. Or Keeler could have. That's why your burglar—what was his name?—"

"Ganzello."

"Ganzello . . . that's why he's a real player in this. What's his story? Where is he now?"

"He's dead."

"Huh?" Brush jerked his chin around, and a strand of sauerkraut escaped his maw.

"Yup. Shot in the back of the head. Two nights ago, as I was about to say. And before anybody could get much out of him."

"Back of the head?"

"Right on the street. Pop, pop."

"Now that's Mafia," Brush said. "Right up close. Dead men don't talk and all that stuff."

He licked his chops and his fingers. The food was lots and good, as my old Jewish neighbor lady used to say.

"It fits. It's perfect, Duffy," he went on. "The Mob hires a guy to set it all up, then they wipe him out. They erase any possibility of a loose tongue. Good God, they're vicious bastards. And smart too."

"Maybe," I said. "And that's where it sits except for the other Huston kid. Griffith."

Brush pushed his chair back and rinsed his pipes with a long drink of beer.

"That's Petey's thread. She's inflamed, Duffy."

"I know. There's real motive there. The guy Beville, the gallery owner—she told you all about him—he's an out-and-out felon. A worm. And he wormed a million bucks worth of fake art into Rupert's collection using his kid to do it.

"Question is," I went on, "did he use the kid to set Rupert up for the kill? I don't know. Petey's sure of it. Putting Monte Beville behind this whole thing doesn't take a great leap of imagination. And Petey has great imagination. But . . . ," I said, managing the last sentence before a beer belch surfaced in a less than mannerly fashion.

"Sounds damn plausible," Brush suggested. "And Griffith was here later than usual that night. He hung around . . . must have been after ten or eleven."

"It's a matter of timing," I said. "When did the kid

really leave? And how? How did he get his old man out to the monuments? According to Lana, Rupert's allergies made him so miserable this time of year that he stayed in his air-conditioned office all the time."

I was thinking out loud, looking out into the stadium and trying to visualize the events of that night.

"Does that sound right to you?" I asked Brush.

"No way, Duffy. When Rupert was here at the stadium, he was in and out all the time. Griffith knew that. Maybe he even knew the burglar . . . this what's-his-name Ganzello," Brush ventured. "Let me run this by you, Duffy: Anybody try to tie the gun to this guy? I mean, maybe it was his job to bring it in. The burglary was an afterthought."

"Judging from the deposit he left, the guy's full of afterthoughts," I said.

Brush sniffed.

"But it could have happened. I'm not discounting anything, John. The Mob. The Huston kids. This Beville character. Especially this Beville character."

Brush balled up a piece of wax paper and tossed it at a corner wastebasket. He missed. Then he thumped the table for emphasis.

"God! I just can't see some *fine-arts* dilettante, some SoHo faggot doing it. It just cuts the wrong way, Duffy. This Monte Beville. An asshole who knows nothing about baseball. Nothing. Or the Yankees! Jesus, a guy like that murdering Rupert Huston just trivializes the whole thing, you know what I mean? Just brings it down to money and greed like every other cheap homicide."

"Whoever said murder had to be high-minded, John?" I asked, my eye catching the Yankee top hat on the outfield scoreboard. That smart, irrefutable logo.

Brush shook his head and began collecting our debris. It had been a hell of a meal, and we were both stuffed.

"Let's take a walk, Duf," he said. "I like this place at this time of night."

We filed out of the press box via the exit into the executive-level concourse. I turned to go to the elevator, but Brush motioned me past it, and we continued to walk down the concourse. The night security lights of the stadium were on now. The shadows were long and the corridors empty. Our steps echoed against the concrete walls as we wound our way down from level to level as if we were general-admission ticket holders. At the main level we went into the stands and stepped down to the aisle that leads out toward left field.

"Who am I kidding?" Brush said as we walked. "Rupert Huston didn't know shit about baseball. Why should his death have something to do with the game?"

"Good question," I said. "Fact is, he died in front of the game's most famous monuments. People tend to read something into that."

"And Albert Anastasia was killed in a barber chair," he rejoined. "So maybe his kid did kill him. Or his kid's pansy friend. Or the two of them together with the help of a Mets fan with overactive bowels. Throw in the Mob too, what the hell?"

He spoke conversationally, the scrape of our shoes being the only competition. We had not passed anybody on our stroll. The concessions and maintenance people had long since called it a day. The stadium's bare-bones security staff, even in these tight-ship times following the murder, was in place but out of sight. It was a situation, I thought fleetingly, not unlike that fateful night. The sky was now dark, as dark as it can get in a city of eight million. Large patches of the stadium's interior were also dark, however, even eerie. I thought about what it must have sounded like: the spit of the rifle, the explosion of bone and brain matter as the shell seared through Huston's head, the sodden thump of his body against the low wall in front of the monuments. Unless, of course, he was propped against the wall before the shot was fired.

"Hell, with Griffith being gay and all that, there were plenty of problems," Brush said, disrupting my thoughts. "I mean, Rupert had a big problem with that. He found it real hard to be a father to the kid. I know, because he tried to be one to me. Don't think that didn't cause a little friction in the house."

"What, between you and Griffith?" I asked.

"Some," Brush replied. "But mostly between me and Keeler. And I know she worked on Griffith—I *know* she did. Lana, she sort of sat back and enjoyed the whole thing."

"I didn't know you got into it that thick with the family, John."

"I tried not to. But when you work for a guy as closely as I did with Rupert, it comes up. He laid the Griffith thing on me more than once. 'Can you imagine my *kid* in control of the Yankees!' he used to say. And I used to think, *Could it be any worse?*"

"A thought you never uttered, I trust."

"You got it, Duffy. I'm shooting off at the mouth now. You bring up Rupert and his family, and I get a little rattled."

By now we were beyond the left-field fence, 387 feet from home plate, walking on the rubber pad that leads toward Monument Park. I had been here a lot lately, yet all the scenes and images of *the* night still rushed back to me.

We passed the white tray-table markers of all the numbers the Yankees had retired through the years.

"Crashes," Brush said, brushing his hand idly over number 1. "First Munson. Then Billy Martin, the poor son-of-a-bitch."

Then we were on the red brick path and in the park itself.

"Do you know Miller Huggins died of blood poisoning?" Brush went on. "Can you imagine? An antibiotic would have saved the Mighty Mite. That's why spiking a guy was such a big deal back then. Get an infection, and you could be a goner."

"Hmm," I said. I turned and pushed the toe of my shoe in the dirt around the flowers, the begonias and dusty millers and geraniums that brightened the park. They had been freshly watered and looked healthy.

Brushed turned to me.

"Some detectives were back today," he said. "Digging around just about where you are now."

"They were?"

I stooped to look at the area. Brush bent down with me, and we idly pawed at the dirt, wood chips, and stones of the area where Huston had made his last flop.

"I can give you an idea of what they were looking for," I said. "If I'm not mistaken, they were checking the soil for blood."

"Blood?"

"Yup. Huston's."

"You lost me, Duffy."

"They want to know if he lost enough of it. See, it looks like Rupert was poisoned before he was shot."

"Poisoned! You're kidding me!"

"No. The lab guys found it. Some kind of mix of prescription drugs—but enough, they say, to deck him."

Suddenly a battery of lights went on. We sprang up reflexively and were bathed in a splash of light that nearly blinded us. The entire area from the bullpen to Monument Park was ablaze in floodlights. The clatter of running footsteps and the jangle of keys came from all sides.

"Don't move!" someone shouted.

We didn't. In seconds we were surrounded by a fleet of panting security guards. An electric golf cart driven by a maintenance man came scooting out of the tunnel behind us.

"It's me, Rick," Brush said.

"Yo, Mr. Brush. Don't do that to me," one of the uniforms said. "We just seen you guys on the monitors. Figured, what the hell is goin' on?"

"Sorry," Brush said. "I should have called. Told you we were out here."

"Yeah, well, no sweat. We're just edgy, you know what I mean?"

"Cow's out of the barn, Rick," Brush snapped.

"Huh?" the guard asked.

"Forget it," Brush said.

With that everybody began peeling off and returning to the sleepy routine of watching an empty ballyard at night.

"You want a ride, Mr. Brush?" said the maintenance guy, who was still perched on the golf cart near the tunnel opening.

"No thanks, Ed," Brush said to him.

"Hey, nobody rides with me anymore," Ed said, and disappeared into the tunnel.

Brush and I began walking back to the front-office lobby. I stayed with him, and as we went, the security lights began to click off.

"He took them, you know," Brush said abruptly. "Pills. Rupert had pills all over the place."

"So I learned. That means he could have done it himself by accident. Or he could have been helped. Either way, if he was poisoned, he might have been dead before he was shot. You follow me? Then he wouldn't have bled much after he was shot. You know, the ticker doesn't pump. That's why the detectives were back here."

"That's incredible. Why didn't you tell me earlier?"

"It's a theory, and I just learned about it. As you said, Rupert could have gulped a few too many pills because he had a runny nose. The police must have wanted to check it all out. It puts a new spin on this thing if he was mickeyed."

"It sure does. Where do you go now?" he asked.

"Not far, I hope," I said.

"Keep me in touch. I'll help if I can," Brush said. "God, it would be nice to clinch this thing."

"Another Yankee tradition," I said.

I was tired and still stuffed. I took Brush up on his offer of a Yankee courtesy ride back to Manhattan, and in a few minutes a club car was out front. It was driven by a clean-cut, quiet young black man who was wearing a navy sweatervest with a Yankee logo on it. The kid wasn't interested in conversation, or perhaps I wasn't much of a conversationalist.

As usual I was turning over the case in my mind, replaying my visit with John Brush and our interruption by the now-vigilant stadium security force. There was something about going back out to the scene of the crime that made it very immediate once again. And something bothered me about it. I didn't know what.

At the hotel I thanked my driver and swiveled to get out of the front seat. As I swung my foot out, my shoe scraped the inside of the door and left a smudge. It was reddish in color, and I reached down to rub it off. It was dirt—damp soil, to be exact—the soil found around the flower beds of Monument Park.

Even as exhausted as I was, I could not turn in once I got back to my suite. I took off my shoes, noticing once again the one smeared with the red dirt. I paced the room. I looked over the notes I'd made earlier. Then I made a phone call. At the other end of the line, Handsome Harry Howell did not sound pleased.

"No, you didn't wake me, Duffy. Telephone calls this late at night mean a death in the family. Didya know that?"

"No death this time, Harry. Just a question," I said. "Tell me what happens to your worn-out equipment bags. The canvas ones for bats and things."

"Now why would you be asking about them?" Howell said, his Irish accent coming to the forefront.

"I'm not sure," I said.

"Fact is, we never have any that get worn out. At the end of the season they get taken like everything else. Cleaned out. Everybody from upstairs to the clubhouse, to where I got to chase those birds away. Why, even Mr. Huston used to take them bags. They tell me he used them for satchels. Can you imagine?"

"Rupert?"

"The boss himself," Harry said.

18

Such Sweet Thunder

I felt like Dave Righetti with his best heat and two strikes on a hitter who was bailing out in the middle of his windup. Petey and I had a lock on this game. She was back in uniform, but sore, still stinging from her wounds, and I wondered if her hip was worse than she let on. But she was not to be kept on the sidelines; she wanted badly to dig more deeply into the toxic side of Monte Beville. I'd called Big Bill Devery and told him everything that we had discovered about Griffith Huston, Beville, and bogus art. Devery was interested, if not a little peeved that Petey and I had uncovered something his dicks hadn't. Coupled with the lab report from Dave Fultz, it all was starting to make sense, he agreed.

"Let's first-to-third this thing," he said, slipping dangerously into my vernacular. "If we find what we want on Beville in some of these other cases, we can pinch him with Huston."

He assigned a detective to assist Petey: the two of them were to turn Beville's dealings with his former and deceased clients inside out. He also decided to bring in Griffith for a grilling.

"You want to jaw at the little bastard?" he asked.

"Not my bailiwick, Chief. But Petey might want to chew on him," I said, and I recounted her run-in in Central Park.

For my part I took Brush's advice and looked into any connection between the AR-15 assault rifle and John

Henry Ganzello, and, to cover the bases, Herm McFarland. It was a crumb, but one I'd take if it was there. Devery also gave me a free run through his database on it.

With this concentrated action, I figured, this thing was only a matter of time. A fastball or two on the fists, and then sneak one across the outside black for the called third strike.

And that's where I was wrong. For the rest of the day I spun my wheels, getting nothing new on the gun, Ganzello, or McFarland. Petey was to have similar results. What she and her police operative—a female at that— found on Beville was suggestive, fishy, downright sleazy, and hideously unethical, but not good enough for a murder warrant. Of Wid Conroy's old ladies, one had died of a stroke, one was a pretty well-documented suicide, and in the case of a third, a greedy nephew was being charged with her murder. He had done it with poison, so Wid Conroy was not totally off the track. Monte Beville had sold them all bogus art, but the trail to him as murderer by poison was suddenly tenuous.

As for Griffith, Devery's detectives were told by Keeler Huston that her brother—and the entire family— was well aware of Rupert's allergies and the prescription drugs he took for them. Wherever her father went, she said, he brought his medicine cabinet along with him. The same detectives, however, could not bring in Griffith for questioning. The kid already had signed on the best criminal lawyers New York money could buy, and they wouldn't let the police get anywhere near their client unless he was to be charged first.

At the end of the day, the same one that had started out so strong, we were three up and three down. Only Devery, who left his private line open to us, was undismayed.

"Game ain't over . . . ," he began—and if he'd have uttered the Yogi cliché, I would have hung up on him— "yet," he concluded.

As for Petey, she returned to the Summit and my suite pretty hangdog. She wanted to end this thing as badly as I did.

"We're gonna nail those bastards, Unk. I can feel it," she said.

"You need a lift, and I got just the thing," I said.

I reminded her of our tab with Red Carney. Her face lifted, but only slightly.

"I can't. I really can't," she said. "As much as I love Red, I gotta take a rain check. I'm hurtin', Uncle Duffy."

"You ought to see a doctor," I said.

"Maybe," she said, and seemed to mean it.

An hour later I was shaved and talced and ready to swap nonsense over prime rib with Red. At the same time I heard noise from Petey's suite. Her shower ran, her television went on, and I detected telltale sounds of activity, the kind made not when someone is down for the night but when someone is doing herself up.

I punched her extension before I stepped out.

"Feeling better?" I asked.

"Uh, kinda," she said.

"Good. You'll join us?"

"Uh . . . no, I can't. John called and invited me over."

"But you're in no condition."

"Well, I guess I feel better," she suggested.

"Dammit, Petey. This is a disgrace!" I barked. "Red's anxious to see you. Where in hell are your priorities?"

"Don't do this to me, Uncle Duffy," she said. "I'm not trying to be rude."

"Well, you are. Hell, can't you check your hormones for a night and spend some time with a couple guys who have a real history with you?"

"I'm sorry," she said. "Red'll understand."

"No, he won't. And neither do I," I said, and hung up before I said something nasty.

Moments later my door chattered with a knuckle-knock. I opened it to Petey in her bathrobe, a towel wrapped around her hair.

"Are you smoked at me, Unk?" she said. She stood like a waif, one recently dipped in bubblebath.

"You bet I am."

She stepped in and hugged me, then drew back and took both my hands in hers. She had all the moves, and I was softening up like a Dove Bar in the hot sun.

"You gotta understand," she said. "I'm crazy about this guy, and I'm crazy about you, and I want you both."

"That's the trouble with your generation, Petrinella. You want everything when you want it," I said, and didn't like the sound of it the second after it left my lips.

"I'm in love, Uncle Duffy, something your generation was pretty good at too."

"We had our moments."

"Let me have mine. Please?"

"That bad, huh?"

"Yes, that bad. You approve?"

"It's none of my business either way, Petey."

"Yes, it is. It makes a big difference to me."

"Thank you," I said, and we went back to the hug.

"Well, if you must . . . ," I said, and got a peck on the cheek for it.

Before she got through her door, however, I added, "But we've got a murder to drain tomorrow. Be fresh."

"I'm always fresh," she said, and stuck out her tongue.

Petey was all but out of my mind when my cab dropped me off at a little place called Periyali on Twentieth Street between Fifth and Sixth avenues. I couldn't pronounce it, and I'm leery of joints sitting three steps below the sidewalk—it's too much like going into a dugout, and I don't have to detail what you find on the floors of dugouts—but Red had said the place was a keeper. Judging from the size of the crowd, I decided he was right. The front bar was standing-room only, and Red, florid-faced and already a little oiled, was one of the mob at the rail.

He spotted me from twenty feet and lifted his beer in the air.

"You're alone, you old celibate," he barked, getting a cheap laugh from the ladies on his elbow.

"Don't mention it," I said, shouting above the noise.

"Where's my true love?" he said.

"Went over to the Yankees."

"Wha—?"

"You heard me. This thing with Brush. He calls, and Petey hops over like a batboy fetching pine tar. She's in love, Red. Gaga. And with a younger man than you."

"This Brush guy? Ah shit. He's a good man, but I hate to see her go over to the American League. Plus, she's easy on the eyes, Duffy, and I was looking forward to treating mine tonight."

"Well, forget about it. I told you, didn't I, how she got banged up in Central Park the other day? So this afternoon she says she can't come along because she's too sore. I'll give her that. I respect the disabled list as much as the next guy. But she gets a call from lover boy, and all of a sudden she's healed."

"Hey, reminds me of the Babe in twenty-one," Red said.

"Whatta *you* know about the Babe in twenty-one?"

"Listen up. Before I come to New York, I do my homework. Ruth had that arm that got infected in the World Series when he scraped it stealing second and third. Stealing bases, can you imagine that? So the press was all over him for dogging it and not playing much in the Series. Afterwards—and the Yanks lost it—first thing you know Babe is going off on one of those barnstorming junkets for extra money, and they ask him how he can do it, and he says, 'I always heal quick.'" Red added a beery guffaw.

"Glad you look at it that way," I said. "I'd forgotten that story."

"So had I until just now," Red said. "Now let's get one of these little Greco-Roman guys to give us a table. Whattaya make of this place, huh, Duffy?"

He didn't wait for an answer and waded off in search of the head table man. He went uninterrupted, which wouldn't have been the case in Chicago, where his mug is plastered in every saloon and on every billboard in town, and you can't sit down with him but some bowser from the boonies is coming over to gab. Here he was recognized only by New York athletic supporters, and this joint, which was hopping with ladies in off-the-shoulder blouses and guys with Dutchboy haircuts, didn't seem to have many.

That was okay, because it had plenty of tables along the wall and a good martini, which I was in the mood for. In no time Red had us seated at a table with linen beneath my elbows and a beckoning waiter whose roots went back to Crete. If it offered something besides squid and goat cheese and grape leaves, I was going to like this place.

Red lifted his beer.

"Damn good to see you again, pal," he said. He was jowly and in great spirits, the hops lubricating that golden voice box of his. "There's gotta be at least a dozen people askin' about you back home every day. 'Where's House? Where's that grumpy old geezer?' Ain't you had about enough of this town yet?"

"The case. I'm just about rung out on the case, Red."

"Criminy! Has Chambliss got you by the nuggets? Beg off! Forget this Dick Tracy stuff and take it easy. Tell him you gave it a run, and it's his baby."

"I'm tempted."

"You *know* you ain't gonna crack it like you did the Wrigley Field thing. This is New York, Duffy, for cripes' sake. They put guys away here, and they stay put. Hell, ain't Jimmy Hoffa s'posed to be planted in the Meadowlands? I figure the same guys did Huston, and they're long gone. You're swinging at thin air, Duf."

"Not so fast, Red. We're getting real close on a few angles."

"Have I read about this?"

"Better not, or it'll dry up like a raisin."

I went on to fill him in on Petey's pursuit of the Beville –Griffith Huston connection. He hung on every word, interrupting only with assorted smacks and grunts from the bread and green olives and cold squid salad he was stuffing into his chops. His lips were wet, and the olive oil welled at the corners of his mouth. Cholesterol and glycerides be damned, Red Carney knew how to eat.

At the same moment and several dozen streets uptown, my niece and her date were nibbling comparable appetizers. As Petey was to relate to me in exquisite detail, Brush had prepared quite a spread for their private little dinner. I had to hand it to the guy, he was good. He could break bread with me one night and break raw cauliflower with my niece the next—and never break stride. This time the edibles were different. Brush had assembled a pantry of assorted and uncooked delectables that I've never heard of but were quite intoxicating to Petey. And, of course, the air fairly breathed romance. Petey, whose hunger was literal and figurative, was game on all counts.

It had not, of course, taken much persuasion to get her there. Petey, I realized from the pools of her green eyes in the hallway earlier that evening, would have joined John Brush over White Castle sliders. This night, however, Brush had yet another attraction, in the form of a vintage piece of jazz that he wanted to show off to her.

Petey, dressed in a sleek pair of black velvet slacks and a charcoal gray silk blouse, her hair pinned up like the tail of a rooster, looked better than she felt. Brush sent a car over, a bit of star treatment that made jelly of her, and she arrived at his building on the Upper East Side feeling nary a throb—at least not from her bruises and scrapes. Brush ushered her into his sprawling duplex digs where the Ellington orchestra was on the sound system, and the smell of garlic, an aphrodisiac in my book, was in the air. He offered her a very long-stemmed and imperially slim glass of Gewürztraminer, and Petey sipped it and drank in everything about her surroundings.

He also sampled some of her goodies, nibbling her lips as if they were pitted green olives, and Petey responded by clamping her free hand on the nape of his neck. The two of them were terribly comfortable with each other, like good wine and great music, like Rizzuto and Coleman.

"The great Duke . . ." Brush said a few moments later, as Petey ran her digits along the teak wall of sound equipment, then perused the plastic compact-disc holder of the Ellington piece.

"Perhaps the greatest composer of American music of his time," Brush went on. "You know, there are tunes and arrangements of his that aren't even published yet. He was a natural—a DiMaggio, a Mantle."

"Ever meet him?"

"Just once—just to shake his hand. They say he had tunes running through his head all the time. He'd write them down anywhere, even on his shirt cuffs when he was traveling and didn't have any staff paper around. Made a staff right on his cuffs! Then, with help from Billy Strayhorn, he'd have the band playing them that night!"

Brush was off and running, talking about Duke Ellington with the same passion he held for his beloved Yankees.

In the meantime he brought out a plate of pâtés and crackers, then a hot artichoke hors d'oeuvre. The two of them, leaning against a counter or sitting on cushions on the living-room floor, alternately plopped food between each other's jaws and giggled and fawned and did things people who aren't in complete touch with reality do, or so I seem to remember. I'm not much at the choreography of coweyed mating games, but Petey said they did them all—and well.

What followed was a dinner of seafood—scallops, lobster, swordfish—all done by Brush over flames on his expensive German grill. He added wild rice and a bunch of sprouts and pea pods, some bread from an Indian bakery, another wine, and knocked Petey's culinary socks off.

"I've been bumped, Red. I'm an also-ran. I'm Wally Pipp with a headache. Sure, Petey's been great on this case. She uncovered the Griffith connection, and she's tireless. Don't get me wrong, I love the little imp. But she's hooked. She and Brush are a battery."

"Great. That's great, Duffy."

"No, it's horseshit. Nothing against John Brush, but he's become a big problem. Petey went to college—that cost her mother an arm and a leg—now she's been accepted into law school. Law school. That's something, ain't it? A girl like her being a lawyer. Maybe a judge? But it ain't gonna happen if she jumps off the boat and hooks on with Mr. General Manager."

" 'Course it will. Who says she don't go to law school if she does stick with the guy? Huh? Who says she won't pay back dividends?"

"Maybe, but I doubt it. The hunger'll be gone. She'll be a missus. Have a long-term contract. Joint in New York. Travel the circuit and watch games in the VIP box. The high life. And she's gonna interrupt that with law school? Hell no. It's like wanting to be a dentist, then signing a million-dollar contract with a big club and telling the world you're still gonna go to dental school so you can look into other people's mouths some day."

"Bobby Brown did it," Red said. "Wanted to be a doc-

tor. So he was always readin' medical books in the clubhouse while the other guys were readin' comic books."

I smiled. He was right, and I could hear it coming.

"Yogi finished his comic book one day—" I began.

"—and said to Bobby," Red continued, " 'Hey Doc,
mine was good. How'd yours turn out?' "

Red gave out a laugh, and I joined him.

"Hey, Duffy. How many guys you think were doing
something they had their heart set on, maybe like law
school or becoming a doctor or a surgeon, and baseball got
in the way? It's gotta be a lot of guys out there."

It was a typical Carney aside, spoken, usually, when a
pitcher was taking too much time between deliveries, or
rain had driven both teams off the field. But it set me to
thinking. It was as if he'd tossed a dart in the center of my
brain and got it going again.

"I say to Petey, 'Go for it,' " Red went on. " 'Grab all
the gusto you can get.' 'Reach for the stars.' 'You only go
around once.' Hey, Duffy, you listening?"

I swung back to him.

"Cripes, Red, you sound like a bad beer commercial. A
whole campaign of bad beer commercials," I said, returning my thoughts to the table.

"She's a beautiful young lady, Duf. If she's found a
great guy, well, that's what life is all about."

"Ah, baloney. She's like a kid in Triple A ball. A can't-
miss. Couple years seasoning before he's ready. Then he
decides he's gonna quit and go to Europe with his girlfriend cuz her daddy owns a ski lodge. Would you say
great, that's what life's all about?"

"Hell no! Not to a *kid*. He's got scouts, the franchise, a
lot of people invested in him! Cost over a million bucks to
get a kid into the majors nowadays—you read that the
other day?"

"Flip," I said. "Flop."

"You know what I mean," he said.

I frowned. "What I do know is there's a lot of people
invested in Petrinella Biggers. And she's making an early
withdrawal. And I don't like it."

"Ah, you're half-cocked, Duffy. You can't hear yourself. She's probably goin' for this Brush guy just to get
away from *you*!"

* * *

"He teamed up with Shakespeare," Brush said.

"What do you mean?" Petey said.

They were done with supper and were sipping cappuccino back in Brush's audio/video/seduction room.

"This is what I wanted you to hear. The Duke and the Bard. Ellington thought Shakespeare had some rhythm in him, and he wrote an entire suite using Shakespeare's characters and themes. Somebody never returned the copy I had in college, but I got a hold of another one—don't ask me how. You've got to hear it."

He pulled a worn sepia-toned record jacket from his shelf of albums. It pictured a thin cigarette-smoking Ellington in 1957 poring over a score.

"Such Sweet Thunder," Brush said, displaying the album to Petey. "Dedicated to the Stratford Shakespeare Festival. Where is the title taken from—?"

"Uh, here it is," Petey said, pointing at the bottom of the liner notes. " 'I never heard so musical a discord, such sweet thunder.' Act Four of *A Midsummer Night's Dream.*"

Brush nodded. "Perfect, isn't it? I mean, Ellington loved the classics—he just *knew* them—and fit his music to them. Look at what he said about this one cut, the one on Lady Macbeth—where is it?—here. Called it 'Lady Mac,' and he says, 'Though she was a lady of noble birth, we suspect there was a little ragtime in her soul.' Isn't that perfect? You can just hear him say it."

Petey lingered over the jacket, noting the lines and characters from Shakespeare interspersed with Ellington's witty and upbeat remarks about the music he had composed for them. She loved the rumpled fedora plopped on his head. Brush went over and carefully cued the stylus up and then back down at the beginning of the record on his British-made turntable. The title selection, full of trumpet and brass in plungers, ushered in Ellington's sweet, inspired passages. It was magical, and Petey, who knew her Shakespeare but had no idea that Duke Ellington knew it too, was enamored.

"He wrote four musical sonnets in perfect fourteen-line sonnet form," Brush went on, talking quietly so as not to obscure the music. "He has sonnets for Henry the Fifth, Sister Kate the shrew, and a tune for Hamlet. He was unbelievable."

"*You're* unbelievable," she said. "You know so much. Jazz. Shakespeare. Fourteen-line sonnets—"

"No, no. Not me," Brush said. "I'm just a fan. I'm a hero worshiper. Like Pearl Bailey once said—she was married to Louie Belson and knew all the jazzmen he hung around with—and she said, 'If jazz is their religion, these are the holiest of men.' "

They listened and alternately read and looked off, letting Ellington's music play the room and wash over them. It was at once quirky, difficult, and powerful. True jazz. Petey loved every note of it. Brush moved behind her and put his arms around her waist. He sought out her neck, and she tilted her head languorously to one side and made his seeking easier. As Clark Terry's trumpet probed the urges of Lady Macbeth, Brush bussed up and down Petey's neck, pausing at the ear, straying to her mouth, her lips, then moving down to her collarbone and related areas.

"Remarkable stuff," he said.

Petey sighed, then turned, and they embraced and all but fused. As Brush's hands caressed and massaged her back and her hips, she grimaced and stiffened.

"What's the matter?" Brush said.

"That damn kid—where I fell when he knocked me down in the park. That spot—*ouch*—right there," she said, putting her hand on his.

"You didn't break anything, did you?"

"I don't know, but it really hurts," Petey said.

He drew back and looked at her.

"That's even more incentive to put the little creep away," he said.

A light line of perspiration had broken out along her forehead. She managed a smile.

"God, how I wish I could," she said. "I am so close. I know why those two wanted to kill him, but how did they pull it off? If we don't find out, they'll get away with it."

He squeezed her hand. The first side of the album ended, and he went to turn over the record. He returned as Clark Terry's muted trumpet became a cool Puck in playing the famous words "Lord, what fools these mortals be." Stepping up to Petey, Brush took her face in his hands.

"It doesn't really matter if you get them or not, does it?" he asked. "The significant fact is that Rupert Huston is dead."

"You gotta be pulling my leg, Duffy!" Red exclaimed as we got back to business and I plied him with the details of the Huston case as Petey and I knew it.

He leaned forward, suspending his fork and a hunk of cucumber midway between the plate and his mouth.

"You say you found a guy who busted into Yankee Stadium and took a crap inside the safe room? Then he plants a Mets' pennant in it? You're kiddin' me, Duffy. You're settin' me up for a punch line, right?"

I would have put a muzzle on him if I thought anybody around us were listening in.

"No, Red. This is straight stuff. And it's hush-hush. Don't go puttin' it over the air."

"Hey, cut it out, Duffy. You're talkin' to Red Carney here. I've kept more things under my hat through the years than Gaylord Perry."

We were slicing into some first-division meat by this time. I had a plate of lamb, and Red had a grilled steak with peppers. The place showed no signs of thinning out. Waiters crisscrossed the floor with plates stacked five deep up their arms.

"Tell me more, Duf," Red said in midchew. "And I'll give you a rundown on the whole thing. I'm good at that."

I went on with ease, leaving nothing out, leading right up to the trail of Griffith Huston and Monte Beville.

"So the kids are your bad guys. The boy and his fruit-cake, and the daughter and her common-law?" he asked, while I dug into my lamb.

"They've got motive, Red. With Griffith, the boy, it looks like Rupert was on to their scam, and they had to get rid of him. The kid was in the stadium that night. Brush saw him. The daughter angle isn't so clear, but she's a schemer."

"So maybe either one of 'em set Rupert up so that a pro could pot him maybe?"

"That's it, I guess, but who?"

"Had to be a pro, Duffy. Hell, I ain't no expert on these things, but I believe in pros. The pros make the world go 'round. If the kid done it, he woulda screwed it up somehow. There's too many variables. It's like givin' a rookie the sign for a suicide squeeze with the bases loaded—something's bound to go wrong."

"This Beville character is a pro, Red."

"So you think he somehow had the son-of-a-bitch poisoned?"

"Yup."

"And you think they somehow had to get the son-of-a-bitch down there after they poisoned him?"

"Yup."

"And you can't just stick him in a bat bag and cart him down there, right?"

"What?" I said, stopping my fork in midair. "What did you just say?"

"You heard me, you can't just stick a guy in a bat bag and cart him down in front of those stones, can you?"

I didn't answer him; my thoughts were hurtling.

"Here's what I think, Duffy," he went on. "Whoever did it, did it in the ballpark for a reason—I gotta believe that. 'Cuz it *means* something, you understand? Here's the owner of the greatest franchise in the game who likes to act like a nut case down by those famous markers, and that's where he gets his head blown off.

"Hell, you're talking about murder in Yankee Stadium! Home of Murderers' Row, for cryin' out loud. There's a hell of a lot of tradition in that, and don't think whoever did this thing wasn't thinking about it.

"I said a pro done it, Duffy. And I still mean that. But it was a pro done it for the right damn *reason*. In the right place. He knew the whole world would see how the son-of-a-bitch was murdered, Duffy, and that meant something. I gotta believe that. Stop trying to put all the x's and o's together for just one minute and look at it from the big picture. You know what I mean?"

At that he motioned for the waiter and ordered coffee for both of us. I nodded assent, but my mind was racing. What Red had said earlier hit me like a line shot in the solar plexus. And once I stopped dancing with the pain, the numb truth sunk in. *Murderers' Row,* for crying out loud!

"Murderers' Row," I said absently.

"Ruth, Bob Meusel . . . ," Red started.

He thumped the table with his coffee spoon.

"Who else, Duf? Huh?"

I looked up.

"Two Wallys. Schang and Pipp . . . then Gehrig and Lazzeri . . . Dickey . . . Hang on, Red! I've got to make a phone call!" I said, and jumped to my feet.

By now the Ellington crew was hard into a "Sonnet for Sister Kate," and Petey, with Brush's help, had propped up her stinging bones on pillows on the floor. She was comfortable and vulnerable, and as long as the action took place above the hips, she and Brush went at it without caution. They nibbled and pecked through the Duke's composition to Romeo and Juliet. At its conclusion Brush lifted himself up onto one elbow.

"Here it comes. Ellington on Hamlet. 'Madness in the Great Ones,' " he said, and scooted over to turn up the volume.

Petey read from the jacket liner about Hamlet's attempt to deceive his stepfather into thinking he was crazy.

"This is great," she said. "Listen to this. Ellington says, 'In those days crazy didn't mean the same thing it means now.' "

Brush nodded, closed his eyes, and tried to follow Cat Anderson's trumpet.

"You know," he said, "Babe Ruth loved jazz. He loved to drink bootleg booze and listen to jazz. He became good friends with Bix Beiderbecke. Bix and Babe. The great ones gravitated toward each other."

Petey eyed him.

"It's amazing how you manage to find a connection to the Yankee tradition in just about everything," she said. "Talk about madness, John, that's madness."

He cocked his head sideways and studied her. Ellington and his cats were blazing in the background.

"Madness? Yeah, maybe it's madness," Brush said. "There *is* a madness in the great ones—in Shakespeare,

Ellington, Babe Ruth—it's there. So maybe I'm like a mad-man trying to touch it with the Yankees. The tradition is so deep, Pete. It swallows you up. It consumes you. You hold everything in life up to it. You realize that it's up to you to sustain it no matter who gets in your way. And that's not easy nowadays. Not with players who wear the Yankee pinstripes and don't think they have to run out pop flies. They're just the tip of the iceberg. The front office . . . ah, damn. You've got to keep pounding it home to people in the organization, people who just don't seem to under-stand the legacy."

Petey exhaled, then ran a hand over his.

"That's dangerous, John. I mean, can anybody ever measure up? Can anybody compare to those giants?"

"If they don't, they have to get out of the way," he said, drawing his hand away.

"Even if they own the team? I mean, what you said about Huston being dead kind of bothers me," Petey said.

Cat Anderson's horn bounded away into the strato-sphere, and the piece was over. For long seconds there was a stillness in the room, one interrupted only by short exha-lations from Brush himself. He was suddenly preoccupied, his expression tense, one fist clenched.

"Nobody can own the Yankees," he finally said.

"Come on, John," she said. "It's a business . . . more so today than—"

"No, it's not," he said. "It's nothing of the kind."

Petey looked at him. Her lips parted slightly, but she was not sure what, if anything, she should say. And Brush, his countenance as cold and rigid as stone, was not offering. She looked down momentarily, and her eyes caught the remainder of the line that had inspired the last Ellington cut: "Madness in great ones," it read, "must not un-watched go."

The phone rang, and Brush reached up to an end table to retrieve a cordless receiver. After a few words he put his hand over the phone and looked over to Petey.

"This is important. A scout. It may take a little while," he said, and moved off into a small room he used for an office.

Petey watched him go, her thoughts now spinning, confused. The music continued, but she was no longer listening. She got up and felt a little dizzy and sore, but her aches were now secondary. Everything was secondary, and she wondered what she should do next.

Carrying the Ellington record jacket with her, she went over to the wall of recordings, compact discs, and tapes. Brush's library of sound was voluminous. At the end of one row of albums, lying sideways against them like a book end, was a wooden plaque. Petey pulled it out.

"Vermont Scramble, Sugarbush Mountain, 1984," it read. "Third place. Biathlon. John Brush."

It was a simple, well-crafted award, and as she ran her fingers over its lettering, Petey trembled.

I had his home number; he had given it to me himself.

"John, this is Duffy," I said. "Is Petey there?"

"She sure is."

"Can I talk to her?"

"No, I'm on the coast on another line, Duffy. She'll have to get back to you."

"No, never mind. Stay right there, will you?"

"Why?"

"I'm coming over," I declared. "I want to talk to you."

"We were on our way out. Can it wait?"

"No."

"It may have to. I've got to go," he said.

With that he disconnected the line, leaving me with a cold receiver that fairly burned in my hand.

Although it may only have been minutes, it seemed as if it took far too long to convince Red to forgo his coffee and cheesecake in favor of a cab chase.

"We got it, Red! We cracked this thing, and Petey's in the middle of it," I said. Red's eyes bulged, and his temperature rose.

"Déjà vu all over again!" he crowed, and jumped from the table, nearly taking the linen along with him.

Red and I had no trouble getting a cab.

"Second and Eight-ninth, and step on it," I said before my seat hit the seat.

At that the taxi stopped dead in the middle of the

street, and the driver, a narrow-eyed black man with, I swear, a toothpick in his mouth, turned and faced us. He was a double, I swear once again, for Cliff Johnson.

"You wanna race, hire a jockey," he growled.

I groaned and longed for Arnold, the Yankee-loving cabbie.

"Oh, for chrissake," Red bellowed. "Can't anybody do their job nowadays! Drive the cab, ya bum!"

The hack eased a thin smile over his mocha-colored mug, and off we went. He drove steadily and directly, over to Twenty-third Street where Madison begins and straight up the avenue. Moving relentlessly, picking his lanes like Gale Sayers in the open field, hitting a remarkable string of green lights, the cabbie ate up the blocks. It was something to see, an artful, seemingly effortless urban skate during which he occasionally fixed us in his rearview mirror with the eyes of a sniper.

In the meantime I filled Red in on everything I knew or had surmised, and a few things I didn't. And together, as we hung onto the straps of the taxi, we worried about my niece. It was not an interminable wait, for ten minutes later we swung onto Ninetieth and pulled back around to the address on Second.

I handed the cabbie a double sawbuck as Red and I scuttled out of the backseat.

"Don't go anywhere, champ," I said. "We may need you."

He nodded.

For her part, Petey wasn't going anywhere. She had all she could do to hold herself in, contain her emotions, try to make her world as perfect and sane as it had been only moments ago.

She was not sure how long she stood in front of the sound wall. It had been long enough for the Ellington record to play itself out and for the tone arm to be skating with a slight hiss endlessly toward the center of the record. It was hypnotic. A ringing phone jarred her. It rang again and again, and she wondered why Brush wasn't answering it.

"John?" she said. "John?"

There was no answer. She went over to Brush's office, but he was not there.

"John!" she called out, now alarmed.

The phone continued to ring, and she went quickly into the hallway and answered it.

"Petey! Are you all right?!" a voice shouted.

It was a familiar shout. It was mine.

19

Pride in the Yankees

I hugged her as I had seldom hugged her before, and Petey wept on my shoulder. Then Red got into the act. He caught her eye and opened his arms.

"Marry me?" he said, and managed to pry a smile from her. The two of them embraced like the old friends they were.

"Where is he?" I finally asked.

"I don't know," Petey said.

"What happened?" I asked.

She led me to the other room and the wall of recordings.

I went to the phone and got the doorman, the same guy who had given us a hard time about getting up to Brush's digs until Petey herself called us up. He swore once again that he hadn't seen Brush, but said that Brush very well could have left through the parking garage. The garage attendant said yes, he had done just that. And not long ago.

"What now?" I said, looking at Red and Petey.

"He could be anywhere, but I'd bet on JFK," Red said.

"Maybe Devery can help," I said.

"Who's that?"

"Chief of detectives," I said. "We've been working with him on this thing."

"Yeah, what the hell. Get a dragnet on the guy, and they'll have a nut on him in no time," Red said, nosing a few steps into the kitchen.

"No," said Petey. "Don't do it, Uncle Duffy."

Her tone of voice was adamant, and she turned to me with eyes as heavy as eyes can get. She was a perfectly beautiful, mature, completely devastated young woman, and I ached for her.

"He'd only go one place," she said, speaking softly once again.

"Of course," I said.

I made another call, this one to Harry Howell, who said he'd do me a favor.

Moments later we were back inside the cab, and without a word, the toothpick in place and with a journeyman's resolve, the driver, whose name was Pruett, pulled out into traffic. He cut over to First Avenue and onto the Willis Avenue Bridge, then he went left onto the Major Degan. Again his progress was sure, as was ours. We sat shoulder to shoulder, saying nothing. The latter was difficult for me, because I badly wanted to compare notes with Petey. I wanted to know how we had come to the same conclusion from two different routes.

Red also kept his peace, which is a chore anytime Red Carney draws a conscious breath. Pro that he was, however, he realized this was no time to jabber. We pulled up in front of Yankee Stadium in ten minutes.

Inside the lobby we met a brick wall. The security guards, one of whom recognized me from the other night, and both of whom recognized Red, would not hear of letting us by. As for Brush, they said they had not seen him or heard from him or gotten any okay whatsoever to allow us inside the premises. They would not even make so much as a call to the general manager's office.

"He ain't here, so who wants to know?" the guard said, not lifting his overweight rear end off his stool.

I wanted to smack the guy, or chew him a new orifice, when my pique was interrupted by the arrival of Handsome Harry Howell, the Yankee clubhouse majordomo. He lumbered in—at least, as well as anybody can lumber wearing a pair of rubber thongs—and gave me a nod. Harry lived close enough to get to the stadium in cut time and get back home, he hoped, before the eleven o'clock news. Beneath his rumpled Yankee cap, he was wearing a T-shirt and a pair of Bermuda shorts that offered a pair of scarred and bowed legs that could have passed for parentheses. At the moment he was about as handsome as an ornery building super at midnight, but he was our grease through Checkpoint Charlie, which, in my eyes, made him Clark Gable. Howell scowled and said something unintelligible to the security mopes, then he signed us in and motioned for us to follow him.

"They *all* with you, Harry?" the guard whined.

"So who wants to know? Rupert Huston?" Howell said over his shoulder. He was a dead ringer for Ed Norton, who was not a great Yankee but was a great New Yorker.

The guards sat and looked wounded, proof that Howell's clout ran deep.

Once inside the main concourse, he turned and faced us.

"Okay, Duffy, so what do you want? What's happening here?"

I gave him a bare-bones recap, and when I finally got to the name of our suspect, Howell's face fell. Then he said, "I wish you hadn't said that. God love the lad."

"Let's go up to the pressbox to start," I said. "Check the executive offices. Bear with me, Harry."

Rather than backtrack through the lobby, we went down the steps to the basement and took the main elevator. Nobody said anything as we rode. Howell ran his hands through his scalp. Petey was biting the skin on the inside of her cheek.

Once off the elevator we walked quickly through the public concourse to the pressbox entrance. Again, except for a few night-lights, it was dark and quiet. I was starting to wonder what Yankee Stadium was like with people in it. The doors to the pressbox were unlocked, and we followed the aisle that runs between the press rows and the executive offices. All were empty. Most had the curtains drawn. Brush's office was dark and locked tight.

"What now?" said Howell.

"I don't know," I said.

"JFK," Red said.

"You wanna look around?" Howell asked.

"Not crazy about it," I said. "I'm a little sick of empty ballparks at midnight."

I turned to go back outside and realized Petey had

lagged behind. She had stepped down to the front row of the pressbox. There she stood, peering out into the dim light of the empty stadium. It was something she had done before, a sight she had viewed at a different time with a different person under very different circumstances.

I went down and stood next to her and saw that tears were streaming down her cheeks.

"There," she said, pointing out to center field.

I strained to see what she saw, and then did.

"Come on," I said.

Hopping back up the pressbox steps as quickly as I could, I motioned to Red and Harry, and we rushed toward the pressbox exit.

"He's down by the monuments," I said.

"What's goin' on?" Howell asked.

"Stay with us, Harry," I said.

"You want me to call your cop?" Red asked.

"No," I said, and wondered about the wisdom of that.

We huffed and hustled to the elevator, riding it down to the basement level and emerging once again at the base of the stadium triangle.

"Can you get out there from right field?" I asked Harry.

"Yeah. There's a delivery tunnel comes out behind the stands," he said.

"Meet us there," I said, and he shrugged and went off.

Red and I went the other way, hotfooting it through the supply tunnel as it led beneath the third-base side grandstands. It seemed darker and stuffier down there than usual, not to mention that we had the length of the ballfield to cover. My lungs were wheezing by the time we emerged into the open night-light of left-center field.

I worried that Brush would see or hear us and flee. I shouldn't have worried. For as our feet slapped against the rubber surface of the park area, I could see his figure. And it wasn't fleeing anywhere.

As we approached the monuments, I saw him clearly, standing with his arms crossed in front of him and his back to the outfield. He was still John Brush, the proud, striking Yankee G.M., one of baseball's new breed of executive. His silhouette cut a sharp outline against the gray New York sky. The sleeves of his custom-made shirt were rolled up, always rolled up.

I pulled up a few feet away. Harry Howell suddenly appeared on the other side of the monuments. I held up my palm to caution him and Red. For long moments we all stood and wondered what to do next.

Brush remained motionless before the stones of Gehrig, Ruth, and Huggins. I looked to my side for Petey, but she wasn't there. Red was alone. Harry Howell, aware now of what was happening, held his position and eyed us all.

I approached Brush.

"John?" I said.

He nodded slightly, acknowledging me.

"Duffy," he said.

I stepped just to the left of him, enough to make eye contact. His eyes, however, made contact only with the granite in front of him.

"I think I know how, John, but I'd like to know why," I said.

He said nothing. He stood like a stone monument, his expression flat, his eyes glazed. Then he spoke.

"Waite Hoyt once told me a story about the Babe, Duffy. It was 1921, and the Yanks were in Shreveport, Louisiana, for spring training. Things were good. Babe had hit fifty-four homers the year before, and the club had picked up Hoyt and Wally Schang from the Red Sox over the winter.

"Babe was driving a new Essex, which the city of Shreveport had given him to use during camp. It didn't even have a license plate, just a sign on the spare tire cover that said 'Babe Ruth's Essex.'

"One night Babe found a roadhouse near Shreveport where he could drink prohibition booze and listen to music. He and some of the Yanks were drinking and carousing pretty good when one of the country boys told them to shut up or he'd shut them up. Or something to that effect. Babe wanted to take him on, and the other guys stepped in and stopped him. But the guy was pretty sore.

"A little later Babe got into his Essex by himself and drove off down the road, probably looking for another bar. Harry Harper, a pitcher the Yanks had just picked up, just happened to see a car start up and follow Babe's down the road. So Harper and the other players jumped in their car and followed them.

"After a few miles they saw both cars stopped on the road. When they got close, they could see the Essex, and in its headlights stood Babe with his hands up. The redneck from the bar was holding a shotgun on him.

"Harper raced the engine and drove right at the guy and made him dodge out of the way. That was enough for Babe to jump on the guy and grab the gun from him. Then the rest of the players ran up and helped take care of the creep. Waite said they kept the shotgun and sent him on his way."

I waited for Brush to go on. He didn't.

"I never heard that story, John," I said. "What's the point?"

Brush turned to me. His expression was now very intense, his eyes focused. He looked at me like an attorney about to cross-examine.

"Babe Ruth wasn't just baseball's greatest star, Duffy, he *was* baseball. He'd taken the game out of the dead-ball era. He'd lifted it out of the Black Sox mess. He made it the national pastime. He loved kids, and he signed autographs for everyone, and he smiled and made people laugh. He was bigger than life. A hero—Babe was a living, breathing hero.

"Yet if it hadn't been for Harry Harper seeing that car take off after him, some random, stupid hick from Shreveport, Louisiana, could have destroyed what he meant just by pulling the trigger. In 1922. It would have changed history. That was obvious to Waite Hoyt, and that's why he told me that story.

"And I told it to Rupert one day. He was standing not far from where you are. And he didn't get it. All the time I worked for him, he didn't get it. And he wasn't ever going to get it. This year he gets rid of Lundgren and Bill Wolfe for nothing, after what we did to get them and keep them, and I thought, *That's him—that's the guy with the shotgun.* Here's a moron who doesn't know why runners are moving on a two-out, three-two pitch. Here's a random fool with a gun to the head of the Yankees, hell, to the whole game, and no one can stop him because he has enough money to come in and do what he wants no matter what it means.

"Harry Harper, Duffy. Don't you see what Harry Harper did? Don't you see what I had to do?"

He stopped, his eyes still searing holes into me, his lips dry and slightly parted.

I could find no words to answer him. No words of consolation or recrimination. I just felt damned sorry for him.

Just then something caught my eye as I looked out to my right, past the outfield fence and the expanse of that historic playing field. Midway up the grandstand, just to the left of home plate, stood a lone figure. Petey had not left the front row of the pressbox. She had not moved from that spot. She stood gazing down at all of us, at the park in the moonlight. At that moment, through the persistent gloom, I sensed that she somehow knew every word Brush had uttered. And she understood.

"He was a hero, Duffy," Brush said. "A hero."

I am not sure of many things in life, but I am sure of this: there is a difference between heroes and the rest of us.

There is a difference.

Boxscore

I tried to get Petey on a plane. Get her out of Manhattan and as far away as possible from the bombshell that was the John Brush arrest. But she wouldn't hear of it, and she stayed in New York in order to stick by him. Without knocking the old stand-by-your-man ethic, I didn't give it much of a run. Not with Petey. Maybe it was just my personal feeling about the kid, but even with her obvious affection for Brush, and her fierce sense of fidelity, she was a Biggers—too strong and too independent to sit the bench during a game that would drag on into many extra innings.

I, meanwhile, hied my tired old carcass out of the spotlight. Somehow the press learned of my roost at the Summit, and the message light on my telephone nearly melted. The *Times* wanted a first-person account of the whole thing. I was briefly tempted but turned them down. I didn't need the money, and I figured the byline would make me a marked man behind the batting cage. What did I need that kind of attention for?

"Stay out of it," Grand Chambliss agreed as I sat in one of his rear offices the next morning surrounded by tabloids and screaming headlines. The marvelous Marjorie insulated us from the press and judiciously screened Chambliss's calls. Together we mulled over how we wanted to handle this thing from here on out.

"Let Big Bill Devery do the blocking on the investigation side," I said.

"The top-cop detective? I don't know the guy."

"He's a fan of mine," I explained. "He personally came up to the Bronx to pinch Brush last night."

"He had to. In this town he had to," Chambliss said.

He paused and took an inquiry from Marjorie, then waved it off.

"You look like a used catcher's mitt, Duffy, but this office has got to hand it to you again."

"This one was a lot of work, Grand, and it took its toll. I liked Brush. A very good baseball man. And my niece, well, she's going to need some time on the D.L."

"What cracked it for ya?"

"Little things. Little things coming together, which they did as soon as I started looking in the right direction. Brush once told me he was studying to be a doctor before he went into baseball. I'd buried that item deep inside this thick head of mine, and it took an argument with Red to dig it out. People who study medicine tend to know something about overdoses, and Huston had a whopper.

"And it was a piece of cake for Brush to administer—with all those antihistamines Huston was taking for allergies. They often come in capsules, you know, and all Brush had to do was pull them apart, dump them, and put his own concoction with the inhibitor in—just like that couple did with the nonaspirin painkiller killings some years ago. The police lab is still analyzing all of Huston's pills they picked up at the stadium. I'm sure they'll find more that Brush tampered with."

"That poisoning bit doesn't sit right with me," Grand said. "Seems like he took too much of a chance."

"Just the opposite, Grand. Brilliant move. Anybody stumbles on him with Rupert in that condition, and Brush only has to say he's taking him for help. In the meantime it was a foolproof way to make sure Huston gets down by the monuments, and in the condition Brush wanted him. Then he covered up the evidence with the gunshot wound. At least he thought he did."

"Seems complicated."

"Well, Brush is just that. Whole thing depended on the timing—who was in the stadium that night and when. Brush first said Huston's boy was there early—around dinnertime; then he changed it and said he was there much later and may have stuck around. In fact, that was a slip, something you don't waffle on."

"It wouldn't convict him though," Grand said. "I bet Brush knew that."

"Yup, he knew just about everything—except for the burglar. He didn't figure on a guy breaking into Yankee Stadium at the same time he was murdering its owner. He didn't figure on somebody seeing him cart the stiff out to center field. Even then, what the burglar told me he saw wasn't a sure thing in my book. A guy in a golf cart with a bag on the back didn't mean John Brush to me, not even with the blue-shirt bit. Not until I got some dirt on my shoe."

"Hold it. Back up now," Grand said.

"Night before last I went out to the monuments again with Brush. We just talked and looked around. Brush was as cool as a cucumber. I started nosing around the flower bed where Huston was shot. The guy at the morgue—the one who told me Rupert was poisoned—said to check on how much blood he lost. He said a dead body, or one with a heart that isn't pumping too well because someone is just about gone, wouldn't gush much blood when it was shot. That's why I was pawing in the flowers and got some dirt on my shoe."

"So?"

"So I remembered that the only thing the sniper left up in his nest, according to the police reports, was a few specks of red dirt. The same dirt is found in the beds around the monuments. That meant that the killer had been down there. And if he'd been down there, it was only because he was putting Huston's body in place.

"That's when the bag on the golf cart made sense. The best I could figure was that it was an old Yankee equipment bag. Turns out Harry Howell said he can't keep the things in the clubhouse. And who takes them? Execs. Front-office types like John Brush. Why, he said even Rupert had one. How do you like that?

"And when you look at them, Grand, those bags are big enough to put a body the size of Huston's inside—as long as the body is still alive and flexible."

"Hey, between you and me, Duffy, I'd a given anything to've been there when he put that schmuck in a batbag," Grand declared.

"Get that big grin off your mug, Commissioner," I said.

He didn't.

"And your niece? Where was she all this time? How can I justify her expense account?" Grand asked.

"On my say-so, you cheapskate. She's golden, Grand. She unraveled this thing like a cheap baseball. Put a bug in my ear about the art-gallery guy and the possibility that Huston was poisoned. When the autopsy said the same thing, we had a whole new ball game. 'Course she was a little blinder to Brush as a possible suspect than I was perhaps. But I had no inclination to look in his direction either.

"She found the proverbial smoking gun," I went on. "You don't win biathlon trophies without being able to shoot real, real well. Petey knew that the moment she spotted the plaque on his bookshelf. At the end it was no problem for the police to find the rifle in Brush's apartment. It's a shame, but it'll slam the pokey door on him, Grand. And Petey is pretty broken up about it."

"She's a smart kid. Is she tough too?"

"As a marine. She'll recover. She's like a Righetti. Good stuff and just keeps bringing it to you."

"Remarkable."

"It was. The whole thing. And here's the heart of it: I didn't want to stay in the ballpark with this thing. I didn't want to, even though everything—my best instincts!—pointed there. I wanted the worst people—the Mob, Huston's crummy family, the burglar, then this sleazy art gallery owner—to have done it. Not a John Brush, for cryin' out loud. This is a hell of a guy. A baseball guy. So he got a pass from me. Of course, he encouraged both Petey and me on our false trails. Cripes, I pretty much spoonfed him everything I knew on the case as soon as I knew it. I don't regret that. I only wish it could have been the perfect crime.

"But then ol' Red comes in again. He says I'm overthinking this thing. 'Got to be a pro,' he said. That was for openers. And then he said it had to be somebody who'd risk doing it right in Yankee Stadium for a reason. Somebody who went to church in the place and worshiped at the altar of every retired number out there in center field. Ed Barrow, George Weiss, the whole lot of them. Somebody who valued Yankee tradition above everything.

"And it hit me like a ton of bricks: another person had

said the very same thing. Brush had! The kid had all but confessed to the crime, but I wasn't listening, Grand."

I finished my coffee after that. Chambliss pondered things, nodded as if he understood, then clapped his hands together.

"Ah, horseshit. You're getting damn good at this, Duffy. Next thing you're gonna want to raise your rates."

"Nope. Just fatten up my pension, Commissioner. I'm finished with the gumshoe beat. Beer, sunshine, and salted peanuts for me from now on."

Chambliss pushed against the sofa and stood up. Marjorie's head appeared and reminded him of his schedule.

"You better be right, Duffy, you washed-up old scribbler. The game has to settle down and get back to gambling scandals, palimony suits, gay umpires—the good old days."

He smiled like Happy Chandler.

"That's right," I said. "Anything violent happens, I'm retired, and my niece is in law school. I enjoyed my stay in Gotham. It was a Ballantine blast, so to speak. I wish the Yankees well, but it's over when it's over. I'm gone."

"The Yankees owe you one," Chambliss said.

"No, they don't," I said, and meant that.

He went for the office door, then paused, turned, and fixed a smirk on his face.

"Why don't you move out to the West Coast, Duf?" he suggested. "Like Casey did. Get some sun. Watch all those good teams and maybe even bleed Dodger blue."

"Impossible. You can always be a Yankee in your heart, but the Bums never left Brooklyn," I said. "Plus, there's too many faults out there."

"Ugh! Too much traffic—"

"—place is so crowded, people don't go there anymore," I Yogied.

" 'Course, it gets late early out there," Grand plied.

"And you could look it up," I said as he closed the door.

ABOUT THE AUTHORS

CRABBE EVERS is the pseudonym for the partnership of William Brashler and Reinder Van Til, a pair of boxscore devotees who admire the poetry of Franklin P. Adams and have spent long hours at the feet of Duffy House.

WILLIAM BRASHLER is the author of eight books, including his novel about baseball in the Negro Leagues, THE BINGO LONG TRAVELING ALL-STARS AND MOTOR KINGS, which was made into a popular motion picture. He has also written biographies of Josh Gibson and Johnny Bench. He lives and works in Chicago.

REINDER VAN TIL, a longtime book editor and free-lance music and art critic, has published a book on regional history and numerous magazine articles. He lives and works in St. Paul.

CRABBE EVERS has recently completed another Duffy House baseball mystery, which Bantam will publish in September 1991. His first mystery, MURDER IN WRIGLEY FIELD, is available wherever Bantam Books are sold.

Murderer's Row is the second in the Duffy House series that began in the Windy City with *Murder in Wrigley Field*. If you enjoyed Duffy's adventures in Gotham, you won't want to miss **BLEEDING DODGER BLUE** where he takes on the City of Angels.

The following is a preview of **BLEEDING DODGER BLUE**, available from Bantam Books in September of 1991.

City of Angels

For years I always felt sorry for the West Coast. Oh, not because they were two and three hours behind the rest of the country—why, we were milking the cows and buying stocks before they were even out of bed—but because they were always in the minor leagues.

The Pacific Coast League was the best they could do. They reared guys like DiMaggio, then had to sit back and watch them go east to fame and riches. They even had a ballyard called Wrigley Field, owned by the same chewing gum mogul, but it too was minor league. A puny version of the real McCoy.

Sure, the people in California had the movies and a lot of sunshine, and most of them didn't know a snow shovel from a rainy day. Yet they had to root for other folks' heroes. Bring their loyalties with them like old photographs when they moved from Brooklyn or Boston or St. Louis. While the rest of the country marked their lives by dropped pop-ups and ninth inning rallies witnessed in official stadiums (some in that glorious October classic), Californians just retired to their lettuce fields.

Being from Chicago, where we had not one but two major-league teams for as long as I could remember, I felt sorry for the westerners. Didn't lose sleep over it, but felt sorry. Let them have Bogey and Bacall, we had Hack Wilson and Ernie Banks.

Those thoughts occupied me as I rode the DC-10 bound for Los Angeles International Airport. The plane wasn't very full, so I stretched out and put my handbag on the seat next to me. Mine is a handbag, not a briefcase, I've never composed a brief and never owned a case to hold one. Advanced age cries out for accuracy.

Inside were a couple of reporter's notebooks, a tape recorder, a proof copy of another paean to baseball written by a Washington, D.C., political pundit who didn't mind slumming in my bailiwick but would probably fulminate were I to invade his—whose publisher begged for my kudos but would probably go on begging—and a volume of Raymond Chandler stories.

For my money you can take Chandler's opening paragraph of "Red Wind"—"There was a desert wind blowing that night. It was one of those hot, dry Santa Anas that come down through the mountain passes and curl your hair and make your nerves jump and your skin itch . . ." —and stack it up against just about any lead on the books.

Philip Marlowe, Chandler's shamus, has always enjoyed a suite in my mind's hotel. Hollywood has cast Bogart, Dick Powell, Robert Montgomery, George Montgomery, and Bob Mitchum among others in the role, and, as far as I'm concerned, has still fallen short.

The more I read, the more my mind drifted off the page. My friend Mike Royko, the testy young Chicago columnist, has long referred to California as the "world's largest outdoor asylum." For evidence Royko points no further than the morning's paper. Every day there is likely to be a curious, cockamamie story of life on America's far West End, a place that remains one of the great magnets for the kooky, the out-of-sync, the flake.

Meet an old acquaintance on a street in Boston or Indianapolis or Dubuque, Royko has written, and ask, "Hey, what ever happened to that goofy brother of yours?" And the answer is always, "Oh, he went to California."

Sometimes you get the feeling that California, that big, rolling nation-state on the big placid ocean, is a basin so immense that the whole country somehow flows into it. Land of wanna-bes, immigrants, dreamers and drifters, of stars, of E.T. The Transient State where everybody comes from someplace else. State of Charley Manson and Squeaky Fromme, of the Night Stalker, the Hillside Strangler, the Zodiac Killer. "Helter Skelter." Land of the editorial "where else?"—as in, "A man with inoperable lung cancer in California *(where else?)* sued to have his head frozen after he dies . . ."

Everybody, it seems, has an opinion on California, especially Southern California. If you keep a camera on yourself all the time, that's bound to happen. And in this video age, even if you haven't been there, you've been there. I've been there many times. It's a pretty place, at least a lot of it is, especially in spring when the rainy season peaks. Storms move from the northern Pacific and soak the coastal area and much of the valleys. The moisture reaffirms the land's remarkable tropical vegetation. The countryside blazes with pink and yellow hibiscus, freeway daisies, the yellow flowers of wild mustard. Ice plants bloom with explosions of magenta and lavender. There are the palms and cypresses, and hundreds of varieties of great, green eucalyptus trees so thick you can't see through them.

The rest of the year, rainfall in the southern part of the state is sparse and the area, which is a desert, grows parched and vulnerable to fires. Southern California's fires, abetted in September by Santa Ana winds, devastate thousands of acres of brush and grasslands and devour millions of dollars' worth of real estate. It is a harrowing phenomenon, and no one is immune. Yet in April, the season of my brief stay, there is no more lush and verdant place. And with the burning season seemingly remote, Angelenos casually pronounce their homeland the best place on earth.

While I have an eye for that sort of thing, I'm not a weather guy. I know that baseball is best played on green grass and in sunshine, but the two are not prerequisites for my continued merry existence. I'll take my share of eyeshade days, wipe sweat from my nape; but when the wind shifts and the seasons flip, I'll dig out the cardigan, give due reverence to a hard frost, and stoke the stove. Cold weather doesn't bother me a bit. For one thing, it stops insects and fleas in their many tracks, just hardens the soil like concrete and allows the pesky critters a bed for their larvae and nothing more. Somebody a lot sharper than I decided there is something to be said for dormancy and hibernation. They do wonders for golf courses. And the Muse, of course, thrives when there is sleet on the window.

The flight west was smooth and unremarkable, which made it remarkable, until an optimistic stewardess with shiny teeth asked me if I wished the chicken or the beef. When I asked her which she recommended, she said that she had not had either. "Young lady," I said, "you have a whole life ahead of you." She looked at me as if I had just removed my lower dentures. I took my chances with the chicken.

Riding that aircraft into Los Angeles from the east, I could see below me the uniform squares of tract housing— the cream and coral colors of little stucco homes with red tile roofs—on the desert floor and up the ravines and mountainsides. Suddenly the plane flew out over the infinite deep blue of the Pacific, did a loop, and hunkered in low for the landing.

With no relatives, wet-eyed loved ones, or limousine drivers holding a scrawled placard to greet me, I shuffled over to the inevitable stop of a West Coast visitor: the rental car desk. I signed away my rights and my future for the privilege of navigating an Oriental flivver on Southern California's freeways. I had no choice. You do not cover this sprawling, fault-lined metropolis any other way.

My mission was simple: to put some flesh on my long-awaited memoirs. My two cents' worth, I'd always considered, was a publisher's gold mine, yet in order not to bore myself with mildewed anecdotes and mealy reminiscences, I decided to add some other opinions. California is a waiting room for a lot of old timers in the horsehide crowd, good baseball people, to be sure, who knew the game as it was played in 1950 and have a choice thing or two to say about the way it is offered today. I'd look a few of them up and barber awhile, take notes, maybe learn something, and thicken the manuscript.

One of my targets was Jack Remsen, the glad-handing, tongue-wagging, fat, and current manager of the Los Angeles Dodgers. I knew him back when he was a stocky minor league catcher whose path to the Dodger lineup was blocked by guys named Campanella and Walker. Why, Jack, who could block the plate and hit his weight, never had a chance. He played alongside Bobby Morgan, who batted over .330 one year at Montreal, the Dodgers' Triple A team, and still rode the big club's bench when he broke in the next season—because of Reese, Robinson, Cox, Gilliam, and company. The Dodgers were on a homestand, and Remsen had said to come on the hell out here.

So that's what I was up to, and why I was risking my life behind the wheel of an automobile on the concrete ribbons of the West. I'm a public transportation person. I like the feel of subway tokens in my pocket; the goose of a turnstile makes me giggle. I can stand in the aisle of a hurtling train with one arm hooked around a stainless steel pole and read a newspaper from front page to back. I understand garbled offerings of mass transit's public address systems. I am immune to the irascible nature of the commuter and the crush of the crowd.

On the other hand, the freeway, the thruway, the underpass, cloverleaf, exit ramp, and turn-off frighten the bejesus out of me. I don't like lane changes, lane closings, merges, squeezes, or yields. Tailgaters haunt my dreams. Throw in a sniper or a freeway shooter, a swell in a Jaguar with a phone at his neck or a dumb blonde with a vanity license plate reading SPOILD 1, and my nerves bristle like those of a rookie crowding the plate against Don Drysdale.

Nevertheless, I nosed out of the parking lot of the car rental agency on Century Boulevard like the little ol' lady from Pasadena. It was late afternoon and I had plenty of time. There would be no San Diego Freeway, No. 405, in my immediate future. The good girl at the rental desk had used her yellow marker to highlight my journey, which sent me north along the ocean via Lincoln Boulevard to Santa Monica. Do not think I drop that or other Southern California locations like some glib late-night talk show host. I wince at the usage "L.A.," and my oafish Spanish raises hell with the street names. I simply read a good map.

My route of choice was Sunset Boulevard, the infamous street that winds its way from the ocean through Beverly Hills and Hollywood to downtown Los Angeles. I had a reservation at the Biltmore, a castle of a hotel that has offered me a plush pillow throughout the three decades that I have come to town to write about a ballclub. When I first began darkening its door, the Biltmore had a midget redcap with a firebell voice who became famous for crying, "Call for Phillip Mor-rees!" in radio and television commercials. That was back in the days when people advertised cigarettes and a lot of them smoked them and nobody apologized for it. Least of all the midget.

So I slogged up Lincoln Boulevard. My old eyes were stapled to the road, and my mitts gripped the steering wheel at ten o'clock and two o'clock as if I were ferrying an oil tanker through a reef. Somewhere to my left was the Pacific. It would have to get along without any gawking from me. There were folks on bikes, skateboards, roller-skates, drivers in chattery Volkswagen Beetles, Jeeps, convertibles, and sweep-finned 1957 Chryslers all around me, but I never saw a one of them. I drove the car and nothing else. The windows were closed. The radio was off.

Which is not to say that I was not mentally considering my surroundings. The City of Angels. The place has a history, and I'm partial to that. It was one of the few cities on earth to have been deliberately planned in advance and ceremoniously inaugurated. The King of Spain ordained it by royal decree—not that that meant an especially auspicious beginning. In fact, despite inducements of land, money, and livestock, the mission Governor de Neve was unable to lure any settlers from Lower California. Finally, a poor and motley group of "nine Indians and one mestizo, two Negroes and eight mulattoes, and two adults of Spanish origin" straggled in from Mexico.

Together with some soldiers, a few mission priests and their Indian acolytes—a roster forty-four people in all—on September 4, 1781, they established El Pueblo de Nuestra Señora la Reina de Los Angeles de Porciuncula—the Town of Our Lady the Queen of the Angels of Porciuncula. That makes the city older than Chicago, my home town, and not a lot of people think about Los Angeles like that. The whole area has always seemed to exist only in the present, its population transient. If you live here, you had to have moved here. History knows otherwise.

But I came to California without blinders, much less a decent pair of sunglasses. In my mind, the state will always rhyme with runaway franchises and expansion teams, two dubious developments in the world of baseball. I know it's been over thirty years since the Dodgers (with Horace Stoneham's Giants riding piggyback) came west, but in my mind, my imagination, and my memories, they will always be the Bums from Brooklyn. I spent too many golden hours in Ebbets Field to think otherwise. I sat at the feet of Mr. Branch Rickey, a wise, gentle, brilliant man, who came to the Brooklyn organization in 1942 and turned that dismal franchise into a contender. I watched Brooklyn become the zaniest member of the National League and Ebbets Field, with Hilda Chester, the babe with the cowbell in the bleachers, become a landmark. I witnessed Jackie Robinson.

Southern California, in my jaded perspective, is Walter O'Malley. O'Malley, that jowly, cigar-chomping autocrat who blustered, bullied, connived and jack-hammered his will on professional baseball as few men before or after him have ever done. The lord of the lords of baseball, O'Malley was as savvy a businessman and politician as the game has ever seen. In 1950 he bought Rickey, his longtime rival, out of the Dodger organization and then forbade employees to even mention Branch's name.

It was O'Malley who seized—I use the term advisedly because other entrepreneurs wanted to go west before him—the fortune that was the California baseball market even though his Brooklyn franchise of the 1950s was the most profitable one in the National League. The old hustler's axiom states, "I saw my openings and I took 'em." and that's just what O'Malley did. He hoodwinked New York politicians and steamrolled fellow major league owners in his planned escape from Brooklyn. Then he managed to keep all other clubs, including any American League franchise, out of Los Angeles. Along the way he picked up allies, but few friends. Bill Veeck, who admired a finagler as much as anybody, said of O'Malley, "He has a face that even Dale Carnegie would want to punch." And to Brooklyn, to the people in the borough, he was a Judas. Wrote Pete Hamill, "The three worst human beings who ever lived? Hitler, Stalin, and Walter O'Malley."

California, a land that had made fortunes for speculators who'd diverted water, drilled for oil, and pocked the hills and valleys full of houses, threw nary a jab at him. The City of Angels and its burgeoning metropolis were ready for the Big Leagues, and in 1958 O'Malley delivered. Thus, the citizenry, those folks who venerated the likes of Howard Hughes and Louis B. Mayer, who tossed around the term "mogul" without shame, embraced Walter O'Malley as if he were a prophet.

Of course, he brought with him a veteran ball team—Reese, Hodges, Snider, Furillo, for crying out loud—and a manager named Alston. He brought Emil "Buzzy" Bavasi, who was probably the smartest general manager in baseball at the time. He brought those white home uniforms with the inimitable "Dodgers" logo stitched across the front. The blue caps had to have "LA" instead of "B" put on the front, but that was a minor, relatively inexpensive problem for the ever penurious O'Malley. Carrying steamer trunks with "Brooklyn" painted on them, Walter's minions unpacked the rest of the team's equipment and the transition was complete.

They gave him parades and let him play in an oval-shaped arena modestly named the Coliseum, which normally hosts a college football team whose mascot dresses as a centurion in a crimson toga and circles the playing field on a snorting steed. It was a joke of a baseball park. The left-field fence was only 251 feet away from home plate and threatened to make PeeWee Reese a home run hitter. Still, latter-day Dodger fans in sun visors and reeking of Coppertone packed the place. On Opening Day over 78,000 of them showed up. Joe E. Brown, a comedian, introduced the opposing managers. On other desert days, as many as 90,000 fans, almost three times the capacity of Ebbets Field, would pay to get in. And in 1959, only a season after their arrival, O'Malley's Dodgers brought the World Championship west by winning in six over the White Sox.

In the meantime, the city of Los Angeles ceded O'Malley a choice chunk of public land called Chavez Ravine on which to build a new ballyard and threw in *carte blanche* as a player to be named later. Despite the delays and the lawsuits pressed by some silly local goo-goos who thought 800 acres of prime Los Angeles real estate might be used for something other than a donation to a private individual with a ball team, O'Malley got his way. He got the Bums out of Brooklyn and ensconced in a terraced, bougainvillea-draped playground with the appropriate address of Elysian Park Avenue in Los Angeles. It was the smoothest piece of highway robbery baseball-style since Jake Ruppert snatched a kid named Ruth from the Red Sox.

So no, I don't see Southern California through O'Malley's wire-rimmed, rose-colored spectacles. A pox on progress, the Dodgers should have stayed in Brooklyn. There were plenty of struggling franchises that could have and should have moved here. Having said all that, and hoping I have not infuriated greater Los Angeles, all fourteen million souls—perhaps including the Orange County mortals who have the Angels to infuriate them—I should hasten to add that I'd be more of a blathering old fool than I usually am if I did not recognize the triumph that is the Los Angeles Dodgers. It is a golden—in every overused sense of the word—franchise; its fans are as blessed and as loyal as any east of the Mississippi. And well they should be, for in three short decades the Dodgers have won remarkable titles in dramatic fashion. There is a glow to the Dodger uniform— the one worn by Garvey, Lopes, Russell, and Cey—to the very *wearing* of it, an aura comparable to the mystique that once resided in Yankee pinstripes. Now that's saying something.

By this time I had taken a left on Santa Monica Boulevard and reached the corner of Ocean Avenue. Here was the western end—or beginning, depending on your point of view—of Route 66, the most fabled of American highways and one of my vintage. In fact, the other end of Route 66, that "colossus of roads," is in Grant Park in my burg of Chicago.

I turned right when I reached Sunset Boulevard and swung northeast over its winding, mountainous route. Its up-and-down, curving feel was green and rich, and it was lined with thick trees and wide lawns in front of expensive residential real estate. UCLA popped up on the right in what may be one of the loveliest campuses anywhere. If ivy and architecture could recruit a kid, UCLA would have a lock on every high school senior in the land.

When my bumper nosed off Sunset and into Bel Air, I was nearly suffocated by the exclusiveness of the neighborhood. The streets said "no outlet," and many of the cars— Mercedeses, Jaguars, and classic Thunderbirds—were covered with tarps. Private drives led past stone entryways.

The specter of security was everywhere; below the security company's name on the signs were the ominous words "armed response." Behind these walls and the thick, manicured shrubbery were familiar faces who wanted to be seen only on their terms, the maps pinpointing stars' homes hawked by roadside vendors notwithstanding. I edged past the private Bel Air Patrol at the bottom of the hill, a posse formed to keep riffraff like me out, and welcomed the sight of Sunset once again.

At Rodeo Drive appeared the Beverly Hills Hotel, a pricey inn known for its lounges and dining rooms and the aura of the deal. An old, wafer thin woman in a blood-red dress, a woman so frail she seemed held together with Scotch tape, minced her way up the drive of the pink hotel. I swear it was the ghost of Bette Davis.

The green lights come fast on Sunset Boulevard, and in a few miles Beverly Hills gave way to the splash of West Hollywood commerce, and the boulevard became the strip known to the rest of the world through television and cinema. There is no more need to describe Hollywood than there is to detail the taper of the Eiffel Tower or Durante's shnoz. Only the Japanese take photos; the rest of us—even we who were not raised on television—have the street's postcard scenes burned into the flaky outer layers of our brains.

Talk of the Japanese and you'll hear of how, during World War II, artists from the motion picture studios were employed to camouflage the rooftops of the huge Douglas defense plants near here. They painted them to look like big pastures and farmyards, complete with cows. Amazing!

Traffic was more frenetic now, and even though it was the stop-and-go variety that I'm used to, I drove like a chicken. It was getting into early evening, and the sun's long rays made the boulevard true to its name. Over my shoulder were Hollywood's hills and the famous white wooden sign on the cliff.

On I drove, winding beneath the Hollywood freeway and into central Los Angeles. In almost no time the street lost its gloss. Its six lanes became crowded with buses, those belching animals Los Angeles is not known for, and bus stops full of dusty faces with the price of a fare and little more. At intersections with streets named Descanso, Silver

Lake, and Coronado there was not even a hint of tinsel or romance. Towering fan palms still cut the sky overhead and the street still rose and fell, occasionally slicing through rocky, cinnamon brown cliffs seeded with jagged century plants. Yet the famous boulevard had become a grid of grimy tire shops and body shops, and the hotels, theaters, and comedy shops had given way to the ubiquitous strip malls with their laundromats and taco stands, tax accountants' offices, furniture stores, tattoo parlors, and liquor stores with wrought-iron doors. Corner buildings were laced with graffiti, the tedious, modern-day script of young street hoodlums who huffed and puffed in the stucco-tough bungalow neighborhoods just off the drag.

At a stop light in front of one of these strip malls, I realized without any profound insight that this stretch of Sunset Boulevard was now just another gritty street in the guts of a big, tough, sun-baked city. A row of haggard old-timers, some of them wearing unmatched shoes with yesterday's clothes, sat along a low wall in front of the mall's parking lot. What we called a bum in my day, but is now referred to as a homeless person, pushed a grocery cart full of aluminum cans and plastic bags against the light, and held up traffic. The bum's face and neck were sunburned, he limped badly, and I could not have guessed his age if good money depended on it.

Billboards with Dodgers on them told me I was getting close to Elysian Park Drive when I got cut off by a bullying sedan that thought it owned the road. I swore out loud. I bellowed a bevy of blue expletives that discolored the windshield before I realized that the auto, barrel-assing in front of me, *did* own the road. It was a squad car, a black-and-white that served and protected on its good days, and mopped up on most others. Now it was in a hurry, its red Mars lights flashing, its engine groaning and tires hissing like something out of the movies. Cars and pedestrians stopped where they were. Some watched the path of the squad car and others looked around for the production crew.

I pulled over to the curb just in time to keep from getting clipped by yet another squad car. I craned to see what the draw was. I didn't have to crane too far, for the commotion seemed centered at the corner of Sunset and

Mohawk, only half a block ahead. Traffic wasn't going anywhere, so I got out and walked. I may be retired, but my reporter's nose is far from cold.

At Mohawk I looked north and saw a half-dozen squad cars parked chock-a-block near an alley. No movie set this, but a crime scene buffeted by the crackle of static on two-way radios and the migraine-inducing blipping of squad car lights. Officers in ink-black uniforms moved about the rear of a *taqueria* and its fetid trash containers. Their concern lay on the oily, stained pavement. It was a still, apparently lifeless body. When I looked more closely I saw that it was that of a slight man, a pensioner with silver hair and dressed in a lime-green, long-sleeve shirt and baggy brown slacks, legs akimbo, a pair of old sneakers pointing at the darkening sky.

But it wasn't the fellow's age or clothes that held my eye, not the awkward collapse of his body with the right arm pinned beneath it, but the gaping wound on the man's neck. In what looked like a gash made by the maw of an axe, his gullet was sliced open almost to bone and from ear to ear, a bloody salad of tissue and cartilage. In my youth I worked Novembers for my grandfather, who operated a live poultry shop on Adams Street on the west side of Chicago. I slaughtered turkeys for Thanksgiving. In a few swift, mechanical motions, I grabbed one fatted bird after another, raised a razor-sharp boning knife to the soft flesh of its crop, and slit it. I then pulled the nearly severed head through a large funnel, and while its torso shuddered and its legs peddled, the dead bird's tepid blood drained to the floor below.

The wounds I inflicted as a boot-clad boy against dumb holiday fowl were no different, and no less effective, than the one I was looking at. The vital and complex food, breath, and nerve tube had been cut and exposed like that of a newly slaughtered turkey. But unlike my quarry, the victim in the street was lying in his own blood. It soaked his collar into a crimson ring and radiated in a burgundy puddle beneath his white-haired head. His eyes were open and his tongue hung out like the tab of a zipper.

I silently stared, transfixed, the sights and, most vividly, the smells of my childhood washing over me. The old man's blood was everywhere, sticky, red, more ghastly than anything in my memory. And no one made any effort to blot it, or cover the source. I was sickened by it, and sad for the old guy. Then in mid-gape it struck me: the indignity! What the hell? Was this Bogota or San Salvador or some pissant banana republic where a leaking corpse in the street is just another piece of terrorist carnage? Was this just a quick piece of TV news footage? A few minutes of cinema?

"Cover him up, for Godsakes!" I barked.

It was the least I could do for somebody of my vintage so ignobly displayed on the pavement. A young policewoman looked at me evenly and repaired to her car. By now people were crowding around in order to see. Adults lifted children on their shoulders as if they were in a zoo. I heard the phrase "Another one?" uttered more than once. Another what? I wondered.

"Happy now?" the policewoman said to me, and I saw that she had covered the corpse with a blanket. She seemed to want a response.

"Who is he?" I asked.

"Number four," somebody behind me said.

"Sunset Slasher, man," came a tobacco-laced gust from over my shoulder. It belonged to an out-of-work movie extra who mimicked the looks of Bob Dylan in his subterranean homesick blues days.

"Dude zaps old guys. Lays 'em out up and down the strip," the actor said, then added a few guttural sound effects as well as a pointer finger across his neck. "It's bullshit, man."

The policewoman bumped into me as she cordoned off the area with yellow plastic tape strung from the nearby dumpster to the lightposts and back again. It *was* bullshit, I decided, for want of a better explanation. From time to time, police, now suit-clad detectives, came over and lifted the blanket and studied the corpse. They jostled photographers and camera crews who rinsed the area with bright camera lights and served as a magnet to passersby. I could feel the crowd pressing against my back.

Through the gathering crowd of cops and photographers my eye caught a last glimpse of the heap. Blood had seeped from beneath the blanket, soaking its edges. Blood, so much blood, it was now black in the artificial light, a viscous, seeping liquid too awful to associate with a human being late in his years who only hours ago could have spoken of Dewey and Truman and Lana Turner.

I had to get the hell out of there.

For some women, motherhood can be murder....

MUM'S THE WORD
by Dorothy Cannell

Several pounds heavier -- and gaining -- blissful mother-to-be Ellie Haskell knows her days as a thin woman are numbered. Time to let out her clothes, put up her feet, and prepare to enjoy the next nine months as a pampered wife. But the first pangs of morning sickness have barely passed when Ellie's handsome husband, Ben, is invited to compete for membership in the world's most exclusive secret society of chefs, and suddenly Ellie finds herself whisked off to America -- to Mud Creek, Illinois -- and to a gothic mansion straight out of a horror movie.

Immortalized years ago in a Hollywood film starring a sexy actress who happens to have the leading role in this season's bestselling exposé, Monster Mommy, Melancholy Mansion is no place for a woman in Ellie's delicate condition. Within its shadowy confines, danger lurks behind every chafing dish. And when murder is suddenly added to the menu, it falls to amateur sleuth Ellie to serve up an unsavory killer with a taste for foul play.

Mum's the Word by Dorothy Cannell
Available wherever Bantam Crime Line Books are sold.